December 21, 20

Hi Kate.

I thank Ann for buying my book. I hope I can thank you for reading it. May wild places survive the twenty-first century.

XXXXX,

Chigger L. Jakes

BETWEEN FORKS & ALPHA CENTAURI

by

Chiggers Stokes

Flying S Press

2674 Dowans Creek Road
Forks, WA 98331
360-374-2444
e-mail: chiggers@olypen.com

Printed in the USA, July, 2006, by Lightning Source, Inc.

ISBN 0-9786941-1-2

Price - $12.95.95 USA

Cover © copyright 2006 by R.J. Mitchell

***Between Forks and Alpha Centauri** is dedicated ...*

...to the early pioneers of the Olympic Peninsula and the wild places that absorbed their lives.

I would like to acknowledge...

...the heroic editing of Deborah Dillon that allowed this to be a readable book. I thank Chris Kloppman, Ralph Jenkins and Justin Knoble for the several photographs which are not my own. I would like to thank Beth Rossow, for her editing, suggestions and support for the publication of this work. Most of all, I thank Beth for revealing to me a real life manifestation of Mossy Stone.

The story is a work of fiction. Historical events in the text are portrayed with accuracy supported by eyewitness accounts or other authors' tellings. In some cases, characters resemble real life equivalents and permission to use their name has been sought. Otherwise, the people, places and events are the product of the author's imagination. Any resemblance to actual persons, either living or dead, or historical events, is purely coincidental.

If within the pages lies affront to any individual or organizations, I remain ready to change the text or personally burn your copy of this book. I am:

Chiggers Stokes
Flying S Press
2674 Dowans Creek Road
Forks, WA 98331
360-374-2444
chiggers@olypen.com

If a man falls in the wilderness, and no tree exists to hear him hit the ground...did that person ever really happen?
- **Mossy Stone**
Fictional character in a modern environmental romance

One

"God's first creature: which was light."
Francis Bacon (1561-1626)
English philosopher, essayist

Hemp Hill Creek, Bogachiel Valley
Monday, June 8, 1987, 05:20 hours

*D*ewdrops hung from the flower buds of the weeping cherry tree like crystal tears, sparkling in the red light of dawn. Through the orchard, which sufficed as the family cemetery, and across the meadow toward the cabin, fog lay like a pink down comforter. Hemp Hill Creek drew a forested and circuitous curtain across the 20 acres, dividing the meadow and orchard, visible from the cabin, from the large garden and fields that stretched off of the property to the Bogachiel River and beyond to Reade Hill.

In the garden, a rototiller growled its awakeness. As the four spotlights trained on the garden surrendered their prevalence to the yawning light of dawn, the woman controlled the course of the machine with one hand while she wiped sweat from her brow with a bandanna held in the other. It would be another scorching day. The pink sunrise confirmed what she had heard on the local radio as she left the cabin: that firefighters were working to contain an escaped slash burn out by Sappho, twenty miles to the northeast. She had left the radio on to mask the sound of the rototiller, so that her daughter, Mossy, would not be awakened by the early morning activity. Likewise, the mother had set a fire burning in the stove, to cook her daughter's oatmeal and to take the morning chill off the cabin. Above the screen of trees, which followed the creek, the woman could see the smoke from the chimney flattening out and hanging over the valley. In the fields, the fog was pressed ever closer to the ground. To the north, in the direction of the river, she saw elk heads bobbing up over the fog line, as the animals stood to face the warm glow of morning. The fog; the smoke; the dew on the grass and leaves: a warm day was coming. She would have to irrigate after planting...

The cabin door slammed shut and the eight-year-old child, Mossy Stone, exploded from the cabin attended by her terrier puppy, Daisy. The two charged into the fog, in the direction of the orchard and the bridge leading out to the garden. The terrier barked and gamboled while the child strode more purposefully: hands clenched; head down; her two braided pigtails arching out behind her head in an uneasy compromise between gravity and inertia. Abruptly, Mossy stopped and stared at the wall of temperate rain forest, which articulated the southern property line of the homestead. The puppy, in turn stopped, and studied her young owner, waiting for a sign of the party's direction. Through the fog that still hung among the spruce boughs, the sun threw great rays that shone from the trees to the child's eyes like structural beams. As Mossy moved, the red beams followed her gaze. "Huh?" Mossy said out loud, walking now through apple trees, with the sun's rays and her puppy for companions. She stopped near the weeping cherry tree that her mother called Mossy's birthtree. Several buds

7

had unfurled into flowers and the pink sparkling dew reminded her of Christmas lights. Next to the weeping cherry, a young pawpaw tree sprouted fresh young leaves, likewise ornamented with the twinkling dew. The exotic pawpaw tree was the wordless epitaph for the father that Mossy had never known. Upon his grave, Mossy turned and ran toward the bridge, over Hemp Hill and along the driveway toward the sound of the rototiller. The puppy abandoned the exploration of deer scent in the orchard and shot across the bridge in pursuit of its mistress.

"Mom, Mom! Guess what?!" Barbara Stone could read the words passing her daughter's lips, though the sound was swallowed in the throaty rumbling of the eight horsepower engine. She bent over and pressed the kill switch and the engine coughed into silence.

"What?" asked Barbara of her daughter, her fingers tingling from the traumatic vasospasm-inducing vibration of the machine.

"My birthtree has five flowers on it and there were sunbeams following me into the orchard."

"The sun must love you almost as much as I do."

"And the sunbeams were coming through those big spruce trees on the edge of our meadow..."

How this kid loved trees! She could have slept for another hour before getting up for school, but she was excited because today her class was taking a field trip to observe silvaculture in Washington State DNR and U.S. Forest Service units along Highway 101 toward Lake Crescent. When Barbara Stone had heard about the field trip, it had seemed like a timber industry whitewash. So she called her daughter's third grade teacher and applied pressure to have the class visit the Sol Duc Valley. Let the children decide which forests had the most aesthetic appeal.

"...but we're going to see trees even bigger than those spruce trees today." The girl was holding her arms straight out and spinning like a top looking straight up. We...are...going... to...see...REALLY...BIG...TREES!" The child stopped spinning and wobbled around dizzily. The puppy had laid down for a quick nap and Mossy stepped on its tail accidentally. The dog yelped and struck out a few feet to a safer place of repose.

"Careful of Daisy," cautioned the mother, abandoning the rototiller. She walked over to the garden fence to be closer to her daughter's morning exuberance and turned off the garden lights to save the battery bank fed by the hydroelectric.

"And, Mom, guess what I heard on the radio?" Barbara expected an update on the wildfire that Mossy's school bus would traverse this morning on the class's field trip. Mossy pulled a face, pinched her nose with her thumb and forefinger and began spinning again. "The lunch menu today is sloppy joe!" She removed her hand from her nose and put her forefinger deeply into her mouth as if to induce vomiting. She actually touched the back of her throat and began coughing as she spun.

"Quit spinning or you really will make yourself throw up." Sloppy joes had been a sore point with Mossy for about a year. While chewing on the shredded meat and bun in the school lunchroom, Mossy had found a tough and rubbery lump in her mouth that defied mastication. She spit it out on a napkin. It looked remotely like a clam. Mossy carried it to her teacher at the head of the cafeteria for identification. The second grade teacher assured Mossy that it was beef and encouraged her to throw it in the trash. Instead, Mossy took it home for the scrutiny of her mother, who had a strong background in biological sciences. Barbara Stone had identified the specimen as a beef heart valve, thereby ending Mossy's appetite for sloppy joe forever. The child grew evermore suspicious of meat and agitated for sack lunches with sandwiches made of vegetables from the garden.

Barbara came through the garden gate to join her daughter for the walk back to the cabin. They walked in silent awe of the morning with the puppy charging ahead to see if she could ambush a deer in the orchard. As they approached the orchard, Mossy spoke. "Mom, how come my weeping cherry tree never has cherries on it?"

"It's an ornamental tree, Mossy. Over the years the people who raise these trees encourage the plant's growth to go into the flower and not the fruit."

"Can they do that with people?" What questions kids asked! Barbara thought briefly of perfume, eye shadow and mini skirts. Her mind flashed on male bravado and all the superficial and hollow human behavior which focused on sexuality while somehow eluding the sensuality and nurturing sensitivity of mutual love or parenting...all flower and no fruit.

"Not really, Mossy. No." They walked by the weeping cherry tree which had been planted and fertilized with the placenta that had been Mossy's lifeline for nine months. The pawpaw tree's young foliage glistened in the morning dew and Barbara's heart ran to another time nine years ago when Phil Stone was in the flesh: his voice, his touch, the smell of him...

"Will Daddy's pawpaw grow fruit?"

"Not unless we get another pawpaw tree, honey. Pawpaws are dioecious. It takes another pawpaw of the opposite sex to make fruit."

"Is that why I don't have brothers or sisters, Mom? Are you...dioecious?"

"Yes, Mossy," said the single mother, amazed at the way children piece together the jigsaw of life. "People are dioecious." The mother and daughter walked past the grave to the breakfasting, face washing and hair braiding chores that awaited them in the cabin. The dew evaporated under the hot gaze of the morning sun.

჻

Bus Stop, head of Dowans Creek Road
Monday, June 8, 1987, 07:55 hours

A sense of unexplained dread filled Barbara Stone's heart as her child climbed up the steps into the school bus. It was one of those premonitions that something was wrong...that catastrophe lay just ahead...the kind of thing that almost always proved unfounded. Still, it was so strong. She almost called her daughter back. She stood watching as her daughter took her seat at the front of the bus and the vehicle lurched forward. She watched the bus accelerating into the blood red sky and felt her insides rumble with nervousness.

"Come back, Mossy. Please come back to me," she said in a small voice and got back into her pickup truck.

ॐॐ

Beaver, WA
08:15 hours
　　The bus driver silently cursed the fog and the payload of young urchins who flounced and bounced in their seats behind him. Couldn't their teacher apply a little restraint? Christ! She was singing Ninety-Nine Bottles of Beer on the Wall along with the little banshees! George Smith had a hangover and just the thought of one beer made him want to regurgitate. He unfastened his seatbelt to relieve his gastric discomfort.
　　Pulling away from the tiny community of Beaver at Milepost 200 on Highway 101, the bus driver accelerated to 60 miles per hour, as if to escape the pandemonium happening just behind his seat, but slowed back to 55 when he saw a police van following the bus. He hated driving a school bus this close to the beginning of summer vacation. He hated the pounding that ran from his head down his spine and the roiling and wild regurgitation that transpired between his sphincter and epiglottis. Every minute seemed like an eternity and every mile seemed like a light year...

ॐॐ

Beaver, WA
08:16

　　In the DARE police van 300 feet behind the bus, Officer Brian Fairbanks could hear Mrs. Bell's second grade class singing *ninety-six bottles of beer on the wall*. He pitied the bus driver if the kids intended to go to term with this song. He could smell smoke from the Sappho fire through his open window. He decelerated partially to give himself more maneuvering room in the fog and also to escape the following ninety-five shrill choruses that would surely issue from the bus. As the junior officer of the Forks Police Department, Officer Fairbanks had been assigned stewardship of the town's DARE program and his love and affection for children did not immunize him from the stress and aural trauma of being around kids at the eleventh hour of their school year. He was driving to the county seat to snooze through another anti-drug pep talk and pick up more DARE pencils and bracelets to hand out to the kids. He saw the school bus cross the yellow line several times and wondered if the driver's seat belt was the only thing restraining the man from running down the bus steps and jumping ship.

Sappho, WA
08:17 hours

　　Dean Hurn had planned to sell the old cow to the Department of Agriculture after she fattened up on the spring grass of his 160 acre farm overlooking the Sol Duc River. Over the last decade the old girl had given the

Hurns some of the best calves in the herd and won first place two years in a row at the Clallam County Fair. For the last two years she had lost her calves. Now she was sloppy joe on the hoof. She had been culled from the herd when the bull was brought into the pasture, but late on in the fall, some old spark had re-ignited and the bull had broken down the fence to get at her. Yesterday, she was stressed by the smoke and the whining of chain saws and fire pumps on the other side of the river. She had gone into labor that night.

ഌൟ

Sappho, WA
08:18 hours

The bloodshot eye of the sun hung over the west running nose of Snider Ridge as the school bus rolled down the hill from the wide plateau of Lake Pleasant. The fog deepened. At the front of the bus, Mossy was too distracted by the red orb of the sun and the blanket of fog to join in the singing. The driver looked like he was going to upchuck. Across the bus aisle and through the bobbing heads of her classmates she glimpsed the pretty, old Beaver school. The grass on the other side of the stone gate had grown over, forgetting the hundred thousand footfalls of students coming and going before the school was closed and students bussed to Forks. When Mossy looked out her window on the right side of the bus, she could see Dean Hurn's cattle pushed up along the northwest fence near the road where they waited for the warmth of the morning sun to push through the fog and smoke. A dozen three-month-old calves gamboled next to their mothers running from teat to tat in utter joy.

One tiny wet calf lay on the ground with stillborn steam rising into the fog. Its mother licked the lifeless lump incessantly...licking and licking in a dumb cow's hope that the calf would rise from the pasture to frolic with the other calves. Mossy watched, waiting for the calf to get up. She strained her neck, looking over her shoulder waiting for the calf to get up. In violation of school rules, she stood up in her seat and peered back over the heads of her classmates waiting and hoping...

ഌൟ

Sappho, WA
08:18 hours

On the eastern bank of the Sol Duc River, twenty feet upstream of the first Highway 101 bridge, the two Hispanic firefighters struggled with the Mark III fire pump. No one had brought a screen for the foot valve and, during the night, gravel had jammed the pump's impellers. A line was dug around the 20 acre blaze the previous evening. This morning half of the firefighters and the brush engine were redeployed to another escaped slash burn to the east. The remaining firefighters called ITT Rayonier for another pump after the impellers jammed, but were told that most of the ITT suppression equipment was committed to the escaped fire and other prescribed burns south of Forks. They were told to

11

"dry mop" through the night, which is the firefighters' equivalent of digging holes and filling them in. After eight hours of dry mopping, Juan and Carlos took the portable lighting and tool kit from the crummy and followed the hose line through the smoke and fog to the bank above the pump. The two spotlights propped in a tree on the bank above illuminated their work as they removed the impeller head. As they worked, a rosy-fingered dawn overtook the artificial light. By 7:30 they were able to spin the impellers with their own rosy fingers. After eating a sack lunch left over from the previous evening for breakfast, they were reassembling the pump in hopes of extinguishing the smoldering flames with the unlimited aquatic resources of the Sol Duc.

"Apagar un fuego sin agua es como jalartela con un pedaso de mierda en la mono." (Extinguishing fire without water is like jerking off with a turd in your hand.)

"¿Que significa?" asked Juan. (How is that?)

"Es sucio, asquroso y es casi imposible de hacer a cabo." (It's filthy, it's disgusting and it's nearly impossible to do.)

"¡Ah! ¡Es daveras!" (Oh! That's the truth!)

ა~ა

Sappho, WA
08:18 hours

Driving down past the old Beaver school, Officer Brian Fairbanks took off his seat belt to adjust the tight wool dress pants, which were riding up his crack. The bus disappeared into the fog and smoke and the cop slowed to 40 mph, putting his seat belt back on. The bus driver was driving too fast for conditions, but the Forks officer was out of his jurisdiction and the violation notice for this infraction was given to operators who had crashed their vehicles and yawned in the face of the investigating officer.

ა~ა

Sappho, WA
08:18 hours

...waiting and hoping for the calf to get up. Through the thickening fog, Mossy peers, hoping to see the steaming little puddle of flesh animate into a calf. While the bus driver's aching eyes try to adjust to the wall of smoke he's driving into...his eyes searching for the familiar green bulwark of the bridge...a dim inclination that *this isn't right* manifesting in his bowels like a fart that goes to diarrhea. Through the white screen emerge two lights, which George Smith takes to be headlights on the other side of the bridge. He removes his foot from the accelerator and steers sharply toward the light, leaving the roadway and missing the guardrail that protects vehicles from caroming off the steep bank down to the river. The bus smashes into and over the road sign announcing *Sekiu/Neah Bay intersection 3/4 mile distant* and slams into a telephone pole at the brink of the thirty-foot embankment over the river. The windshield explodes as the driver and

12

a student are thrown through it and the telephone pole simultaneously cracks and heaves over, under the momentum of the bus...

৩৵৶

Sappho, WA
08:18 hours

" ¡Chihuahua!" says Carlos. " ¡Es como el camion en en que viajamos de Chih!" (It's like the bus which brought us from Mexico!)

Carlos and Juan hear the cracking of the signpost across the river and look up from the pump to see the school bus crash into the telephone pole. The windshield explodes and a young girl flies through it, rear first. As she is sailing over it, the hood is buckling and heaving up. The driver is likewise coming through the windshield face first, but is slowed down in a launch over the steering wheel. As the girl plummets down the steep embankment, the driver is pushed up against the jagged edges of the hood cowling. There is a half second of silence as the telephone pole begins falling and then the bus begins slithering down the steep slope following the tumbling girl with the driver hung up on the crunched metal of the hood. The girl's head impacts a rock at the river's edge and she comes to rest on her back, feet downstream. The wheels narrowly miss the supine child as the bus collides with a large alder at the shoreline and rides part way up the tree. The driver slides over and off the end of the hood trailing what looks like a glistening rope and painting the hood with red and brown. Forward momentum is finally exhausted and gravity pulls the bus back down off the leaning alder tree. The right front tire of the bus comes to rest on the girl's abdomen.

৩৵৶

Sappho, WA
08:18 hours

To the ears of the old cow comes a strange sound, which makes her lift her head from her ministrations to the lifeless calf. It is a cacophony of human calf cries. The old cow sniffs and, through smoke, smells the blood and fear on the wind. It is like the sound and smell of a human veal herd being led from the feeding stanchions to the slaughterhouse.

৩৵৶

Sappho, WA
08:19 hours

In the smoke and fog, Officer Fairbanks slows to 25 mph to drive across the first Sol Duc Bridge and nearly runs into two Mexican firefighters who are running toward him in his lane. Maybe the fire had blown up and he wouldn't have to go to the pep talk at all. The Mexicans motion for him to stop and get out of the car.

"¡El camion escolar choco!" one is screaming. "¡Los ninos estan heridos!" (The school bus has wrecked! The children are hurt!)

"¡Sal del carro, policia huevon!" yells the second. (Get out of your car, you lazy cop!)

He activates his emergency lights and steps out of his vehicle. At once he hears the crying and screaming. He jumps back into his vehicle and yanks the radio microphone off the dash. "Forks, Five Zero Six, I need ambulances and all available rescue vehicles for a school bus accident at the Sol Duc Bridge, milepost two zero two. I'm going to the crash site, which is non-blocking and almost in the river. My vehicle is on the bridge with emergency lights. Five Zero Six going to portable."

Fairbanks runs to catch up to the firefighters at the west end of the bridge. The Mexicans clamber down the steep slope and Brian Fairbanks tumults after them, ripping the seat of his pants. When he gets to the bus he waits as the Mexicans are kicking in the door. Across the crumpled hood is splashed a unit or two of blood mixed in with what looks like the sloppy joe mix they make the kids eat at school. A slithery, glistening lariat is draped from a dagger-like fold in the cowling over the hood and into the river. Officer Fairbanks recognizes the rope as human intestine. While the firefighters charge up the steps and begin shouting in excited Spanish, the cop walks around the deformed engine compartment and finds the eviscerated driver lying face up in shallow water. His belly is as open as a punch bowl and the man, who Fairbanks recognizes as George Smith, is trying to get up. "Be still," advises the cop, trying to remember the appropriate therapy for these kinds of wounds from his ARC one-day Standard First Aid training. Officer Fairbanks figures on coming back to that one and goes back to the steps to help the Mexicans sort out the mess in the bus. Just as he starts up the stairs he hears the breathy, whispered words, "Help me...please...help." He turns around, half expecting to face George Smith carrying his coiled intestines, but there is no one. He looks down and sees the red puffy face of Mossy Stone, her eyes locked on his. The tire is resting directly on her pelvis and it's difficult for Fairbanks to imagine how she is alive.

"Get...it...offfff...offf," pleads the child. The cop remembers stories of adrenaline crazed mothers lifting cement trucks off their entrapped children without even putting down their groceries and runs back around to the front bumper. He counts to himself, *one, two, three,* and lifts with all his might. His pants split from the bottom of the zipper to the back of his equipment belt. The bus does not budge.

The cop sighs, "Hold on, Mossy. We'll get you out of there." Officer Fairbanks temporarily leaves Mossy Stone and George Smith behind him. He walks up the steps further into the nightmare, adding his weight to the already terrible load, which is crushing the bones and rupturing the organs of the young child.

❦

Forks, WA
Monday, June 8, 1987, 08:30 hours

Richard Stokes, the editor from the small town newspaper, had opened the office at 06:30 that red morning and read over a couple of letters to the editor from local citizens. The contributing writers were inflamed over the preservationists' latest ploy to use an obscure owl to lock up the sylvan resources of public lands and commercial forests. Stokes had been the editor of <u>Knives, Spoons, and Forks</u> for almost a decade and had followed the economic shifts and mood swings of the lumber town like a kid chasing a run-away dog: calling out the town's name with affection, but not daring to guess where it was headed.

He finished with his letters and checked out a couple of human-interest stories from the UPI subscription service. Nothing from UPI seemed more interesting or germane than the biographical sketch of a German emigrant named Chris Morganroth he had found in the small newspaper's morgue. Morganroth was the first of his race to settle the upper Bogachiel and had enlisted as a Forest Ranger in the early days of the Olympic Forest Reserve.

When Terri, his secretary, came in at 08:00, Stokes walked 500 feet north on Main Street to take his breakfast at the Pay and Eat Coffee Shop. He had finished reading the <u>Port Angeles Daily News</u> at his booth and his order had just arrived when he heard three or four police cruisers rolling out of Division Street, hammer down. The fire hall siren sounded and several small town businessmen ran out of their stores in the direction of the fire department. To the wailing sirens was added the shriek of the Forks Ambulance as it charged out Bogachiel Way to chase the police east on Highway 101. Stokes began wolfing his food. The second-out ambulance howled through town and individual police cars began converging from all over town as off duty officers from Forks, the Sheriff's Office, and State Patrol were being called on duty from their residences. The rescue rig from Forks Community Hospital with "*The Jaws of Life*" rolled out. It sounded like a coyote convention on the night of a full moon. Something had happened which was summoning every response resource in the area. Stokes figured that a story of this magnitude probably justified walking away from his second egg, second sausage, fourth slice of toast, and fifth cup of coffee. He hurried back to the newspaper office, where his secretary had the presence of mind to turn on the scanner. "It's a school bus accident out at Sappho," announced Terri. "They're calling in everything from Aberdeen to Sequim."

"Is it bad?" the editor heard himself say and couldn't believe the words had escaped his mouth.

"That DARE cop, Fairbanks, was the first on scene. I heard him say that there were over thirty injured third graders. One of the kids is pinned under the bus and the driver's guts are spread all over the hood. Does that sound bad?"

Richard Stokes considered the impact of such a scene upon the one egg, one sausage, three slices of toast and four cups of coffee that he had on board and decided that it was in his professional interest to risk it. He grabbed his camera and went outside to his rig. After crossing the Calawah Bridge he accelerated to 70 mph, figuring that most cops on the road wouldn't have the time to deal with a speeding ticket. Even at 70, he had to pull over three times for emergency rigs coming up behind him.

Traffic was completely blocked on Highway 101 and Stokes had to walk half a mile or so to the accident scene. With his press card, he was able to get out on the bridge by walking through the traffic barriers and gain a view of the rescue efforts. A steady stream of rescuers were bringing kids up the hill one at a time. They were using the bridge as a staging area where the casualties were being assessed by ambulance personnel and a limping doctor who had arrived from Forks Hospital. Tags were being attached to the patients' toes to indicate their priority and destination. The green-tagged kids were hollering like hell and being loaded like cordwood onto ambulances taking them back to Forks. Between assessing the patients, the doctor, Richard Dickson, limped among the four red-tagged children awaiting airlift. He set up IVs and quietly reassured the children without regard to their varying levels of consciousness. Dr. Dickson knew what it was like to be a child facing overwhelming and terrifying medical obstacles. As a young boy, he had suffered the ravages of polio.

Briefly, Dr. Dickson explained to Stokes that, when the helicopter from Airlift Northwest arrived, the most severely injured of the four high priority patients would be loaded into an ambulance and transported to the empty park-and-ride, a half a mile down the highway. There, they would be dusted off by helicopter to Childrens' Orthopedic in Seattle. Turnaround time from Childrens' to the park-and-ride was about forty minutes, and the air ambulance could only carry two patients.

Looking over the railing from the east side of the bridge, the editor could see that someone had thrown a partially opened body bag over the bus driver like a sheet. His shoe was removed and a black toe tag fluttered in the warm, smoky breeze. A glistening tether ran from the still driver up to the crumpled cowling on the bus's hood. The two sausages in Stokes' belly began thrashing about and swimming up his throat when he realized that he was looking at human sausage casing. Several rescuers were fitting what looked like a beanbag under the front frame of the bus near where a child was pinned under the front right tire. A long hose ran like an umbilical cord from the bag to the exhaust pipe of a rescue vehicle on the bridge. An ambulance attendant was putting a cervical collar on the child's neck. Dr. Dickson dragged himself to the railing on his deformed left leg and stood beside Stokes to check the flow of patients. The EMT saw the doctor and called out, "She's got a one-inch depressed skull fracture just posterior to her right ear! Looks like C.S.F. in the ear. Pupils are equal and reactive but we're getting a spread in BP: 130 over 60. Christ! She's starting to convulse!"

Doctor Dickson fought the anxiety and grief that welled up as he recognized another child that he had delivered into the world in the birthing room of the Forks Community Hospital. "Keep watching her breathing after you get the bus off her and bring her up the hill," advised the physician. "Her blood pressure may bottom out when the weight comes off - just like cutting off a pair of MAST pants. Assist ventilations, but if she codes, just put her next to the bus driver. We don't have the resources..."

"Doctor Dickson" called an EMT back on the bridge. "This patient is urinating blood." A child who had been screaming a minute before was quieting down and shivering in the warm breeze on the bridge. Where her pants had been cut away to expose her legs and pelvis, the doctor could see her panties stained with the pink color of bloody urine. The doctor pulled off the green tag from the

16

child's toe and put on a red one. He was searching for a vein to start an IV line on the child's forearm.

"Doctor Dickson! Doctor!" called Officer Fairbanks as he and an Hispanic firefighter carried Mossy onto the bridge, duct taped to a backboard. The attending EMT was giving artificial respirations. Dr. Dickson noticed that the EMT was performing mouth to mouth without benefit of a rescue mask. Most of the emergency personnel were handling bleeding children without protective gloves. The cop carrying the backboarded child had his pants split and shredded. Only his belt kept either pant from going independent ways. Two other crying, bleeding children were being carried on to the bridge by firemen.

"Red tag for Mossy Stone!" yelled the EMT in between rescue breaths. "She needs the next airlift."

The physician's eyes burned as he examined the young patient who, from birth, had always been so full of life. The depressed skull fracture, crushed pelvis with acute abdomen, the certainty of internal injury. Maybe it was the smoke causing his eyes to tear. He sighed and caught his breath. "If she's not breathing on her own when the ambulance gets back for the next two airlifts, put a black tag on her. We've got to concentrate on the patients we can save here."

The editor turned away from the grim scene on the bridge and looked over the railing at the bus. Two police officers were putting George Smith into a body bag. A fireman was coming up the hill carrying a boy with a pneumatic splint on his ankle and forearm. A Park Ranger above him was rigging a handline to a tree and told the fireman to wait. The fireman continued up the slope, slipped on the steep bank, and slid fifteen feet on his bottom holding the crying child to his chest. A vehicle pulled in behind Stokes and he turned to see the child with the bloody underwear being loaded onto an ambulance. The EMT with the girl called Mossy was still doing artificial ventilation and the cop was quietly disobeying the doctor's orders and attaching a red tag to the child's toe. They loaded her onto the rig and the EMT began talking as another ambulance attendant took over ventilating the young patient. "Crushed pelvis; unknown internal injuries; depressed skull fracture medial to the right ear. She quit breathing just after we got the bus off of her ten minutes ago. She needs high-flow O2 and Lasix. She convulsed, but we're not seeing any posturing..." The ambulance doors were pulled shut from within and the ambulance pulled away. "Godspeed," said the EMT in a small voice.

"Amen," whispered Officer Fairbanks.

❧

Hemp Hill Creek
10:46 hours

Barbara Stone came back to the cabin from the garden for some relief from the sun. Her T-shirt was glued to her skin with sweat. She had been drinking water all morning from hose bibs as she moved starter plants from her greenhouse to the garden. But in the cool, relative darkness of the cabin, she sat with a filled quart jar of the same water that drove the small turbine that electrified the property. Barbara thought about turning on the radio to see if the Sappho fire

17

had been contained, but decided that the quiet went with the dark. She was one and a half pints into the jar when the phone rang.

"Stone residence, Barbara speaking."

"This is Forks Primary School. Have the police been in touch with you about the accident?"

"What accident? Is Mossy all right?"

"Barbara, the school bus that was taking Mossy's class on a field trip was involved in an accident and your daughter was flown out for medical attention. The helicopter was bound for Childrens' Orthopedic in Seattle, but a fire south of Sequim blocked visibility and her airlift went to Olympic Memorial in Port Angeles. I have the phone number..."

"Is Mossy all right?" asked Barbara, knowing that if Mossy was airlifted, she was all wrong.

"We don't have any more information about any of the children. Most of them were taken to Forks and Olympic Memorial Hospital, but seven made it to Children's Orthopedic. I have the patient information number for OMH. Do you have a pencil, Barbara?"

"Yes, go ahead." Barbara picked up a pen in trembling hands and looked about wildly about the desk for something to write on. She opened the family Bible given to Barbara by her mother and wrote the number 360-417-7000 on the title page of the heirloom.

"I wish I could tell you more, but that's all we know and we're only half way through the notification list. Our prayers are with Mossy and the other children. Good-bye."

The line went dead and Barbara dialed the number for Olympic Memorial's patient information. She learned that Mossy had arrived at 09:30 and that she was being stabilized for surgery. The faceless person on the other end of the line said that Mossy's condition was serious, but would not discuss the specifics over the phone.

"Serious?" asked Barbara. "Is her condition critical? Just tell me, is she dying?"

"We're assessing her situation right now and it's serious. That's all I can tell you. Until you get here we will proceed with the assumption that we have your permission for all life-saving procedures. Will you be coming to the hospital this morning?"

"Yes, of course," said Barbara, with a brief vision of the starter plants she had set in the morning shade baking in the high afternoon sun. "I'll be there in an hour and a half."

"Mrs. Stone, please be very careful about driving here yourself. We recommend you take a cab or have a friend drive you."

"Of course," said Barbara Stone, hanging up. Sure, wait an hour and a half for a cab from Port Angeles and then drive the speed limit or less all the way back trying to raise the fare. *Of course.* She threw a few articles of clothing, a hairbrush, and toothbrush into a day pack. She put the dog in the kennel with a week's worth of food and water. She was climbing into her green GMC pickup when she stopped and bent over to vomit a pint and a half of clear fluid. She pulled a bandanna from her rear pocket and wiped her face clear of the sweat and tears that stung her eyes so badly she could hardly see. She jumped into the pickup and drove by the little plants that called out for water without even turning on the sprinkler.

శ్రా

Main Street, Forks
11:00 hours

Officer Brian Fairbanks hadn't had to go to the DARE training after all. He was stopped at the only traffic light in town, waiting to make the left-hand turn onto Division Street which would take him back to Town Hall and Forks P.D. and a well needed shower and change. The oncoming GMC pickup didn't even slow down for the full red light. Fairbanks could see the driver - what appeared to be a 30 y.o.w.f.d.u.i. (year-old white, female, driving under the influence). Her face was sweaty and she had the cow-pie-eyed look of a binger on a full-blown drunk. He still hadn't been able to change his pants and his hands were covered with crusted blood, but DUI enforcement was an integral part of his job, so he made a U-turn, swinging out after the green truck. He accelerated and had caught up to the speeding violator before the vehicle reached the north town limit. He was traveling 70 mph across the Calawah Bridge to get the license plate number to radio it in, waiting for the license plate computer check before activating his lights to make the stop. In a few moments the dispatcher came back with his 10-28/29.

"Five Zero Six, Your Washington three seven six one one tango comes back to Barbara Stone, mailing address of Forks. No wants or warrants, and tags are current and clear. But, be advised, registered owner is on our ATL (Attempt to Locate) list for the bus accident this morning. Maybe the school has already notified her that her daughter was flown to OMH."

Fairbanks thought, *What the hell, I'll pick up the DARE pencils and bracelets, after all.* He floored the accelerator, reaching 85 mph, in order to pass the GMC. The DARE Officer activated his emergency lights and led the old green truck in its blind chase to close the distance between a mother and her injured child only 56 miles outside his jurisdiction.

శ్రా

Two

"It is not the things we do in this life so much as the way we do them."
Chris Morganroth
Olympic Pioneer/U.S.Forest Ranger

Olympic Memorial Hospital, Port Angeles, WA
June 8, 1987, 15:10 hours

*B*arbara Stone paced and paced in the waiting room of the Hospital, in a dumb mother's hope that her child would rise unscathed from the bed to again frolic with other children. A doctor named Brown had met her and asked if her daughter had any identifying marks. Barbara said that Mossy had a birthmark on her left knee. The doctor briefly discussed Mossy's condition, giving Barbara little hope for this scenario. He had alluded to the necessity of cerebral drains and blood transfusions. The EMTs had observed the crepitus of the crushed pelvic girdle. The acute abdomen meant there was certainly internal injury. The internal bleeding was being stemmed in surgery and within a couple of hours, Barbara would get word of her daughter's prognosis from this perspective. A CAT Scan would be required to determine brain damage caused by the subdural hematoma, but that would have to wait until Mossy was more stable. Barbara had asked to see her daughter, but the patient was in surgery. She asked if she could see Mossy when she was finished with surgery; and the doctor saw a sweat plastered T-shirt, dirty fingernails, and a muddy, tear-streaked face.

"Your daughter is totally vulnerable to infection at this time. Germs from you could go straight into her brain through the open drain in her head. We can't afford to bombard her with antibiotics. Believe me, she's not suffering. She's out like a light. We're totally committed to saving Mossy and we need your trust and cooperation. We'll let you see her as soon as it won't jeopardize her chance of survival...or, on the other hand...if things go wrong and we feel we can't save her...then you can see her." Then the doctor hurried off to participate in what might be the closing chapter of Mossy's young life.

Friends and family of other patients were made nervous by Barbara's pacing. She couldn't sit still. She was terrified of what the future held for Mossy and her. She paced to escape the claustrophobia of the present, which closed in on her like an iron maiden. As she paced, she felt herself being pulled into the past like a tear drawn back into the eye. The book of her existence appeared. As she speed-read the major events of her life, it occurred to her that every sentence was punctuated with grief:

Barbara, the small girl, owns and loves a dog (grief). A father comforts his daughter and the bond between them grows stronger (grief). Barbara, the young woman, falls in love for the first time (grief). She overcomes the turmoil and complications of first love and marries the target of her amour (grief). The fruit of her widowed marriage is a perfect daughter and friend, Mossy, with whom she shares the wonder of a homesteading life on a frontier (grief, grief, oh GRIEF).

Barbara paced and paced, falling back in time as the minutes moved inexorably forward on the wall clock of the waiting room...

21

୬൶

Rose Lodge, Oregon
November 11, 1967

Ten-year-old Barbara Beyers paced the narrow floor space of the 10' by 14' upstairs bedroom she shared with her sister. Tears streaked her face and her breath caught in uneven gasps. Roscoe, her Bernese mountain dog, had been her best friend for as long as she could remember. On this Saturday, Roscoe and Barbara had crossed the highway to play over at the millpond. Later in the afternoon, when they re-crossed the highway on their return, Barbara had hurried across the road with the dog as a log truck approached. The smell of a rabbit or deer must have drifted into the dog's olfactory because Roscoe turned around and ran back into the highway and right under the wheels of the charging log truck. Her logger father, who was accustomed to sewing up the family pets and heaping gauze over the bleeding wounds of his four children and coworkers, was at a loss at how to deal with Roscoe's injuries. He gently loaded the old dog into the family station wagon, told Barbara to wait inside the house and drove for the vet in Lincoln City.

Two hours later, there was a knock at her door and Glen Beyers stood, without words, in the doorway. The look on his face confirmed her deepest trepidation and she ran to the refuge of her bed bursting into convulsive sobbing. Her father sat on the bed beside her, laying his calloused hand on her shoulder, waiting for the quiet of her subdued grief. There was nothing in the Lutheran view about pet heavens and the logger looked far into the horizon without seeing a silver lining. When, after half an hour, her sobbing had subsided and her broken breathing took cadence with the ticking of the wind-up alarm clock by her bed, her father spoke.

"Barbara, honey... to own and love a pet... you have to accept the reality that one day you'll lose it. Enjoy them while you have them. What you feel right now is the price of love. Roscoe is at peace right now. So don't cry for him. Pets die. That's part of life."

"Daddy, I know that pets die. We **all** die. But I wasn't ready for Roscoe to die. **HE** wasn't ready to die. Roscoe and I had so much fun at the millpond today... (sniff)... running... (sob)... exploring... (sniff)... playing. I miss him and there isn't any end to it. I never got to say 'good-bye.'" And the ticking of the clock was lost in a fresh bout of sobbing, which the father bore in silence.

When the ticking of the clock was again audible, the father spoke. "The coho are in the river right now. I'm going to drift a few miles of the lower river tomorrow and thought you might want to come along: just you and me. Your mom could pack a lunch for us and maybe we'd catch a big fish. At least we would have time together and enjoy the river. What do you say?"

Barbara said nothing for a while and the ticking of the clock measured the silence between the two. Fishing and hunting had always been the province of her older brother, Paul. Barbara strongly identified with her father and was jealous of the quality time that these male members of the family spent together, tromping the forest and plying the waters in pursuit of game for the dinner table. Her grief would not be ameliorated by the promise of a fishing trip, but it was an opportunity not to be spurned...as long as she could be assured that her obnoxious siblings were not to be part of the outing. "Just you and me?"

"Just us two and the river."

ৼৡ

Salmon River near Rose Lodge, OR
Sunday, November 12, 1967

The drift boat glided down the water of the Salmon River, stern first. At times Beyers put down his pole to lazily pull the craft to one side of the stream or the other to avoid the rock shoals and log strainers. Barbara sat erect and attentive at the bow of the boat with her pole straight in the air, like an antenna. She seemed more interested in talking than in catching a fish, but that was OK.

"Why are the salmon only in the river this time of year?"

"It's an early winter run of coho. In winter, there's more water in the streams to keep them from dragging on the rocks, like what this boat would do if the water was low. Each run of fish has its own river or stream. These fish are coming back to where they were born after living out in the ocean for several years. Get it? Different rivers have different runs."

"Why do the fish come in from the ocean? Don't they like it out there?"

"The salmon return to their own spawning grounds - where they hatched and over-summered - to...procreate. The hen, that's the female fish, makes a nest in the gravel and lays her eggs. The male fish comes along and fertilizes the eggs. Sometimes the male fish fight over who gets to fertilize the hen's eggs. It's like the fish have no control of their lives when they get the call to mate - kind of like people on that score. They get the call somewhere out in the ocean and they use their noses to find the river from where they came. They follow their noses all the way up the river to their birthplace. It's amazing when you think about it!"

"Do they go back to the ocean after they mate?"

"No, honey. It's all over for them after they spawn. It's the end of the line. They begin to die when they come into fresh water. The Salish Indians out by Depot Bay - for that matter, all the coastal Indians - believed that God lives in the ocean. This time of year the Indians believe that God dresses himself in salmon flesh and swims up the river to feed the Indians and woodland creatures."

"Is that what we believe?" asked the child, recalling the scant lessons she had learned in the few Sunday school lessons of her life.

"No, princess. We're Lutherans. I guess you could say we believe that God dressed himself in the flesh of Jesus to feed us spiritually. There's something about 'Take, eat. This is my body...'" the father felt self conscious and ill prepared to talk to his child about religious matters and drifted into silence. After a minute he began on another track. "When I was a kid there were thousands of spawned out carcasses along the shoreline this time of year. I remember drifting the river then and you would see bear, coyotes and even cougar down along the river at the all-you-can-eat buffet. There's only a handful of fish compared to what there was back then...but we're lucky to live here. Most places are a lot less wild than this."

"Do the cougar and bear go hungry?"

23

"There's less of them, too. People move into an area and they build their homes along the rivers...like ours is. They take away the homes of the wild animals. They fish the rivers and commercial fishermen are sent out upon the high seas to catch more fish for people to eat. More people means less fish and less habitat and that means less wildlife. You can tell a lot about what's wrong with the world by looking at the fish."

"If too many people is the problem, why don't they stop having so many babies and give the fish and the wild things a chance?"

Beyers mulled this one over, reflecting on his own brood of four squirming fingerlings. "It's like I said about the fish. People are like the fish. Once they get a whiff of the urge to mate, everything else is out the window..."

Suddenly Barbara's pole was nearly pulled out of her hands. It doubled over and she clenched onto it with white knuckles.

"Set the hook! Jerk the pole!" Her father was yelling, but Barbara sat there terrified and in a moment the fish became suspicious of the lure and let go.

The fish left the two drifters to attend to its own business of procreation and the quest for salmonhood. Aboard the boat, after a discussion of how to set a hook and reel in a large fish, there was time for reflection and a few moments of silence.

"I miss the wildness this country used to have," the father continued. "It reminds me of a cowboy story I heard which occurred in Texas some years back. The countryside was being settled and most of the wild horses that had roamed the countryside were being captured for riding stock or dog food..."

"DOGFOOD?" exclaimed Barbara in protest.

Beyers continued..."A group of cowboys started chasing this one, fine-looking white Pacing Mustang that they all agreed would be a fine ride for the man lucky enough to capture it. That wild horse could run like the wind and none of the cowboys could get close to it. So they pooled their information and resources, and showed up as a team, to chase down that white Mustang. From their talk among themselves they knew the horse's route and they spread out on their own horses along 200 miles of wild Texas countryside. On the agreed day, a cowboy at one end began chasing the white Mustang and that horse ran for a day and a half without stopping for food or water. It got to the end of the wilderness and turned around and ran back for a day and half with the cowboys all chasing.

"The cowboys gave up after three days, figuring someone would get killed, or lame a horse chasing that crazy Mustang. Another cowboy, unrelated to the pursuit, came along a while later and saw that lathered up white Mustang drinking out of a watering hole to quench the thirst that he had worked up running for three days straight. Now any creature that's shipped aboard three days worth of water can't run for horse pucky and that cowboy had no trouble chasing down the Mustang and getting a rope around its neck. He took the Mustang back to the prize stall at the ranch where he worked. He laid out the finest alfalfa and nice clean water for the Mustang. He called all the other cowboys to come admire his catch. But everyone noticed that the Mustang wasn't eating his nice alfalfa. Days went by and the Mustang wouldn't eat or drink. The cowboy tried bringing in water from the Mustang's old hole and bringing in the scrub brush from the desert. The wild horse wouldn't eat or drink and after ten days, that magnificent wild Mustang laid down and died..."

"That's a horrible story, Daddy!"

"I don't think so. The Mustang was captured, but never surrendered it's wildness. Maybe its hooves are tearing up the desert of some wilderness heaven. Maybe Roscoe is lying by some cozy hearth in the hereafter. The Bible doesn't talk much about what happens to animals when they die, but there must be a place for their souls. Where do these fish end up? They certainly show spirit in their fight. Is it too much to think they have soul?"

"What was that white Mustang's name?"

"It didn't have a name, princess. What was that fish's name you had on the line? Wild things don't have names. You take away a wild creature's spirit when you give it a name..."

The father's ruminations and ponderings were interrupted as his daughter's pole bent over again. This time, Barbara gave it a jerk, setting the hook. She struggled with the fish, alternately letting the fish pull against the resistance of the pole and taking in line as her father directed. In about five minutes, the fish was brought alongside of the boat and her father reached down to pick up the net. Barbara pulled again and brought the fish's head out of the water; the lure stuck on the creature's lip, its eye looked unblinkingly at Barbara. Through the unyielding gaze of the fish, Barbara perceived that she viewed the coho's soul: its quest for procreation; the spirit that pushed it forward into the poisonous fresh water. In catching the fish, Barbara had interrupted the journey much like Roscoe's journey had been interrupted by the log truck. She was stealing a precious carcass from the wild things whose cubs and kittens would, in turn, go to bed hungry. She began to cry.

Her father watched for a moment and shook his head. Without taking the fish out of the water, he removed the hook from its lip and held the creature's head into the current for a minute, letting its gills gulp oxygen from the fresh water. When the fish began to struggle, Beyers let go, and the fish disappeared into the current. "Good as new," reported her father, stowing the two poles. "Maybe we should forget about the fishing and just explore this river a little bit."

"I'm (sniff, sniff) sorry, Daddy." Barbara worried that this might be the last excursion her father would want to take with her.

But the rest of the afternoon was a total success. Her dad landed the drift boat and they walked up a side channel where he pointed out salmon redds being guarded by the hens and bulls. They saw a skunk and a raccoon eating carcasses further up the channel. They had a picnic in a meadow with deer grazing in plain view - even though it was general buck season. All in all, it was one of the best days of Barbara's life and, when they pulled the drift boat up on the launch to be met by her mother, who brought the trailer along with Barbara's two brothers and sister, she felt like a salmon being inexorably pulled from the current.

"Dad, this was the best day of my life," said Barbara hugging her father's waist and burying her face in the wool shirt he wore. "Can we please do it again?"

"Yes, honey. It was really fun. I'll be out hunting next weekend, but two weeks from today, we'll drift it again and talk more about the fish." The hook was set. What began as a fishing trip on a river behind her house, resulted in a lifetime preoccupation with salmon and the protection of their habitat.

৵৶

The following week, Beyers returned to the meadow with a 30-06 carbine and Paul, his eldest. The deer were still in evidence, browsing brush and, from a vantage behind the trees, Beyers set up an easy shot through the rifle scope. "Here you go, Paul. He's a four-point buck and it's a sure shot." Beyers passed the carbine to the 13-year-old boy, who watched the deer for a few moments through the scope. Beyers could see tension and anxiety forming on the face of his son as he took off the safety; the finger trembling as it curled into the guard. Paul held his breath for fifteen seconds; then gulped air and went to set up the shot again. His son was not enjoying this. "Wait a second." The father took back the carbine and looked through the scope. It was an easy shot. He glanced back at this son whose face was still screwed up in anticipation of the shot; the blood; the butchering.

He set the weapon down. They needed the meat on the table, but the killing could wait. "How about if we forget about hunting for a while and just watch the deer. I can show you where they bed down and we can check down by the slough and maybe see a bear or otter feeding on the salmon carcasses."

There was relief in his son's face. "Sure, Dad. Whatever you say. That would be great!"

It was the best outing Beyers had ever had with his son.

ঌৣৄৢ

Sunday, November 26, 1967, 12:30 hours

"Daddy, let's just go!" whined Barbara, standing next to the drift boat which would have to be dragged across the lawn and into the woods to the river. Already, their lunches, a camera, binoculars, a magnifying glass, and other tools of the young girl's trade had been carried across to the put-in.

"I told you, that my partner Dave was coming over for a brief visit after his church meeting. His son Brian, will be with him. I want you to play with him for half an hour without killing him. Normally, I'd give that honor to Paul, but he's over at his friend's for the weekend, so you'll have to fill in."

"But, DAD! You promised we'd go exploring and Brian is a nerd!"

Glen Beyers silenced the child with a scalding look. A few moments later, David and Brian pulled up in the Jones' four-wheel-drive pickup on their way back from church in Lincoln City. Barbara looked over the fine Sunday school raiment worn by Brian and settled on an idea. "Let's go to the millpond and explore a bit."

"Wait a minute!" interjected Beyers. "That millpond's no place for a kid in Sunday school clothes."

"I brought his farm boots," said Brian's father, husking off his son's shiny brown shoes and replacing them with oversized boots, which went above the knees of the child.

"A size bigger and the whole kid would be in the boot," remarked Beyers watching nervously as the two children crossed the road going in the direction of the millpond where God-only-knew-what was in store for Brian. "Remember what I told you!" he called out. "Be careful with Brian!"

26

"They'll be OK," theorized Jones, offended at the affront to his son's sensibilities. "Listen, Glen, we have to talk about this Cape Perpetua contract we're working. The only way we're going to get to that pocket of timber in the southwest corner of section 13 is to short haul the logs on the Cat road. To dump gravel and punch in switchbacks for the log trucks...we'd never make up the costs of the road."

"It's almost a mile of road. It'll cost more than the logs are worth to skid them out with the Cat."

"I figure we'll bring in Beckner," reasoned Jones. "He's got a self loader on that old all-wheel-drive troop carrier..."

"That old rattle trap! It's more work keeping that junkyard-on-wheels moving than it would be to put **us** in traces and mush the logs out ourselves..."

"What is it with you and Beckner's truck, Glen?"

ᔕᘓ

Meanwhile, at the millpond:

"I can jump from all the way up there and not get hurt," announced Barbara. She pointed twelve feet above the pond to a little crow's nest built over the cutting deck of the old mill. All the mill's equipment had been removed decades ago, after the first cutting of the trees around Rose Lodge. Remaining, was the wooden skeleton of the lost industry; the rotting remains of culled lumber and the pond itself, where the logs had been stored awaiting their fate. At the edge of the pond, about eight feet out from the pier that supported the cutting deck, was an invisible peninsula of cedar saw-chips which offered more ballast than the rest of the muck around the pond's edge. Barbara climbed up the old step way, picked her target from the crow's nest and launched herself out for the spot she knew would support her impact. She landed on her feet, sinking in a few inches, and held up her arms. "Ta da!" Barbara followed the peninsula back to dry land.

"That's nothing," said Brian, climbing the steps to take the leap.

"Oh, it takes practice," Barbara's voice taunted Brian. "I'm supposed to look out for you...don't jump off there."

"It's no big deal..." said Brian, gulping in awe from the distance he had attained above the shore. He was having second thoughts, but knew there was no way around the jump if a girl had done it first. He looked straight ahead as he stepped off into space. He felt like he fell forever, but had a nice soft landing when he impacted the shoreline. When he looked down, his eyes were about three feet above the mud and his farm boots were wholly swallowed by the hungry muck. "Hey! Get me out of here!" cried Brian indignantly.

"I told you not to jump," chided Barbara, throwing Brian an old rotten 4" by 4" for floatation.

"Did not!" contradicted Brian, slipping further into the muck. "My feet are stuck! **Hey, this is quicksand!**" He looked worried now.

Fifteen minutes later, Beyers and Jones had concluded their business and were talking about fishing when Barbara led what looked like Swamp Thing across the road to the horrified adults. "I said, 'Don't jump off there,'" claimed

Barbara as if she were talking about an individual with a severe developmental handicap.

"DID NOT!" erupted the Swamp Thing, apparently contesting that it was instructed not to jump. Beyers brought over a charged garden hose and gave it to the Thing's father.

"Did too! His boots are still over there." This was news for the adults who, for all the hosing off, were not sure there was a child inside all that walking muck.

"DID NOT!" cried Brian being loaded into the back of the pickup, shivering.

"I'm sorry about this," offered Beyers as Jones climbed into the driver's seat. Barbara and I will go back and look for the boots."

"DID TOO!" called out Barbara, politely waving good-bye.

෨෴

Cape Perpetua, Oregon
Friday, December 1, 1967, 11:15 hours

The old truck was in the middle of the make-shift landing, squatting under a full load of logs. Glen Beyers picked a spot in the sunshine and sat down to eat his lunch using one of the rear wheels of the old, World War Two troop carrier for a backrest. The truck had been converted with a jury-rigged self-loader and cobbled together log bunker. It was being used to short haul logs from a little unit, which was accessed by a four-wheel-drive road, to the main landing almost a mile away. Beyers had an uneasy relationship with the troop carrier.

In July, 1944, following the bloody wave which broke upon Normandy Beach, Beyers had completed basic training and been sent to clean up the crumbling opposition of the Third Reich. Moving from France to Germany in canvas-covered cages on the bed of troop carriers like this one, the Americans had been like ducks in a barrel for the handful of German infantry that persisted in resisting the Allied onslaught. The sudden chatter of a 50-caliber machine gun answered by one or two tank rounds: several wounded or dead American GI's were pulled from the carriers and some poor scout got sent up to make sure the fifteen-year-old German kid on the machine gun was dead.

There was no joy in the liberation for Beyers' Division. The release of the prisoners from Dachau..."It's over. Es ist doruber." the GI's kept telling the prisoners. There was no jubilation in the skeletal faces. A soup kitchen was set up in the cafeteria previously used by the S.S. officers that were the camp's administrators. Young Beyers had asked one of the interpreters from military intelligence about a paragraph of German calligraphy on the wall over the mess area. "It's Luke 11," said the bespectacled interpreter. " 'Our Father, who art in heaven...' "

"The Lord's Prayer," grimaced Beyers. "What religion were these animals, anyway?"

"Lutheran, mostly."

The survivors moved about like robots, mechanically moving their spoons from the soup bowl to their faces without satisfaction or relish. They

28

continued to die in spite of rescue efforts. It was like death was some kind of pillow or net for them. There had been a destruction of hope; a trampling of human spirit. "Es ist doruber, God damn it..."

"How are you and my truck getting along today?" Burt Beckner, the owner and driver of the troop-carrier-turned-log-truck, sat down beside Beyers, resting his back on the second set of rear wheels and opening his lunch box.

"It's an uneasy truce, Burt. I'll feel better when we finish with this little pocket of timber and aren't staking our lives and fortunes on a piece of equipment held together with bailing wire and chewing gum."

"Ha!" retorted Beckner. "This truck will dance on your grave."

" That's what these old deuce-and-a-halves are best at: grave dancing," grimaced Beyers.

"Are you two still arguing about this poor old truck?" called out Dave Jones, reaching into the cab of his four-wheel drive pickup to retrieve a tin lunch box. Walking from the cab, seeing both sets of rear wheels occupied, Jones sat down, forward of the cab, and rested his back on the front wheels. "Let's at least argue about something worthy of our wind."

"Like: what's the best way to save our immortal souls?" offered the lackadaisical Lutheran, Beyers, to the fire breathing Born Again.

"Like: where are Brian's farm boots?" countered Jones, sitting down and opening his lunch pail. He let it drop. "Let's see what the wife put in the old nose bag." He pulled out a turkey drumstick and began gnawing on it like a coyote on a road kill. Beyers pulled out a second piece of his wife's homemade pie. Beckner slammed shut his lunch box and threw it in the cab of the troop carrier. He pulled out a three-foot pipe cheater bar to help him cinch down the load binders, which kept the log payload in place down the precipitous and bouncy four-wheel-drive road to the landing.

Beyers finished his lunch and pulled away from the tire to lie on his back stretching out on the ground. On the other side of the truck, Beckner grunted and muttered, tweaking down on the front binder. Beyers looked up at the deep blue sky and thought happily about the great times he had been having with his kids.

'Where are Brian's farm boots?': Beyers had accompanied his daughter back to the millpond to look for the boots directly after the Jones' retreat last Sunday. There was a rotten 4" by 4" timber laid out in the muck and a huge crater where the child had struggled to extricate himself.

"Get the boots," the father ordered quietly. Barbara walked out on the rotten timber and knelt over to bury her arms in the muck. She tried several times, but came out dirty armed, but empty-handed. "Get the boots," repeated the father. On the fourth try Barbara fell face first into the muck. She struggled to get her feet under her and, failing that, tried to turn around to reach the 4" by 4". Her father watched with respect as his daughter worked without complaint to effect her own rescue. When he stepped out on the timber to help her, he in turn fell into the muck. It took ten minutes for both of them to get out and the boots had been hopelessly beaten into the primal ooze, maybe to come out in some rice paddy in China. He and Barbara started laughing as they hosed each other off and, all afternoon, they would burst out laughing at the thought of it. They had such a good time, checking out the fish in all the side channels...but they couldn't stop laughing.

ৎৡ

Cape Perpetua, Oregon
Friday, December 1, 1967, 11:45 hours

"What's so funny?" asks his partner, Dave, pulling Beyers back to the present.

Glen Beyers looks straight up into the blue sky, hearing Beckner grunting and mumbling as he reefs down on the rear load binder and says, "We looked for those boots, Dave, we really..."   Beyers hears the rear chain snap and the log payload explodes outward, tearing apart the log bunker like a Tasmanian Devil breaking out of a hamster cage. Before Glen Beyers can wipe the smile off his face, his view of the blue sky is eclipsed by ten tons of logs rolling off the truck. In slow motion, Beyers begins to roll and is still rolling as the logs start hitting all around him. He feels a log come down square on his shoulder. For a moment he cannot roll, but then he is rolling into the darkness...there is no blue: only dark...*salmon swimming upstream...*"GLEN!"...*there's light up ahead...I'm in the river...a wild, white horse running across the wilderness... a warm seat by the hearth and forge of Creation...swimming...*

"GLEN! Hang on, we're getting to you. Burt! Get the other peavey so we can get these logs off of him."...*it's the voice of my partner, What's-his-name.* "Jesus, it's his arm! Christ Almighty!"...*leaving the salt water of creation and swimming up the river of Life...*"Glen! I know you can hear me! Open your eyes, man. Jesus, look at his shoulder. He's not going to make it, Burt!"

Beyers struggles to get his eyes open, but the message his eyes are sending to his brain is all static and nonsensical...like a TV picture when a squirrel chews through one of the feed wires to the roof antenna. His partner is holding a huge turkey drumstick...no, a HUMAN ARM! Beyers recognized his wedding ring and shut his eyes again.

"Glen, hold on. You're going to be all right!"

It is all light. Who is this Glen, anyway?...fish swimming upstream into the headwaters of Creation: our flesh is dying. From the time we leave the salt water of our birth, we are dying. "DYING."

"What did you say, Glen? Burt! Help me get him in the back of the pickup...hurry it up! He's bleeding to death! What did you say, Glen? Talk to me!"

In the fresh water of life we are all..."DYING..."

"No, Glen. You're not dying. Is that what you asked? **Don't forget the arm, Burt! Watch his head; don't let his head dangle like that! Talk to me, Glen! Hang on for your kids' sake!**"

...fish swimming upstream in the River of Life...he wasn't leaving his mate or spawn: they were just further downstream as he approached the shimmering Light...into the fire and forge of Creation...other fish swimming beside me...without names, but I know them...the friends and family that were called upstream before me...into the timeless Light, past the roe of future generations...

"Give me a towel or something to hold on his shoulder, Burt! You still with me, Glen? We're going to the hospital to have you sewn up. The Lord is my Shepherd, I shall not want. He maketh me to lie down in the green

30

pastures...Don't forget the arm, Burt...GLEN, STAY WITH ME!...put it back here with us, Burt so it doesn't fall out when you get in or out of the rig..."

...there's the Lord's House upstream in the side channel. It's all light. We're all swimming into the Light...

"Our Father, Who art in heaven, hallowed be thy name...GLEN! LET'S PRAY, OK?...Hallowed be thy name. Thy kingdom come... GLEN! Glen? It's over, Burt! Hold on, I'll ride up front with you!"

...swimming into the timeless Light...

૭৵৵

Rose Lodge, OR
Monday, January 8, 1968, 08:45 hours

It was not easy for Barbara, returning to school. It was not easy for any of Glen Beyers' family to return to normalcy. Watching her mother prepare breakfast this morning, Barbara knew that it was all the woman could do to hold on long enough to get the two older kids out of the house. Her mother needed time to be alone with her grief. Barbara knew she had to be strong for her family, so she left for school before her brother. She was not comforted at the sight of Brian Jones, coming down the steps of the school to greet her.

"We never found your boots, Brian."

"My whole family feels terrible about what happened to your dad. We wish to express our regrets," said the young hypocrite, saying what he must have rehearsed for hours.

"We'll make it," said Barbara trying to get by Brian to the school's entrance.

Finished with the rehearsed spiel, young Brian entered the ad-lib portion of his condolences: "I mean the way your dad's arm came off and everything was horrible and I know how you must feel..."

"My father's arm didn't get knocked off in the accident and I don't know who started that story..."

"Oh, it got knocked off, all right. My dad forgot to carry it in when he dropped off your dad at the funeral place and came home with it. He was telling my mom and us about what happened when our dog, Pepsi, started scratching to be let in. I opened the door and Pepsi was dragging your dad's arm. My mom fainted..."

"OK, Mr. Smarty Pants," retorted Barbara, with her eyes stinging with the tears she was fighting back - revisiting her father's open casket in her mind: "If your dog ate my dad's arm than how come he had both arms at the funeral. You were there, you little liar! He had both arms!"

"My dad got the arm back from Pepsi and took it to the funeral parlor. They sewed it on like you would sew the arm back on a stuffed chair. I swear to God! My mom won't let Pepsi have bones anymore and my father threw out a leftover turkey drumstick. They're really upset. Your dad's arm got pulled off in that accident same as you would pull the leg off a Daddy Long Legs..."

"DID NOT!" Barbara could feel her certainty slipping. She gave up going into the school building and began pacing outside.

31

"Did not, did not, did not."

"Did too," countered her tormenter.

"DID NOT!"

"Did too"

"DID NOT!"

Did, too. Barbara, it certainly did, is, and will always be.

ౚౚ

Olympic Memorial Hospital
June 8, 1987, 17:20 hours

Barbara Stone was pacing the waiting room like a caged animal. While others in the waiting room read newspapers or engaged in private conversation, few were finding sufficient distraction to escape the uneasy atmosphere created by Barbara's incessant stalking. A receptionist approached Barbara.

"Ms. Stone?"

"Yes?" said Barbara with real fear in her voice. Would a receptionist carry the news of her daughter's demise on the surgery table?

"I just got word that your daughter is out of surgery. She's doing...as well as can be expected. The doctors would like to meet with you in about an hour to discuss Mossy's condition and some strategies for her treatment."

"Is she expected to live? What are her major problems?"

"The doctors will discuss her condition with you. I'm really not informed of these things. As far as it goes, Mossy made it out of surgery and that's a really good sign."

"Thank you," said Barbara in a small voice, the knot in her stomach unclenching only slightly.

"There is a cafeteria down the hall to your left, if you would like to get something to eat or some free coffee..."

"No!" At the thought of eating, Barbara's stomach splashed acid. She became aware of her thirst and her thoughts of water brought her to washing her hands. She became aware of the garden dirt under her fingernails; the dry dust on the back of her hands. She looked down at the sweat stained T-shirt she still wore from her gardening. "No, thank you. Is there a washroom around where I could clean up before I talk to the doctors?"

"Yes. Just across from the cafeteria."

Barbara picked up her day pack and headed down the hall following the international symbols for toilet/sink. Her body walked purposefully, but her consciousness toggled from the joy and anguish of the past to the anxiety and uncertainty of the future. She followed the sign of a person standing in front of a toilet into the bright, blue-tiled room.

She stood in front of the sink for a moment letting the cold water run and looking at herself in the mirror, trying to collect herself to the here and now. There was a film of garden dust over the pretty face with little muddy streaks leading down from her eyes to her chin. Her long, brown hair was tied back, but was escaping its mooring and having a bad day. Barbara sighed and pulled back her hair into a ponytail, which she held with her right hand while she put her mouth to the spigot to gulp the cold water. She was immediately overwhelmed by the taste of chlorine, which was absent from her liquid intake on her farm. She rinsed her mouth and spit into the sink. She became aware of the person using the sink next to her looking at her in the mirror. Drinking from the spigot was something she had done since she was a child... something Mossy did about a million times every night before going to sleep...running back and forth from her bed to the bathroom, drinking little sips of water from the sink like a humming bird...

Dear God, please let her be all right. Please let my little precious child live...

Barbara took off the dirty T-shirt and stood in front of the mirror in her bra. She removed a wash cloth from her day pack and began sponge bathing her torso. A toilet flushed behind Barbara and the occupant of the stall waited to use a sink. The person who had stared at her in the mirror left, vacating the sink to the left. Barbara put the damp wash cloth back in the pack and turned around to use the toilet, almost bumping into the person who was somehow missing that the left sink was available. Barbara left her day pack on the floor and went to use the stall. She found that she was constipated and made a resolution to drink more water, even if it tasted like sewage. She flushed the empty toilet and went back to her pack while two people used the sink. She pulled out a T-shirt to put on and a man at the sink said gently, "We can leave if it would make you more comfortable."

Quickly, Barbara donned her clean T-shirt and fled the men's room. A nurse met her outside the door, evidently summoned by the staring face in the mirror. "Is everything all right?" asked the worried nurse.

"Yes," lied Barbara and then broke down into great heaving, quaking sobs...crying uncontrollably for her loneliness and fear. She missed Mossy; she missed Phil; she missed her father...she still missed Roscoe...*Sweet Jesus! Is there nothing for this unrelenting loneliness and fear?*

ومي

Olympic Memorial Hospital
June 8, 1987, 18:40 hours

"Ms. Stone, I'm Dr. Knoodle, a neurologist. This is Dr. Baker, an orthopedic surgeon; and Dr. Brown, our emergency room surgeon. I would say that we three represent the team entrusted with your daughter's care, except we are part of a much larger team, which includes this entire hospital and, certainly, yourself. We three are going off shift in about an hour. Before we discuss Mossy's care with the doctors who will replace us this evening, we knew that you would have questions and want a full report. We know how stressful this is for you, Barbara, and we want to remind you of the counseling and support services available to you.

"Mossy is a very strong girl and, though she is a long way from out of the woods, that she has survived this long; that she is breathing on her own; the results of the CAT scan: these are all good signs that give us hope. But we still list her condition as critical and our optimism will be on better ground when...**if** she regains consciousness. That your daughter survived the accident is a bit of a miracle. The bus ran over her. She was trapped under the tire for over an hour. She sustained a depressed skull fracture and the concussion was aggravated by the engorging of the vessels in her brain from the blood being pushed up from her abdomen. A human body just can't suffer such insult without sustaining some permanent damage." Barbara slumped.

"We have to remain realistic in our outlook. There is a chance that Mossy will not survive the next twelve hours. Her liver was severely lacerated by a piece of her shattered hip and we transfused five units of blood during our surgery. Her bladder was ruptured and required surgical repair by Dr. Brown.

Dr. Brown interrupted, "Behind and just above the bladder is where the uterus develops. In Mossy, this will be all scar tissue and we can say with confidence that she will never develop a normal, fertile uterus. Our agenda for the next few days is keeping Mossy alive. When she is stabilized Dr. Baker will use the same surgical incisions to rebuild and pin her pelvis."

Dr. Knoodle continued, "Because of the tremendous pressure from the swelling in her brain, we had to open two drains through her skull which is routine procedure. If all goes well, we should be able to close them tomorrow. We just plug the hole with the bone we cut out. It sounds much more dramatic than it really is.

"The CAT scan is good, but there is some tissue damage in the area of the concussion. I don't know how much you know about the human brain, but maybe I should say a few words about the process of thought. It's a little bit like an enormous playing field with half a billion players on it corresponding to brain cells. There are hundreds of games going on, corresponding to every function of the human body and every process of our conscious and unconscious thought. The different functions are sometimes discrete, but a lot of times involve passing the ball from one game to another, such as encoding a message from the ear, formulating a response and sending a message to the lungs, larynx and mouth to respond. Even with all these functions, there is more ground and players in the field than there is game to play. As players become casualties, new players move in to keep up the games. If an area of the playing field becomes too muddy or is fenced off, the game that was being played there is moved to a different part of the field.

"The playing field of the human brain has been mapped and we know where the different games are played, which account for survival of the organism and behavior of the species. In the right quadrant of the brain are located the areas that participate in the regulation of emotions and the development of personality. The problem is that the game being played here is always one of transferring the ball to some other part of the playing field. Because the ball moves so fast across the right brain, when casualties occur, there is a lack of perception that new players should come on the field. The ball is thrown erratically and sometimes fumbled.

"Mossy sustained right brain injury in the area most typically associated with the development of personality. Assuming she survives and recovers, she may present atypical human behavior for some time to come. She faces a long and painful rehabilitation. Socially, she may become somewhat eccentric, but that's the least of our worries right now. That's it in a nutshell. Can we answer any questions?"

Upon the playing field of Barbara Stone's brain, almost five billion players stood quietly, dumbfounded and grief stricken. The few players that were still in the game called for a brief huddle and the quarterback initiated the psychogenic shock game plan. Between the brain and the heart, the ball was thrown faster and faster; the skin begin to sweat in a diaphoretic glow and Barbara caught her breath in a hypoxic reflex. The players, who had staged the uncontrolled crying forty-five minutes earlier, still had enough energy to push a tear from a duct in Barbara's right eye and clamp down hard on the vasculature of her stomach.

From the biology lesson offered by the neurologist, Barbara had gained nothing. Four years as a premed student at Oregon State University had left her with a stronger anatomical appreciation for the subtleties of cellular damage and brain waves than that offered by the neurologist's primer. Her husband had died of a head injury. How could this be happening?

"Ms. Stone? Barbara, do you have any questions?"

This **was** happening! Barbara struggled against the dizziness and rising nausea. The players in the field turned to one another asking questions, voicing their anxieties and began passing the ball to the speech center.

"Barbara, would you like to sit down? Can we get you some water or prescribe a sedative?"

"**WILL**..." started Barbara in a loud voice, stopping to modulate her speech and gain control of the pandemonium, which was breaking out across the playing field.

"Excuse me?" asked Dr. Knoodle, waiting for the mother to compose herself.

"Will she...walk. Will Mossy be able to walk?"

Dr. Baker fielded this question. "It's much too early to say anything about her mobility. We see here a patient with remarkable tenacity and determination and that's a good sign. Still, the pelvic girdle was shattered and radically displaced. As Dr. Knoodle mentioned, rehabilitation will be a long and uncomfortable process. We want to focus on the more immediate concerns relating to your daughter's survival." To himself, Dr. Baker added, *If she walks again, without crutches, it will be one of the true miracles of my career.*

"Can I see her now. Can I be with her?"

The neurologist answered, "We think it would be a very poor idea. We definitely need her defended from any contamination for the next twelve hours until we replace the burrs taken from her skull. You could see her through glass, but we strongly recommend against it. You are an important member of this team working for Mossy's recovery. We need your hope and strength. She's breathing on her own, but she's still attached to a ventilator for better oxygenation and control of her breathing environment. She's hooked up to the IV and to a heart monitor. With the cerebral drains I mentioned, she's quite a sight and our experience has been that it's overly traumatic for parents to view this degree of medical intervention. She is unconscious and you won't help her. Wait until tomorrow when you're rested and Mossy is somewhat recovered from the ordeal of the accident and surgery. If her condition changes, you'll be notified and you can see her."

All of a sudden the players on the field were throwing questions at the speech center faster than the balls could be put into play. Balls were being fumbled everywhere and Barbara stood in silence. Then Dr. Knoodle looked at his watch and left the room followed by Dr. Baker. Dr. Brown stood awkwardly waiting for a final word. All the players on Barbara's field scrambled to formulate a question that would tear down this sad wall...a wall which somehow deflected all the balls thrown into the court that a mother reserves for her child.

"Is there nothing I can do for Mossy? Nothing at all?" the mother pleaded.

Doctor Brown stood up as to leave. "Ms. Stone, are you a religious person?"

"Yes," Barbara answered reflexively. "I'm Lutheran...or I was raised Lutheran, though I don't attend church much."

"Then," said the doctor in a quiet voice, "you can pray for Mossy. I know I will."

ক৵৶

God in Heaven, please let my child live. The words were somewhat garbled as they left the mouth of Barbara Stone. She knelt on the floor of the chapel room of Olympic Memorial with her eyes clenched tight and spoke in a faltering, mostly unintelligible voice as she spoke directly with her Host of Hosts for the first time since her childhood. With her dog, Roscoe, as a witness, she had prayed out loud for her older brother to get run over by a logging truck. This evening at Olympic Memorial, a man and woman with problems of their own, sat in embarrassed silence at the front of the chapel as Barbara bore her heart to God. To the couple in front, it seemed like the woman kneeling in the back in a T-shirt and blue jeans was sometimes speaking Hebrew or gibberish. But the message from Barbara's heart to God was: *Please let my child live. I have had enough tests of my faith: the loss of my father and husband...I have never stopped believing in You. But my faith is not strong enough to lose my daughter. She is the most precious gift You have ever given me and I just can't go on without her in my life. She will not give me grandchildren. I had looked forward to that, but I accept this change in our lives. They say that it will be a long, hard rehabilitation. Dear God, please give us the challenge...and let my little girl walk again. Please let her life and health be a temple to hold my worship. I will thank You with every one of my daughter's footsteps. I will praise You with every ring of Mossy's laughter and song. If I could give my life or my health for hers...Give me back the miracle of my daughter's life and health and I will take it as a sign from You - a foundation upon which to build faith. My belief and gratitude will never falter. But, God, Lord, Jehovah, answer this one prayer, please: I must...have...my little...girl back.*

Barbara continued to kneel on the floor, her head resting on the oak bench in front of her. Exhausted and wrung out, her mind ran across the wide field of memory: looking for a happier time in which to find comfort and rest. Every happy moment recalled from the last decade called up the joyful face of her

36

daughter. The image of her effervescent daughter stung Barbara's closed eyes and knotted her empty stomach. She drifted back to a time before Mossy: a time of exploration, of discovery...of newness and hope. Barbara quieted her mind, focusing only on the memory. The tired players on the field of Barbara's consciousness sat down exhausted on the dusty field and watched the mummery of memory.

Three

"When 'knowledge' enjoys the entirety of our present situation as 'space' and 'time', this same 'knowledge' is able to remain undeceived by time's apparent passage; the partitions which mark out discrete, temporal points and the feeling of moments having elapsed are recognized as UNREAL. Everything - whether past, present, or future - is seen to be unoriginated, because 'knowledge' perceives that, in point of fact, THERE IS NO MOVING TIME."
-Tarthang Tulka
Indian author/philosopher

"The clearest way into the universe is through a forest wilderness."
- John Muir
Founder of the Sierra Club

Highway 101, Quinault, WA
Tuesday, September 12, 1978

Barbara drove her old green GMC pickup north along Highway 101 through the horizon-to-horizon clearcuts of the 200,000 acre reservation of the Quinault Indian Nation. Abruptly, the road corridor plunged into a finger of old growth timber. Gargantuan, moss-draped spruce and hemlock curtained either side of the highway like a parting of green sea. A roadside sign welcomed her to Olympic National Forest, the target of her peregrination, but she would be working further north, in the Soleduck district of the Forest. Passing Lake Quinault at Amanda Park, the road climbed to a vantage over the lake basin, which revealed the stark, brown boundaries of the reservation with the tall, green, rain forests of the Colonel Bob Wilderness behind.

Barbara had answered a flier at the Oregon State University advertising for post- grad biologists to study forest ecology, specifically the impact of logging upon fisheries. She called the number from the campus Career Development Office and had been forwarded to Rick Larson, a U.S.F.S. biologist who had overviewed the Bear Creek Study on the Bogachiel River. He had forewarned Barbara of the desolation evident across the Reservation. Larson had explained that the Bureau of Indian Affairs had managed the sale of the timber resources from the Reservation. It had been a rape and run operation, conducted in the days before the statutes requiring replanting within three years of harvest. The tribe's heritage, a major piece of the most productive forest in the world, was rapidly converted to a 200,000 acre stump ranch, a fleet of rusted out four-wheel-drive pickups and a mountain of empty beer cans. The Quinault Nation sued the B.I.A., arguing bad forestry and mismanagement of the trust. The defense argued that, while the 200,000 acres would lay fallow for some time, by not replanting a singular crop of Doug fir, the B.I.A. foresters had allowed for a more natural and healthy forest succession. The court found in favor of the B.I.A.

Larson had gone on to explain that the Forest Service was responsible for remaining on the cutting edge - ha, ha, no pun intended - of forestry science. Replanting was a basic precept of forest management and greatly reduced the time required to grow a crop of trees, but, in the long run, did monoculture produce the healthiest forests? As an Agency, the Service was convinced that forest practice could parallel natural science to sustain a healthy environment within a commercially viable frame of land management.

The Bear Creek Study on the Bogachiel River proposed a detailed and thorough inventory of the factors relating to wild fish propagation in a controlled environment. For the last two years, the pristine creek had been studied from every angle. This winter, a swath of trees would be removed along the riparian zone, without roads, yarding, or other logging intrusions. The indicators would be closely monitored. Then the roads would be developed, the fallen timber removed, the trees further back from the creek harvested and the indicators revisited. The study would have significant relevance to forest practice in managing for fish habitat. Did this sound like the kind of post-grad work that Barbara was seeking?

It was (now).

"Good," said the biologist. "Then let me explain to you one of the downsides of the study. We have to work on-site, of course, and, without four-wheel-drive, you're pretty much cut off from the outside world. There's a little shack with a wood stove and kerosene heater, but there is no plumbing, electricity or phone. Does this still sound like anything you'd be interested in?"

"Sure. I like primitive conditions."

"Well, you'll love this, Barbara. You'll hear the coyotes howling most nights, there's cougar and bear all over that country. It's wild and it's lonely...too lonely. We've lost a couple of researchers who just couldn't hack the social deprivation of it. That's another part of the problem: We're recruiting for two biologists but, if you take the position, until we find you a partner, you're it. Are you still interested?"

"I'm OK working by myself. It sounds like my kind of place," said Barbara prophetically, not yet aware that this squat, green, amphibious bulge - the Olympic Peninsula - would swallow her life like a frog taking a bug.

So yesterday Barbara had her transcripts sent from O.S.U. to Washington State University who managed the internship. She walked away from four years of pre-med, to prepare her for veterinary medicine, to follow an interest that was born a decade ago in a drift boat with her father. She negotiated with her older brother, who lived in Corvallis, for the old pickup truck, loaded it down with camping gear and food, and set out for Rose Lodge to spend the night with her mom and explain her decision to change her life.

ᔥᔉ

Undi Road
Tuesday, September 12, 1978

The Undi Road, which in 1978 terminated at the pioneer road and would become USFS 2932, crosses Bear Creek several hundred feet from its mouth into the Bogachiel River. Just east of this lies a full-fledged cedar swamp with large, placid water. The smooth water serves as a mirror to reflect light. On September 12, 1978 an upside down universe glimmered from the surface of the swamp, hiding the fingerling that lurked beneath. Barbara pulled her truck over to gawk. A blue heron waded along the shore bobbing its head to overcome the false front presented by the reflection. From Barbara's perspective the creature appeared to be Siamese herons joined at the legs. In the reflection, a bald eagle swam through the blue sky and curtains of moss and fern hung upside down from the cedar sentinels. Barbara approached the swamp to see what she could see beneath the reflection and she saw an upside down young, smiling woman standing at the edge of this reflected universe. After a few moments the upside down woman glanced at her upside down watch and realized she was late for her upside down rendezvous with the biologist at the road's end.

ഏ

USFS 2932
Tuesday, September 12, 1978

Rick Larson laughed as the four-wheel-drive pickup bounced and spun its wheels charging up the southern flank of Reade Hill. Below, the Bogachiel River slithered through the timbered slopes like a jeweled snake on the rain forest floor.

"I had a filling fall out two weeks ago when I drove up to pack out one of the students who quit." The bearded biologist with blue-grey eyes looked at Barbara and smiled. Barbara looked away self-consciously.

"I'm just as happy walking if you want to park the truck."

"Naw. I have to pick up a propane tank and the cabin is still two miles from here. It's better to drive as long as we have the dinosaurs to burn."

Fifteen minutes later the pickup ground to a stop and Rick Larson jumped out to grab a box of Barbara's supplies from the bed of the truck. As the biologist secured the box to a packboard, Barbara looked out over the headwaters of Bear Creek. It was awesome! The cabin situated where the little spring of Camp Creek fed into Bear, was not visible and nowhere was there sign of human intrusion. The vast expanse of montane forest was unbroken except by swaths of creek-side alder burned banana yellow under the bright autumn sun. At this elevation, the fern and moss had been replaced with the light green lichen of Witches' Hair, which clung to the trunks of the ancient forest. Barbara could hear the roar of a waterfall below.

"The falls keeps out salmon and steelhead. Our study population is cut throat and sculpin, but the findings of our study will translate directly to anadromy."

The biologist further explained the intricacies of the study on the walk down to the cabin. There were stations every 200 meters along the 1.2-kilometer study area. Each station along the creek was measured for temperature, canopy, large and small organic debris, insect fallout, macroinvertebrates, creek flow, and turbidity. The fish population was determined by electroshocking the creek, marking the stunned fish, which floated to the surface, and extrapolating total population from the percentage of marked fish that turned up in subsequent censuses.

"We're finishing up with the control this fall. In February, Mayr Brothers Logging will send out their finest to fell all the trees within a 70-meter corridor of the creek without anything falling into the stream. You'll be involved in the re-monitoring until spring. The next year, the four-wheel-drive track we came in on will be developed into a full-on road and Mayr Brothers will yard out all the bucked timber and finish logging the unit.

"You're going to systematically rape the headwaters of this creek?"

"Well, except for the proximity to a riparian zone, it's a regular Forest Service sale. Mayr Brothers bought the stumpage along with the stipulations which support our study. The information we gain here on Stream Management Zones [SMZ] will be invaluable in harmonizing timber and fishery management in the future." The biologist smiled and shrugged. "I prefer to think of it as a vivisection. But, if you want to call it "rape," it's going to be an extremely well-organized and disciplined gang bang."

છ૭જ

Bear Creek

Sometimes time does not seem to behave linearly, but lurches ahead like a pickup truck, bouncing and spinning its wheels as it charges up a steep slope. This is how it was for Barbara Beyers and this research project. Four months had gone by since she arrived, and her absorption in the details of the survey had jarred her sense of time. With other researchers demonstrating a transient interest in their comings and goings, Barbara dug in and took to the project as if salmonhood hinged on her perseverance. She was just getting comfortable in the routine of the stream monitoring, when Thanksgiving approached. Rick Larson had invited Barbara to take Thanksgiving with his family and she had declined. She called her mother while she was in Forks on a re-supply run to say that she would be unable to join the family at Rose Lodge for the annual feast. On Christmas morning she came out of the research cabin to tend the monitoring stations and found a little wrapped gift at the door. The biologist had come all the way out here to sneak her a set of wool mittens and a rubber rain hat.

As the tires of time spun over January and settled down on the tread of February, Barbara left the research station for the sixth time since her arrival, to make the three-mile walk to her pickup truck, then on to her re-supply in Forks.

As Barbara began walking out on the four-wheel-drive road overlooking the creek, she heard an approaching vehicle. It could be Rick Larson, making one of his trips to check up on the progress of research, but it could be game poachers, wood thieves or other gate crashers. Barbara hid herself behind a large hemlock.

The orange four-wheel-drive pickup pulled to a stop at the end of the grade. On the red door of the crummy, which swung open, was the Mayr Brothers emblem. A bearded man wearing black suspenders climbed out, saying to the other occupants, "What I'm saying is that it's _all_ an illusion. It's like a mirage. It seems like it's there, but it's only our perception."

A clean-shaven man wearing red suspenders got out of the front passenger's side and came around to stand beside the first man, pulling chain saws and ruck out of the bed of the truck. "So if it's all a mirage, and you're part of it, if I ignore you long enough, you'll disappear."

The driver, wearing green suspenders, got out and came back to help off-load gear. "I wish there were some way to harness the energy you two waste arguing. There's no end to it."

The man in red suspenders addressed the driver. "Were you listening to this bullshit coming up the hill? Time, space... things: they're all a mirage! Philip has finally flipped his mortarboard!"

"I told you: DON'T CALL ME 'PHILIP!'" The bearded man with black suspenders was clearly provoked.

"Leave it alone, Rod. You go berserk every time Phil brings up you dropping out of high school." The man in green suspenders shouldered his knapsack and saw and started down the hill. The man in red suspenders caught up to him.

"Lucky I got out of school when I did, George. Look what higher learning did to Professor Phil. It's all a mirage...Jesus!"

The bearded man in black suspenders delayed lacing up his corks. He reached in to pull out his saw and canvas knapsack when he turned around as if he heard something. His eyes slowly scanned the woods as if he knew someone was watching. Barbara ducked fully behind the tree. In a minute she heard the man whistling as he went down the hill toward the creek. Barbara waited a little longer and hiked out on the pioneer road.

ৡৣ

Forks, WA
Thursday, February 1, 1979

In town she morosely went about the business of picking up her General Delivery mail at the post office and shopping for her re-supply. Around noon she called her mother to commiserate over how she felt about the logging incursion into her pristine environment. Her mom reminded Barbara that the study was predicated on the harvest and that, until the death of Glen Beyers, the timber industry had put food on their family's table. It didn't help.

Barbara finished the call and went back to her pickup, which was parked in front of Art's Place Tavern. Not wanting to return to Bear Creek in the midst of timber falling, Barbara turned away from her pickup and, uncharacteristically, entered the tavern. At 12:40 in the afternoon, she was the only one at the bar. She ordered a pitcher of draft. Having never drunk more than two beers in a row, she was lined out for a drinking party with her mail.

Two hours later, she was finished with all her mail, but still working on the pitcher. A man about her age, wearing a hickory shirt, came in. With all the empty stools, he chose to sit next to Barbara. He briefly studied Barbara and the two-thirds empty pitcher. "I'll have another of whatever the lady is having."

Barbara gathered up her mail. "I can't finish what's there. Why don't you just get another glass and drink what's left in the pitcher." Barbara got up to leave.

"Hey, don't leave on my account," protested the fellow.

43

"I've pissed away half the afternoon in here trying to drink all that beer. You have it. I've got a research station I've got to get back to."

As Barbara came out through the heavy wooden door into the light of the February afternoon, she felt the impact of the four beers she had ingested. She decided to walk down to Tillicum Park and back to sober up enough to drive.

 ᧞

USFS Road 2932
Thursday, February 1, 1979

It was past 4 p.m. as Barbara hiked up the long hill on the rutted Cat road. She heard the rumble of the truck coming down the road and stepped upslope, well off the grade. The man in green suspenders was driving. He stopped and rolled down his window when he saw her standing on the slope with her backpack.

"Howdy," said the driver, pointing to the logo on the rear door behind him. "Mayr Brothers Logging, at your service. Can we turn around and drive you and that fat pack back up to the research cabin?"

"No, thanks," said Barbara. "I spent all afternoon drinking and I need the walk to sober up."

"Did your boyfriend just dump you or are you just a party girl?" asked the passenger in red suspenders in the passenger's seat.

Barbara began walking along the slope to get around the truck.

"No, I'm *not* a party girl and it's nothing you'd understand!"
The bearded man in the back, wearing black suspenders, laughed out loud and held up two fingers in a V sign. Their eyes met and there was something in the way the logger smiled at her...Barbara continued around the pickup and started back up the road without saying anything more.

"We'll see you around, miss," called the driver, and proceeded down the hill with the crew.

 ᧞

It was twilight as upper Bear Creek came into Barbara's view. About fifty linear feet along the upper creek had been logged, revealing several tributaries forming the headwaters of Bear Creek. With the creek exposed, the head of the creek seemed somehow lower. It appeared to Barbara like a young girl hanging her head in a crisis center: The pretty green dress of the forest was torn and pushed aside to expose the bruises and wounds of her assailant; the privacy and dignity of this young watershed, violated. Across the bared slopes, water ran from tributaries like tears across flushed cheeks. Barbara's eyes stung and her stomach burned as she passed the logged unit and dropped off the Cat road to the cabin. She wished she had brought the unfinished beer with her in a doggy bag.

 ᧞

44

A week had passed and the Mayr Brothers bushlers had cut almost half of the "treatment zone," and had worked their way within 600 meters of the research cabin. It was impossible for Barbara to gather data from the control stations while the falling was going on and she found it necessary to work mostly in the dark. At about eleven every morning, the loggers stopped the raping and pillaging of the creek shore to take some lunch. They repaired to their crummy up on the road for their mid-morning feast. During this hour, Barbara would scurry out to take turbidity readings and electroshock studies, which could not be done accurately in artificial light. It was strange, but the preliminary results showed no change in the cut throat population, though temperature and turbidity had climbed steeply.

On this Thursday morning, she had finished the readings of the three stations still in the woods and was re-calibrating the turbidimeter, when her third cup of tea finished percolating through her kidneys and announced its reunion with its two friends in her bladder. A "MICTURATE NOW!" message, which could not be ignored, flashed on her brainpan. Barbara retreated from the stream shore and pulled down her pants. She took care of her business and wiped herself with a piece of tissue, which she placed in a plastic bag she carried to pick up snoose cans and other evidence of the barbarians up the hill. Something tickled her consciousness and she pulled up her pants and looked around the woods self-consciously...

৵৵৵

Up on the road, Rod Hill had burped venison and looked down with his binoculars upon the clearing, which he had created only this morning. He had taken to spying on the pretty, young researcher, who scrambled about during their lunch hour, to liven up Rod's digestion. As he watched, he took out the almost full can of Copenhagen from the holster on his red suspenders and put a generous pinch into his lip. "Here she comes!" announced Rod, to his two coworkers who lay, recumbent, in the warm February sun.

"Leave her the hell alone, Rod," said Phil Stone, picking his teeth with a spruce toothpick he had fashioned with his folding Buck knife. Stone had to find something to occupy himself after lunch to stay awake. A bushler's usual workday in the woods was from six in the morning until noon. That didn't include the marathon commuting time spent chasing around in the crummy. This job was a hurry-up affair working dawn to dusk. This siesta was a safety precaution, as much as anything, but Stone always had trouble staying awake with a full belly in the middle of the day.

"Look at that!" exclaimed Hill, from behind his binoculars. "She's collecting empty snoose cans! Maybe she's studying us! I bet she would like to study this!" exclaimed Hill rubbing his crotch.

"Through a magnifying glass, maybe," taunted Stone, returning his folded knife to its leather holster on his black suspenders. It bothered him that Hill was spying on the researcher. It was a violation of the privacy guaranteed by the great northwestern forests.

"Leave it to Professor Philip to grab for a magnifying glass when pussy is on the table."

"Get it through your thick skull that I don't want to be called 'Philip.' And about the only pussy on your table is your wife's cat eating leftovers in your dining room..."

"Would you two please give it a rest," said George Redding, the foreman, from under his tin hat, which he had pulled over his face to shelter his eyes from the noonday sun. This particular contract was a demanding job. The Forest Service had been clear on the environmental issues. They were using hydraulic jacks to fall the trees away from the creek and, after bucking the logs, every branch had to be dragged out of the flood plain. That biologist guy, Larson, had been nosing around almost every day to check on compliance. It was hard work.

"I get so tired, listening to your nonstop bickering..."

"Oh, Jesus! Here it is!" interrupted Hill. "She's pulling down her pants! She's taking a leak! She's wiping her tush!"

"Let me see that!" ordered Stone. He had no interest in watching the young women micturate, but Hill's intrusion into her privacy was insufferable. Stone had to get the binoculars away from him.

"For the love of God!" Hill was getting worked up into a high degree of agitation. "She's putting the used toilet paper into the bag with my snoose can! What the hell do you make of that?"

"Let me see that!" said Stone again, grabbing the binoculars from out of Hill's white-knuckled grip. Once he had the binoculars, Stone realized the line of least resistance was to look through them and pretend to be interested in the spectacle of the young woman's toilet.

"Give back my binoculars you son of a bitch! You're not even looking at the girl! Give 'em back, God damn it!"

Stone focused the binoculars on the researcher. He could see the bag she was putting under her belt and recognized it for what it was: a litter bag. She was keeping her research area tidy and would not even leave the degradable toilet paper behind. Stone wondered what the young woman thought of his lot when she picked up Hill's snoose can.

"Give back the binoculars, Philip!" Hill was growling at Stone and the binoculars were snatched from his face. Stone prepared to grab them back, but it had been the foreman Redding who snatched them.

"If you two are going to fight like kids, I'll take away the toy," said Redding, picking up his empty lunch sack and going back to the truck with the binoculars and trash.

"Okay by me," said Stone standing up and picking up his garbage, getting ready to get back to work.

"That's because they're not your eye pieces, Philip!" Hill threw his empty lunch sack into the woods below the road.

"Pick it up, Rod. God-damn-it, I'm tired of you throwing your trash all over the place!" Stone walked over to Hill with his fists clenched, ready to trade blows.

Redding got between them. "I give the orders around here!" Redding huffed in Stone's face. Then he turned around, "Go down there and pick up your trash, Rod. This contract says we can't leave anything but bucked logs on the ground. If you two can't quit fighting, one of you is going to be history."

"It's <u>him</u> that's messing with <u>me</u>!" protested Hill. But he went over the bank and retrieved his lunch sack. He glared at Stone on his way to the truck where they all picked up more saw gas and chain oil for their respective saws, which awaited them down in the unit.

కాం

Olympic Peninsula
January 29, 1921, 11:10 hours

The wind had begun to wash across the Peninsula in great currents: tumultuous rivers of air. In Beaver, surveyor Rixon watched limbs and other widow makers hurling through the air in the woods at the end of his little meadow. He checked the barometer on his porch and watched it visibly drop to almost nothing. He hurried inside and extinguished the fire in his wood stove by pouring salt on it. As the wind picked up, Rixon's neighbor, Charley Hahn, had a harder time of it. His stone chimney was blown over and his cabin blown off its foundation and along the ground. The wind roared up the upper Bogachiel Valley sending the only two settlers within five miles scurrying to their cabins to put out their stoves and hunker down for the blow. Safe in the large fields along Hemp Hill Creek, Otto Siegfried watched the ash sapling he had brought all the way from his fatherland in Germany bending low to the ground in the pneumatic tsunamis. A mile upriver, in the old Morganroth cabin, young Jim Reade watched nervously as the giant spruce and hemlock waved around like eelgrass in a riptide. Surrounding the cabin in all directions were mighty sylvan giants standing almost 300 feet tall, in defiance of the inexorable force of gravity. Over the roar of the storm he could hear the thunder and crashing of the ancient forest, as the wind tore and uprooted the colossal plants, giving them at last to gravity.

Up at Coons Bar on the Hoh, Leroy Smith and "Kobe" Koberlin were hunting, or "elk poaching" as the Forest Rangers called it. As Smith squeezed the trigger in the freshening wind, he heard a mighty crack. A huge fir limb came crashing down right beside him, spooking both him and the quarry. The main front came crashing through and the forest exploded with the splintering of huge tree trunks. Monstrous limbs, the size of roadside trees, were swept from their arboreal anchors and sailed through the air. The men ran for safety in the clearing of Kobe's homestead and watched from this vantage as thousand-year-old trees were blown asunder.

Further down the Hoh at the Moritz homestead, where Smith lived with his wife Theodora, the stove pipe blew off before the fire could be extinguished by the settlers who had taken refuge there. The log cabin caught fire. Dora Smith threw salt on the fire in the stove while Leroy's brother, Herman, climbed onto the roof and put out the fire with buckets of water passed from below.

Just north of Forks, three hundred feet from the Calawah Bridge, a Model T truck, bringing the mail delivered by ship to Clallam Bay, was blocked by a large fir falling across the road. The driver, Didd Klahn, stepped out of the Model T to see the trees along the road being knocked down like tenpins by the bowling ball of the storm. A huge tree, six feet in diameter, slammed across the bed of the mail truck. He ran for the shelter of the bridge.

Didd's brother, Pat, was taking the mail to Beaver, where Charley Hahn was kneeling on the floor, praying to be spared from the apocalypse, as the cabin toppled off its foundation. Like his brother, Pat was stopped by a tree across the road, but there was no bridge for shelter. As the trees piled up like pick-up-sticks across the road grade, Pat climbed under the shelter of the blowdown. Klahn joined Hahn in prayer.

At least seven barns were blown over in the Forks area, with cows and horses pinned down and injured inside. Stock were struck down and bleeding from the rain of wind-driven projectiles. The bawling of cattle joined the bleating of wildlife. On the wind was this cacophony and chaos as cabins burned and the ancient forest toppled.

On the morning of January 30, 1921, these West End pioneers looked out over ten billion board feet of windfall. They saw the rubble of destroyed outbuildings and of roofs that had become kites. The roads and trails which connected their communities were buried under a sea of fallen trees. They began cutting out with misery whips. They carried the loads for rebuilding on their backs. They doctored or butchered the injured stock. They checked on their neighbors. They accepted their losses and threw themselves at the task of reconstruction. Like other pioneers across the space-time continuum, they had no choice.

ဢ

Tuesday, February 13, 1979
Downtown Seattle

The Lincoln Day broke gray and drizzly at the ferry landing of the Emerald City. Twenty-two-year-old Richard Stokes sat in his Volvo station wagon, waiting in the line of other Peninsula-bound vehicles to cross the water to 'the Last Wilderness.' At the tollbooth, he rolled down his car window just enough to pay his fare and asked the ticketing officer if his position in line guaranteed a place on the next sailing. The State employee had difficulty hearing Stokes through the little louver in the window and stepped out into the light precipitation to assure the driver that there was room on the next ferry, which would be boarding in ten minutes. Stokes sat in the line of cars with his engine running and the heater/defroster running full blast while he perused the headlines of the Seattle Times. Stokes felt a rush of exhilaration as he again reflected that, within the week, he would be editor of his own newspaper. His father, a wealthy Seattle gynecologist, had purchased controlling interest in a company which held, as one of its assets, the small town, weekly journal of Knives, Spoons and Forks. Stokes had graduated the previous year from the University of Washington School of Journalism and been moping about the Stokes house, drinking his father's beer and piling up laundry for the maid. His father had given him the paper as a 'late graduation gift' to push the empty beer bottles, the mountain of dirty laundry, and the baby bird out of the nest. Stokes' day trip was exploratory, in that he would meet Tracie Cattel, the office manager, and look over the equipment.

Stokes looked up from the paper to see the ferry pulling in. On the pilings, in the freshening wind, a family of cormorants stood with their wings spread in the funny yoga-like posture that this species of bird assumes to dry its plumage of the rain and salt water that dominates its habitat. The cars loaded onto the ferry. Stokes locked the Volvo and went up two flights of stairs to the upper deck. He left the shelter of the passenger compartment to stand on the foredeck and face his new destiny. The ferry disembarked into the chop of Puget Sound and a wind cut across the deck driving Stokes back into the passenger compartment to drink coffee and eat a doughnut.

సా

Bear Creek
February 13, 1979, 12:45

Loggers work in all kinds of hostile and extreme weather. About the only kinds of weather they don't work in are: prolonged dry weather, when the woods are closed down because of fire danger; and strong wind. A faller's job and life depend upon his ability to gauge the structure and dynamics of the towering biomasses upon which he saws, to lay the tree down within few-inch tolerances. Wind changes every aspect of the engineering problem with such suddenness that there is no correcting for it. It overstresses the hinges that the faller fashions to accomplish his work and the results are unpredictable and deadly.

Rod Hill, George Redding and Phil Stone sat on the landing after their lunch and killed time, waiting for the wind to die down. Hill was focusing his binoculars on the coed researcher, who had offered him diversion for the previous week.

"Look at that! She's shampooing her hair! She fetches a basin of water, takes it 30 yards away from the creek, washes her hair in it and now she has to go 30 yards back with soapy hair to fetch the rinse! Where's the sense in that? Whyn't she just stand by the creek or plunk her head in the creek?"

Phil Stone dove into the speculation. "It's so she doesn't get the soap in the creek, you dope. The phosphates in the shampoo change the chemistry of the creek she's here to study."

"Leave it to the professor to figure out someone else's flakey behavior with his own flakey answers. Anyhow, she won't have any trouble blow-drying her mane in this hurricane..."

The sound of an approaching four-wheel-drive interrupted Hill's conjecture. The USFS biologist bounced along into the landing, turned his rig around so it was facing out, and hopped out of the vehicle. He called out to the three loggers, "Blowing hard enough for you?" Rick Larson went to the bed of his pickup and shouldered a pack. He walked over to where the three were sitting at the edge of the landing.

"I think you guys will have to shut it down for the day. Weather report is calling for a regular wind event." Rod Hill continued to focus the binoculars. Larson looked out over the clearcut and tried to see what occupied Hill's attention. "Watching the elk hunker down for the storm?" he asked.

"Welllll...," started Hill in the tone that let his coworkers know that whatever came out of his mouth next would be bullshit. "There's this one cow I've been watching all week. She ain't bedded down just yet but..."

"Manure-for-a-mind here is spying on the intern," interrupted Stone. "He's been doing it all week and can tell you everything about her toilet, which is where his brain is, anyway."

"She's finishing up with her shampoo and towel drying her hair," ignoring Stone's taunting. "Maybe she'll take her sponge bath now. I like that part the best!"

"Eat your heart out, boys. I let her know last week that I would be coming out to talk to her and she's prettying herself up for the visit."

"Do you have flowers and candy in your rucksack? That'll help you get in the door." George Redding offered the mature advice of an older, married man.

"Naw," answered the biologist. "Better than that. I've got her resupply. And I threw in some delicacy items like wine and smoked oysters."

"Smoked oysters! She'll throw you out on your butt," cautioned Redding.

"We'll see," said Larson, continuing down the hill towards Camp Creek. "Anyway," he called back, "if you boys want *my* advice, you'll clear out while you still can. Things are pretty cozy down there in the research shack and, if we all get stuck up here from windfall closing the road, you might be staring at the 'No Vacancy' sign."

The loggers sat on the landing in their hard hats and rain gear and watched the biologist heading down to his rendezvous. The wind continued to increase in roaring waves. "Say, Rod, give up your surveillance for a few minutes and turn on the AM radio in the truck. See if you can get a weather report on KVAC. If they're calling for fifty-mile-per-hour winds, we better shine it on for the day, like the biologist said." Hill reluctantly put away the binoculars and repaired to the cab of the crummy.

"It drives me wild how he spies on that poor girl!" yelled Stone to Redding into the wind.

"Everything about Rod makes you crazy!" Redding yelled back. "You seem like an intelligent guy, Phil! Can't you put your squabbling and petty grievances aside? It would make working with you two a lot easier for me!"

"What did you say! I can't hear you over the wind!"

"Quit fighting with Rod! QUIT FIGHTING WITH ROD! OK?"

"NO! We were born to fight with each other! Look down at the cabin! That crazy biologist and coed started a fire in the wood stove! The stovepipe will blow off and they'll burn the place down! Maybe one of us should go DOWN AND WARN..." Stone was interrupted by a roaring gout of air with the crashing thunder of falling trees. Two trees attached to the same root wad had fallen across the P-road.

Hill jumped out of the pickup. "Nothing but country music on the radio, but my personal forecast calls for us to didi mao while we still can move.

Phil Stone was still studying the 'what's wrong with this picture' of the research cabin next to Camp Creek. "LOOK AT THE CUT LINE DOWN BY THE CABIN, GEORGE! THERE'RE THREE SNAGS IN THAT LINE THAT COULD SMASH THE CABIN! THE WIND'S PUSHIN' THAT DIRECTION!"

Redding appreciated that what was unfolding was a full-blown wind event. He gave up on hopes for progress and concentrated on the details of life, property and getting his ass off the mountain. "ROD. TAKE THAT OH FIVE SIX OF YOURS DOWN TO THE CUT LINE NEXT TO CABIN CREEK. GET THE COUPLE OUT OF THE CABIN AND WAIT FOR ANY LULL IN THE WIND. KNOCK DOWN THOSE THREE DEAD HEMLOCKS AND ANY OTHER TREES YOU CAN THAT COULD REACH THE CABIN IF THEY'RE BLOWN OVER." Redding was screaming in Hill's ear. "YOU GOT THAT?"

Hill nodded and ran to get the chain saw with the 36-inch bar out of the bed of the truck. "TELL THEM TO PUT OUT THE FIRE!" Stone yelled at Hill.

"GRAB YOUR OH SEVEN SIX AND LET'S GET THIS GOAT TRAIL OPEN SO WE CAN GET THE FORK BACK TO FORKS!" yelled Redding grabbing a limbing axe and chain saw with a 48-inch bar before walking down the dirt road towards the windfall. Stone followed him with his own saw with a 3-foot bar. These saws were too big for this job, but the smaller saws were down in the woods. Arriving at the fallen hemlocks, the men started their saws. Stone marveled at the mighty roar of the wind, which he could hear over the 110 decibels of his saw.

The wind pushed harder and threatened Stone's balance. He let go of the saw and squatted down to get out of the main thrust of the wind, holding onto the brim of his hard hat. He heard the crashing of more windfall. When he looked up, he saw more fallen trees out where Redding had been cutting. Redding was not in evidence. Stone left his saw running in the middle of his cut and walked the fifty meters to check on Redding.

As Stone approached he could see his boss pinned under the fresh windfall. Stone ran to the fallen man. The recent windfall had knocked Redding down, over the log he was bucking, and scissored across his thighs. Redding's legs were pinned under the weight of the windfall and he was held face down. "GEORGE! CAN YOU HEAR ME?"

"MY LEG'S BROKE, OH JESUS, GET THE WEIGHT OFF ME, PHIL!" Stone found his partner's chain saw, but the pistol grip had been broken off by the tree fall, making the throttle inoperable. "HOLD ON, GEORGE, I'LL BE RIGHT BACK!" Stone ran back and grabbed his saw. Another huge current of air almost knocked him over and more trees crashed upon the landing. He heard a metallic crash and looked back down the road to see that a tree had fallen across the crummy, crushing the bed and splaying out the rear wheels. He ran back to Redding with his Stihl still running. Stone studied the foundation of the log jumble for a moment before beginning his cuts, so that he wouldn't release a crushing load upon his partner's legs. After making a couple of cuts, he sawed off two pieces of spruce limb approximately the size of a man's leg and, with the flat head of the limbing axe, drove them between the logs holding Redding's legs. Another gout of air charged across the road, knocking over trees and showering limbs.

"GEORGE! REACH DOWN WITH YOUR HANDS TO CATCH YOURSELF IN CASE YOU FALL FORWARD! I'M TAKING THE LOAD OFF YOUR LEGS."

"BE CAREFUL! AT LEAST ONE LEG'S BUSTED! IT HURTS LIKE HECK!"

Stone made the cut and the released log rolled down the ramp he had made with the Spruce limbs. Redding slid forward catching himself with his outstretched arms. Over the wind, Stone could hear his partner screaming in pain. Bright, arterial blood was splashed all over his left thigh. Stone took out his folding knife and cut along the left inseam of Redding's tin pants. A broken bone end of his femur protruded from the left thigh. Stone took out a bandanna and cut off the material of Redding's pant leg and his suspenders. Stone made a crude pressure dressing, and anchored it with the suspenders. "WE BETTER GET TO THE HOSPITAL!" Redding yelled. "GET THE CRUMMY AND YOU CAN CUT YOUR WAY OUT AS WE GO. HILL WILL HAVE TO OVERNIGHT IT!"

Stone shook his head, "THE CRUMMY'S FUCKED! A TREE NAILED IT! THERE ARE A HUNDRED TREES DOWN BETWEEN US AND UNDI ROAD!" Stone needed more room to work. He finished cutting out the log that Redding had been working on and removed the limbs that intruded into his work area. Then he shut down the saw and stared down at the injured man, trying to structure a plan out of the chaos that raged around him. Stone tried to clear his head and assess the options that remained available. I could use his good leg for a splint...I could saw some tree limbs for a splint...I could wait for Hill to get back...

"I'M BLEEDING TO DEATH HERE, PHIL. YOU BETTER DO SOMETHING!" Redding was screaming at him, but Stone ignored the distraction and persisted in weighing the different options that availed themselves to him. We need a traction splint. I could... The idea revealed itself to him like a dancer in a stripper bar. At first it was just the promise of an idea, but in the privacy and quiet of his mind, layer after layer of gauze was removed until he viewed the naked brainstorm.

He ran back to the truck for a scrench and first aid kit. He used the scrench to remove the 36-inch bar from his saw and the 48-inch bar from Redding's broken saw. He tied the 48-inch bar to the outside of the injured leg using Redding's outer belt loop and a piece of roller gauze through the stud holes to anchor the bar. He padded Redding's crotch with a four-inch compress. He took another compress and removed the suspender strap. Stone covered the bandanna dressing with the compress and used a two-inch elastic bandage to anchor the works to the wound. Then he took two triangular bandages to tie the bars together above and below the fracture and made a stirrup for Redding's left foot with the remaining triangular bandage. Stone joined the two sprocket noses of the bars with adhesive tape and made loops of roller gauze from the heel of the stirrup over the tape.

Stone took out a pencil from his front pocket to make a windlass and yelled out to Redding, "I'LL BE PULLING TRACTION BY WINDING THE GAUZE WITH THIS PENCIL! IT MAY HURT LIKE HELL FOR A LITTLE, BUT IT WILL GET TO A POINT WHERE IT FEELS BETTER. LET ME KNOW!"

As Stone wound the windlass he watched his partner roll his head in pain, drawing his face in a grimace. Suddenly, Redding stopped and looked at Stone with a surprised expression. Redding held up his thumb in an all's well sign. Stone tied off the windlass and yelled to Redding, "I'LL BE RIGHT BACK!"

Stone ran back to the trucks. Gas was spilling all over the landing from the ruptured 100-gallon tank fuel carrier in the bed of the crummy. Phil checked the Forest Service rig, which had been locked up by the biologist. He picked up a rock and threw it through the passenger's side window. Inside the cab, he got a tool kit and opened the hood. Stone cut out a piece of the horn wire and went back to the driver's seat. He pulled out the ignition switch by driving the retaining washer with a screwdriver struck with the rock, which lay conveniently on the seat. He used the horn wire to close the circuit to the primary side of the coil. Stone opened the hood of the truck and went back to the crummy. He ducked under the windfall which had crushed the bed to remove a 150-foot coil of manila rope, which was starting to soak up gas, and a tow chain. Stone carried the rope and the chain thirty meters back up the road to the Forest Service rig. Stone took off his wool jacket and threw the rope in the bed of the truck. He hooked one end of the chain onto the positive battery cable, put the excess chain on the nest of his jacket and reached down with the other hook and held it to the starter motor. The Forest Service vehicle's motor coughed to a start over the roaring wind. Stone went to the crummy one more time and removed the last saw from the bed, which appeared to have escaped the wind damage. He turned the Forest Service rig around and backed up to the windfall that he had been working on when Redding was injured. Stone finished his cuts, opening this section of road. Driving to where his boss lay, Stone brushed the glass off the seat and turned the car heater on full blast.

He leaned over and said to Redding, "ALL RIGHT, GEORGE, I'M GOING TO HELP GET YOU INTO THIS RIG. YOU'RE GOING TO LIE ACROSS THE FRONT SEAT UNTIL ROD GETS BACK. USE YOUR RIGHT LEG TO LIFT UP AND THEN HELP DRAG YOURSELF IN WITH YOUR ARMS WHEN I GET YOU TO THE DOOR." In a minute the injured logger was resting on the seat of the Forest Service pickup.

ഋഄ

Highway 101, Discovery Bay, WA
February 13, 1979, 16:15

Richard Stokes had given up on his meeting with Tracie Cattel, the office manager for <u>Knives, Spoons and Forks</u>, and fled the splintering trees and falling limbs for the protection of the concrete canyons of the city. Or, more accurately, he had tried to flee. He had driven a hundred miles through a pneumatic maelstrom. It had taken him three hours to drive this distance because of the windfall that blocked the road corridor. Stokes would arrive in a line of cars waiting for windfall to be cleared and hunker in his Volvo with the radio blaring, hoping to get a report about the Hood Canal Bridge. The bridge would be closed if the winds were this strong on Bainbridge Island.

Here, just west of Discovery Bay, a Doug Fir had blown over across the dead power lines and blocked the road at about eye level. Stokes was the first to arrive at this windfall and he rolled down the window of his Volvo to look around for a phone to call the beleaguered Department of Transportation. There was no phone in evidence.

Studying the tree, Stokes perceived that the trunk of the tree was higher than the roof of his Volvo. If the branches yielded, he might be able to drive under the tree and leave the obstruction for the next unfortunate traveler. He drove forward into the wall of branches. Suddenly his radio turned to static and Stokes cursed when he realized that he had knocked the antenna off of his hood. The branches swallowed his vision and he drove forward. Suddenly there was a metallic popping sound and the roof buckled several inches. Stokes slammed his foot on the brake and cursed. He tried to back out, but the engine died. He restarted the car and tried to back up, but the tree had a grip on the Volvo and the engine died again. Stokes tried to open the door, but the limbs of the fir held the door closed. He rolled down the window and stuck his head out to assess the situation. He could see a flashing yellow light and he heard a chain saw being fired up. Around him, limbs began to fall off of the tree and from the hood of the car emerged a view of the road ahead. Stokes rolled up his window. There was the throaty roar of a chain saw next to his rig and an employee of the local Public Utility District wearing yellow rain gear knocked on the driver's window.

"YOU LOST THIS!" the P.U.D. employee yelled over the wind, holding the truncated aerial in his gloved hand.

"The tree pushed in the roof of my car," whined Stokes, pointing to the four-inch bulge in the ceiling. The P.U.D. employee leaned in to better hear what Stokes was saying and saw the dent to which the driver was pointing. He dropped the antenna on Stokes' lap and made a fist with his gloved hand. He reached by Stokes to make a sweeping upper cut to the ceiling. There was a popping sound and the big dimple inverted to its original shape.

"ALL BETTER!" said the P.U.D. man.

"Thanks," muttered Stokes, starting his car engine.

"JUST A MINUTE, GUY!" the employee hung in the window making Stokes think for a minute he expected a gratuity. "SEE THOSE POWER LINES THE TREE IS LEANING ON OVER THERE?"

"Yes?" said Stokes.

"IF THAT TOP WIRE WAS HOT...YOU WOULD BE TOAST IF YOUR FOOT TOUCHED THE GROUND GETTING OUT OF THE CAR! NEXT TIME WAIT FOR US!"

"Thanks," said Stokes putting the car in gear. "I know better than to try to get out of my car in a situation like this." Stokes drove on towards the Hood Canal, in blind hope that the bridge would be open, accessing his return to his urban home.

Bear Creek
Tuesday, February 13, 1979, 16:30 hours

The two men were screaming into each other's faces - partly to be overheard over the deafening roar of the wind and mostly because their hatred for one another engendered this level of confabulation.

"WHAT DO YOU MEAN YOU DIDN'T FALL ANY OF THOSE SNAGS!" demanded Stone. "THERE'S STILL SMOKE COMING OUT OF THE CHIMNEY, YOU WORTHLESS FUCK!"

"THE WIND NEVER LET UP FOR ME TO KNOCK THEM DOWN. I DIDN'T FEEL LIKE INTRUDING..."

"LIKE YOU REALLY GIVE A SHIT ABOUT THAT COED'S PRIVACY - ALWAYS SPYING ON HER..."

"I'M GONE FOR A COUPLE OF HOURS AND COME BACK AND THE CRUMMY'S SQUASHED AND THERE'S SPILLED GAS EVERYWHERE AND GEORGE IS FUCKED AND ..."

"ROD!"

"...YOU'VE STOLEN THE FOREST SERVICE RIG AND YOU'VE ROBBED THE BARS OFF THE SAWS TO SCREW AROUND..."

"ROD!"

"...AND THE ROAD'S STILL NOT OPEN, SO OUR ASSES ARE STUCK OUT HERE..."

"ROD! HOLD ON A SECOND! WE DON'T HAVE TIME TO WASTE ARGUING! WE'VE GOT TO WORK TOGETHER..." Stone removed the coil of manila rope from the bed of the Forest Service pickup and flaked out a zigzag of rope articulating ten bights three feet across. "WE CAN'T LEAVE GEORGE IN THE PICKUP LIKE THIS! THERE'RE TOO MANY TREES STILL COMING DOWN! WE'VE GOT TO GET HIM DOWN TO THE RESEARCH SHACK!" Stone tied off the end of each bight with a clove hitch and then took the remaining 20 meters of rope to run in a continuous loop through the eyes of the bights. The finished product was a soft litter. "HELP ME LOAD GEORGE INTO THIS AND WE'LL CARRY HIM DOWN THE HILL..."

"WHAT THE FUCK! ARE YOU NUTS! CARRY HIM DOWN THE HILL..."

"ROD, WORK WITH ME ON THIS ONE DEAL! WE HAVE THE REST OF OUR LIVES TO FIGHT. TOMORROW WE CAN FIGHT. YOU CHOOSE THE WEAPONS: FISTS, GUNS, CREAM PIES...LET'S JUST GET THROUGH THIS FIRST!"

৩৽৵

Camp Creek/Bear Creek
February 13, 1979, 17:15 hours

Barbara sat on the far edge of the makeshift couch next to the wood stove. The biologist, who sat in the middle of the couch was invading her personal space and making it hard for her to think. The roar of the wind outside made it hard to hear what he was saying. An hour and a half ago he had been alluding to the idea that her work was done here at Bear Creek and that she should be finding an office to prepare her thesis work. Then she had discovered the logger spying on them through the window. It was the man who made the obnoxious remark about her being a party girl ten days ago. He came in for a few minutes and said he was waiting for the wind to die down to fall some hazardous trees next to the cabin. Rick Larson and Rod Hill had gone out to study the trees, but the wind never subsided and the logger had left.

Over the din of the wind she had heard something metallic being blown across the roof and wondered if it might be the stovepipe. She was beginning to wonder if having a fire going was a good idea. She got off the couch to open the firebox and see how much fuel was left.

"I'LL GET SOME MORE FIREWOOD," offered the biologist, having to shout, even indoors, to be heard.

"NO, I DON'T THINK WE SHOULD BE..." the door flew open and Rod Hill stumbled in carrying the feet of the logger in green suspenders in some kind of jury-rigged litter. He was followed by the logger in black suspenders who had given her the V-sign.

"SORRY TO INTERRUPT YOU LOVE BIRDS, BUT OUR FRIEND HAD A TREE DROP ON HIM." The two loggers set down their injured partner and the logger in black suspenders took the fire extinguisher from its spot by the doorway and came over to where Barbara was squatting next to the open firebox.

"HI," said the logger. "SORRY TO RAIN ON THE PARADE, BUT YOUR STOVEPIPE BLEW OFF AND YOU'RE ABOUT TO BURN THE PLACE DOWN." The logger let go with the dry chemical extinguisher and in two seconds the fire was out. He shut the stove door to keep the chemical from blowing out in the down drafts.

"OH...INTRODUCTIONS!" said Rod Hill, pointing to the logger with the fire extinguisher. "THIS IS PHILIP. PHILIP MEET BARB. BARB MEET GEORGE," said Hill pointing to the ashen-faced casualty.

"HI," said Barbara.

"HI," repeated Phil. "GEORGE HAS AN OPEN FEMUR FRACTURE. HE'S KIND OF SHOCKY. I NEED TO GET THAT ROPE FROM UNDER HIM TO TAKE CARE OF A CHORE OUTSIDE. UNTIL I GET BACK EVERYONE SHOULD STAY AS CLOSE TO THE WALLS AS POSSIBLE IN CASE A TREE COMES THROUGH THE ROOF." The four worked to scoop up the patient and lay him down in a sleeping bag on the couch, which they had dragged over from the stove. The logger in black suspenders gathered the rope and went back outside. Barbara and Rick placed a couple of cinder blocks under the foot end of the couch to Trendelenburg the patient. Barbara checked on the circulation of the injured leg by pinching a toenail and watching the capillary refill to the nailbed. She felt the dorsalis pedis pulse on the top of the foot of the injured leg and the subtibial pulse on the inside of his ankle. The makeshift splint was good. There was nothing else anyone could do for the patient until he got to a hospital. Barbara put on her rain slicker and went out to see what the logger in black suspenders was doing outside.

Barbara found the man in a stand of hemlock snags. The logger had cut off a twenty-foot section of manila rope and had tied himself in with a bowline. The logger tied off the short end of his rope with a bowline and put the long end around one of the snags and back through the bowline to form a carrick bend - a knot Barbara's dad had shown her twelve years ago. "I HOPE THE TOP DOESN'T BLOW OFF WITH ME ON IT!" yelled the logger, planting his cork boots into the bark of the tree and leaning back. "BETTER STAND CLEAR IN CASE THE SNAG COMES APART UNDER MY WEIGHT! I'LL BE DROPPING LIMBS AS I GO!" Barbara stood back and the logger climbed. The tree pitched about wildly in the wind as the logger climbed. He lopped off limbs with the chain saw that Rod Hill had left earlier. When the man got 75 feet up the trunk of the tree, he secured a bowline around the trunk with the end of the 120 feet of rope he was tailing. The logger came down the tree in about thirty seconds. He ran the rope around a solid spruce downstream of the cabin and cinched down on the hemlock snag with a truckers' knot. He used the saw to cut a face out of the snag and as the wind came around from south to north he made his back cut, allowing the tree to fall perpendicular to its lean towards the cabin. It took forty minutes to knock down the first snag. The logger noticed that he still had Barbara's audience and yelled out in a cavalier voice as he went up the second snag, "DON'T TRY THIS AT HOME!" Barbara knew enough about it to appreciate the danger to which the man was exposing himself. In another hour, he had fallen the third snag. He was untying the rope from around his waist.

"THANKS FOR SPOTTING ME, BARB." he said to Barbara as if it were he that was indebted to her. "'BARB' IS IT?,' he asked, gently screaming. There was something about this courageous, resourceful man...

"Mrs. Stone?"

"IT'S 'BARBARA BEYERS.' 'BARB' REMINDS ME OF A FISH HOOK THROUGH THE LIP. 'PHILIP' IS IT?" Barbara asked looking into the logger's eyes as the forest heaved and swayed in the roaring windstorm. There was something about this man that called to Barbara from the past and out of the future.

"Mrs. Stone. Are you all right?"

"'PHILIP' REMINDS ME OF MY DAYS AS A PUMP JOCKEY AT A FILLING STATION! PLEASE CALL ME 'PHIL.' 'PHIL STONE." He smiled and there was a whirling cyclone of past, present and future.

"HI," said Barbara, moronically.

"HI," said Phil again, fading in the wind...

"Mrs. Stone, please wake up! The doctors are ready to meet with you and to have you visit Mossy."

...fading in the roaring maelstrom of time and space. "HI."

Four

"We abide in the presumption that we think, when, in the larger picture, it is just as plausible that WE ARE THOUGHT."
Fredrich W. Nietzsche (1844 - 1900)
German philospher

Olympic Memorial Hospital
Tuesday, June 9, 1987, 08:35 hours

This is not happening. *This is just a dream.* Through latex gloves, Barbara Stone gripped the hand of her daughter, Mossy, and wrestled with reality. There was an occasional reciprocal squeeze from the little hand that emanated from the array of tubes and wires that was Mossy. As Mossy drifted in and out of consciousness her eyes reflected the fear and angst of the mother.

After making so much noise about seeing and attending her daughter's condition, Barbara was having trouble being here now. The nurse had found Barbara in the little chapel room, sleeping or lost in memories. She had gently pushed Barbara to a shower, where she washed off the remaining grime from the garden in preparation for this antiseptic meeting with Mossy. The doctors had briefed Barbara, saying that Mossy was resting comfortably. However, it was too early to predict to what degree the patient would be impaired by the detected brain damage.

Now, finally, in Mossy's presence, Barbara felt powerless to contribute to the healing process. It would be such a long road: waiting for a healed child to emerge from all these catheters and gizmos...like planting a tiny Doug Fir seed and waiting for the advent of the forest giant.

Barbara wanted to let go of the little hand and burrow into the plastic and gauze to embrace her daughter...To clutch her daughter to her bosom and, thereby, resist the Fear and Pain which gripped both mother and daughter.

While Joy lay dashed and battered, and Hope hung by a thread with drains burred into her skull, Pain and Fear seized the pulpit of Barbara's bowels and exchanged sermons. "You're going to be OK, Mossy," Barbara feigned unwarranted optimism. "We'll be going home soon," Barbara lied and then lapsed into silence.   Waiting...waiting...waiting with the pain clock on the wall ticking out interminable seconds.

Waiting, Barbara thought about the inane simplification the neurologist had made yesterday about the complex workings of the human brain. Waiting, Barbara reflected about the prognosis the doctors had given her half an hour earlier: that the bones would mend, that there was no spinal/neural damage, but that her ability to walk, talk, smell or interact socially or sexually might be compromised. There would be no grandchildren: that was a certainty.

Waiting, Barbara attempted to review her own battery of knowledge on the subject of the human brain. She felt herself escaping the walls of the Critical Care Unit and entering the O.S.U. classroom, waiting for Professor Jake Nice to further her knowledge of the workings of the cerebral cortex.

༄

Oregon State University, Corvallis
February 15, 1977

Waiting, Barbara looked out of the classroom window on the warm February day in 1977 and wished that she could be out of doors. Professor Nice arrived, "Good afternoon, students and I'm sorry I'm late. Of course the condition of lateness is relative and, from my perspective, I'm right on time and you all are five minutes early." Some of the kids laughed politely.

"Yesterday, we were looking at the temporal lobes which are the center for olfactory, taste, social inter-activity and, most importantly for you rambunctious students, the center for our species' complicated and bizarre sexual behavior. A famous brain surgeon won the Nobel Prize for manually stimulating his patient's motor and memory responses. By touching parts of the open brain of his conscious patients, he could cause them to raise their arms involuntarily. He could invoke a memory response that was so vivid, it was almost indistinguishable from reality. These were brave experiments! Imagine the complications if he had accidentally stimulated the region of the temporal lobe accountable for sexual reflex: a female patient escaping the moorings of brain surgery to chase the doctor around the operating room, missing the top of her skull..." The students laughed at the picture. Barbara waited for the class to be over so she could be outside.

"Have you ever wondered why a dog rolls on something long dead, or why a bear will smell you before it sees you or why a monkey will turn around and smell its feces after defecating? It is because all of these creatures have a sense of olfactory quite beyond our pitiful sense of smell. If our sense of smell were as developed as the canine, after showering, you ladies would spurn the *Jean Nate* and splash on the *Essence de Road Kill*. It's a fact: our olfactory ignorance causes us to cover up all the smells of Nature with perfume.

"If we evolved from monkeys, which is the debatable foundation of your studies in your Biology curriculum, what became of our sense of smell: of our ability to defecate and smell a prescription for health on the vapors of our excrement? Now I know enough about my subject to know that not all of you students are listening to me. Every four seconds most of you are having a thought about sex...well, at least the guys. For some it is more than a transcendental thought: it's a preoccupation. You would rather be having sex than sitting in this class. Hey, am I right? Well people, homo sapiens, guess what got your sense of smell? It was taken over by the part of your brain which tells you to splash on *Jean Nate* instead of road kill. It was gobbled up by the growing monster of your species' sexual behavior. When women learned to shave their legs they forgot how to smell honesty and sincerity on a suitor. When men invented the cod piece they forgot how to smell rut. When man stalked woman with a club in his hand instead of a box of candy or flowers, he had only to follow his nose to the pheromones. We dump perfume on everything because, in the development of our complicated sexual behavior, we have crowded out that portion of our temporal lobe: the part of the brain which gives window to the wide and immensely satisfying olfactory world...in which the so-called 'lower animals' so frequently dwell." Waiting for the class to end, the stuffy room continued to close in on Barbara.

"We have turned our heads to the sense of smell, but what about the other senses we employ as the dominant species of Planet Earth? Last year, at the Harvard School of Behavioral Science, researchers separated two groups of test kittens. One group was placed in a room with exclusively horizontal stripes, while the second group was isolated in a room with all vertical stripes. When the kittens grew to maturity, the cats in the horizontally striped room could jump on a couch, but could not see a tree or scratching post. The cats from the vertical stripes could hit a tree or scratching post, but were unaware of the presence of a couch. WE ONLY SEE, HEAR, SMELL, TASTE OR TOUCH THAT WHICH REINFORCES OUR PRECONCEIVED NOTION OF REALITY! It is called 'precognitive commitment.' In this room; in this University; in this LIFE, you will only perceive and retain that which conforms to and reinforces your conceptual reality. You ignore ninety-nine point nine nine nine percent of the total stimuli available to your senses and process only that which conforms to your status quo of reality: of time, place and things."

"Take, for example, our perception of time. Have you noticed how it flies by when you're at a party and drags on when you're at class? How...slow...each...moment...can...pass...when...you're...bored? Or how, when you're in a dream state, you can experience several hours worth of dreams in a few minutes? This relates to the brain waves we were discussing yesterday. At normal speed, at ten hertz, you experience ten reality checks a second, and time passes at an average speed. When you're in R.E.M. sleep, or bored, or severely frightened - like in a near death episode - your brain waves accelerate to process more information. Time seems to slow down. When you are having a good time, you are centered on it alone and your brain waves slow down to accommodate the focusing. Time accelerates. If you could speed up your brain waves to fifty hertz, which, God forbid, can be done with drugs, your reality of five minutes would be our reality of one minute - or maybe two minutes for some of you who appear to be getting bored with this." Waiting in the classroom, with the students pressed together in their seats, the clock ticked second after interminable second.

"Biologically, it's a proven fact, that different species assimilate light information differently. A movie, which is twenty-four still frames a second, appears to us to be a moving picture. To a fruit fly, with a life expectancy of only several days it is a slide show. To a turtle, a frame every second would appear as a movie."

"Consider this for a second," the professor held up a picture and wobbled it back and forth. The students in front perceived that it was a three dimensional image of an Oregon landscape. "It's called a hologram. It's produced by shooting a laser beam through a splitter and bouncing the second wave off a mirror to create an interference beam. Holograms are not common now - as a matter of fact this one is worth several hundred dollars, but one day they will be so common they will be on everyone's drivers' licenses. One of the most amazing aspects about this holographic plate is not the obvious - that it is three dimensional – but that, if I were to cut it in half, I would end up with two half-sized pictures of the whole scene. If I cut it in hundreds or even trillions, I would end up with that many pieces of the whole scene." From her position towards the front of the room, Barbara studied the landscape in the hologram and longed to be there.

"Why am I wasting your time with this? Two things: If three dimensional images can be expressed digitally or on a holographic plate, how long will it be before computers extend to us a virtual reality and what will be our reaction when we come to find that the greater reality of the whole does not fit our tiny model of perceived reality?"

"The second point relates to vivisection experiments conducted in the 1940's by Lashy Prograhm in which he taught mice to perform a simple chore by exposing them to the routine rewards and torture of the scientific horror chamber. After the initiates were fully indoctrinated in the task, he began removing portions of their brain. In an effort to avoid torture and secure reward, the mouse brain would communicate to other portions of the brain the details of the task. The end result were mice reduced to little more than their Medulla Oblongata, performing a task that had been inculcated to Cerebral Cortex. THE BRAIN IS A HOLOGRAM. You can damage or cut away piece after piece, but each part reflects a piece of the whole. In your brain is the memory of not only your entire life back to the socks you wore to school on the twentieth day of class in second grade...In your brain is the entire genetic memory of your species. The miracle of life, of healing, of regeneration, of Creation - these great mysteries that defy science and elude the laboratories - the answers to these and every other question are inside of your gray matter."

"The crazy old hippy," muttered a student beside Barbara. She looked at the wild-eyed professor and wondered if anything he was saying would bare relevance in the world of veterinary science or fishery biology.

"Stay with me a moment longer, students, and we'll all excuse ourselves to go out into this unseasonably wonderful February weather...What I'm saying is part of a question: If we are experiencing conscious thought as the result of ten brain waves a second - which is proven fact - where are we for the greater balance of our lives when that brain wave is not peaked and we are in the world of another consciousness?" Students began gathering up their books and papers in expectation of the approach of the minute hand to the top of the clock.

"Some call it our subconscious state, but more accurately it is our superconciousness. It is this state of total memory; of total recall; of total mind over matter, bodily control that we retreat from with every conscious thought we make..." the bell rang and the students stood up to exit the class, while Barbara remained seated, relieved of her claustrophobia, suddenly making a connection. "...it is this field of infinite wisdom between each thought to which the mystics and the enlightened gurus refer..." Barbara, alone, sat in the classroom as the professor rambled on.

"Excuse me, Mrs. Stone..."

"...It is this field of infinite possibility which will allow you fifteen years from now to recall every word of this lecture..."

"Barbara, excuse me for a minute..."

"...in that field of infinite recall you will remember every scent, every subaudible whisper, every refraction of light, every pin prick, every caress, every lollipop, every lima bean..." The bell rang, indicating the beginning of the next class, while Barbara remained transfixed in the chair of this class.

"Please let go of her hand, Barbara, while I re-do the IV"

"...every word that you ever heard, spoke or read, is written indelibly upon the pages of your superconsciousness. Your impression of reality is the edge of the page as you leaf through the book. Look at the writing between your conscious thoughts, and you will really be reading the book instead of leafing through the pages."

৩৩

Olympic Memorial Hospital
Tuesday, June 9, 1987, 10:30 hours

The alarm was silenced and the nurse gently pushed Barbara aside. "Her IV infiltrated which is what set off the alarm on the pump. Are you all right, Mrs. Stone? Would you like to lie down?"

"Yes. I'm OK."

The nurse had pulled the cannula out of the back of Mossy's hand and was prepping the next vein over on her hand to stick in an over-the-needle catheter. "I'm not sure why this IV infiltrated, Barbara. Did you move her hand?"

"I don't think I did. Maybe, I'm kind of spacey right now."

The nurse found the vein, removed the stiletto, hooked up the venoset and turned the pump back on. As she disposed of the sharp she said, "Here, Barbara, come around this side of the bed and take Mossy's other hand. I'm going to get you some orange juice and I'll be right back."

The nurse returned with a glass of O.J., which Barbara drank. "You don't have to stay here if you don't want," said the nurse. "Mossy is far enough along in the sedation so she is probably pretty much out of it for a while..."

"I'll stay," said Barbara holding onto Mossy's right hand. "It's important to me."

"I'll be at the nurses' station if you need me," said the nurse, leaving Mossy's room.

"Thank you," mumbled Barbara, reentering the long wait.

৩৩

"...is written indelibly upon the pages of your super consciousness."

Thursday, 1 p.m.

Dear Barbara,

It was really fun spending time with you the other night during that wind event. I've been busy taking care of some stuff for George who got back from the hospital yesterday, but the cretin, Rod, and I should be back to finish this cut tomorrow.

Hey, I'm not doing anything tonight after I finish helping George. I'll pick up some pizza and beer and drop by here hoping to share it with you if you, likewise, are doing nothing in particular.

See ya.   *Your friend,*
          Phil Stone

Barbara found the note pinned to the door of the research cabin when she returned from a re-supply run to Forks. She put her groceries inside and carried the note and some other mail she had already read over into the sunlight on the south side of the cabin. She sat on one of the stumps left when Phil Stone had fallen three hemlock snags during the windstorm. She had a copy of <u>Knives, Spoons and Forks</u>, which had just come out. The paper had acquired a new editor and was in a downhill plunge from its former mediocrity.

Barbara reread the note from Phil with some trepidation. As a matter of fact, she did have a previous commitment for this evening. Before Rick Larson left with the loggers two days ago, carrying George up the hill to the Forest Service rig, he told Barbara he would be back about 4 p.m. this evening to discuss something important. Barbara sensed that Rick had been trying to hit on her since shortly after her arrival last September, but he was a gentleman and had always separated his personal life from their work. She guessed he was coming to discuss the latter. Her stomach roiled a bit and she picked a sprig of wild mint next to the cabin and chewed it.

It was the meeting with the logger that excited her interest. As she opened the newspaper to the opinion page, she had trouble focusing on the words as she anticipated the company. An article citing the Harvard School of Behavioral Science caught her attention, but it turned out to be pulp. She glanced over the self-introductory remarks made by Richard Stokes, the new editor. Her thought was that, as surely as a peanut rancher was in the White House, an egotistical and pompous ass was editing the town's newspaper.

❦

"Hi." Phil Stone's voice startled her from her hard-won concentration on the small town newspaper.

"Hi...I mean Hello." She hopped off the stump and turned north to face her visitor who stood with a six pack of beer and a large cardboard box.

"Pizza's here!" announced the visitor. "The pizza and beer have achieved almost equal states of molecular activity, proving again the laws of thermodynamics."

"The pizza is cold and the beer is warm," Barbara smiled. "Is that it?"

"That would depend upon your point of reference, but, from the perspective of someone who hasn't eaten all day and could sure use a beer...Let's dig in."

The couple turned to on the dinner disk and the sextet of beer. After a brief frenzy, in the manner of a couple who doesn't want to deprive each other of their fill, a couple of beers and two slices of pizza remained. Phil caught the movement of something on the hill beneath the landing. He stood up and studied the picture of someone coming down towards the research cabin.

"It looks like more pizza on the way. Are you expecting company?" he asked Barbara.

"Yeah," said Barbara, wiping pizza smear off her face with her bandanna. "Rick Larson said he needed to come out on some business matter."

"It would appear to be the same business matter that has occupied our attention for the last ten minutes."

In a few minutes, Rick Larson knocked on the door of the research cabin and announced, "Pizza's here!"

"Back here, Rick," called Barbara. Rick came around the research cabin and was obviously surprised to see Phil Stone.

"Oh, hi, Phil," Larson stood self-consciously with the pizza and what appeared to be a bottle of wine in a paper bag. "I think I brought enough for three. Anyone have a bottle opener or should I use my Swiss army knife?"

"We're not going to be much help, Rick," said Barbara, holding up the almost empty box. We're just wrapping up a large pizza Phil fetched down here. I'll get an opener and a glass."

As Barbara disappeared inside the shack, Phil and Rick sat in silence. After a few moments, Phil spoke to break the silence, "Mayr Brothers is sending out a wrecker for the crunched crummy tomorrow. I hope you're not pissed off about how I hot-wired your government rig..."

"Heck, no. You do what you have to do in circumstances like that windstorm."

"Hill and I will be finishing up the job starting tomorrow. We'll be coming up here in my four-wheel-drive pickup."

"It's too bad the wind pushed so many of the remaining trees into Bear Creek. If the wind could have held off another few days, you guys would have had her whupped. The windfall in the creek may bias the study..." Barbara returned with the opener and a glass. "Am I the only one drinking here?" ignoring the five empty cans on the ground. Larson popped the cork and poured.

"We're drinking beer," said Phil, popping a beer and trying to pass it to Barbara, who shook her head. Stone gathered up the empty beer cans and offered the last two pieces of his pizza to Larson who declined and threw open the lid of his box.

The three ate pizza 'til it hurt. Eventually, Barbara went for two more glasses and, as dusk surrendered to night, the two liters of wine went the way of the beer.

"One of the reasons I came out this evening," Rick spoke to Barbara, "Was to talk to you about the spotted owl studies we'll be undertaking in this District over the next decade. It's the kind of research that may interest you."

"Fish are kind of my thing," said Barbara, with a note of finality.

"Still," went on the Forest Service biologist, "The spotted owl is relevant to fisheries and all other forest ecology. You must be familiar with the O.S.U. studies. The owl is a habitat indicator which reflects the health of an old growth forest."

"I don't understand," interjected Phil Stone. "Wildlife habitat seems to be enhanced by logging. Bear, elk, deer, and all the large mammals, like the brush that succeeds a clearcut. The small creatures like the cover and succulents that go along with a transitional forest..."

"Well, that's how it looks at first glance," the biologist interrupted the logger. "And that's what we used to think, all right, but the emergence of several indicator species proves otherwise. That's one of the reasons I came out this evening: to set up some spotted owl study plots and practice my calling..."

"Isn't it possible that the less esoteric species are better indicators than the spotted owl?" Phil again interrupted Rick. "I don't think I've ever seen a spotted owl...

"For a while after a clearcut, the herbivores come on like gangbusters, but once a uniform canopy eclipses the ground, re-prod areas become a wildlife desert. You need a multilayered canopy to sustain an old growth ecosystem. The decline of the spotted owl in this forest zone shows that logging has had a deleterious impact on the old growth forest community as a whole..."

"Well, what has this study at Bear Creek shown?" demanded Phil. "What's been the impact of tree removal to the stream environment here on Bear Creek?"

"Well, the study is not finished," Rick was evasive. "We don't know what the long term impacts will be. That's why this project will be going on for another two years while the roads are built and the logs are yarded."

"Barbara," Phil demanded. "What measurable difference have you detected to fish biomass from the pristine forest to the removal of trees along the Streamside Management Zone (SMZ)?"

"Well, none...yet."

The logger went on, "What decline, if any, have you detected in the macrovertebrate biomass?"

"Well, actually, it's gone up slightly."

"What change has occurred to turbidity?"

"None detected..."

"So, where's the impact from logging here on Bear Creek?" asked the logger.

"That's why the study goes on from here," answered Barbara. "We believe from the declining fish runs that logging impinges on fisheries. If you guys have proven that you can remove the trees from the creek corridor without hurting habitat, we need to know exactly what phase of the logging it is that screws up the fish. Probably the road building..."

"Or the yarding," Rick Larson joined the counterattack. "And the slash burning sets up an environment for sediment washes. You guys just go ahead with knocking down trees and leave the research and resource management to us experts," Larson attempted to joke with the logger.

"Hey! We just cut them. GRAVITY knocks the trees down! And fire was historically a major element of the forest ecology here on the Peninsula. That's why Doug Fir is the predominant tree species. If fire causes sediment washes, then it was a recurring attribute of the habitat. Clearcutting mimics what happened here naturally before man ever entered the picture. It's just that we take out the logs before burning the slash and replant prime species to hurry up the succession.

Stone threw his hands up. "Hey, I didn't come out here to argue with you two. I'm glad you're looking at the issue. If there's a way to make logging complement fisheries, I'm all for it. Say, Barbara, want to take a little walk? I want to show you something."

It was pitch dark and the prospect of a hike through the rugged, trailless terrain would intimidate most slickers of the urban or suburban type. "Sure," said Barbara. "I'll get my headlamp."

Rick Larson began protesting, "Actually, there's something we need to discuss, Barbara. And I was thinking you would be interested in setting up the spotted owl survey grids."

"How long will you be setting up the survey?" asked the logger.

"We'll be at it most of the night," answered the biologist.

"Well, my part of the agenda will only take an hour," reasoned Phil Stone.

While the two men sat in silence, Barbara went into the dark shack and came back with a lit Coleman lantern and a headlamp. "We'll be back in a while, Rick," she said leaving him with the lantern. "There's plenty of wood by the stove if you want to make a fire."

"Barbara..."

"There's plenty of wood..."

"Excuse me, Mrs. Stone..."

"...by the stove..."

৵৽

Olympic Memorial Hospital
June 9, 1987, 10:42

"...if you want to make a fire."

"Barbara, are you sure you're all right? You're under a lot of stress. I'm going to recommend that you sit down with one of our counselors."

Barbara looked at the nurse as if she had just arrived on a space ship or time machine. And there, in Barbara's hand, was the tiny hand of her daughter, Mossy. And attached to the hand was the frail arm leading to all the tubes and wires and the small, pale face and...this is not happening. *This* is just a dream.

"You were saying something about a fire, Barbara. Do you know where you are right now?"

"Yes, I'm in Olympic Memorial Hospital with my daughter, Mossy, who was injured in a bus accident."

"What was that about a fire?" asked the nurse.

"I was reminiscing about Mossy's father."

"I read about her father's accident on her chart," said the nurse in a kind voice. "You've experienced a lot of stress and it's all cumulative. The doctors will be coming in a few minutes. If Mossy is stable, they may decide to remove the ventilation. Why don't you and I go get a cup of coffee and then we'll talk with a counselor? Oh, I almost forgot! This came for you Federal Express." The nurse gave Barbara a large square envelope.

Barbara opened the envelope and a check fell out on the floor. She bent over to pick it up and glanced at it as she stood up. It was made out to the amount of $750 and was signed by George Redding. She opened the card inside which read,

Dear Barbara,

The prayers of Forks are with you, Mossy, and the other injured children. We put out jars at, Thrifty Save and around town. Every crummy from Port Angeles to Aberdeen carries a collection tin. We'll send more money next week to help out. Your friends and neighbors are with you now and always will be.

With love,
George

৩০৫৫

Olympic Memorial Hospital
June 9, 1987, 12:30

Barbara sat erect and rigid upon the comfortable couch in the Counseling Services room. "It's important to channel all the emotions you're experiencing right now into positive avenues," the counselor droned on. The nurse had made sure that Barbara ate something for lunch and then delivered her to this closed, airless room where the pleasant counselor was trying to exorcise the demons which engulfed the grieving and worried parents that wandered these halls. "There's no room for guilt here..." Barbara sank deeper into the couch. Through the open window, looking out to the Strait of Juan de Fuca, she could see a breeze blowing across the water. Barbara wished the window could open. Barbara tasted the cheese sandwich and yogurt she had had for lunch and wished that she could brush her teeth. Somehow, there was a growing aftertaste of pizza and beer and a distant memory of wild spearmint.
"What did you want to show me?" interrupted Barbara.
"Excuse me?" questioned the counselor, thinking that the subject was definitely flipped out and a candidate for heavy duty tranq intervention...
"What specifically is it that you wanted to show me out here?" asked Barbara, again.

৩০৫৫

Bear Creek
February 16, 1979, 18:45 hours

"What, specifically, I wanted to show you out here was me *not* being defensive like I was getting back there at the research cabin. Listen, Barbara, nobody has all the answers. Surely something as dramatic and intensive as logging has impacts associated with it, but so does wildfire; wind; earthquake; flood; drought...So does Nature. You and Mr. Wizard back there can heap all the woes of the world on us loggers, but Nature is apocalyptic and timber extraction mimics Nature. Logging depends on healthy forests. Forests are habitat. Timber lands provide habitat opportunity for deer, elk, bear and the fish you've come up here to study..."

"It looks to me like you're still defensive out here," Barbara swept her arm across the headlamp beam at the virginal forest they were traversing on the eastern upper slope of Reade Ridge. "As far as bear habitat goes, did you know that the Olympic Peninsula used to host the largest black bear concentration in the lower 48 states? Black bear eat re-prod. Timber companies have paid a bounty on bear to local hunters and the result is that bear have been all but extirpated outside of the Park. How is that like flood, or drought, or wind, or Nature?"

"Well, species' populations have their booms and busts just like the timber industry. But I'm against bear control. I'm not denying that the Timber Industry has made mistakes in resource management. What I'm saying is that, of all the extractive industries, logging is the most similar to Nature. You can look through a microscope and pick it to pieces, but the big picture is that timber ties up vast acreage, and that vast acreage is habitat."

"I'm not down on loggers. My father was a logger. Where are we going, anyway? What did you bring me out to show me?"

"I just wanted to talk with you without being defensive and, you're right, I'm still being defensive. Your study on SMZ will help to make logging less destructive to fisheries. I'm all for it. We're on the same side: research and progressive logging. I asked you to come out here so I could say I'm not a bad guy because I'm a logger. Maybe you understand that already if your dad was a logger, too. Here, let's sit down here for a while."

Barbara's headlamp revealed a mossy, flat spot next to a small drainage, which ran steeply downhill to Bear Creek. A rough-skinned newt, aroused from hibernation to courting by the mild weather, moved across the forest floor in her headlamp. She sat upon a soft sponge of moss and oxalis while Phil rummaged through his pack and pulled out a blanket which he tossed over to her. "You may want to sit on the blanket if that moss is wet from all that rain two days ago."

Barbara let the blanket fall next to her without trying to catch it. "I'm all right." This rendezvous was starting to smell like a cheap date. Half a pizza, a couple of beers, the guy tosses her a blanket...Barbara wished that she had put on a bra when she went into the cabin to grab her headlamp.

"I'm all right, really." She repeated and tossed the blanket back to him. Phil caught the blanket and walked over to her. He unfolded it and sat on it next to her. Barbara turned off her lamp to conserve the batteries. They sat for some hundred seconds in silence with the moisture wicking up into Barbara's blue jeans. In the warm, February air, a frog crawled out of its boggy winter abode in the mud and croaked its sexual keening.

Barbara felt awkward with the frog doing all the talking. "So, what gives between you and your partner, Rod Hill. It seems like you guys aren't on the best of terms."

"The guy gives mental retardation a bad name. I would rather not talk about him." The frog again gained control of the conversation.

"When you guys first pulled onto the landing above Bear Creek to do your logging, you were having some deep conversation which I overheard...something about time, space, matter...It was a pretty strange conversation for a logger."

"I spent five years at New York University, studying nuclear physics before I decided that I didn't aspire to be an atomic engineer stoking the furnaces at some nuclear reactor. The picture you get when you look out at the universe from the perspective of the electron leaves a lasting impression."

"Nuclear engineer turned logger," Barbara remarked. "That's more than a little vocational shift." Silence. A screech owl cried out through the dark in the sweet, lugubrious song which sounds like a single, ever quickening note, bouncing off the forest floor like a Ping-Pong ball. "Maybe we should get back. Rick is wanting to set up this spotted owl survey."

"Our perception of our environment is all sensorial," began Phil. "But our senses only reaffirm what we, as a species, have come to believe about our universe...and our senses lie. We totally misunderstand the fundamentals about our cosmos. Time, space, matter: western society is totally confused on the relationship of these axioms. Try to imagine the passage of time without some movement of some sort. Without movement, time stops. Actually, it's the movement of light at 186,000 miles per second that serves as a clock for our universe. One of Einstein's paradoxes was if you travel away from a clock tower in a train car at the speed of light and could continue to see the time on the clock face, it would remain the same time indefinitely. Traveling at the speed of light, which is how fast an electron moves about a proton, our time is stationary..."

"That doesn't make much sense," remarked Barbara.

"Let me put it this way: is time infinitely divisible? Can you divide a second into a billion parts and those billion parts into a billion subparts and so forth?"

"Well, I suppose you could."

"Relativists feel that you can divide it that far and no further. If you can divide a moment in time indefinitely, then there is no substance to that point in time. There is nothing you can call the present. You are always either before or after that point, but never on it."

"I see," said Barbara, suppressing a yawn.

"You're familiar with the expression of a "light year," the distance light travels in one year. It illustrates the relationship between time and space because we use a year to define a distance - 186,000 times sixty seconds, times sixty minutes, times twenty-four hours, times three hundred and sixty-five days. It equals two hundred forty-four billion, four hundred and four million miles or two hundred forty-four point four zero four to the ninth power miles..."

This time Barbara did yawn, "Excuse me," she said.

"Let's go the other way: A light inch. It's the unit of time it takes a particle or photon of light to travel one inch. So, multiply the number of feet in a mile, five thousand two hundred and eighty, by the number of inches in a foot, twelve, multiplied by one hundred and eighty-six thousand. The number is about eleven point seven eight five to the ninth power."

"Are you doing this in your head?" asked Barbara, with growing dread that she was frozen in time with a nerd.

"Hell, no. These are numbers I memorized years ago. They're magic! If you picture a hydrogen atom as roughly a billionth of an inch, or an angstrom, in circumference, then an orbit is one billionth of a light second or ONE 11.785 to the eighteenth power of a second!" Phil exuded enthusiasm for the number.

"What does that number represent again?" asked Barbara, bewildered.

"It's a particle of time! One epoch! Just like a stream of photons make up the information we assimilate as sight, time is a string of moments, X times eleven point seven eight five to the eighteenth power!

"Go back to Einstein's train car. We see ourselves in time as being strapped to the front of the train engine, hurtling down the track. The railroad ties pass so quickly we can't identify them as individual pieces of wood. They're a blur, just like particles of time. We can't see what's coming up around the bend, though it certainly exists. We can't see what's behind us, though that certainly exists because we passed through it. We can only see a little bit of where we are at the moment on the track, but by the time we recognize them, they are a ways behind us. The individual ties don't cease to exist because of the blur or because we pass them or haven't reached them..."

Barbara joined the conversation. "You're saying we live in the present, but actually our awareness is in the past. If you want to express it in light seconds, if you are three feet from me and I can see you in the starlight through these clouds, it is thirty-six light inches before your image hits the surface of my eye, about eleven point seven eight five to the seventh power light inches before the image is transferred to my brain via the optic nerve, and about eleven point seven eight five to the eight power light seconds before that image manifests in my consciousness. Average reaction time being what it is, you could turn into a starbeam and flash out of here. It would be almost five billion light seconds and you would be ninety thousand miles away before I jumped up and said 'hey.' Sight is one of our most immediate senses. We live in the past."

"Exactly," murmured Phil, smiling, as the curtain of clouds parted to expose a piece of starry heaven.

"If you want to talk about light and time," continued Barbara, "biological science has proven the connection between a species' perception of light and its time environment. With a seventy-year life expectancy, homo sapiens perceive fluid motion in movies shown at twenty four frames a second. Desert tortoises, which enjoy a longer life expectancy and a slower world, cannot perceive visual shifts occurring faster than once a second. The well-studied fruit fly, which lives for a few days, would see a twenty-four frame a second movie like a slide show.

"It's our brain waves that metronome our perception of time. Roughly, we experience ten brain waves for every heart beat. Time just is. It's the intersection of our peak brain waves across the plane of time which gives us the sense of its passing.

"I had a professor at Oregon State who used to compare our brain wave activity with swimming underwater and coming up for air. While we are between peak waves, we are subconscious and underwater...we are one with the water: with the fish and other aquatic creatures. When we come up for air, in his example, your head comes out of the cosmic soup and for a split second you look around and say, 'I'm swimming and I'm one with the water.' The irony is that you are amnesic about your subconscious experience where you really were one with the cosmic soup...It's kind of hard to explain. Professor Nice thought that dreams were a window into another reality..."

"That's what I believe!" declared Phil. "A nuclear or cosmic perspective confirms that belief. Matter and energy can't be destroyed. What is the human spirit? It's more energy than matter. You can't extinguish the human spirit with

71

physical death...you just scatter it. Space-time is not a line, it's a curvaceous plane and our lives are painted on that plane like the stroke of a paint brush. From our point in the space-time curve we cannot see Abraham Lincoln or the fiftieth President, but they both exist on the cosmic easel.

"You've heard energy expressed as foot-pounds? Well, E equals M C squared. The energy represented by your physical being is your body weight in pounds multiplied by thirty-four billion, five hundred and ninety-six million, multiplied by five thousand, two hundred and eighty. If you weigh one hundred and twenty pounds, your human spirit is packaged in an engine which can develop 23 quadrillion foot-pounds. We know a bullet with thirty foot-pounds can stop that engine, but it can't destroy the energy or the matter represented by your physical presence and it can't destroy the human spirit."

"Are you doing these numbers in your head?" Barbara asked again. "You're saying that mass relates to kinetic energy, but the size of a person doesn't reflect their spiritual potential or the size of their soul. An elephant isn't closer to God than a mouse..."

"Naw, the big multiplier is the speed of light, squared. Whether you're a mouse or an elephant you represent an enormous envelope of energy. How you focus that energy in a relationship with the Creator is a function of a tiny part of your brain. How much of the brain do we use, anyway?"

"About 10 percent," answered Barbara, going on perusing another thought: "Our senses lie to us about reality! We say that blood is red and chloroplasts are green. But our impression of the color is based on the reflected light. Blood absorbs green and reflects red. Chloroplasts absorb red and reflect green. What we see is the opposite of what is...just like a photographic negative.

"Hear that frog croaking down there in the mud? The ambient temperature warms up five degrees Fahrenheit and the frog perceives the temperature shift buried under four inches of mud. The frog was hibernating under that cold mud: its heart beating four or five times a minute and holding his breath for months at a time. If I stick my hand in the mud, it's so cold it hurts, but to the frog, it's a down comforter on his winter bed. A shift of five degrees and he throws off the covers and tosses around on top off the bed singing his lonely, horny old song..."

"Like a red hot iron is only a representation of molecular movement," interjected Phil. "Heat is molecular movement, so our fear of burning is only our emotional response to the sensorial message transmitted by molecular movement."

"God had to instill us with the tactile sense of pain before He gave us fire or we would have burned ourselves up standing too close to the flames..." Barbara offered and then faded into thought.

Phil continued, "This is the illusion of matter: that it exists somehow independently of movement. It is the movement of electrons around the field of a proton which define matter. The only difference between two hydrogen atoms, an oxygen atom and a molecule of water is the course an electron takes as it careens around the three atoms. The only difference between matter and energy is the trajectory of the electron.

"For that matter, if you had a camera that took pictures with a shutter speed of one billionth of a light inch, you would be looking inside one epoch of time and your picture would be nothing but vacant space. If you took the picture through an electronic microscope, you would see the frozen electrons and protons swimming in an enormous sea of ether. Matter is almost entirely space and it depends on movement, across the field, for existence. You don't think of electricity as having substance, but electrons are the basic units of matter or electricity. In a time event occurring at the speed of light, there is no matter or energy. The view from inside the atom is the view from inside a particle of time: it is infinity!

"You can't conceive of space without matter to measure it. Let's say that you're measuring the space between two stars with a mile-long yardstick. Halfway into the measurement, double the mass of the stars, double the distance in between them and double the size of your yardstick. Complete your measurement and your sum will be the same as if it were never doubled..."

"Obviously," said Barbara. From the direction of Camp Creek, an owl cried, more harping than the beautiful, lugubrious call of the screech owl.

"Now, take away the two stars and start measuring empty space..."

"Between what two points?"

"Exactly!" exclaimed Phil. "You need at least two points to define space. Without these points, space doesn't exist! It's why relativists believe that the universe curves back on itself.

"It's like if you took a flat map of the known universe and placed it out on the desert floor with a rock in the middle. The gravity of the rock would keep the middle down, but the edges would start to curl up in the sun. Eventually, the chart would fold in on itself. Beyond the material universe is vacant empty space, and that curls back on itself just like time does. If you go out to the most distant star in the known universe and follow a light beam away from matter into deep space, it will come back to matter.

"A graviton, which is one of the four quarks found in an electron, has authority over light, space, and even time. Astronomers study black holes, which are just burned out supernova stars, and they see matter and light being swallowed by the intense gravitational field. Where light is bent, time is likewise bent. We know that an infinitesimal graviton quark, a kind of particle, inside the electron kind of particle, inside the atomic particle can feel another quark half a billion miles through space." Phil lay on the blanket with his hands behind his head looking up at a layer of clouds which parted to give a starry glimpse of the heavens. "It seems like if two quarks a universe apart can do it, we ought to be able to harness and focus some of our kinetic energy to communicate with our Creator..."

"How do you prove that a quark can feel another quark a half billion miles apart?"

"How else do you explain Mercury orbiting around the Sun. It's all quarks. The gravitational field of the Sun is the product of all its quarks upon the product of all the quarks of Mercury. It's a huge multiplier, but ONE quark on the Sun has to have some measurable effect on ONE quark on Mercury or the combined effect of ALL quarks would be zero. Like if, in a vacuum, you set three pendulums in motion at different times. Eventually, they synchronize..." An owl hooted more closely and, on the slopes below, a rock was dislodged and tumbled through the forest obedient to gravity.

73

Barbara dragged her wet rear end closer to Phil and set herself half on the blanket beside him. "Like women living together who end up having the same period, more often than not. It's called biological entrainment. The fact that women have their periods every month is obviously a carry-over from the tidal effect of the moon, which is gravity. Homo sapiens haven't lost the diurnal, seasonal and random biorhythms which connect the species with the cosmos."

"Maybe not, but we use our senses to reinforce our precognitive conception of reality. We use our sense to corroborate major deceits about the cosmos. For example, our senses tell us that we are lying still on this blanket under a veil of clouds that separate to give us glimpses of the distant starry heavens. In fact, the ground is spinning at a thousand miles an hour on its axis. We are orbiting the sun at 6,000 thousand miles per hour and our solar system is exploding from the epicenter of the universe at a speed many times greater than that and has been since the Big Bang ten billion years ago. Our notion of place, which is pivotal to our reality, is totally flawed. From the moment of our birth to our death we never come to the same place. It's movement, which defines matter, time and space. Any place on earth is no more than a seat on a spaceship.

"Picture yourself praying. You look up into heaven to face your Creator. But our Creator is within us. Outer space is the same as inner space. The idea that God or the far heavens can be externalized totally disregards the system of reality we have known since Copernicus. Place is a myth and through all of our reality washes a torrent of fresh space...like the winds of a hurricane blowing through a barn with all its doors open.

"Biologists try to take apart life until it is a dead pile of flesh and bones. It's not flesh and bones that make up life...it's spirit and motion."

Barbara's head had come to rest on Phil's shoulder. "I agree that there is more than flesh and bones to life," she said. "We use our senses to confirm what we already believe about our universe. If we could quiet our minds and pause between brain waves, we could see our universe from a nuclear perspective. It's like the mother deer finding her fawn in the woods. The fawn is conditioned by genetic memory to be very quiet so as to not attract predators. I think the mother finds the physical location of the fawn by first going to a quiet place in her dumb mind, where she and her fawn are one spirit. Whales find each other in the enormous ocean and, though they have wonderful sonar, they instinctively find one another without it. Animals are more in tune with their environment. We've spent two hours talking about what two dogs would settle in a five second whiff from each other's rear ends..."

As Barbara lay with her head on Phil's shoulder, she smelled the sawdust of cedar and spruce on his wool Filson jacket. It was the smell of her father coming home in Rose Lodge: Of her father knocking off the saw chips and taking off his calks on the porch before coming in to greet his family. The familiar smell picked her up and held her to its chest and asked, "How is my princess this evening?" This man electrified her. This man electrified her. She took his right hand and held it upon her bosom.

In the cool quiet of the forest, Barbara's heart lay like a poem longing to be read. She felt her heart, her heart, her heart beating like the wings of an owl as it flies in the direction of the mating call, discerned in the deep, dank silence of the forest. Her sexual libido crawled out of the cool mud of shyness and croaked boldly in the warm air of her longing: Herrrrr hearrrrrrrt, herrrrr hearrrrrrrt. Her heart: gone a courting, did it ride and glide like a rough-skinned newt across the forest floor.

Her heart, her heart, her heart. In her heart: the swimming of a whale searching for its mate in the deep silence of the wide ocean floor... Her heart was a jumble of longing and desire in the tangled forest of her emotions. Pheromoning and hormoning, her heart was the feral moaning of a wild beast...behind the thorny, dense underbrush of her mores and inhibitions... in the wet woods, waiting without words. Her heart tumbled and rolled like rock, exposing the same longing, as it crashed through the brush, descending from her bosom to her viscera...her heart. Her stomach gurgled.

ॐ

Phil Stone almost apologized when he heard the gurgling stomach. He was experiencing difficulty separating where he ended and Barbara began. His hand had insinuated itself upon her breast and she held onto it tightly. Whether she clutched it so tightly out of some spontaneous affection for him, or to restrain his hand from some mischievous wanderings, he could not be sure. Through the fabric of her sweater and pullover, Phil felt the warm, living swell of her bosom. His cosmic ponderings changed gear. "Is she not wearing a bra?" he wondered, as the tactile senses of his hand sent wild and bawdy messages to his brain. "What does a woman wish who holds you to her breast?" the brain inquired of the hand. The hand became diaphoretic and trembled slightly.

Phil Stone's brain became overwhelmed with the biological responses which overtook him. His heart began to race. He could not concentrate or put together a sentence. He felt a pang in his loins somewhere between a gentle stirring, and having his testicles caught in a blender. *"This could be really good,"* came a leering message from somewhere south of his belly button, while a part of his brain pleaded, *"She's just a twenty-two-year-old kid, for crying out loud!"*

The silence that had enveloped the reposing couple was temporarily interrupted by another owl hoot somewhere between Camp Creek and their mossy bench on Reade Ridge. An argument raged in Phil Stone's brain between the pleasure center and the portion of the temporal lobe which pretended to control ethical behavior. A 'go/no go' situation had developed with the temporal lobe shrieking, *"Don't! Stop!"* while the autonomic control at the back of his brainpan pulled the plug and the oxygenated blood which supported an exploration of cosmic reality ran down to pool in Phil's penis.

In the inner commotion and lightheadedness which was overtaking him, Phil attempted to drag his consciousness out upon the plane of infinite possibilities. He tried to survey the 360-degree course available to him. *"I could remove my hand and say, 'It's late and we should get back.'"* Phil's right hand rejected this direction. *"I could excuse myself under the pretext of having to go into the woods to micturate. That would give us a cooling-off period and we wouldn't be rushing into anything..."* Phil's penis would have nothing to do with this scheme and stood resolute saying, *"I couldn't piss right now if you held a gun to my head."*

"I could...I could...I could remove my right hand from Barbara's grip and make a run for it under the sweater and shirt. I'm sure she's not wearing a bra, so the only interference here would be if her pullover is well anchored by a tight belt." Phil's hand continued to sweat and tremble just waiting for its marching orders.

"I could...I could make the same move, but change directions with my hand and go south. Then we would know in a moment where this evening is taking us..." The right hand liked this idea even more and began to extricate itself from the custody of the ten female digits.

The temporal lobe of the brain stilled the right hand as it began to stir with stark embarrassment tactics. *"What if it's her period, huh? Did you think of that? What if she slaps you into next week and goes crying to the Forest Service that you shoved yourself down her pants?"*

The penis feigned sage-like wisdom. *"Women that hold your hand to their bosoms aren't having their period. Women that don't wear bras don't go crying to the Forest Service..."* The nose attempted to distract the brain with the intoxicating perfume of her washed scalp and the soft scent of mint on her breath.

The temporal brain sought the ego as an ally. *"You know how you like to be respected. So does she. Whatever happens here, you have to respect her if you want to be respected or respect yourself..."*

"Well, kiss her then," suggested the penis. *"Yeah, kiss her,"* agreed the right hand.

"Kiss her!" yelled the brain, throwing adrenaline and endorphins like confetti and party streamers.

From the field of infinite possibilities emerged only one degree. There was no retreating, no running off into the woods to micturate. There was commitment and consensus. Phil Stone rolled over to kiss Barbara. Barbara's lips met his and there was consent. There was more than consent: there was hunger... an earnest eagerness...the fitting of two pieces in a biological jigsaw puzzle.

Clothing began to be shed like tufts of elk hair falling onto the forest floor in the spring. There was grasping and gasping. The shed clothing became a bed and the blanket was just being deployed for warmth and shelter for their growing nakedness when a beam of light searched them out and lit on Barbara's naked bosom. Rick Larson's voice at the other end of the beam said, "Jesus! I'm sorry, guys. I had no idea! I just came to check up because I was worried when you didn't come back."

Pulling up the blanket, the shed clothes were clumsily retrieved and put on. But there was no way to cover the deep, penetrating embarrassment of the moment. Barbara's sense of NOW bucked and kicked like a Wild Pacing Mustang trying to escape its stall.

❧

If celestial bodies could recoil in embarrassment the way we humans do, the mortification that Barbara felt, gathering her clothes and fumbling for her headlamp, would knock the sun backwards a couple orbits, dragging time with it.

The dizzy earth would jump off the backward merry-go-round and stare dazedly at another warm day in February, 1977.

ৡৣৢ

Five

"What then is time? I know well enough what it is, provided that nobody asks me; but if I am asked what it is and try to explain it, I am baffled. (Time) can only be coming from the future, passing through the present, and going into the past. In other words, it is coming out of what does not yet exist, passing through that which has no duration, and moving into what no longer exists."
Augustine
Greek philosopher

Oregon State University, Corvallis, OR
Monday, February 14, 1977

*B*arbara felt slightly nauseous sitting in the classroom, listening to Professor Jake Nice drone on about R.E.M. sleep and the relationship of the unconscious to reality. Her roommate had started her period this morning and that meant that the same phase of the moon would find Barbara cramping, menstruating and floundering in gastric distress. It was funny how the celestial bodies cast their influence over their inhabitants, thought Barbara, chewing on an antacid tablet from her pocket...

"I know you students are having trouble staying with boring, old me after your weekend fun and frolic," Professor Nice was always so self-effacing. "We believe that wakefulness is a higher manifestation of reality than sleep because it is a shared experience. For those of you in the class that are still awake, we agree that this classroom is reality. Those of you that are dreaming about making out in the woods or the kegger you're going to have next weekend are said to be dreaming.

"But, when we dream in R.E.M. sleep, there is an acceleration of brain waves. We perceive a minute as several hours and the eye movement tracks the motion of inward experiences that go by in a twinkle. If we could put the images of Mr. Wilcox, as he sleeps peacefully there in the back row, on a screen, they would fly by so quickly that we would all agree, they are nonsensical and all just a blur..." at mention of his name, the student Jack Wilcox stirred and opened his bleary eyes. "But, we know from our own experience, that R.E.M. sleep carries a powerful sense of reality.

"Those of us who are awake in this classroom, are applying many filters to remain focused on the task of learning. We filter out our rear ends, which are getting tired of sitting." For a moment the room was silent. "We filter out distracting sounds like that distant chain saw or the traffic noise out on the street. We filter out the rumblings of our stomachs, the beating of our hearts, the ventilation of our lungs...

"When we sleep, these filters behave differently. The sound of a distant chain saw can become the central theme of a dream. It is a proven fact that the

77

sensory perception of subjects in sleep can become far more acute than in a wakeful state. In sleep you can hear and process auditory stimuli which, in the waking state, would be totally filtered.

"Look at all the documented cases of precognition and telepathic communication which have attended the dream state. Dreams are another picture of reality. In some cases, they are a clearer and more accurate picture than wakefulness. Go back to sleep, Mr. Wilcox. You won't fail this class by sleeping through it..."

ঙ৵ড়

Bear Creek Research Station
Friday, February 16, 1979, 15:00 hours

Barbara lay restless in her sleep. It had been difficult to find sleep since she was able to lie down at one in the afternoon after spending the night with Rick Larson, walking the forest, hooting for spotted owls. She was mortified and just wanted to lie down next to a nurse log, pull the moss over her and let the trees grow, sucking the sap out of her.

For his part, Rick was all business. He dropped a bomb shell: that her part of the Bear Creek study was finished and she should be planning on clearing out of the research station to make room for the couple who was moving in for the third phase of the project. This, she had known was imminent, though it gnawed at her insides to think about leaving the Olympic Peninsula, which she had come to think of as the center of her universe. Rick Larson had suggested that spotted owls might become a heavy piece on the chessboard of conservation law and timber management. He seemed eager to recruit her as the vanguard of what he felt would be a standing army of owl hooters. But fish were Barbara's thing...

They had come back to the research shack at about noon and had breakfast in silence. After eating, Rick had begun transcribing his notes while Barbara went into the next room and tried to find sleep. She had tossed and turned for a couple of hours in the clothing she had worn to bed, coming out of her warm sleeping bag. Just as she would begin to doze, she would feel the tickle of a flashlight on her naked bosom and yank the sleeping bag up to her chin. Her mind chased a sweet dream of drifting down a river with her father, like a child chasing a butterfly. A loud, gurgling ripple threatened to upset the boat and Barbara woke up to realize it was her own stomach, roiling in agitation.

By 3 p.m. she slept and the dream she found was vivid and clearer than wakefulness. *She lay in bed in the dark as her father put on his wool jacket and calk boots by the door before heading out in the early morning to work: The soft latching of the door as he left...into the dark...beyond her sight.*

Her home was surrounded by wilderness: bear, cougar and salmon, swimming upstream. In the distance she heard the rumble of a pickup motor rumbling into the wilderness. Was her father home already? No, it was her husband coming home to her. Coming through the dark...She could not see his face, but he carried something...Her husband smelled like...her father.

She lay surrounded by the maze of wilderness, and the simple home of her childhood became a labyrinth. In the huge maze, she lay dozing in one room as something precious lay frightened and injured, separated by many walls...something innocent and cherished...an entity that called out to Barbara in a tiny voice that thundered in portent.

Her husband was coming for her. She looked down like a bird on the figure of the man she loved coming down from the landing to the research cabin, in a clean hickory shirt and reeking of aftershave, he carried a gift in each hand. She couldn't quite see his face, but he whistled cheerfully...the shrill sound cutting through the wilderness and reaching her in the maze where she waited.

Her husband was coming down the hill to her, whistling, as her employer walked slowly up the hill to the landing. From the sky above, she watched as they met on the trail. Her husband self-consciously concealed the gifts behind his back.

"Hello, Rick," said her husband guardedly.

"Hi, Phil. I hope you're not holding a gun behind your back. Barbara and I were just doing owl census stuff all night. Listen, I'm really sorry about last night. I was just checking because Barbara said you'd be back within a couple of hours. I didn't mean to rain on your parade." Her husband's left hand came into view, clutching a half dozen long-stemmed roses. "Flowers!" exclaimed Barbara's employer. "Now that's an elegant touch! I hope they go over better than my smoked oysters."

"Is Barbara down at the cabin?" asked her husband.

"Yeah. I think she's sleeping, but maybe not. She called out 'Good-bye, Daddy' when I left. Listen, Phil, no hard feelings here. Barbara interested me, but it's obvious she likes you. Last night I was just looking out for her as a friend and as her employer...OK?" The Forest Servant held out his hand to her husband.

"It's all right, Rick," said her husband, bringing out his right hand, which carried a box of opened chocolates. The edge of the box caught on her husband's hip as he shifted the gift to shake hands. The candy fell out on the ground. Her husband and employer bent over to pick up the spilled candies.

"Hey, half of these candies are missing, you cheap bastard," joked Barbara's employer. "When she sees this, maybe there will be hope for me, after all."

"That pig, Rod Hill, found them in the back of the crummy this morning and scarfed half of them."

"Maybe he'll get a big cavity," commiserated Barbara's employer.

"He's already got a cavity the size of the Grand Canyon between his ears," said her husband.

"Well, good luck with everything," said her employer, continuing up the hill to the landing.

"Thanks," said Barbara's husband, starting down toward the research station. But somehow his face was sliding into the dark. In her darkened labyrinth, the walls separated her from her husband; from her father; from the cherished ward that lay in terror and agony separated by so many walls. The walls pushed in like a horse stall confining Barbara's spirit; stifling her soul. She was a Pacing Mustang, kicking at the prison walls of its stall. She could hear the hooves kicking against the walls, the boards rattling with every kick...

"Barbara," called the man's voice. *The kicking continued.* "Barbara, it's me, Phil..." She woke up sweating under the sleeping bag in the tiny bedroom of the research cabin. She went to answer the knocking of the door and there stood Phil Stone in a clean hickory shirt with a half dozen long-stemmed roses and a half-eaten box of chocolates. "Hi, Barbara, did I wake you up?"

"No, I was awake...kind of." Barbara stood at the door's threshold, not receiving the gifts and not inviting Phil's entry.

"I brought you these," said Phil, lamely, holding up the gifts.

"Thanks, Phil, but I'm really not into cut flowers. Give them to someone else."

"That stupid idiot Rod ate half the candy..." said Phil, apologetically.

"Thanks for the sentiment, Phil, but I don't need the candy either. What I really need is some sleep. We just got done with that owl stuff a couple hours ago."

"Yeah, I'm kind of bushed, too. I got two hours of sleep before I had to go to work at a unit along the Ozette Mainline. They had light banks set up so we could start cutting before dawn. Hey, I was wondering if you would like to come to Forks with me for dinner..."

"I'm sorry, Phil, I need sleep right now more than food."

Phil shifted uncomfortably. "I'm sorry to intrude, Barbara, but it's not like I can telephone ahead to announce my visits. I'll leave you to your sleep and I'll take my dumb presents, but when can I see you again? When would you like for me to come back?"

"I don't know, Phil. I got the word from Rick that my part of the study is over. I'll be leaving in a couple of days..."

"That son of a bitch!" exclaimed Phil.

"No," said Barbara. "It's not what you think. My part of the project was finished with your cutting. It's time for me to go..."

"Barbara, I need to spend some time with you before you leave." She was tired and irritable. Was Phil saying that he wanted to take up where they left off last night when Rick's flashlight found her naked bosom? She recoiled at the thought, the Pacing Mustang of her soul kicking at the confines of the moment.

"Listen, Phil, what happened last night was not me," Barbara heard her voice saying. "I hardly know you and I can't understand why I started behaving like an alley cat."

The stall boards imprisoning the Pacing Mustang are held to the walls by the nails of hours and days. "In two days I'll be back in Oregon and there doesn't seem to be a lot of point in persisting in a flash romance with a life expectancy measured in hours. I'm sorry that I gave you the wrong impression and caused you to develop unwarranted expectations..."

"Ms. Stone...Barbara..."

ॐ

Olympic Memorial Hospital
June 9, 1987, 16:30 hours

"You've been asleep for a few hours now," intoned the counselor. "I didn't wake you because I knew you needed the rest and I had a lot of paperwork to do. But I've got to see another patient now and it's time we spent a few minutes discussing YOU instead of your daughter. Would you like to be admitted? We could put you in the same room with your daughter as soon as she stabilizes..."

"No!" Visions of a padded cell, Valium drip, and wire screen on the windows pressed in on Barbara's consciousness. "No, thank you. It won't be necessary," said Barbara, extricating herself from the gravity of the couch and making for the door. "Thanks for your time and for the chance to rest. I feel a lot better now," Barbara lied.

She made her way into the halls and arranged a motel room on the telephone. She called George Redding, thanking him for the support from the logging community and arranged to have George check in on Mossy's pup, incarcerated in a kennel back at the farm.

She returned to Mossy's floor, but was dissuaded from entering her room by a charge nurse. Barbara carried a chair to the threshold of the door and sat herself down to begin the long wait. In the brightly-lit halls of the hospital, Barbara waited. Amid the comings and goings of doctors and nurses, with the passing of so many other terrorized parents, in view of the arrivals and departures of other child casualties...Behind these doors the spark of life sputtered against a black night of parental despair.

From a sterile motel room, to the brightly-lit halls of the critical care unit, to the frightened and drug dazed face of her daughter, Barbara waited on a recovery which she prayed for with every breath. She waited...

And waiting also, is the wilting new corn in the burning afternoon under the June sun. Waiting is the tongue of the lactating cow upon the cool hide of the stillborn calf. Waiting is the dust of despair that gathers with time over the inner furniture of our hope.

The loooooooooooooooooooooooooooonnnnnnnnnnnnnnnng waiting ... The weary, worrisome, waiting without words. Barbara waited...

ॐ

Rose Lodge, OR
February 28, 1979, 10:35 hours

In her tiny bedroom, Barbara tried to concentrate on her notes and the thesis she was trying to write on the impact of timber felling on a SMZ. While she labored to focus her attention on her writing, her heart waited. Her heart waited for the noon delivery of mail that might bring an answer to a letter she had written last week: A letter addressed to a logger sent c/o a Forest Service biologist. The letter had apologized and attempted an explanation. The letter had tried to open a door that had been slammed shut at a research shack next to the headwaters of Bear Creek overlooking the wilderness of the Bogachiel Valley. Her heart counted the ticking of the clock, waiting.

And her waiting was the Silver salmon hen, arranging her nest in the gravel. Her waiting was the silence between the croakings of the frog. Her waiting was the feathery seed of the dandelion that waits on the wind. In the keen wanting without words, Barbara's heart pined and waited.

81

৯৵৶

Olympic Memorial Hospital
June 20, 1987, 16:45 hours

Barbara waited by her daughter's hospital bed while Mossy dozed. It had been five days since she was removed from the Critical Care Unit. One by one, tubes had been withdrawn from the child until only the IV drip remained infusing the child with dilute sugar water and Darvon painkiller. The attending nurse was shutting down the Darvon piggyback on the IV in preparation for the therapy, which would begin in two days. Barbara had given up staying at the motel, sleeping, when she could, in the chair next to Mossy's bed. Though Mossy's survivability seemed assured at this point, the sedation had kept her groggy and Barbara had to rely on the doctor's opinion that the child had escaped without brain damage. The doctors would offer no assurances regarding Mossy's future ambulation. To Barbara's persistent questions, they replied that they would have to wait and see how the patient responded to rehabilitation and therapy before making a prognosis on her future mobility.

Barbara arranged five little toy ponies with fluorescent manes on the roll-away table in front of her daughter's face. The toys had arrived in a box from George Redding, who had somehow remembered Mossy's birthday. The "My Little Pony" series was somehow a favorite with female homo sapiens of Mossy's age, regardless of their grasp of nature or familiarity with equestrian coloration or anatomy. Mossy opened her eyes and smiled feebly.

"Honey," said Barbara, talking around the toys and nurse who worked on the IV, "tomorrow is your birthday and I wondered if you had any ideas on ways we could celebrate."

"I want to go home...please," came the child's small voice.

"Mossy, we've been over that. You need to stay here so the doctors and nurses can help you walk. You had a serious accident and you've gotten a lot better, but we need you to get all better before we go home..."

"It wasn't my fault! The accident wasn't my fault..."

"Of course it wasn't, Mossy. No one said it was. But these things happen and you have to try hard to get better..."

"Mommy, if I die will I go to hell?"

"Of course not, honey, why would you ask such a thing? In the first place, God loves you and in the second place you're not going to die. Who's been filling your head with these spooky things?" Barbara cast a hard glance at the nurse who mouthed the words, "NOT ME."

"Janice Star told me two days ago during recess that kids who aren't baptized go to hell when they die." Mossy's reply indicated that she was unaware of the two weeks she had lost since her accident. "I'm not baptized am I?"

"No, Mossy. But you can be, if you want. Just decide on a church. In the meantime, I thought I would get some books and we could study some and read the Bible together. It would be fun and we could pray together."

"But if I die..."

"Mossy, YOU WON'T DIE. You can't die on me."

"But some day, I'll die."

"Someday we all will die, yes. But there is no room in hell for a sweet, young thing like you. I can't quite picture where it is that we are going, Mossy, but when you do finally die, I promise you...your mommy will be waiting for you on the other side. And you'll get to meet your daddy, too."

"Will Daisy be there?"

"Well, I don't know about Daisy. She isn't always so innocent. But there's no hell for her either..."

"Can you get Daisy and we'll have a little party here in the room?"

"George Redding is taking care of Daisy and I don't know if they allow dogs here in the rooms." The nurse nodded "yes," so there went that excuse.

"Mommy, you asked what I wanted for my birthday and what I would like is to see my dog and for you to bring some real food from the garden for me to eat. The food and water here are yucky!"

The nurse reacted defensively, "You hadn't eaten for ten days while you were on the NG tube, so we had to start off slowly with soup and pureed food. Anyway, tonight we're having a dish that all kids love. Guess what?"

"What?" asked Mossy with trepidation.

"Sloppy joe!" announced the nurse expansively and left the room to fetch the same.

"Mommy, I'll die if I have to go on eating this junk!"

The nurse returned with Mossy's dinner and removed the ponies to place the tray. The little girl went to work with her fork to push the macerated flesh into a pile at the corner of her plate so it didn't touch any other food and then went to work on the jello, mashed potatoes and corn. "The vegetables don't taste real," complained the little girl.

"All right, I'll go home tonight after you're asleep and bring back some stuff from the pantry. I'm afraid that the garden's a write-off this summer. I need to check in on things, anyway."

"Don't forget to bring Daisy," the child was brightening.

Barbara sat beside her daughter to await the results of the child's withdrawal from Darvon, which might or might not present in the next three hours. The ponies were brought back to share in the vigil.

"Mommy, tell me a story," asked the child, settling back into a pillow and the drug-induced drowsiness that lingered in her veins.

"What kind of story do you want to hear?"

"Tell me a story about ponies. Tell me a story about My Little Ponies."

Barbara charged ahead confidently, "Well, once upon a time, there was a herd of wild, little ponies that lived in a beautiful, little valley in the deep forest..."

"A valley like our valley?" asked the child.

"Yes, just like the Bogachiel; a valley with grassy meadows and huge spruce trees. A wild, clean valley with sweet grass and crystal clear water...with fish." The child shut her eyes, and Barbara also shut her eyes, dabbing at the palette of her imagination and recall. "A fresh breeze always blew up the valley in the afternoon, blowing the tall sweet grass like waves on the ocean..."

"Just like hommmme," came the child's small voice drawing out the word, which was her center of the universe.

"Yes...and the frogs croaked, the owls called one another and, in Fall, the ponies liked to stand in the meadow and listen to the elk bugle. It rained, just like where we live, and there were biting flies and sometimes the ponies tripped in holes made by the mountain beavers...But the ponies were very happy and glad to be alive. They had each other and they had the whole world to play in..."

"What games did they play?"

"They ran as fast as they could across the wide, flat meadow and they played hide-and-go-seek in the surrounding ancient forest..." Barbara fell quiet, looking for a serpent in the garden: some conflict upon which to hang a story line.

"And then what happened, Mommy?"

"One day the ponies smelled smoke for the first time, and it was strange and frightening to them..."

"Was the forest burning? Was it a wild fire?" the child's eyes widened in fear for the ponies.

"No, honey. Man had come to the valley. The settlers were clearing the land and fencing in their gardens. At first it was just a few wisps of smoke, but then every afternoon breeze brought the choking smell of smoke. It was more than the ponies could bear and they sent the lead pony downstream to ask the settlers to please stop all the smoke..."

"Was the lead pony named 'Fiver?' What were the ponies' names?"

"They didn't have names. These were wild ponies without names and they knew each other by their smell. They had no language, as such, and the alpha pony could not make the settlers understand by gesture or olfactory what was so obvious, that the smoke was hurting the valley..." Barbara fell silent for a moment trying to sniff out the direction for this story line, borrowing from a chapter of Native America.

"And then what happened?"

"Well, there were more and more settlers and more and more smoke. The smoke choked the trees and clouded the water. The smoke began to kill the grass. And the settlers continued to advance on the ponies, pushing them evermore upvalley, until the ponies had arrived at the last meadow...the last place they could live. And behind the settlers was all scorched earth and blacktop and concrete...no place for wild ponies. And still the settlers advanced trying to push the ponies further upvalley and out of the last meadow where the ponies could live."

"What did the ponies do?"

"The ponies prepared to fight for their home. They practiced their kicks and they sharpened their hooves and they prepared for battle. But they were peace-loving ponies and they could not make warriors out of themselves, so they sent the alpha pony out one more time to try to talk...I mean to communicate with the settlers that were flooding into the valley."

"Did it work? Did the settlers listen...I mean understand?"

Barbara realized that she was painting herself into a corner. There was no happy ending to the picture on this easel. She was silent as she searched for the elusive silver lining.

"Mommy? Did the settlers understand?"

"No, honey. And there were so many of them. The alpha pony looked out over a sea of settlers. There was no turning them back. There was no point in fighting so many. There was no way for the ponies to defend their home or preserve their way of life..."

"So what DID THEY DO?" asked Mossy, agonizing over the prognosis of the ponies, just as her mother had anguished over the prognosis of Mossy.

"They smelled each other very carefully and made sure that they could find each other wherever they went by smell. They shared one last nibble from the grass that had lost its nourishment and a sip from the water that no longer tasted of freshness...they lay down in the meadow and they waited and waited."

"FOR WHAT? WHAT WERE THEY WAITING FOR?" Mossy was very apprehensive.

"Honey, they waited for it to be over. They waited for the end which comes without food or water..."

"THIS IS A HORRIBLE STORY! WHY ARE YOU TELLING ME THIS! HAS SOMETHING HAPPENED TO OUR HOME?"

"Mossy our home is just fine and this is just a story, but hear the end of it. One by one the ponies woke up on the other side. They woke up back in a wide, expansive prairie that was like it was before. The river ran clear and cool and the air was sweet and pure. The ponies followed their noses to find one another and they ran like the wind across the wide prairie and played hide-and-seek in the old growth forest..."

"They lived happily ever after?" asked Mossy, calmed with the resolution of the story line.

"Well, this is the other side we're talking about, so they EXISTED in happiness for eternity. But, your home is fine, Mossy, and it's waiting for you. This is not a time for you to quit and lie down in a brown meadow. It's a time to be sharpening your hooves. You are the alpha pony and you have to struggle against all odds to walk again. The doctors, the nurses, your mommy...we're all here to help you win this fight. Please do what they tell you to do in therapy. Help us to get you walking again."

"I will, Mommy," said the little girl, settling in. "Tomorrow you'll bring fresh food and Daisy and my birthday will be OK. Soon I'll be going hommmmmme."

"Yes," said the mother, knowing that weeks of therapy and postoperative surgery separated the child from hommmmmme. The child's head was pulled by gravity into the pillow and sleep found her. "Hommmmmmme," said the mother softly to the sleeping child.

᮫᮫᮫

Olympic Memorial Hospital
June 20, 1987, 23:45 hours

"STOP IT! STOP IT! NO! NO! NO!" Barbara woke up in the chair beside the screaming child. "STOP IT! PUT OUT THE FIRE!" The child's diaphoretic face thrashed about in the pillow. She was having withdrawals. Barbara rang the nurse's call button and shook her child awake.

"Shush, Mossy, you're only dreaming," as Barbara spoke Mossy's eyelids parted to reveal the terror of a pony caught in a barn fire.

"Mommy I can smell the smoke! I CAN HEAR THE SCREAMS OF ALL THE PONIES!"

"It's just a dream, Mossy. You're all right. I'm here with you..."
Barbara realized the bedtime story a few hours ago had been a big mistake.
"You're awake now!"

"NO! I heard the pony scream: 'Stop it, no, no no.' I HEARD IT and I
smelled the smoke!"

"No, Mossy. There's no smoke in here. Everything is fine!" Barbara
tried to comfort her daughter. The nurse arrived and shrugged helplessly. The
therapists couldn't afford to have the young patient drug-addled as she made her
attempts to regain mobility. She could overstress a surgical pin. The drug
withdrawal was a dragon that had to be slain.

"Mommy, I HEARD THE PONY SCREAM, 'STOP IT!' You were
wrong! The ponies can talk!" Mossy would not be placated.

"Mossy, that was YOU. You heard your own voice."

"The pony TALKED IN MY VOICE, trying to stop the smoke! And
then the pony was falling and hurt its head and legs!"

"What's this about the pony falling?" asked Barbara, trying to engage the
child. "You had an accident and you hurt your head and legs. You were falling in
the bus accident..."

"NO! This was something else. It happened a long time ago! The pony
fell out of the tree and hurt itself. The pony tried to stop the smoke, but THEY
WOULDN'T LISTEN!"

"Mossy, you're not making sense. It was all a dream from that story I
told you. I never should have made that story up. Cut it loose. Cut yourself loose
from the tangle of that story!"

"Mommy, the pony was talking in my voice," said Mossy, beginning to
weep miserably.

"Shush," said Barbara. And as she held her daughter's sweaty, shaking,
little body in her arms she tried to comfort her with a lullaby and the smell of her
closeness. "Row, row, row your boat..." As the child quietly wept, the mother
sang, while the nurse stood by the door. "...life is but a dream..." The nurse left
the room and the mother sang the same verse over and over and over until sleep
again triumphed over anguish.

After a couple of hours the mother left the sleeping child. It would be a
three hour round trip journey home to satisfy Mossy's requests.

ᱬᱬ

Highway 101 Milepost 216
Sunday, June 21, 1987, 01:15

Listening to 'oldies' on her car AM radio, Barbara struggled to stay
awake as she drove her old GMC. She tried focusing on the road, but her mind's
eye flashed between her injured child behind her and the neglected farm at the end
of the road in front of her. Like her daughter, she longed for home and the inner
peace of that sanctuary. In her mind she was standing on the bridge over the
gurgling water of Hemp Hill Creek. She could see the meadows and her garden.
She looked out across the river and up Reade Hill to the old growth timber on the
ridge. She saw, in the picture of home, the sun glistening on a large boulder

nestled in the big trees toward the top of the hill. She was being pulled into the picture and started as her truck crossed the center line, proceeding in the lane of oncoming traffic. She tuned out the music and searched the dial for a talk show.

"...welcoming you back to B.B.C. radio and welcoming you to the first day of summer. We're an hour and fifteen minutes into the longest day of the year and continuing our discussion with Dr. Adam Tromell, formerly of the United States National Aeronautics and Space Administration from Houston, Texas. Our discussion appropriately focuses on global warming and the impacts we may expect to see in the next fifty years. Dr. Trommell, the last two weeks appear to be vindication for the people who share your view that global warming is a reality. What other indicators do we have to substantiate that this theory is being borne out?"

"Well, I'm uncomfortable with the word "theory" to describe global warming. It's like saying, if you lay down for a fifteen-minute nap on a train track ten minutes before the arrival of the train, the THEORY is that you may get hurt. It's just reality. Carbonic gases and the other unfortunate byproducts of our transportation and industrial systems are stacked in our upper stratosphere. It's elementary science. It's not theory. Some of us say that the impact of our wholesale reliance on fossil fuel is as certain as that of a large man passing gas on a crowded elevator on a hot day. The effect is surely predictable and not theoretical in the least.

"Another component in the reality of global warming is the diminution and destruction of the ozone layer due to chlorine out-gassing from swimming pools, drinking water and, largely, from sewage treatment. Chlorine, and not the aerosol propellant you find in deodorant cans, is the bad guy here..."

"Excuse me, doctor," interrupted the moderator. "But for a couple of decades the implication of aerosols and fluorocarbons in ozone depletion was accepted as fact. If this is not the case, what substantive proof do you have to tie chlorine to the process?"

"Thanks for the question. Ozone is created by lightning. It is absolutely critical to the screening of the face of the planet from ultraviolet rays of the sun. NASA has two satellites dedicated to monitoring the condition of the ozone, Cirrus One and Two. Both satellites have been sending back data that indicates the ozone layer has been disappearing at a rate three times faster than our worst model. The Vice President of the United States is in charge of federal science and research, which makes Dan Quayle in charge of NASA. His solution to the global problem of ozone depletion and warming was to have NASA tell the media that the Cirrus satellites were out of calibration. THE HOTTEST THREE YEARS IN RECORDED HISTORY OCCURRED DURING THE BUSH/REAGAN ADMINISTRATION! It's Vice President Quayle that is out of calibration. Believe me, a warmer day is coming..."

"Dr. Trommell, I understand that NASA is no longer your employer..."

ॐ

Reade Hill
Moon of the Melting Snow, 8,025 B.C.

Wolves howled in the growing light across the valley. The dog-thing began barking as the hunter/gatherer ran out from the large overhang in the huge granite boulder, which sufficed as the family's shelter. The man slipped in a pile of canine excrement at the opening of the overhang and came down in the snow with a grunt. He picked himself up and ran a few more feet before lifting his fur robes to defecate diarrheatically. The liquid feces ran down his leg.

Too many dried berries. Not enough meat. This was the consequence of being left behind by the Tribe. The hunter/gatherer had planned to eat the dog-thing, but the child-thing protested and the woman-thing would not allow it. To die eating berries and bark: This was the price of being spurned by the Tribe.

The hunter/gatherer began cleaning his leg with snow, but it made his hands cold. He had tried to make the Tribe understand that a warmer day was coming. He had taken them upvalley to the large lake impounded by the ice dam and shown them the melted glacier. But there was not the sound or dance to make them understand its significance. A WARMER DAY WAS COMING! There was not a need to continue the trek into the noon sun. His fingers were cold. He put them in his mouth, but pulled them out when he tasted the excrement on them. This was the price of exile.

The Tribe had come from a country under the star, Turba.[1] The enormous granite rock which sat on the side of this hill was likewise from that country and proved this man's theory: that a warmer day was coming. The Tribe had not understood and there were not the sounds to explain.

The man looked down, from the short forest of Engelmann spruce which covered the hill, to the savannah across the drainage. This was a perfect killing field for the woolly giant thing. In his mind's eye, he could still see a line of Spruce cut down and stacked up to corral the woolly giants that came to feed in the savannah. He could see shelter, built not of rock, but of thatched Spruce. There would be shelter for all the Tribe. But there was not the sound or dance to make them understand these things that he saw in his head. They could not understand that there was no need to press on. And press on they did, exiling the man and his family for his heretic vision.

It was impossible for one hunter/gatherer to take a woolly mammoth by himself. Even a small one was defended by the herd and required teamwork for the slaughter. The woman and female child-thing could not be counted on in the hunt. To survive, the family would need another hunter. The woman-thing had missed one or two blood flows, but this was probably due more to the lack of meat, than to being with child. The hunter/gatherer wiped his hand on his furs and steeled himself for the task of making another child. Gods willing, it would be male. He followed the smoke back under the overhang and into the rock shelter.

---

[1]The orientation of the North Pole under the star Polaris is a temporary stellar arrangement dependent on the wobble of the Earth's axis and stellar arrangement. Eight thousand years B.C., the North Pole aligned with Turba. Twelve thousand years later, it would align with Vega. In the twentieth century it aligned with the star, Polaris.

From inside the shelter came the angry sound of a woman's shriek. The hunter/gatherer was chased out from the rock, with the woman in pursuit. She pointed to him and held her nose with the other hand. The hunter/gatherer pointed to the soiled mukluk on his foot and the smashed pile of dog excrement. The woman-thing pointed to the cold drainage down below which ran white with glacial milk in the morning light. The hunter/gatherer began walking down to the icy bath, grumbling to himself about the family thing to which he had been relegated. After several minutes of descent, the sun peeked through the valley from the northeast in the direction of the huge lake. The water was running much swifter and whiter than he had seen it.

Of a sudden, there was the crashing sound of ten fingers, times ten fingers, times ten fingers, times ten rampaging woolly mastodons, charging down upon the man. The sound grew in pitch and ferocity until the wind joined the sound with such violence, it knocked the hunter/gatherer to the ground. As he looked up in the direction of the sun, the last thing he beheld as a hunter/gatherer on the third planet from the sun, under the star of Turba, was a huge moving cliff of rushing water.

Some eight thousand years later, under the star of Polaris, men, who studied such things on a different continent of the same planet, would coin a sound to describe this event. It happened in Scandinavia, with the same frequency it occurred in the American Northwest. They would utter the noise '**Jokulhlaup**' which was the single most profound event to explain the geology and landscape of certain river valleys. It was not the sound made by the hunter/gatherer as he joined the debacle and apocalypse of infinity.

১৯৯৯

Hemp Hill Creek
June 21, 1987, 04:20

The first day of official summer is the longest day of the year. Barbara stopped at the garden. She threw a switch, turning on a bank of old car headlamps, which served as floodlights to augment the growing daylight. The seed and starter plants, which she had put in the ground the day of Mossy's accident, had gone to feed the starlings, jays and crows. The lettuce, kale, broccoli and other succulents lay wilted and desicated by the fierce heat of unofficial summer. But the berry patches were thriving and the fruit hung like dew-adorned Christmas ornaments in the sparkling artificial light. She grabbed a bucket and began picking berries, until the puppy, Daisy, began to bark and howl pathetically from the kennel.

Barbara set down the bucket, turned on the sprinkler to salvage the thirsty corn and tomatoes that were established before the accident, and hurried on to liberate the puppy and raid the pantry. Daisy exploded from the kennel, jumping in the air and micturating herself with joy at relief from the incarceration. Barbara hurried through the cabin, ignoring the dishes with dried-on oatmeal, and the mice that scurried out from the sink in the dazzle of house lights. Barbara found a box and began loading jars of green beans, peas, rhubarb, corn. She loaded the entire pantry into twenty cardboard boxes which she began carrying out to her truck. She brought out five-gallon buckets, which she used to use for hauling water to the garden before the gravity-feed sprinklers, and loaded water. She grabbed a few more T-shirts, some clean blue jeans, and a few of Mossy's favorite toys. She glanced around the cabin one last time, longing for the normalcy of home, and turned off the lights. She picked up the pup, put her in a portable kennel and seat belted the kennel onto the front, bench seat of the pickup. She drove out to the garden, turned off the sprinkler and hurriedly finished picking the berries in the half-filled bucket. She threw the berries into the bed of the pickup and was just climbing into the cab when the powerful hand of home reached out to arrest her flight.

She stopped and gazed in moonlight over the meadows and the wall of trees that defined the creek's course through the fields. She stood beside the truck with the engine running and let the feeling of home wash over her. Suddenly she keened for something just for her. Barbara needed some reward for all the waiting. She turned off the engine and left the pickup truck, walking slowly back to the cabin, savoring the earth under her feet. She closed her eyes on the bridge and heard the tinkle of Hemp Hill Creek as it pushed its way to the Bogachiel and then out to the Pacific Ocean. Barbara reflected briefly on a lecture from Professor Nice who had told the class that human consciousness was akin to a stream: you could stand at the same place in the creek, standing on the bed of memory, but the water of consciousness was ever changing and fresh. Barbara longed to revisit one part of the creek bed. She hurried on to the cabin. She entered the cabin and climbed the inclined ladder to the loft of her bedroom. With the first hint of dawn illuminating the room through the skylight she went to the bed she had left unmade two weeks ago and knelt. From under the bed she pulled a small chest built out of western red cedar. She opened the box and peered in at a pile of neatly folded, but dirty men's clothing. On top of the clothing was a silver ring, which she removed and held to her cheek for a moment with her eyes closed. She set the ring aside and carefully removed the stack of clothing. She opened a hickory shirt upon which were dark brown stains of long dried blood. She put her face into the shirt and breathed in through her nose. The smell of cedar and sawdust filled her nose and the smell of her man wafted up from the past. Barbara felt herself cut adrift and floating downstream in time. She felt herself trying to stand up on the slippery streambed of her memory with the clear, clean memories running between her legs.

She set the clothing aside and took up a small bundle of paper which lay at the bottom of the chest. Unfolding the top paper, she carried it and the silver ring to stand under the skylight. The illumination afforded was insufficient for the human eye to read the handwritten scrawl, but the eye of Barbara's memory read every word. As she read, the middle-aged widow metamorphosed into the young virgin standing by the mailbox in Rose Lodge trying to read the letter through waves of infatuation and anticipation. She read:

Wednesday, February 28, 1979

Dear Barbara,

It really made my day to get your letter yesterday! They've got us staged out in a few trailers on a logging show in Olympic National Forest overlooking Lake Cushman on the east side of the Peninsula. George Redding got my mail in Forks yesterday when he went through and was I was really happy to see your letter in with the pile of junk mail he brought back. I will thank Rick Larson for forwarding the letter from you.

I felt so bad for the feelings you expressed at the research cabin before you left. I know the incident the previous night was really embarrassing for you. It was embarrassing for me, too, but I guess the male gender gets used to living with that sort of thing. The goofy little gifts I brought that day were just a way of apologizing and I'm sorry if it looked like I was trying to re-ignite smoldering embers from the night before.

I can be patient, Barbara, but the waiting can be tough. You mentioned that you might be returning to the Peninsula in June after you're done with your thesis and to work on spotted owls. I can't quite figure what all the focus is on that particular bird, but I'm glad for any excuse that brings you back.

I look at the calendar hung on the wall of this trailer and there seem so many days between now and June. On my time off, I look at my watch and the hands seem frozen in place. In my mind's eye I look at the ecliptic clock of our movement through the solar system. Looking down at Earth from 93,000 million miles above the sun, is the face of a clock with a day for every degree (or, more accurately, 0.986 day/degree). The Earth moves counterclockwise, while the twelve "hours" of the clock face are counted by orbits of Earth's moon. Three months seems like forever, but it's coming at me at 18.511 miles/sec (the Earth's speed across the ecliptic plane.) June is coming at me at one ten thousandth the speed of light and I can live with that progress. I'm sorry. That's how my mind works when I get impatient.

Thanks for the local news in your life at Rose Lodge. I'm sorry that you're having trouble getting going on your thesis and your mom is not feeling well. I hope the biopsy doesn't reveal cancer. Speaking about parents, I got a letter a few days ago from my mom who was cleaning out her files and came upon two essays I did for a creative writing course I took in high school. I'm sending them along to you in hopes that you might enjoy them more than the teacher who graded them. I can't have that kind of stuff lying around a logging camp! If that stupid idiot Rod Hill were to find them, he would die my hickory shirt pink. I don't need them back. But I sure look forward to YOU coming back! I've got to head off to work, but I'll write in a couple of days, before our next mail run.
Your friend, Phil Stone

Briefly, Barbara passed over the two essays paper-clipped to this letter. One was called "The Classroom" and the other was called "Tears of Joy." Both were so typical of her late husband, suggesting that the mold was cast and the concrete of his personality set barely beyond the years of his adolescence. She had tried to read "The Classroom" aloud at Phil's funeral, but it had become more of a private reading.

She shuffled through the pile of seventy-four letters, diving deeper into the chronology of what had become the second-most agonizing wait of her life. As the clock of the June 21 sun cut the horizon, illuminating the temperate rain forest visible through the skylight like green stained glass, Barbara went to the bottom of the pile. She read:

Wednesday, July 4, 1979

Dear Barbara,

We got off work today owing to the National holiday and I spent the day in Forks, which is kind of a happening place on this particular occasion. A group of bikers showed up from out of town and kind of took over Art's Place. They pushed a logger around, which, they should have seen, would lead nowhere near a profitable end for themselves. The guys from Bogachiel River Timber found the bikers drinking beer down by the Calawah bridge just outside of town and all the Harley's ended up in the Calawah along with most of the bikers. The loggers confiscated the beer for the bikers' own good and for the protection of society in general. George won third place in his weight class in the arm wrestling. His leg is all healed up, though he still walks with a limp.

I got first place in the pole climb. Some of the competition had been involved in the police action upon the bikers and had committed themselves to the disposal of all the confiscated beer. And maybe that tree climbing without spurs in that windstorm toughened me up a bit.

Barbara, I am praying for your mom. I am glad to hear that her prognosis is improved and that the chemotherapy is working. I understand that you're the only one available to be with her during her recovery and I appreciate your dedication. I sure miss you. I think about you all the time and have never looked forward to anything in my life as much as I anticipate your return.

Love, Phil

P.S. I can stop by the research cabin next Friday whether or not the weather breaks, putting us back to work. I'm sure looking forward to seeing you and talking with you face to beautiful face. There's something important I want to ask you (hint, hint.) xxxxxxx, Phil

---

Sunday, September 9, 1979

Dear Barbara,

Tomorrow is Labor Day and we would have had a paid holiday, but the woods are shut down due to fire danger so State unemployment is underwriting my vacation. Unless the weather breaks, I won't be working when you get here next week, which is fine with me.

It's neat the way things worked out so you can go back to the research shack at Bear Creek to work spotted owl. I guess you heard from Rick that the first Spotted Owl Management Area was established at Rugged Ridge and the idea is sniff out Reade Hill for the second one. I don't know where it all will end, but I suppose I can always go back to stoking the nuclear furnaces if that's what the environmentalists want. Just kidding! Ha, ha.

Anyway, I did my own little exploration of Reade Hill yesterday. The USFS 2932 Road now runs all the way to the research cabin and, eventually, will connect with Forks and the A-Road out by Rugged Ridge. Up on the north side of Reade Hill above the road is a huge glacial erratic - a piece of granite that rode in from Canada on the ice cap which buried the Peninsula in ice ten thousand years ago in the thousand year winter of Milankovitch cycling. The slow wobble of the earth on its axis put the north pole under the star of Turba as in 10,000 years the north pole will lie under the star, Vega. From up on the hill you can see that the ice flows of the Hoh and Bogachiel came together just below Willoughby Ridge. You can see from the terracing that there was a lake. I wish I could view earth from a star ten thousand years distant and watch the show.

Love, Phil

❧

Bear Creek Research Cabin
Friday September 21, 1979, 10:15

Barbara sat on pins and needles on the wooden chair as Rick Larson tried to explain the current direction of the spotted owl survey. Rick had come out to Bear Creek to welcome her back to her old haunts and to brief her on the work she would be starting Monday, after getting settled in over the weekend.

"All the young have fledged, of course, but they continue to occupy the nest with the parent owls having moved on. We're still trying to get a handle on the survival rate of the fledglings and, with the young still occupying the nests, we have found it the best possible time of year..."

Barbara fidgeted and checked the end of her hair for split ends. She had recently returned from the bedroom after changing her shirt which had got a little sweaty carrying her pack down from the landing, but she still felt caged and claustrophobic. She had never been in the research cabin in the hot, dry weather of Indian summer. She was having trouble focusing.

"It looks like less than fifteen percent of the little guys are surviving the first year. More than half the nests we've visited are twins which is consistent with the OSU figures that you read back in Corvallis. For whatever reason, when one twin goes down, the other usually follows..."

Barbara felt like she was suffocating. She got up and began to pace. It was as if her diaphragm couldn't move enough air to sustain her. Her stomach was doing little flips. In her anxiety and distress, she barely recognized the culprit organ in her chest. THIS was the threshold of the moment upon which her sense of anticipation had feasted for months...in her visceral panging; in the spinning of her imagination; in the yinning and yanging of her heart...

How, in her fantasy, she had sat like a sweet, young flower about to be picked... But now, she paced the floor with a sheen of sweat covering her brow, her stomach growling, and unable to catch her breath at the exertion of the final wait.

"...with just Rugged Ridge and Reade Hill for Spotted Owl Management Areas, it's premature to draw any demographic conclusions, but there remains a clear connection between the nesting sites and old growth forests..."

Barbara was listening through the words at the sound of a Ford pickup arriving at the landing above the research cabin; at the sound of a truck door being slammed shut; at the whisper of the salmonberry being pushed aside by her lover as he came down the hill to the cabin.

"...It's an exciting time, really. The Forest Service has been guided by mandates from above to increase production and push yield way beyond sustained limits. Spotted owl brings us back to biological realities of forest management..."

The knock at the door: Barbara throwing open the door with Phil standing in the burning light of midday. The embrace and the clutching. The smell of laundry soap on Phil's clean hickory shirt and tin pants. The question from Phil's mouth, "Well, will you m..." (...as Barbara planted a big kiss on the lips that attempted the proposal).

"Yes! Yes!" said Barbara, before kissing him again.

"'Yes' what? I didn't hear him finish his question," Rick Larson was feeling excluded from the unfolding developments.

"Yes! I'll marry you!" said Barbara, addressing Phil as if Rick wasn't there.

"Marry him! Jesus, what's this all about? Barbara, do you have some personal agenda here that you haven't told me about?" The biologist was disappointed and a little angry. Romping through the woods day after day and sitting on owl sites all night long took a special breed of independence that was strongly eroded by outside romance. As the couple embraced and kissed, Rick realized that, on this day, he had not gained a partner, he had lost an intern. "Excuse me," mumbled the biologist pushing by the couple to trudge up the steep hill to his government truck. Tomorrow, on his day off, he would begin the job of re-recruiting for the position.

Hemp Hill Creek
Friday, September 21, 1979, 12:30 hours

Ed Vannausdle wiped a sheen of sweat off his brow as he sat in the noon sun waiting to show two loggers the twenty-acre parcel which represented the unsold half of the Goakey Ranch Ed had bought in 1968. The family had given up on the spread after the kids were mostly grown and the husband had died in an industrial accident at Allen's Mill. Before the Goakey's, the property had been settled by a German immigrant named Otto Siegfried who gave the property the name, *Flying S Farm*, in honor of man's discovery of flight.

Ed owned a hardware store in Port Angeles, but dabbled in Bogachiel real estate to supplement his retirement a few years away. Gypo logging companies were now buying anything they could get their hands on, harvesting the trees, and unloading the property to mushroom pickers, shake bolt cutters, fern pickers and other transient woods workers who set up travel trailers and called it home. The woods were booming and, along with it, the real estate market. Ed glanced up at Reade Hill. For a moment he focused on a large granite boulder 300 feet upslope. A bull elk bugled upriver, signaling the beginning of rut. Across the meadow the wings of grasshoppers chattered as they flitted from stalk to stalk. A cloud of dust rose up mid-slope as a pickup rattled down the Forest Service Road below the boulder.

ဢ•ঔ

Barbara's teeth chattered as the Ford pickup bounced down the steep, washboard road under the granite boulder. Whether her teeth chattered from antagonism between the truck's momentum and the uneven tread of the road, or from her personal momentum across the uneven surface of her life, she could not be sure.

"That's the glacial erratic up there I was talking about," Phil was saying. "Imagine a moving sea of ice that carried a rock the size of a house on its back all the way from Canada! A mile upriver you can see where a rampart from the east side of Reade Hill stretches out to Willoughby Ridge. It had to have been a huge lake basin, bigger than Lake Crescent..."

Barbara glimpsed the shiny granite boulder uphill through the old growth Douglas Fir as the truck descended into the Spruce/Hemlock forest which skirted the Bogachiel River. Barbara shifted her gaze down to the river and to the wide, green meadows and orchard that adjoined the south side of this section of river. "Phil," she interrupted. "Can we get our own place? I don't think I'm suited for life in an apartment. How much is real estate around here, anyway?"

"There's some stuff for sale at the end of the road on the other side of the river. I saw signs when I was back there bow hunting last week. That homestead down there got broken into lots. That would be a place to start..."

"Let's go take a look. Please."

"I thought we were getting married."

"Hey, Washington State is not the Love Chapel of the Union. It will take a couple of days to get a blood test and license. It's a good day to look for a nest. The license, we can get another day."

96

"Sure. We can drive down there and get the phone number off the signs."

༜☙

Ed Vannausdle was standing under the sign waiting for them when the couple arrived.

"Know of any property for sale in these parts?" Barbara asked the man standing under the "FOR SALE" sign within sight of the collapsing Goakey cabin.

"I hope to be selling this twenty-acre parcel in the next hour," replied the hardware man.

"That would be soon enough for us," said Barbara.

"Well, I'm supposed to be meeting a Mr. Harper and a Mr. Tuinstra to close the deal, but they seem to be delayed. You can look at it if you like."

"Is that a map and legal description you've got there?" asked Phil.

Ed Vannausdle passed Phil the documents he held in his hand. "You can start walking the line right here. It will take you about twenty minutes to get around it. But, I warn you, it may be sold when you get back."

Beginning at the northwestern corner of Government Lot 10 Barbara followed Phil who took out a compass and began walking south, 179 degrees, 0 minutes, 14 seconds, along an old logging road through tall, butt-swollen spruce, amid a green riot of ferns, moss, and lichen. The rocks and stumps lay under a thick, green carpet. From prostrate logs sprang curtains of young trees. Green, green, green: the longing filled Barbara's heart like the biomass of the rain forest that occupies every square inch with green life. They crossed a rickety, fern-covered bridge over Hemp Hill Creek on their way to the northwest corner of the property. From this point on, thence, the couple proceeded east on a line 89 degrees, 0 minutes and 14 seconds for 1,900 feet or 380 of Phil's paces[2]. With a small meadow on the left, the couple walked through moss-draped arches of vine maple that broke like green waves upon the shore of the meadow. "We could put a cabin right over there," Barbara's voice was more a plea than a statement.

They again found Hemp Hill Creek, realizing that the stream made a dramatic oxbow on the property. As they waded across the gurgling creek, Barbara saw the old flagging marking salmon nests. "This is an anadromous stream," she said with awe and respect. They found the southeastern corner and, thence, headed north along the offset course, roughly following the creek. On their right was blowdown from the windstorm seven months previous. Barbara was overwhelmed with her want for this land. She was frustrated over her lack of control over the acquisition of the property. She had no money to contribute for a down payment.

It took her back to a Sunday afternoon in 1966 when she had convinced her father to take her to "just look" at a litter of Bernese mountain dogs she had seen advertised in Lincoln City. The dog breeders had wanted $75 for each pup, which cinched it for Glen Beyers, who had never paid a dime for dog flesh in his life. Barbara's heart went out to one of the furry little boxcars, which pounced on her shoelaces and lay on his back at her feet with his paws kicking in the air. She used every promise and guile in the book to gain her father's assent for the

---

[2] Two steps

acquisition, but he had stood firm. When it came time to go, she faced the biggest challenge of her life. She could not cry because it would make her father angry. She wanted the furry little pup more than she had wanted anything in her life, but she could not cry and embarrass him. She sat, dry eyed, but dazed in the car, while her father studied her face. He went back into the house and came back out with the puppy. As she drove back home with her father, the puppy sleeping on her lap, her joy effervesced. "Daddy, I'll call him 'Roscoe' because he reminds me of a colored man. We will be a family, you, me, and Roscoe forever. And he'll follow me, wherever I go, forever. Forever and always..."

From the southeastern corner near the creek oxbow, they walked along the southern property line, cutting through the orchard and waist deep grass of the large 30 acre meadow which stretched off the property and out to the river on their right, with the Hemp Hill Creek still on their left. Barbara was pulling on Phil's hand, in her eagerness to get back to the owner/seller of what had just become her center of the universe. Ed Vannausdle saw the couple approaching and walked east to meet them. "Well, what did you think?" he called out.

"We'd like to make an offer," called Barbara, not waiting to reach him.

"Maybe we can arrange something. Mr. Harper and Mr. Tuinstra haven't shown up yet."

The deal happened so fast, Barbara missed it. Barbara stood for a minute, looking out across the meadow, wistfully. As swallows swooped frantically around the sky, gorging themselves on insects in preparation for their migration, Phil walked over to his pickup and got his checkbook. Phil studied the easements on the title for 30 seconds and talked about financing with the hardware man for another 30 seconds. Phil wrote out a check as they talked. The two men shook hands.

Barbara heard a car engine start and turned to see Ed Vannausdle turning his car around. She ran to the moving vehicle and he called out, "Nice meeting you, Mrs. Stone!" as he drove away.

"Please wait!" she called out dolefully, but the hardware man was rolling up the window to keep the check from blowing out the window as he accelerated.

Phil put his arm around Barbara's slumping shoulders. "We bought it! Or, more accurately, we're buying it...for the next ten years. You and I are now the landed gentry..." Barbara planted a big one on Phil's lips. In her heart was the excitement of a child on Christmas morning; of the high school girl picked up by her date on the way to the prom; of the swallow returning to her nesting grounds; of the cow elk joining the harem; of the grasshopper on the ripe seed head of grass; of the dandelion seed lighting on fertile soil; of the child holding her new puppy...They walked together, hand in hand, through the meadows and into the front orchard. The warm breeze of Indian summer blew visible waves across the deep grass.

They stood in silence for several minutes just inside their property line in the expansive meadow under Reade Hill. Grasshoppers chattered in flight, swallows swooped and caromed. A shrill, single cry from a red-tailed hawk cut through the sound of the stirring grass on the wind and, moments later, came the impossibly high and resonant call of a bull elk.

"That's the one that got away," joked Phil, breaking the quiet between them.

"I'm glad you're not," said Barbara and Phil was still trying to figure out what she meant when all of the sudden they were kissing and groping. Upstream, in the clearing of the old Morganroth orchard, came the distant clashing of elk antlers as two bulls battled for the harem. As one, Barbara and Phil descended into the sweet, soft grass and there began a great fumbling with clothing.

Remembering the previous experience of coitus interruptus and its impact upon Barbara, Phil sat up and asked unsteadily, "Do you want to go back to my place?"

Barbara sat up unashamedly, leaving her T-shirt where it lay on the bent over grass. "This IS your place," she murmured, pulling Phil back down into the deep green curtain. And as the rest of the creatures of the meadow and rain forest went about the business of life, Phil and Barbara conjugated their emotional longings and fleshly cravings under a sun, that on September 21, gave twelve hours of daylight and twelve hours of dark to every corner of the planet.

And for Barbara, there was no going back, as she plunged into the maelstrom of unvirginity. Her flesh was a raging wildfire in August, driven by the dry east wind of her desire. Her sexuality rained like the November monsoon, over-running the gutter of her sexual fantasies. The lake of her craving overtopped the icy dam of her inhibition and in the resulting **Jokulhlaup**, the timbers of her mores were snapped and thrown aside like twigs. Her voice and breath was the call of the elk, the song of the dandelion seed, the cry of the hawk, the splash of the salmon swimming upstream...

$\wp\!\!\sim\!\!\wp$

The two loggers pulled alongside the silver Ford four-wheel-drive pickup in their own Ford crummy. "That's Phil Stones' rig isn't it, Fred?" Tuinstra asked his partner Harper.

"Yeah. Maybe he's out trying to poach an elk with his mighty bow. This is the neighborhood for it."

"More likely he's tied up in a knot in some kind of crazy yoga position with an olive in his belly button," remarked Larry Tuinstra, walking with his partner past the old Goakey homestead and standing next to the large meadow of their intended purchase. "Jesus! Have you ever heard that guy talk about his vision of the universe? He smoked too much dope back in college or stuck his head in a nuclear reactor one too many times..."

"The son of a bitch can sure get up a sparring pole," remarked Fred Harper taking off his tin hat to pat his forehead with a red bandanna. "George Redding says he could fall a tree right on the back of a log truck and he's never missed a day of work. George says that Stone about saved his life when that tree dropped on his leg in that blow last February..."

"Where the shit is Vannausdle, anyway?" interrupted Tuinstra, standing under a mountain ash planted by Otto Seigfreid. "We can't wait here all day. Half this property is fields, anyway. The Indians already stole the cedar off it for their dugouts and burned off the rest of the good stuff for firewood. Let's go down to the lower Hoh. Charlie Anderson ran into hock with that feed store he tried to run in Forks. He's cutting loose another 160 acres of his family's farm. We could take a million board feet off it and still resell it as wooded property."

"You're right," said Harper. "Vannausdle is a no show. Let's go. There's no electricity back here, anyway, and that would make resale tough." The two men walked back to their pickup.

"I wonder what that fucker Stone is up to, anyway," said Tuinstra walking by the silver pickup to climb into his own crummy.

❧

...and, afterwards, Barbara lay in the deep grass with her head on Phil's chest looking up at the swooping swallows into the deep azure sky which whispered infinite possibilities. In the throes of passion, the couple had not noticed the insects, with which the swallows were preoccupied, but, in their nakedness they were attracting much attention on the part of the mosquito nation. A grasshopper landed in Barbara's hair and she fumbled to get it out without hurting the creature.

"Can you get the grasshopper out of my mane? For some reason my hands are like hooves"

Phil plucked out the grasshopper, which flew off. He stood up, naked, and held out his hand, "Come on. Let's take a little swim."

"Shouldn't we put on our clothes? What if those loggers show up?" asked Barbara.

"We'll tell them to take off their clothes and join us or get the hell off our property." Phil Stone put on only his Romeo slippers and led Barbara off their newly-acquired property and through the 400 feet of deep grassland that separated them from the Bogachiel River. On the bank, Phil left Barbara for a moment and splashed out through the knee-deep water on his way to a deep pool behind a large rock. An enormous Chinook salmon spooked and drove upstream revealing its back as it charged through the shallows. "Come on!" called Phil, ignoring the fish.

❧

A simultaneous science story:

Under its enzyme helmet in total darkness, the gamete swam for all its soul in the acidic waters of the strange upstream current. Already 80 million of the gamete's compatriots were dead and washing downstream. The gamete and his kind were hated in this environment, just as they had been loathed at the address of their previous world. There, the white police had killed them indiscriminately and they were kept in a facility outside of the host entity. The temperature inside the entity was too hot to sustain life for the gametes.

Since being taught to swim by a nurse some fourteen Earth days earlier, the gamete had swum over two million times its body length - the equivalent of a Homo sapien swimming back and forth across the Pacific Ocean. An army of these gametes, equaling the human population of the United States, had set off less than an hour ago, with only a tiny dose of fructose for energy. Each individual carried in its bosom a message too large for a modern Cray computer. Each of the 200 million dead and dying carried half the blueprints in a package of 24 envelopes...blueprints for a temple...blueprints for a Temple to the Creator.... Following a course set by genetic memory and the strange upstream current, the

100

gamete swam for all its soul through the strange and poisonous water in total darkness...

Meanwhile...

An entity the size of a grain of sand on Earth was being pushed downstream against the tiny eddy current. The entity had been with Barbara as a ten-year-old, sitting in a drift boat on the Salmon Creek, as Glen Beyers talked about wild places and Pacing Mustangs. For the last hundred and twenty-two orbits of the Earth's moon, such an entity had set out in search of life and finding none. In 24 envelopes, the entity carried the other half of the blueprints for a Temple to the Creator...

Phil dove into the water of the deep pool and was upside down in the water, kicking in the air with his Romeo slippers splashing, as he tried to overcome his buoyancy. The bubbles escaping his mouth and nose tickled his belly on their way to the surface causing him to guffaw and lose more air. The Cosmic God that resided in Creation rode the bubbles to the surface. Phil popped up to the surface and recharged his lungs. "Come on in, Barbara! You can see four trout holing up behind this rock!"

He's just like a big kid, thought Barbara. And from the inner space of her thoracic and visceral cavity, the Lutheran God that had guided Barbara's life, looked out upon the situation in which she found herself. As she stood in the water up to her ankles, the Lutheran God pointed to the wall upon which no marriage license yet hung and tapped His watch with a stern finger.

Even in total darkness, the gamete sensed the bifurcation in the stream. The eddy was pulled into two currents both leading further into aquatica incognita. One channel led to a one in a hundred thousand chance at the Miracle of Life and the other channel led to a 100 per cent certainty of the Miracle of Death. There was no vision, no smell, no audible clue for the gamete; there was genetic memory and dark fate in the gravity of the cosmos.

"Please, Barbara! Come into the water. It's wonderful!"

Barbara followed the voice of her lover out into the clean river watching the water move between her bare legs like a liquid jewel. Phil left the deep pool and lunged over to meet her. They met in the waist-deep water and embraced. Barbara smelled the clean river on Phil's face and beard. She felt the cool beads of water on the warm skin of his neck and back as it reflected the radiant heat of the blazing sun...

And there ahead loomed the entity, 195,000 times bigger than the gamete. Only a few thousand of the 200 million gametes had arrived at their destination. In the dark, the swimming swarm formed around the sphere. And suddenly the creature was inside and no longer swimming. And in that spark of time, on the first day of Fall, nineteen hundred and seventy-nine, under the blazing sun, in the total dark of Barbara Beyers's left fallopian tube, was conceived the life of a child that would be born unto a widowed mother. And while the parents of this Miracle of Life celebrated their flesh in an embrace, held under the bright sun, standing in the cool, clean water of Creation, only the God of the dictionary would dare call the Miracle, that would carry the name 'Mossy,' a 'bastard.'

Hemp Hill Creek
June 21, 1987, 07:40 hours

    Barbara could taste the kiss on Phil's mouth. She felt the cool water moving between her naked legs and smelled the clean river. The bright sunlight beat down, warming her skin and as she pulled back her head from the embrace to look into her lover's face, she stared at a letter written by him...eight orbits around the sun gone by. Under the longest gaze of sunlight, in the year of nineteen hundred and eighty-seven, in her bedroom loft, Barbara carefully folded the letter and replaced the contents of this precious chest. She checked her watch uttered "OH!" in the knowledge that her daughter would be waking without her, injured and hurting in a scary hospital, on her birthday. Barbara hurried from the room, down the ladder, out to her pickup, and back into the present tense.
    She drives like hell for Port Angeles...

Six

"And so if you think of (the Olympic pioneers) as having been in some kind of battle with the wilderness, then I guess you'd have to say that after the years they fought with the country and the folks they buried in it, all they ever did was lose. But I think what they did was win."
-**Don Moser**, author/seasonal Park Ranger, Kalaloch about 1960 from **The Peninsula**

Olympic Memorial Hospital
Sunday, June 21, 1987, 12:40 hours

*B*arbara heard Mossy's shrieking, through the heavy hospital door, from the hallway. The volume rose by many decibels as the charge nurse opened the door from inside and hurried out carrying Mossy's mostly uneaten lunch. Against the white backdrop of the nurse's uniform were spatters of what appeared to be blobs of mashed potatoes and flecks of ground beef.

"She really doesn't like the food here!" said the nurse in greeting, hurrying out of the room. "She didn't even go for the cake!"

"I brought some food she'll eat," said Barbara from behind the gifts she had bought at Thrifty Save, the only open store, on her way through Forks. "Did Mossy throw food at you?" Barbara asked incredulously. The nurse scurried off remarking over her shoulder, "There was some spillage, yes."

Barbara entered the room with the gifts and the mail which had accumulated over the last half month. She also carried a copy of a book called In Search of Jesus - An Historical Perspective which she had found in the general store. It was her intention to begin a little Bible study with her daughter which seemed consistent with a fervent prayer she had uttered in the chapel of this hospital two weeks earlier. From the noise emanating from the room, her daughter would have to be bound and gagged for the instruction.

Seeing her mother coming in the door, Mossy found new focus for her vocalization. "How could you, Mother!," she shrieked and sobbed. "Oh, how could you leave me alone in here on my BIRTHDAY!"

"Mossy, I'm so sorry. It took longer than I thought to put things in order at home and I had to stop to get these presents..."

"THEY'RE TRYING TO POISON ME!" Mossy bellowed loud enough for the hospital's administrator to hear from his home a mile away. "Last night it was sloppy joe on a bun! Today it was left over sloppy joe on mashed potatoes. They called it "shepherd's pie" and it looked like something a shepherd might put his foot in!" Mossy screamed again her declaration, "They are trying to poison me!"

"Would you like to open a few gifts or are you not in the mood right now?" said Barbara hoping she could help effect a mood change.

"NO! I don't want to open gifts. I want my dog! Where's Daisy? I want some real food! My right leg doesn't work!" Mossy began to sob pathetically. "I want my little Daisy dog."

"Your little Daisy is in a kennel out in the car. I'll get her and I'll get the food I brought. But what's this about your leg?"

"This leg here doesn't work," cried Mossy pointing to her right leg which lay on top of the sheets. "It's full of pins and needles and hurts. But I can't move it."

"I'll get your dog and some food from the garden. I'll leave the gifts right here and you can open a couple while I'm gone, if you like. There are some get-well and birthday cards for you in that stack of mail." Barbara left her daughter and hurried out to the big parking lot.

A few minutes later she was stumbling down the hall with the pet kennel, a box of jarred food, and the Beyers' family Bible which Barbara's mother had given her as a gift during Mary Beyers' convalescence from a cancer operation nine years ago. Doctor Baker, the orthopedic surgeon, saw her in the hall and stopped her.

"Good afternoon, Barbara," said the doctor smiling. "I just talked to the nurse on Mossy's floor and she reports that there is nothing wrong with Mossy's ability to vocalize complaints or her ability to move air. That's a good sign."

"I want to talk to that nurse and apologize for..."

"No, Barbara, we're used to the moods that attend rehabilitation. I was with Mossy this morning and, I can assure you, the frustrations she's facing are healthy and normal. There's a problem that we detected with her right leg, which we need to talk about."

Barbara interjected, "Mossy says that she is having pins and needles pain and that she can't move the leg. Will she be able to walk? Listen, I've got to get back to Mossy or we will have another scene out of The Exorcist. Can you walk with me?"

"I'm on a forced march myself to see my other patients, Barbara, but I'll stop by your room in an hour or so to check in." Doctor Brown pulled away and called over his shoulder, smiling. "If you stand next to Mossy's bed, watch out. There's still shepherds' pie fallout raining down from the ceiling."

Coming back into the room, Mossy was still snuffling and had moved on neither the gifts nor mail. She lay on the bed on top of the sheets with her arms crossed over her little chest. Barbara set the kennel on the chair next to the bed. At the sight of her mistress, the dog Daisy, pushed her face to the screen door of the kennel and wagged her tail furiously. Mossy brightened. "Let her out, mom. Let her out!" Barbara opened the door and the pup rocketed out, licking Mossy in the face, and charging around the bed to catch ubiquitous scraps of food - the aftermath of the earlier holocaust.

Barbara picked up the plate with a piece of cake on it, left by the nurse on her retreat, and was about to put the cake in a trash can. Mossy said, "Wait! Give the cake to Daisy." Barbara gave the piece of cake to the dog, who wolfed it down, and then set out a plate of home-canned vegetables. Mossy cleaned the plate, eagerly eating with her fingers. Barbara loaded the plate again. She re-filled the plastic hospital cup with water from Hemp Hill, which Mossy gulped to wash down the food. Mossy belched loudly and said, "Excuse me." The child burrowed into the bed snuggling her squirming puppy. Mossy put her nose to the dog's fur and sniffed. "Daisy has been stuck in the kennel the whole time, since my accident. It's not fair to her!"

"Hey, I've been stuck here in Port Angeles and you've been stuck in bed. It's not fair to any of us. We just have to make do. Anyway, here are some get-well cards and a few birthday cards. Do you want me to open them and read them to you?"

"That's OK, I'll read them to Daisy." Fed and watered, the child seemed more ready to stand on her own. Barbara passed the pile of mail to Mossy who began opening the cards one at a time after announcing to the dog who the cards were from and what relation the sender was to their family. "This card is from George Redding, the nice man who's been dropping by to check on you, Daisy. He says, 'Get better soon. Your dog and I miss you.' Well, he's half right. This card is from our Grandma Mary. She usually sends candy with each card. The puppy perked. Mossy finished opening the card and sniffed the empty envelope. "Nope. No candy this time. Mom, Grandma was crying when she wrote this. I can smell the salt."

"You can't smell salt, Mossy," challenged Barbara.

"Sure I can. Smell for yourself," said the child passing over the card from Barbara's mother. Barbara shut her eyes and smelled. She could catch a vague whiff of the perfume her mother wore. She could see a couple of watermarks, one on the handwriting and one on the envelope...most likely it was raining.

"It's your grandmother's perfume. That's what you're smelling."

"No, mom," the child patronized. "The perfume covers the smell of the crying. Can't you smell it?"

Barbara gave up the argument and left the child to her private review of the cards with her puppy.

Killing time before Doctor Baker's visit, Barbara searched for home and normalcy by scanning the latest copy of <u>Knives, Spoons and Forks</u>. An article caught her interest. It was about the family that occupied her farm a quarter century previously.

Stories from the Frontier
from <u>Knives. Spoons and Forks</u>

"Mommy!" cried young Ed Goakey, looking out the window of his pioneer home at the end of the Dowans Creek Road. "Daddy's home early!" But there is no joy in this news to a logger's wife. For an early return usually foretells a problem in the woods, meaning bread is not being won. Or, more seriously, the early return of the family vehicle can be the harbinger of injury or death of the woods worker. When young Ed ran to the back window looking out toward the family garage and Hemp Hill Creek, he yelled, "Mommy, it's not Dad in the car! It's Whitney Stevenson!" Edith Goakey, the mother of seven children, the husband of Howard Goakey, knew her husband was in serious trouble.

The Goakeys had settled on Hemp Hill Creek in 1946, long before the days of public power and telephone. Today is still a day before public electricity in that neighborhood. George Siegfried, son of the old German immigrant, who first lived on these banks, sold the land to Howard and Edith and the work began: digging a well, setting fence posts, planting the garden, building the roofs that would shelter the young couple and their growing family in this rain country.

This was how Howard spent his time off: In the woods, he really worked his butt off. And on this fall day in 1954, he had worked half his butt off, plus one of his legs. A sliding log slid off a steep ridge over the Calawah River and pinned Howard Goakey beneath. There would be no more logging for this pioneer and he would learn to walk on a prosthetic made of the wood that was previously the target of his employment. The family endured five tough years as Howard retrained as a millwright and eventually found employment as the "grease monkey" at Allen's Mill.

The children were mostly grown and gone by 1968 when Edith looked out to see Lloyd Allen's car parking in the garage in front of Hemp Hill Creek. She knew that he was not there to talk about a raise for her husband and, as Lloyd walked from the garage to the door, he carried the grimmest news he had ever had to bestow on the family of his mill workers. For as Howard had lain on the conveyor to the igloo incinerator, greasing each roller fitting, a careless worker had thrown the switch to the powerful motor. Howard Goakey had been fed to the fire.

ᔫᕊ

"Good afternoon, Mossy." Dr. Baker greeted the patient first, coming into the room after a cursory knock. "Are you feeling better with your mom and puppy here?"

"Yes," said Mossy, clutching her dog.

"Too bad we can't turn this room upside down and let your dog walk on the ceiling. I bet he would like to eat that shepherd's pie that's still up there..."

"Daisy is a *she*."

"Oh, excuse me, Daisy. I couldn't see you under the covers." The doctor addressed the mother, "Barbara, has Mossy always had a developed sense of smell?"

"Yes, probably better than most kids."

"You know we use these little jars full of coffee, orange peels, flower petals and the like to spot check for damage to the temporal brain. This is the area of Mossy's subdural bleed, so we've been running this simple test along with the Magnetic Resonance Imaging."

"Is there something wrong with her olfactory?" asked Barbara.

"No, it's the other way around. She was able to smell the coffee and orange peels in the jars before they were opened. With her eyes closed and not touching, she could distinguish the difference between my hand and the nurse's hand. I've never seen anything like it. We all tend to block sensorial information. In fact, a major function of our nervous system is the filtering and suppressing of all the intelligence brought to us by our senses. Without this filtering, we wouldn't be capable of thought because we would be constantly bombarded by sensorial information. What's happened here is that Mossy has a broken filter. It can be rebuilt.

"It's like the little...," Dr. Baker chose his word carefully, "...demonstration we had about the shepherd's pie. The same part of the brain which connects to olfactory prescribes our social interactions and behavior..."

"Shepherd's pie is YUCKY!" declared Mossy with finality.

106

"Be that as it may," continued the Doctor, "Mossy's behavior seems somewhat out of character to you, Barbara?"

"Well, yes. She's never thrown food that I can recall, except at a dog that wanted to eat it."

"What's happening is that there has been a shake-up in the part of her brain that transmits messages of smell and messages regarding behavior. Her brain is catching scent messages that most of us would filter out and selecting behavioral responses that she would have previously ruled out."

"Will she develop normally?" asked Barbara, taking her daughter's hand.

"Well, when you think about it, there is no 'normal' because we are all different from one another in so many ways. My guess is that Mossy will always have a sharp olfactory and may turn out to be unusually shy on some things and remarkably bold in others. She can be taught not to throw food, at least at humans," said Doctor Baker shaking his finger playfully at the child who pulled the bed sheet over her head and the dog's.

"There is something more serious than a little spilled shepherd's pie that we need to talk about, Barbara. Are you comfortable talking about it here, or would you like to go to my office for a little chat?"

Mossy came flying out from under the sheet and reversed the grip on her mother's hand, holding on like a lifeline. "NO! Stay with me! I want to hear about me!"

"It's OK, I'm right here," Barbara comforted the child, then spoke to the doctor. "We're OK here, unless you have a problem."

"Well, about the referred pain and diminished motor skill to Mossy's right leg...I say referred pain because the only organic problem we have is a tearing and contusion of the sheath of the sciatic nerve as it passes through Mossy's pelvic girdle. Now there is nothing wrong with the nervous system or circulation below this injury, but the brain is playing a trick on the leg. Every time the brain sends a motor message to the right leg, part of the message comes back as a pain message as it passes through the damaged sheath. The brain doesn't like to get these messages, so it's telling the whole leg that it's hurt and that it can't move..."

"But the sheath can heal, correct?"

"Yes, a nerve sheath can heal. Though nerve cells themselves can't regenerate, the nerve sheath restores itself very gradually. The problem is that, while the nerve sheath is repairing itself and the brain is sending out this "don't move message" to the leg, the patient forgets how to walk."

"But you can always learn to walk again," reasoned Barbara.

"Not necessarily. You are born with the ability to wiggle your ears. In our society we don't practice this skill and we lose it. We are born with a developed sense of smell similar to what Mossy is demonstrating. We develop filters that shut it out and usually it's gone. Mossy needs to be walking or she may develop a block that will paralyze that limb or at least give her a debilitating limp.

"On the other hand, to engage in therapy just now would subject Mossy to a lot of pain. She needs to be engaged in rehabilitation, but she will suffer a lot of discomfort, unless..."

"Unless what?"

"Well, I would recommend oral administration of pain suppressants preceding her courses of rehabilitation..."

"NO!" interrupted Mossy. "NO MORE PAIN KILLER! It messes with my mind!"

"Mossy," pleaded the doctor. "You need to be using that leg and it will hurt you to move it without the medicine..."

"I'll learn to move it. I'll make it move. NO MORE PAIN KILLERS!" said the child.

"No more pain killers," agreed her mother.

"I worry about this decision," said Doctor Baker getting up to leave. "We'll talk about it later. For now, Happy Birthday, Mossy."

"NO MORE PAIN KILLERS!"

ॐॐ

Olympic Memorial Hospital
Monday, June 22, 1987

The therapy center looked more like a health club than the wing of a hospital. Everywhere young patients were walking on treadmills, pushing against resistive loads and testing their afflictions against the invented work of therapy. The grim reminder that this was not a kid's spa, were the prosthetic limbs attached to the children's bodies, the gain of real pain and the expressions on the young faces as they struggled and attempted to adjust to, what for many, would be lifetime disabilities.

Mossy's hospital gown had been traded for a bathing suit, which barely covered the fur of surgical stitches, covering her abdomen. As she was putting on the suit, Barbara had noticed that Mossy's color had returned and she seemed focused and committed to the task at hand. Just twenty-four hours of the child's normal diet and the reunion with her puppy had effected a very positive change.

She was led to a set of waist-high parallel bars, which led down an inclined plane into about two feet of sterile water. The idea was to remove half the patient's body weight through buoyancy and reduce the risk of sudden jarring movements with the viscosity of water. Mossy was led down the plane by the sincere and encouraging voice of the young female therapist, who remained a foot away on the tile shore. Mossy charged into and out of the water using her arms on the bars and hopping along on her left leg. She occasionally winced in pain, but seemed to be enjoying the exercise. The therapist called her down into the deeper part of the plane and had Mossy sit down and stand up in the reduced gravity of water. Both the therapist and the mother watched anxiously for movement of the hemiplegic leg, which seemed to follow the child like a wooden dummy.

"Wheeeee! This is FUN!" called out Mossy over her shoulder to her waiting mother. And through the anxiety that surrounded and engulfed her; through the concrete walls of Olympic Memorial Hospital; across the time and tribulation that separated Barbara from the recovery of her daughter came a message from the Lutheran God. As Barbara heard her daughter call the word 'fun,' she received into her heart confirmation that her daughter WOULD WALK AGAIN. In less than a second, Barbara was instilled with the certainty that the psychoneuoroplegia which dragged Mossy's right leg like a ball and chain would be cut free. Before the therapist, before Doctor Baker, even before Mossy; to Barbara, was revealed a truth that no empirical observation or medical authority could refute: Her precious daughter would walk without crutches and would run chasing her dog across the grassy meadows of their home. Barbara stood amid the working, straining child victims of trauma and disease and wept with joy. Her child would walk and run again...

֍

Olympic Memorial Hospital
August 22, 1987

Two months of therapy and healing and Mossy's leg did not move. There was no discernible pain associated with the affliction, nor was there any apparent connection between the inanimate limb and the will of the young patient. There was nothing more to be achieved at the hospital and it was the patient's fervent will to return to her home. Mossy sat quietly in a wheelchair with her full-grown, little dog on her lap, while her mother spoke with the neurologist.

"You have to see Mossy's recovery from the perspective of her condition when she arrived. When she came to us ten weeks ago she was comatose with a head injury; she had a crushed pelvis with massive internal bleeding. Of course, we were hoping for more progress with her right leg, but, in the big picture, I'm sure you will agree that there has been remarkable recovery while she has been in our care."

"Doctor Baker, I remember two months ago when you approached us about the problem in the limb. You felt that, if we resumed pain medication, there might be some improvement. Is it too late to..."

"No, mother!" interrupted Mossy. "No more pills and stuff. We're going home and that's final!"

"She's right, Barbara," continued Dr. Baker. "There's nothing to be achieved by medication at this point. The sciatic nerve sheath is healed. Put simply, her brain has taught the leg NOT to move. My hope is that, as her life regains normalcy, the brain will overcome the neurological barrier."

"How much chance do we have of that," asked Barbara.

"I'd say less than fifty per cent."

"How much less?"

"Between one and fifty percent."

"Closer to one or closer to fifty?" the mother pressed.

"What do you want me to say?" the doctor reacted defensively. "Pain medication two months ago probably would have made a difference. There's a one in a hundred chance that the leg will regain its former mobility, OK? But you have a living, beautiful, happy, all-be-it tempestuous, little girl..."

"Thank you, Doctor Baker," intoned Barbara. "From the bottom of our hearts, thank you for all you and this hospital have done for us." The mother pushed the crippled child out of the hospital and across the parking lot to the waiting pickup truck.

❧

Prince of Peace Lutheran Church, Forks, WA
Sunday, May 14, 1989

After church services, Barbara read in the pickup truck, waiting for her child to finish up with her Sunday School. Mossy looked so pretty, in her little Sunday dress, coming out of the church and hobbling along with her steel crutches across the parking lot. She looked more serious today. She leaned the crutches against the seat, climbed into the car, pulled down her skirt and sighed. In the bed of the truck you could hear her dog's tail begin to beat against the inside of the pet kennel at the sound of Mossy.

"Mom, what's a gimp?" asked Mossy.

"Why? Did someone in your Sunday School class call you a 'gimp?'"

"Yeah. They always call me a gimp when the teacher is not around."

"That's not right, Mossy. I don't like that word and I'm going to talk to the teacher about it..."

"Mom, please DON'T! It will just make things worse and you can't change kids. Remember when Jesus said, 'Suffer the little children?'"

"He said, 'Suffer the little children to come to Me.' He wasn't talking about obnoxious kids or children being mean to other children."

"Mom, didn't we learn from that book at the hospital that Jesus was dark complicated?"

"The Israelites of Jesus' time were dark-*complectioned*, yes."

"Well, I told Amy Burt that Jesus was black and that they didn't crucify people on crosses but on straight posts. I told her that Jesus wasn't born on Christmas and that the early Christians were Communists..."

"Well, it wasn't a political party. The book didn't say they were Communists. They shared everything, is all."

"Amy said I was going straight to hell for that kind of talk!"

"Did *she* call you a 'gimp?'"

"Mom, *most* of the kids call me a gimp!" Mossy began to make little sobs. "I hate it! Can we just do Sunday School at home like we studied and prayed at the hospital? Please..."

❧

Hemp Hill Creek
May 21, 1989

The child turned the family Bible over and over in her hands. Barbara and Mossy had continued with their Bible study, which they had started in the hospital. They had just finished the last two chapters of Genesis and the child appeared to be uneasy with the lesson.

"Do you have questions you want to ask about, Mossy?"

Mossy opened the book to its title page and read, "*'To Glen, from Bill and Vicky with love. Stay away from the back of troop carriers and come home to us when it's over.'* What's that about and who are these people?"

110

Glen would have been your grandfather, my father. I already told you that he died when I was about your age. His parents gave him that Bible when he went off to fight in World War Two."

"But he didn't die in battle, right? He died in an accident in the woods?"

"That's right. Mossy, do you have questions about what we've read in the Bible?"

The child was quiet for a while, formulating a question. "Mom, how come if God is all-knowing and all-powerful...why did he let Satan tempt Adam and Eve with the Apple? And why would God not like Cain's offering of fruit, but accept Abel's fat sheep? When Abraham and Sarah came into the land of the Pharaoh, Abraham said that his wife was his sister. When the Pharaoh took Sarah in marriage and gave Abraham gifts for her, God punished the Pharaoh, leaving Abraham and Sarah to go with the silver and cattle? Why is God mean to the Egyptians? And it says that all the men in the town of Sodom where Lot lived were...*gay*. How can that be...I mean how do they have children? And weren't women and innocent children burned up by the fire and brimstone that God rained down to kill the gays? And poor Lot's wife turned into a pile of salt for looking back at her burning home? And Lot going off to live with his two daughters in the mountains where they had sex? Isn't that as big a sin as being gay? Mom, on the first page here it says that God created day and night on the first day and then God waits until the fourth day to make the sun, moon and stars. How can there be day and night without the sun and stars? How can..."

"Mossy, **sweetie**, don't let these questions come between you and your Creator." Barbara paused to organize her thoughts. "There is a lot of discussion about whether the Bible is literal or symbolic. Let's take a scientific approach. Most scientists agree that all matter in the universe exploded from a single point about ten billion years ago. It was a very simple universe, lacking the ability to form carbon, water and other biological necessities of life. The stellar system we see in the sky is the second stellar system since this beginning of time ten billion years ago. Geologists say that the earth is five billion years old and simple viruses came to be billions of years ago. The human race, scientists say, can be traced back two million years. Doesn't that look like a deliberate path, from a sterile universe to a living planet, in seven or eight billion years.

"Consider your eye, Mossy. Think about how it works and what joy it brings you. With all of mankind's laboratories and hospitals, there is no place on earth, except inside the human body, where an eye can be manufactured. Look at all the miracles around you! Our universe is a creation and every creation has a creator. The Bible puts it, 'All things were made by Him; and without Him was not any thing made that was made. In Him was life; and the life was the light of men. And the Light shineth in the darkness and the darkness comprehended it not.'

"Look deep inside your heart and you will find that Creator. And when you find the Creator...Mossy, I promise you, the Creator loves you. The Creator loves Cain, the Creator loves the Egyptians, the Creator loves the Sodomites...because the Creator is Love. God **is** Love.

"Let's give up on the Bible study for a while and try a half hour of silent worship. Let's just sit here and count our blessings and inventory the miracles we know about. OK?"

"OK, mom. I can be quiet. I've got stuff to work out."

And the mother and daughter fell into silence, sitting in their primitive living room, with sunshine streaming through the skylight and a living green wall of temperate rain forest swaying in the afternoon breeze. As Barbara, began to count her blessings, first was her daughter, sitting beside her. And the second was the brief marriage, that had given her the first.

§∞§

Hemp Hill Creek
Friday, September 28, 1979, 12:20 hours

The newlyweds stood like Adam and Eve, surveying for the Garden of Eden. Facing south in the large pasture and looking at the creek where they were building a bridge, Barbara pointed to a sunny corner of field and said, "That's where we'll put the garden."

Phil looked over at the spruce growing on the other side of the creek and walked to the edge of the creek. He did an about face and strode 10 paces toward Barbara. Phil turned around once and pulled out a compass from his front pocket. He looked up at the top of the spruce over the edge of the compass, using the built on clinometer like a sextant. He strode towards Barbara another ten paces and put a stake in the ground.

"Why are you putting the stake there, Phil? The garden should be closer to the creek so we can get water."

"Water in this country is not a problem. Sun is. We'll have a gravity-feed system for irrigation. This stake is where the shadow line will be on September 28, 2000. That big spruce will intrude much sooner. We'll have to move the garden back into the sun or cut down the trees. And I thought you didn't want me taking out the big trees on this property. Better to keep it away from the creek."

Barbara tried to envision the elaborate formula for Phil's prediction: the spinning and whirring of stars and planets. The spot she had identified was fifty feet from the shadow line. "How do you figure?" she asked simply after a minute of studying the picture.

"A spruce which has escaped the alder canopy like those ones across the creek will grow easily three feet a year. From the edge of this side of the creek is forty feet to the base of those smaller spruces. I paced out another sixty feet and checked with my clinometer. They're about 100 feet tall and will all go over 160 feet by 2000. It's simple."

Barbara felt as if she were losing control of her dream. "I'll worry about the garden, you let me know when you need help winching the fourth stringer on the bridge."

"Suit yourself."

There was no time to argue during the daylight. The bridge had to be completed before work could begin on the cabin. Phil had weekends off. When he got back from work about four p.m., they worked until dark and sometimes several hours afterwards by Coleman lantern.

The bridge became the doorway to a hundred other vital projects. Since the couple were spending almost all their time and money on the property, they gave up Phil's apartment in Forks. As soon as the foundation and floor of the cabin were constructed, Phil pitched their tent in the middle. It was a dry, secure nest. They hoped to have a roof over their heads before January, but there were so many other projects to be planned and executed. Phil was buying thousands of feet of two-inch pipe to run up the creek above Hemp Hill Falls. This would power a nano-hydroelectric for lights and offer them water for household use and irrigation. Barbara worked on applying for the water right, by lantern light.

They built the superstructure of the cabin entirely out of two-by-fours from Allen's Mill on the Hoh River. Purchasing structurally deficient lumber that would otherwise be chipped for pulp, they laid out the two-by-fours like bricks. They bragged that their cabin would cost four cents a pound and they would build a 1,200 square foot structure for just over a dollar a square foot. They could build the walls at a rate of just under a vertical foot a day, and occasionally outworked the supply of dunnage from the mill. They dug an enormous hole next to the cabin site for a septic tank and several hundred feet of drain field in the glacial till. The digging was easy. On Sundays they poached pickup loads of rock from the Anderson rock pit to build up a road through the meadows. Whenever there was a spare minute, Barbara went back to the front pasture to dig fence posts.

It was all backbreaking work, but Barbara had never felt better in her life. They were getting by on about five hours of sleep a night. As darkness would overtake their industry, they would bring the lanterns into the confines of the newly constructed walls and heat up gallons of water on a Coleman stove. They would clean the mud off of each other and toast their daily accomplishments. They would eat and prepare a lunch for Phil to take to work and climb into the tent to plan the next day's work from the foundation of each other's embrace. Occasionally, they found time to scratch out notes on Phil's project to develop a primer on the biological perspective on space-time.

Barbara began to wake up feeling not as well as the previous day. She felt hungover. She did not join Phil in the evening's libations. In the mornings, she didn't feel well. She had missed her period. She vomited, after Phil left for work, several mornings in a row. She drove into Forks to find a doctor and scheduled an appointment with Dr. Richard Dickson, the limping young doctor fresh out of medical school. The diagnosis was easy, and Barbara laid in supplies for a special dinner that evening.

Hemp Hill Creek
22:30 hours, Friday, December 14, 1979

"Wow! After a dinner like that we deserve the usual before-bedtime dessert," said Phil, pulling Barbara toward their tent/bedroom.

"Hold on there, big guy," argued Barbara, allowing herself to be dragged into the tent. "You still haven't gotten the report from our first dessert binge."

Phil pulled her down into the open sleeping bags and rustled around with a box of condoms at the head of the sleeping area. "Whatever it is, it can wait five minutes."

"It can wait five minutes," answered Barbara. "It can wait six months. But it looks to me like you're about to waste a perfectly good condom."

"What are you talking about, honey? Did all that food make you crazy?"

"I'm pregnant, you big dummy!" Phil dropped the partially opened condom and gawked. "I've been dropping hints all night. For a nuclear scientist, you're kind of slow."

"But...but...it's impossible. We've been using contraception all along...Except that Sunday in September just before we got married."

"Bingo," said Barbara. Phil was dumbstruck and lay in silence for a few moments. "Does this come as a big disappointment to you, honey?"

"No, I'm excited, really. It just takes a little time to adjust. There are so many things to do. This will be a big commitment and require significant adjustment in our schedules. You can't be working as hard..."

"Hard work is good for me...for us...for the baby..."

"Well, for example: stay away from the creosote we've been painting on the foundation piers. That stuff is genetic poison. Our kid could be born with an arm coming out of the middle of her forehead."

"Why did you say 'her'? Why do you think it will be a girl?"

"It just came out of my mouth. Anyway, if it is a girl, let's call her 'Mossy.' That's a great name for a girl born in Forks."

"Well, if it is a girl, we won't be naming her 'Mossy.' There's already a 'Mossyrock' in Washington."

"'Mossy Stone,'" mused Phil. "I really like it. Don't be so closed-minded about it..."

"Closed-minded? I'm the person who gets stuck carrying this kid. Already it feels like a big hangover. I'm stuck with nine months of pain, discomfort and looking like a beanbag and you want to name the fruit of my labor 'Mossy?' What do you want to name the kid of it's a boy? 'Rolling?'"

"Hey! That's a good name, too," answered Phil, happily.

Barbara rolled onto her side facing the wall of the tent. This was the closest they had come to an argument. She needed respect and support right now, which she didn't feel she was getting. The couple lay in silence for several minutes. Phil broke the silence.

"Barbara, we should have a family cemetery."

"What's this about? First you're seeing a baby girl. Now are you seeing me die in childbirth or killing myself in postpartum depression?"

"No. Hey, I'm eight years older than you and a male. I'm a logger! What are the chances of you dying before me? It's just that we are going to be a family. We need a family cemetery. I want this property to swallow me in death the way it's swallowing me in life."

Barbara said nothing and remained pensive, breathing against the wall of the tent. Minutes passed and Barbara said in a quiet, tired voice, "I'm talking about new life, and you want to talk about a cemetery." She paused. "I wanted tonight to be special for us..." Minutes passed.

Barbara was beginning to drift off to sleep when Phil began to speak again. "A family cemetery is like your garden. Pay yourself a quarter an hour and you buy food cheaper from the store than grow it on your place. But the produce from your garden will come from OUR soil. It's like when I hunt. Eating the elk or deer makes me part of the forest. A family cemetery is the same process in reverse..."

Barbara was quiet. Phil continued, "Remember when we were talking above Kahkwa Creek last February? You talked about peak brain waves?" Barbara didn't answer. "It's like ego is what separates us from the cosmos. Erase ego and you join Creation. Every epoch of time; every moment: they are forever. But as we whir through time and space our lives...and after-lives...require an anchor. Soil, that's an anchor. Are you following me?" Barbara was quiet.

"Mortuary science is exactly opposed to this. They embalm the human remains to keep them from returning to soil. They put up stone monuments with the name of the deceased carved on them attempting to permanently separate the ego from the Cosmic Creation. It scares me to think about it. It's like being separated from life. It's like...Barbara?"

"Mom?"

"...Barbara?..."

"...Mom?..."

Barbara was falling awake through time and space.

ᕙᕗ

Hemp Hill Creek
Sunday, June 4, 1989, 12:40 hours

"Mom, were you sleeping when we were supposed to be worshipping?"

"Yes, Mossy. I guess I kind of drifted off." Barbara was having trouble returning to the present. "It's such a nice day, let's take a walk out to the front pasture before dinner."

"OK!" agreed Mossy, grabbing her crutches.

They walked across the bridge with the full June sun illuminating their spread. Looking back at the garden from halfway out the driveway, Barbara noticed that the shadow line had finally retreated all the way out of the garden. In a month, the shadows would be back, haunting the sun starved-produce she labored to cultivate. "Mossy, you really like having fresh produce from the garden, don't you?"

"I depend on it," answered the nine-year-old girl, simply.

"Well, our garden isn't doing so well because of those trees across the creek...Particularly that big spruce. How would you feel if that big spruce and a couple more were to disappear and we were to have a lot more light on the garden for growing..."

"No! I love the trees on this farm! Just move the garden!"

Just move the garden, thought Barbara. No small feat. She thought of the days she spent digging fence posts, the tons of soil amendments she had added to the rain-washed till, the composting and weeding. "Mossy, moving the garden is not that easy. Just think about it..."

"NO!" spoke the child.

ೋ

Hemp Hill Creek
Monday, June 5, 1989

With Mossy away for her last days of school, Barbara decided to work fast to resolve the tree issue. In the morning she made a few phone calls to arrange the pick up and sale of the spruce. She studied the angle of the biggest spruce and it grew towards the southern pasture, away from the creek. With a big enough saw she could fall it and still keep it out of the creek without disturbing the silver salmon fingerlings that over-summered in the spawning grounds. She went to the shop and got Phil's old 056, which hadn't been run in five years. She gassed it up and cleaned the spark plug. She took the saw out of the shop and tried to start it, holding the saw to the ground with one hand and pulling on the starter cord with the other. She couldn't overcome the compression. She took the saw back to the shop and put the bar in a vice. She got up on a stool and reefed on the starter cord. It started after the third pull. She took it out of the vice and walked out of the shop towards the creek. The saw died. She took it back to the vice and started it again. This time she got all the way to the spruce. She made a face cut in the direction she wanted the spruce to fall. She kicked out the face and began her backcut. The tree groaned and, as she looked up, the top began to tip towards the south meadow. She left the saw and ran for the bridge. The tree crashed out into the meadow. Barbara flush cut the stump, cut three, thirty-foot logs from the trunk and bucked the limbs off the trunk. For two and a half hours she piled up the limbs and then it was time to pick up Mossy at the bus stop out on Highway 101.

"HOW COULD YOU? MOTHER, HOW COULD YOU DO THIS?" wailed the child when she saw Barbara's trespass. When the skidder arrived to pick up the logs, Barbara went inside to cook dinner while Mossy moped around the bridge. Two hours later, Barbara went out to find Mossy. There were her crutches lying next to the stump. The child was lying on the flush cut, still weeping. When Mossy saw her mother, she kicked her good leg in the air pitifully and lamented, "Oh, mother, how could you? This tree was like a brother to me! How could you?"

Barbara walked across the bridge to the garden and began digging postholes 200 feet north of the current garden.

ೋ

Hemp Hill Creek
Sunday, June 11, 1989

By the following Sunday, Barbara had worn herself out digging fence posts. Though Mossy couldn't help with the digging, she would fetch the level and hammer and provided company and supervision to the labor force of one. Sunday morning, before their little worship, Mossy was out in the front pasture, checking for tools her mom might have left out in the rust-encrusting dew, when she saw a deer lying on the freshly turned soil. Since the deer did not move she hobbled closer to see if the deer was all right. Lying beside the deer, in the soup of birth, was a tiny newborn fawn. Mossy was close enough to see the new fawn was white on its hindquarters. She hurried back on her crutches to get her mother.

Barbara was cleaning up the breakfast dishes and preparing their afternoon dinner. She received the report with good humor, but refused to participate in a rescue. "Mossy, I'm sure the little fawn is fine. They get born around here all the time and the best thing we can do for them is leave them alone. We don't want to harm the deer..."

"But MOM! Of course I don't want to hurt the deer! But the little fawn couldn't walk and it's rear end was all white!"

"Appaloosa deer are a sign of inbreeding. Since the wolves were killed out of this country the deer get too settled and too lazy with their gene pool. Newborn fawns need a few hours to learn to walk..."

"Their mommies teach the fawns how to walk in just a few hours?"

"It's called genetic memory, Mossy. How to walk is printed on their brain. The deer will be fine. Let's start our little worship early so we can take advantage of the fine weather this afternoon."

୭ℛ

Mossy sat quietly under the skylight with her crutches stowed under her chair. She had become accustomed to this manner of worship. Her mind jabbered about summer vacation and about her impending birthday. Her ebullience clouded as she reflected briefly on the accident which took her mobility two years previously. She began her private worship in earnest:

I can pray, amen. And I can talk to God, amen. Ahhhhhhhhhhhhhhhhhhhhhhmen. And I can slow my breathing. Ahhhhhhhhhhhhhhhhhhhhhhhhhhhhhhhhhhhhhhhhhmmen. I can slow my heart with my breathing. Ahhhhhhhhhhhhhhhhhhhhhhhhhhhhhhhhhhmmmmmmmmmmmmmen. God? God, are You there? Of course, You're there. You're always there. It's just us that stray. But, I'm coming, God. Ahhhhhhhhhhhhhhhhhhhhmmmmmmmmmmmennnnn. It's Your friend, Mossy. I want to thank You for our farm, and for my mom, and for my little Daisy dog... Ahhhhhhhhhhhhhhhhhhhhhmmmmmmmmmmmmmmmmmmmmmmmen. And for each precious breath I take and for the clean water and air...and for the soil that gives us stuff from our garden. Ahhhhhhhhhhhhhhhhhhhhmmmmmmmmen. And if I can't run and jump on that ground, You maketh me to run and jump in my mind, which is where I am right now hobbling on my crutches across the bridge to meet You, amen...towards the garden, where the little fawn lays next to its mommy, amen.

Thank You for new life, God, and meet me by the new fence post next to the driveway, because the ground is uneven and hard walking on crutches and we don't want to frighten the deer. And...God? Thank You for being my Friend. And for teaching me how to pray, ahhhhhhhhhhhmmen.

As Mossy sat under the skylight, a high cumulus cloud was pushed to the west by the high-pressure ridge, which had enveloped the Pacific Northwest. Sunlight poured down upon the bowed head of the child and she was enveloped by a state of mind to which the child referred to as 'God.' And in this state of mind, the child watched the sunlight move across the large meadow, feeding chlorophyll, circulating water, moving air. She watched the sunlight touch the baby fawn and the tiny creature began to stand on wobbly legs. The Light took the child in Its embrace and the crutches dropped like dried limbs in the spring breeze. The Light lifted up the child to show her the land and as Mossy's consciousness rose over the farm it was caught by the up-valley wind of an early summer and carried up the Bogachiel. She could see the river valley from a vantage missed by the backpackers and fishermen that were the human visitors above Mossy's farm. She saw countless waterfalls pouring out of the glacially-cut valley into the river. From the bosom of the Light she could see the fabric of life and the great inter-activity. She saw the Light melting the snow, to feed the waterfalls and flush the little salmon fingerlings out to the ocean. The Light carried her upstream. And the Light spoke with the same love and tenor as Mossy's mother. The voice asked, "Mossy, are you with Me?"

Barbara watched her beloved daughter lose herself in concentration. She saw Mossy take very slow, even breaths and, as sun reflected off her blond hair, a blissful expression covered Mossy's face. The child's breathing seemed to stop and she sat rigid.

"Mossy, are you with me?" asked Barbara.

"Yes. For always and forever. Ahhhhhhhhhmmmmmennnnn," murmured her daughter.

Barbara settled into her own reflections, which most usually took the form of powerful reminiscing.

Hemp Hill Creek
Saturday, December 15, 1979, 16:15 hours

Phil couldn't understand why Barbara was so moody. She had fallen asleep on him the previous evening when he was trying to explain how important a family cemetery was to the big picture of the homestead they were building. Most of the day they nailed down the two-by-four walls in silence. They would need at least two weeks of dedicated work to complete the roof before the new year, but Phil would be working right up to the Twenty First and several days between Christmas and New Year's Day. The clear weather had left a frost on everything, which had lasted all day. The last sunlight of the day filtered through the trees from the west. They had finished nailing together the walls for the upstairs wall and Phil climbed down the ladder to retrieve his chain saw, a chalk line and another quart of beer. The couple scribed the eave line on the stacked two by fours and Phil picked up the saw to make the cut.

"I'm going to go pee," announced Barbara. "The sound of that saw gives me a headache, anyway."

"Sure," agreed Phil. "It's safer for me to do it alone." He swallowed half a quart of beer and belched loudly. "There's one that will never make it to farthood," he remarked of the burp. Barbara grimaced and climbed down the stairs.

Phil started the saw and began the cut standing on the floor. To cut a level line towards the ridge, he stood on a sawhorse. Cutting the eave line beyond the south wall required that he climb up on the sloping west wall, standing on the three-and-a-half inch wall as he made his cut. He finished his cut and turned off the saw. The silence that washed over him was wonderful. The frost on the trees was winking orange in the twilight beams of the sun. Phil sensed something overhead and looked up. Two bald eagles cavorted with one another. They came together, grasping talons, and spread their wings to slow their descent. They came down slowly, spinning like a six-foot pinwheel, in their mating ritual.

"Barbara, look!" called Phil, beginning to point with the hand which did not hold the saw. Phil's balance was offset as he brought his gaze down to his wife who returned towards the cabin from the treeline. He shifted his right foot further up the eaveline to support a squat, but a piece of the cheap two-by-four tore out and the uncobbled arch of his left foot slipped on the thick frost. Both of the logger's feet went out over his head and he plunged headfirst and backwards off the twenty-foot wall.

A human body falls through space with an acceleration factor of 32 feet per second per second. Though a twenty-foot fall is measured on a stopwatch as 00:01:12 (seconds) it can feel like infinity to the body and mind in motion. Phil thought of the fang-like teeth and dagger dogs on his saw and tried to push the saw away. He thought of the tools that were stowed beneath his fall line: a pitchfork for unloading saw chips, a spear-like digging bar, an axe, a pulaski. What a stupid mistake! He should have built some interior scaffolding with the sawhorses. This didn't have to happen. He would be killed or crippled.

As Phil fell with his eyes wide open, the adrenaline which caused his brain waves to accelerate, caused his heart to race, and his optic nerve to constrict the flow of information to what was directly before the pupil. Phil was seeing something clearly, but could not understand the visual message. *The eagles!* Phil was falling through space, looking straight up at the eagles, which were still dropping slowly with their wings outstretched. Phil realized that he was making futile kicking motions with his feet and swimming motions with his arms. He relaxed his legs and brought his arms around his head. Phil was still looking at the eagles. He flexed his head forward and WHUP! The fall ended abruptly and Phil's thought was *I'm alive...but I can't...breath.*

ॐ

Saturday, December 15, 1979, 16:15 hours

"Barbara, look!" called out Phil as she came out of the woods walking towards the cabin. It looked like he launched himself off the roof and got rid of his saw like a Saturn Rocket ejecting a stage. He flailed wildly as he fell, but halfway down he collected into a backwards dive into the pile of Doug fir chips they had gotten from Allen's Mill for the orchard. Barbara heard the wind go out of him like an elephant stomping on a whoopy cushion. He lay motionless in the saw chips. She dropped the used toilet paper she carried in her left hand and ran to where his body lay. His face was red and turning blue.

"I can't..." he stammered. "I can't..." He was turning blue and she was just moving to give him mouth to mouth when there was a sudden implosion of breath and she felt the negative wind of his inspiration on her cheek. "I love you, Barbara," Phil said with the air from his first breath. He kissed her and said, "But look!" He pointed straight up over her bowed head. She looked up and saw two eagles falling through the sky, grasping one another's talons. Barbara raised her right hand reflexively and pointed with Phil.

"They're mating," said Phil, pulling Barbara into the sweet smelling wood chips. "That's what we should be doing," he said, kissing her with breath that smelled partly of beer and mostly of the man she loved. Their two pointing hands embraced and clutched like the talons of the falling birds.

How often she returned to that kiss: that long sweet kiss on the pile of saw chips, which radiated heat from its own metabolism. That kiss that started under the shadow of two eagles, that continued through the orange beams of the cabin's doorway and ended in the dark of their tent/bedroom. A kiss that promised the love, devotion and hope of a lifetime together. The sweet kiss of reconciliation against the backdrop of abated fear...
Falling through time and space, Barbara's memory would grasp that kiss like an eagle talon holding on to its mate.

The Wednesday following that weekend, Phil had come home with what he thought was good news. Mayr Brothers had been awarded a DNR sale just across the river and downstream. The fallers would start cutting on the following day. With a fifteen-minute commute, Phil would have two more hours of daylight every workday to give to their projects. The couple might be under their own roof by New Year's after all. Barbara had some news of her own: the nano-hydroelectric the couple had ordered from Canyon Industries had arrived. Phil tore into the box and removed the tiny power plant. This was very exciting for Phil, who temporarily forgot about the roof and insisted on laying out one of the ten 300-foot sections of two-inch penstock they had bought for the project. The pipe resisted being laid out flat, but, as one partner held down the recalcitrant black plastic, the other laid down branches and pinned the pipe to the ground with rebar and hose clamps. They came back to the cabin in near darkness.

Thursday morning, Phil ran by a checklist for Barbara's attention. They had placed the rafters on the downstairs the previous week and Phil had in mind Barbara making all the bird's eye cuts, so the upstairs rafters could be placed in a manner of a few hours. Phil reminded Barbara to run the public notice in <u>Knives,</u> <u>Spoons and Forks,</u> in pursuit of their water right on Hemp Hill. He asked her to contact the State Cemetery Board about setting up a family cemetery; to get some more Coleman fuel, 16 penny nails,and beer in town; to finish framing in the front door and upstairs windows; to clean up the dropped and bent nails out by where they parked their rigs; to remove the pitchfork, rock bar, and pointy things from the west wall of the cabin (where he liked to land) and put them under the floor; to pile up the loose two-by-four ends into a heap under a tarp; to...

"Phil, honey, I've got a doctor's appointment today and I was hoping to write my mother and do some laundry in town."

"Well, call your mom instead of writing, forget the dirty clothes because we'll just get them dirty again, and go into your doctor appointment one hour late and, that way, you won't have to wait forever to see Dr. Dickson. We're in a hurry and so am I, kiss, kiss!" Phil ran out to his Ford pickup and threw himself into the driver's seat. He pulled out with a honk and a wave.

෨ஷ

Flying S Farm
2674 Dowans Creek Road
Forks, WA 98331
Thursday, December 20, 1979

Dear Mom,

I've only got a few minutes to write because Phil and I have been so busy building our place. I wanted to be sure you had our address since we don't have a phone and may not get one out here for sometime. In asking around I find our farm was called "The Flying S Farm by Otto Seigfreid, the German immigrant who first settled these meadows burned out of the rain forest by Native America.

Phil came home last week with a case of dynamite from work and blew a bunch of holes out where we are putting our tiny hydroelectric. When the holes are full of water from the race, salmon fry will have protected backwater habitat, which is important. Phil tried to help me with my fencepost digging with the dynamite, but that got really messy.

I've never worked so hard in my life! There will be plenty of time later on in life to use my college degree, so please don't be mad about me not finishing up with my post-grad work. This is what I'm doing now.

I stopped off at the Forks Pound today and got a little Toy Fox Terrier. Oh, and by the way, I'm writing this card in the waiting room of Dr. Dickson's office. I'm pregnant.

Love,

Barbara

121

❧

As Barbara drove up to the high point overlooking the river on the Dowans Creek Road, returning with 16 penny nails, beer and, (she hoped) everything else her husband had ordered, she had a clear view of the trees coming down in the DNR unit at the end of the Undi Road. To her amazement and horror, they were falling right up to the river's steep bank. It was a violation of forestry practice laws. The puppy whined nervously from the front seat of the car. From her vantage she could see the red suspenders that held up her husband's tin pants, crouching beside a large spruce tree just above the cut bank. She could hear the growl of his saw; the silence as he turned it off; the whack, whack whack, as he drove in his wedges. She heard the tiny voice of her husband yell, CLEAR!, the snarl of his saw and the crash of the mighty giant to the floor of the retreating rain forest. Barbara was not happy...

❧

Hemp Hill Creek
Thursday, December 20, 1979, 16:00 hours

"What do you mean you forgot the Coleman fuel? You remembered to get a puppy, but you forgot fuel so we can't see and cook dinner! How are we supposed to work? This is the second to longest night of the year and we've got about an hour left of usable light. How could you forget to get fuel?"

"I got beer, nails, and all the other stuff you asked for! If it's that big of a deal, I'll go to town right now and buy some. And I'll report Mayr Brothers for violating a riparian corridor on a stream of statewide significance. What are you doing knocking down trees right next to the river?"

"Hey, I just cut them. Gravity knocks them down. And I cut them where the blue flagging tells me to saw them. I don't decide what trees to cut..."

"Every one of you is in violation of Washington Forestry Practice Act. It doesn't matter that some bonehead strung blue flagging right along the riverbank. You're the one who is destroying habitat! You're the one who will bear the ten thousand dollar fine when State Fisheries stumbles on your little show. Who do you think you are? Cutting down trees next to a major anadromous stream..."

"I'm a logger. Barbara, honey, you married a logger. I haven't exactly tried to hide that from you. I cut trees for a living. Someone else makes a living telling me where to cut trees. I don't ask questions, I just cut trees. If you want to report it to Fisheries, be my guest. But without guys like me cutting trees, we would be building our cabin with recycled tires instead of lumber. You would be wiping your pregnant ass on owl feathers instead of toilet paper..."

Barbara picked up the puppy and stormed out of the unfinished cabin to get in her pickup and drive her pregnant ass to town.

Seven

"I wouldn't say that getting out in the country always makes a man happy. Life here is full of disappointments as it is anywhere else - in fact, around here the disappointments are part of the scenery."
The Peninsula by **Don Moser**, author/seasonal Park Ranger, Kalaloch about 1960

Hemp Hill Creek
Thursday, December 20, 1979, 21:00

*W*hen Barbara got back, the cabin was in complete darkness and Phil had evidently repaired to the tent. Using her headlamp to find the lantern, she refueled and put their "living room" into the white glare of the Coleman. She noticed two empty quart beer bottles. Phil had been busy, after all. "Are you in the tent?" she called out.

"There was no point in staying up in the dark," came the disgruntled voice from inside the tent. The puppy whined from Barbara's car. She fetched the dog, set out some food for the dog and crawled into the tent. Phil lay in silence.

"The puppy is a female, or, was, before she got spayed. I was thinking about naming her 'Mossy,'" said Barbara to break the ice.

"That's a nice name for a baby girl. How about 'Gawnit' for your dog. As in, 'Have you seen my dog, *Gawnit*?'"

"I like 'Mossy' better for a dog."

"Well, whatever her name is, she wants to come in the tent. Leave her outside and she'll wander off and the coyotes will get her."

Barbara let the pup in and it ricocheted around inside the tent making it difficult to talk. "Do you want to get up and have dinner and do some work?" Barbara asked. "I'm not hungry, myself. And I'm sorry about forgetting the fuel and calling the State Cemetery Board. I don't understand the big deal about it, anyway. I mean, it seems like our focus right now should be building a family rather than planting one in the ground."

Barbara grabbed onto the little dog and pulled it to her to quiet it down. It settled into her embrace and they lay quietly in the tent with the lantern hissing outside. After some moments, Phil stirred. He rolled over to face Barbara. "I guess my problem is I feel I'm being ignored. When I was a kid, my parents were totally preoccupied and I had trouble getting their attention or approval. Maybe 'Mossy is a dumb name for a kid; maybe a family cemetery is a misplaced priority; maybe forgetting the fuel is no big deal since we need a rest, anyway. It's just that...the Brer Rabbit complex...I like to be heard *and* answered. We're here on earth for such a short time, anyway, and I want to be heard. I need you as a sounding board...Barbara...Barbara?" Phil listened to the deep breathing of his human and canine company and realized he had lost his audience. It irritated him that she had fallen asleep on him, leaving him unheard and unanswered. He felt a strong obligation to micturate.

He crawled out of the tent into the lantern glare and the cool, December evening. He padded across the two-by-four subfloor in his bare feet. He opened the front door, which Barbara had hung today, and was about to relieve himself. It was beginning to drizzle. Something tickled the hairs on the back of his neck and he was certain that he was being watched. He looked back inside the cabin, but Barbara and the pup were still in the tent. He was sure he felt a presence and, looking once more around, he saw a pair of glowing eyes looking down at him through the open rafters. He walked back to the lantern and held it up to see to whom the eyes belonged. The lantern revealed a small brown owl with white spots and chestnut eyes. From pictures Barbara had shown, Phil recognized this visitor.

"Barbara, there's a spotted owl out here visiting on the rafters." From inside the tent, there was no response. Phil went closer to the tent and the puppy growled, as if Phil were an intruder to his own tent. "Barb, there's a spotted owl out here."

"Mmmmm," came the reply from inside the tent. The puppy growled again. "Shush!" Phil wondered if the dog or himself was being quieted. He walked off to take care of his business under the gaze of the owl. He smelled excrement and, on his way back to the tent, saw feces oozing up between his toes! He was wearing a shit moccasin on his right foot!

"Your damned puppy shit the floor out here and I stepped in it!" Phil complained to the slumbering tent, limping over to the coffee tin the couple used to store their toilet paper. NO TOILET PAPER! Barbara had forgotten to get toilet paper! "YOUR DAMNED PUPPY SHIT THE FLOOR, I STEPPED IN IT, AND YOU FORGOT TO GET TOILET PAPER!" Phil raged at the tent entrance.

The dog growled and Barbara murmured, "That's nice," still processing the news that an owl was visiting them on the rafters. She was dreaming of the kiss the couple had shared a few days previously.

Phil limped around the inside of the cabin looking for something with which to wipe his foot. There was only a pint of drinking water left and he didn't feel like marching down to the creek in his bare feet. And he sure as shit on a bare foot was *NOT* going to stink up his corks. His mood became darker and darker. There on the primitive dining table was a blue bandanna sitting out in the drizzle. He used it to clean the gross material off his foot and washed his foot with soap and the remaining drinking water. He set the bandanna aside to clean later. Then he was thirsty so he drank a quart of beer. The owl was still there watching him. He went out to his truck and got some newspaper to clean up the floor. He drank another quart of beer. He talked to the owl. He worked on the latch for the front door and drank another beer. At midnight, he climbed into the tent, drunk.

৯৽৶৶

Hemp Hill Creek
Friday, December 21, 1979 05:00

Barbara could not understand Phil's dark mood the next morning. She got up in the dark a half hour before him to make his breakfast and lunch. He was late leaving for work, ignoring breakfast and taking the lunch pail without a 'thank you.' "Bye," he said, without a kiss. She missed being kissed and couldn't understand Phil's dark mood.

She fed Phil's oatmeal to the hungry little puppy. Before light, she found the latch at the front door that Phil had been working on. The strike plate was on backwards and the knob was oriented to lock them in. It took Barbara an hour to take apart the assembly, reorient the strike plate and put the knobs back on the correct sides. She couldn't make the locks work and the door wouldn't stay closed, so she took it all apart and put it back backwards *a´ la* Phil. Probably they didn't need a lock, living this far from human populations. The next time Phil tried to leave her without a kiss, she could lock him in and have her way with him.

In the growing light, Barbara began to straighten the inside of the cabin. She put the breakfast dishes in the sink. She fetched more water from the creek. She began sweeping the cabin of all the wet sawdust and found her bandanna wadded up on the floor. She straightened out the bandanna to dry and there was a turd inside! WHAT SHIT WAS PHIL PULLING HERE!? Barbara was really upset. She went out to her car and brought in the toilet paper she had purchased the day before and cleaned the bandanna. She washed it out with soap and water and spread it by the stove to dry. The puppy scratched at the new door to be let out. Barbara was so upset she followed the puppy outside and took a walk through the meadows to collect herself.

శ్రీ

Undi Road
Friday, December 21, 1979, 10:45 hours

Across the river and slightly downstream, Phil Stone was having a hard morning. Somehow he attributed the raging ache in his head to his wife's forgetting to get Coleman fuel and toilet paper. Even through the earplugs he wore, the sound of the chain saw cut to the quick of his pain center. Even the sound of the rain hitting his tin hat hurt. A big leaf maple's branches interfered with Phil's intended fall line of a huge spruce about twenty feet from the cutbank. Phil dropped the maple like pushing over a matchstick and stood back as the butt of the maple bounced up to head level while the trunk of the tree rested on slash. If no one poached the tree as firewood, it would burn with the slash, anyway.

Phil began clearing the vine maple away from the huge butt of the spruce and threw the chain off his saw. He pulled a scrench out of his saw kit and took off the clutch cover to put the chain back on the sprocket. When he began putting the side cover back, he had lost one of the two large nuts which hold the cover and bar in place. He spent ten minutes looking for it before he found it buried in the duff.

Then the saw wouldn't start and, as he pulled the spark plug with the scrench to see if the saw was getting fuel or flooded, the spark plug broke off. Checking his saw kit, he didn't have any plugs for a 056. He went back to the crummy and got a couple of spark plugs. He felt his pulse like a hammer in the suspension system of his tin hat. He put in a new plug, pull-started the saw and it growled to life, emitting a cloud of blue-grey smoke. He cut into the large butt of the spruce tree, cutting a face to direct the fall of the large tree. This done, Phil made his back cut and stopped the cut two inches from meeting the cut of the face. He killed the saw engine and placed his falling wedges, as the tree had a slight backward lean seeking the light in the clearing of the river. Driving the wedges, the tree leaned forward, indicating its willingness to fall on the slash pile which would keep it off the ground and make it easier to buck up.

"CLEAR!" yelled Phil and pulled the starter cord, which broke off with his tug. What else can happen? marveled Phil. It's like Nature doesn't want this tree on the ground! Phil removed the saw from the cut and took a length of starter cord from his saw kit. He took the other side panel off the saw and replace the cord. He tested the saw and it started right up.

Almost noon, with no wind to blow over the tree. Phil sat down on the maple stump and opened the lunch pail, which Barbara had packed for him. Looking at the carefully arranged food, Phil felt shame for the blame he had projected onto his bride. He bit into a sandwich and looked around behind him at the river. Barbara was right. They shouldn't be cutting here. The river was too unstable. He would finish this one cut and check with George about why Forestry Practices were being ignored on this sale.

Almost noon on the shortest day of the year. Sitting on the maple stump, Phil thought briefly about how, south of the sixty-sixth degree, thirty minute parallel, south, the sun would be defining the highest point of an arch on a day which had lasted three months. That would be enough light to finish the roof on any cabin. Phil ate some fruit and cookies, which Barbara had lovingly stowed in his nose bag. *How lucky I am to have Barbara for a partner*, thought Phil. I'll make up for my moodiness tonight. I'll tell her that I protested cutting in a riparian zone. Maybe we should just walk away from our projects this holiday and celebrate life...

ঙৃৎ

Friday, December 21, 1979 11:45 hours U.S. Pacific time

Close to the Sagittarius-Carina spiral arm of the Orion Spur of the Milky Way lies an average size star. It is neither a dwarf nor giant and, with a spectral type G2V, is largely unremarkable from the other stars it passes in a stellar year on its orbit around the galaxy. On the third planet of this particular star, the terrestrial inhabitants call their star "the sun" to distinguish it from the ten to the 20th power other stars in their known universe. On earth, they count the orbits of their planet around the sun as the star plods across the galaxy in its own orbit. Two hundred million earth years equal one stellar year in the Milky Way.

At the sun's core, with temperatures of a hundred thousand degrees centigrade, electrons have dissociated from the atomic structure leaving the lonely hydrogen protons searching for the only other vestiges of matter that exist in their universe: other hydrogen protons. Under the considerable gravity of the sun's mass, the hydrogen plasma is quite dense by earth standards and a 12 ounce by volume Coke bottle filled with it and carried to Earth would weigh more than any Coke-guzzling Earthling. Yet the potential space of matter is such that, on an average, the proton looks for two billion Earth years before making contact with another proton. A four-stage, chain-fusion reaction occurs in which the protons are bonded together to form a helium proton and a gamma ray is released. Enough protons are looking for one another in the loneliness of inner space so that, on any given second on Earth, 4,500,000 tons of matter are transformed into energy, or 1 to the 24th power of foot-pounds a second.

For ten million earth years the particular gamma ray released in the fusion reaction of the chance encounter of the two hydrogen protons bounces and ricochets around in the radiative zone inside the sun. By the time the particular ray emerges through the convective zone it has been metamorphosed into x-ray and ultraviolet light. Leaving the photosphere at 186,000 miles per second, which is the speed it has been traveling since its inception as a gamma ray, long before monkeys pondered their opposable thumbs on the third planet, this photon cut through the chronosphere and into the Corona of Earth's star. In a process that had taken 5.05 stellar years (2,010,000,000 earth years), a photon had been conceived, born and thrown out into the world of the known universe.

This photon bore a course toward the northern hemisphere of the third planet, a distance of 93 million miles. To an entity for which every earth inch is an eon, the trip through space to the tiny blue-green, third planet was epoch. On earth the trip from the Corona to the surface of the planet would be measured in eight minutes and twenty seconds.

৵৽

Undi Road
Friday, December 21, 1979, 12:01 hours

Phil had finished his lunch, but was not anxious to get back to work. He sat on the maple stump, smelling the spruce sawdust and looking around at the woods that he was beating back. It stopped drizzling. Looking up into the dense boughs of the spruce tree which was about to fall, Phil was amazed to see the outline of a feathered creature. He had worked ten years in the woods without seeing a spotted owl and, in the last twenty-four hours, he had seen two. Phil wondered if the bird's nest was in the spruce he was about to fall, but remembered what Barbara had told him, that their nests were vacant from August to May. "Better beat it, guy!" called out Phil, putting his saw back into the cut and hitting the wedges a couple of times with his axe. The tree wobbled, but the owl stayed where it perched. "Better fly! I mean it!" called up Phil to the bird. "CLEAR!" yelled Phil, starting his saw. He cut for ten seconds before the top of the tree began falling to the north. He ran with his saw to the "safety" of where he had taken lunch by the maple stump. He turned around to see the owl take wing as the tree fell on its prescribed path towards the slash pile.

The huge tree crashed into the pile of slash. The bowed top of the big leaf maple was driven down into the pile. It pivoted to the west, bringing the butt in an eastward arch like an enormous baseball bat. Phil heard the whoosh of an incoming limb and held his hard hat to his head as he crouched and looked up. Behind him the butt of the maple closed the distance of forty feet at a speed of sixty miles per hour: roughly, half a second or 93,000 light miles.

৵৽

Hemp Hill Creek
Friday, December 21, 1979, 12:01 hours

Across the river and slightly upstream, Barbara was doing the breakfast dishes and thinking about the relationship with her husband. Her walk had made her feel much better. Phil was feeling under pressure to make shelter for the couple. He was under pressure at work to keep up production. Though he said he was happy with it, he might need time to adjust to their pregnancy. Phil was the most wonderful man she had ever known and she would make sure that tonight was a special night for him. She would drive into town and get supplies for another mega *celebration of life* dinner. She would call back the State Board and rattle their cages to see what was required for a family cemetery. The clouds had parted and the sun made a valiant effort to illuminate the valley. From the window in front of the sink, the ferns and moss at the edge of the meadow sparkled in sun-washed coats of rain. She paused mid-dish, looking out at the beauty of light versus gloom. "How I love you, Phil," she said out loud. "How much I look forward to our lives together..."

৩৵৶

Friday, December 21, 1979 12:01:50 hours U.S. Pacific time

If a photon could see as it approached the northwestern hemisphere of the third celestial body from the sun, it would see a living, shimmering, blue-green globe...an island of life. Approaching the ionosphere, it was the ozone layer that absorbed so many of the other infrared photons that had accompanied this photon on this ninety-three million-mile leg of its journey. Still, seven million light inches remained before this photon would reach earth. On the ground, this final hundred and eighty mile leg would be measured as .001 second. It was in the last .0001302 second that most of the photons arriving from the sun were intercepted by the organic gas of the stratosphere, causing molecular activity, or heat, and thereby creating weather on the planet earth. But a photon cannot see. For more nearly, a photon *is* sight...

৩৵৶

Undi Road
Friday, December 21, 1979, 12:01:65 hours

A body in motion tends to stay in motion and a body at rest tends to stay at rest. This was the conflict which developed when the butt of the two thousand-pound maple tree traveling at 88 feet per second arrived at the space occupied by Phil's helmeted skull. The human eye and perception of space-time would suggest that the butt of the tree pretty much knocked the logger's head off and killed him instantly. However, in the perspective of light/time/space, an event occurring in .01 second could fill the pages of a Michener novel.

For millions of light inches, Phil maintained his upward gaze, as the butt of the tree collapsed the shell of his tin hat; increasing pressure was placed upon the suspension system of the hat until it developed a pain threshold upon the neurosensors of his forehead and temple. These neurosensors attempted to communicate with the brain via a pony express system, which required the electrochemical telegraphing of the message across each gap or synapse in the straight, neural road to brain headquarters. These nerves carried the most relevant and important message that any nerve was privileged to carry: PAIN.

During the state of average human awareness, brain waves occur at a rate of approximately ten hertz (no pun intended). When the nerves call the brain with messages, usually the brain is not home and the brain checks an answering machine for pain/pleasure messages ten times per second. The brain doesn't usually respond to one isolated message and must receive several reports from the nerves before the messages are processed into a thought. Two or three billion light inches are required for the slow computer of the brain to process the most primal recognition: PAIN!.

After about a billion light inches the tree butt had closed the distance between the top of the tin hat and the logger's hair. Even with the extraordinary force which had collapsed the tin hat like an empty beer can, the body of Phil's head was stationary relative to the momentum of the tree butt. The tree butt began pushing the skin of the tin hat into the skin of the scalp and more pain emissaries set out for the brain. The skin began to dimple and push against the subcutaneous tissue. Now the envelope of tin, skin and underlying tissues began an inexorable push against the bony shell of the logger's skull. Pain messages were sent out from every square inch of the scalp. Finally, after several billion light seconds, the body of the head began to move. Surrendering its inertia, the skull began to accelerate wildly. The brain was thrown violently against the seat of its compartment. The skull began to cave in like an eggshell. Inertia continued to apply brakes while momentum pushed ever harder against the resistance. The pressure inside the compartment climbed steeply.

All incoming messages carried the PAIN message, but the bridges to the brain were being blown up and all was in chaos in the cortex where the messages arrived. The increased pressure traveled as a shock wave through the brain, which was pinned to the driving force of the tree butt by inertia, and the sides of the skull began to buckle under the fantastic force.

As the skull of the logger shattered and the gray matter encompassed previously therein flew out across the forest floor, his brain processed its last message. His gaze focused up for incoming limbs and his eyes pushed across an incoming beam of sunshine from photons arriving coincident with celestial noon. *LIGHT!* said Phil's brain. "Light light *light,*" echoed infinity.

ഉൟ

Hemp Hill Creek
Friday, December 21, 1979, 18:40 hours

Barbara paced the floor under the open rafters, waiting for the return of her husband. A special dinner was drying out next to the stove. She had set it on the table, and then put it back by the stove to warm up, several times. Against the cold night air, she was dressed with a heavy coat over a bathrobe. Her idea was to shed the coat and flash Phil at the entrance to their cabin. The lock was set so that he couldn't get away.

The puppy growled and Barbara heard Phil's pickup approaching up their long driveway. She put the food on the table and took off the wool coat. She heard a second engine coming in behind Phil's Ford and put her coat back on. She crawled inside the tent to find some long johns to cover her legs if Phil had brought company.

Incongruously, there was a knock at the door and George Redding's voice called out, "Barbara? We're looking for Barbara Stone."

"Come in," she said since she couldn't open the door. She held up the lantern to illuminate their threshold and Redding appeared in the doorway. Rod Hill was coming out of the crummy carrying a tin hat. "Hi, George," she said, wondering why her husband was waiting in the pickup.

"Barbara," said George Redding, "there was an accident at work this afternoon." In the lantern light, Barbara realized that the tin hat that Hill carried was Phil's and that the crown of it was contorted like a tree had hit it. She could see that the inside was painted in blood. Her face contorted into what may have looked like a smile of greeting to Hill.

"Hi!" said Rod Hill, as if it was a pleasure to be visiting a new widow on this evening four days before Christmas. "We brought his brain bucket to show you that he didn't feel any pain at..."

"Oh, my God, NO!" blurted Barbara. "Please no. NO! NO! NO..."

"Barbara, I would like to send my wife over to be with you tonight," continued George. "I don't think you should be alone tonight. Right now I just want to tell you that I'll be coming by to explain your benefits tomorrow. You'll be taken care of financially...you AND your child, so don't worry about that. Phil was a great worker, but ours is a dangerous business and he let his guard down for a minute.

"We didn't find him until the end of our shift. His saw was still running. The coroner said that it happened instantly...Phil didn't feel anything. They took his body to Forks Hospital. We'll help you to make arrangements."

"We didn't know where your place was, is why we didn't get here sooner," offered Rod Hill - as if it was OK for Phil to be killed in the woods, but regrettable that the report was delayed by several hours. Hill began to study the door knob assembly and strike plate, as the three stood in silence in the doorway.

Barbara's grief was a huge, frigid lake, which was beginning to overtop the ice dam of her facade. "That's...that's OK, George...about your wife. Your family will want to be together this close to Christmas. I'll...be all right..."

"Hey, it looks like this door was originally set up to lock from the outside. What was Phil thinking of when he set that up!"

"Are you sure you don't want Angeline to come over, Barbara?"

"Yes."

"Would you like us to say a few words of prayer right now?" asked Redding gently.

"Yes, please."

130

Rod Hill headed back to the crummy and called out, "Later!" like he was leaving a keg party. George Redding and Barbara bowed their heads. George spoke quietly:

"Father in Heaven, please accept unto your bosom our beloved Phil Stone, who was a loving husband and faithful worker. We know that Phil was on a spiritual search and we pray that he has found the object of his quest in You. Be with this woman, God, in her grief...and protect her against loneliness and despair. Help us to understand why the things we find in life that mean the most to us are taken away...Help me, God, because Phil was my friend and already I miss him..."

The dam burst and Barbara walked away from the prayer into the cabin, sobbing. "Amen," said George hurriedly. "I'll send Angeline out tonight," said George reaching out to close the door.

Through her tears, Barbara could see her pup on the table eating the dinner. She pushed the dog out the door with her foot. "GET OUT OF HERE, GOD DAMN IT!" screamed Barbara at the little dog. "Not you, George," she sobbed. "Just go back to your family...I need to be alone."

George shut the door quietly and left. Barbara took the remaining cold half of leftover dinner and put it by the stove. She began pacing the floor under the open rafters. The lantern ran out of fuel and she paced in the dark. Occasionally the clouds parted to reveal a riot of stars. The full moon rose to illuminate the valley in a black and white dazzle. She opened the door and left it ajar for the dog's return.

She paced and paced and paced, twelve hours into the second trimester of her pregnancy. Barbara stood in the living room with her eyes clenched shut trying to dam the tears that would not stop. With moonbeams bouncing off her tear-washed face, she was clutching the memory of a kiss that had visited her lips just one week ago. Falling, through space-time...grief, howling, grief.

While on a crow's foot of Willoughby Ridge, touching the headwater of Hemp Hill Creek, a family of coyotes howled a chorus under the stars in celebration of their full stomachs. They had much enjoyed half of Barbara's *celebration of life* dinner. They had enjoyed the envelope in which it had been delivered. The puppy - "Gawnit" or "Damnit" or "What-Ever-You-Call-It" - never came back to join Barbara in her long loneliness.

ॐ

Hemp Hill Creek
Sunday, June 11, 1989, 11:58 hours

Barbara opened her eyes and beheld her precious daughter sitting under the skylight in the living room of the cabin. It was like the child was in a trance, breathing slowly with an expression of rapture on her face. In the brilliance of sunlight, Mossy's face glowed like an angel. The room had become quite warm and Barbara opened the door on the north side of the living room to let in a cooler breeze. Barbara went into the kitchen to ready their Sunday dinner. She called to her daughter in the next room, "Mossy, it's time!. Come!"

131

৩৵৩

As Mossy soared like an eagle up the Valley of Muddy Waters, she alighted on a high point overlooking the headwater. From this high point, she could look out over 360 degrees. She looked back down the valley, all the way to the ocean. To the south, a huge river of ice glaciated from the craggy summit of Mount Olympus. To the north was the lake-speckled country of the upper Soleduck. As she looked around, there were so many intriguing places to go, so many exciting things to explore. A cool breeze filled her nostrils with the wonderful secrets of these places. Just out of the range of her ears, she smelled a waterfall, pouring out of the subalpine basin of the upper Bogachiel and into the temperate rain forest below. Of a sudden, she realized that she had forgotten her crutches and was standing unassisted upon this promontory. At first she wobbled, but she recovered her balance. Surrounded by Creation, Mossy felt the spirit of her Creator very close to her. "Mossy, it's time!" said her Creator in the voice of her mother. The Creative Force wafted like a spirit-wind down into the basin below and rode the water over the falls into the valley that Mossy called home. "COME!" commanded the Spirit of Creation.

And as the Spirit moved down the valley upon the water, the weather gathered over Mossy's head. And from the towering cloud came a bolt of electricity that connected the rod of Mossy's body with the Creation upon which she stood. And the connection was complete and grounded. Mossy's legs began to follow the Spirit, that she called *Father in Heaven*, Which talked with the voice of her *Mother on Earth*.

"Come home to me!" commanded the Spirit again, and Mossy's legs worked to climb down from the high place onto a trail that paralleled the watercourse. One leg in front of the other, Mossy checked the birthmark on the left leg to make sure it was her own.

Running for home now, each pace consumed six feet of the 2.16 million inches that separated Mossy from her farm, one leg in front of the other. One leg in front of the other, amen, one leg in front of the other, amen, leg, amen, leg, amen, leg, ahhhmmmmmmmm...

Until Mossy was running down the driveway, towards the bridge, passing the garden...And she stopped in wonder to watch the fawn, which followed its mother on shaky legs. The voice of the Creator called from the cabin...

৩৵৩

Hemp Hill Creek
Sunday, June 11, 1989, 12:01 hours

"Mossy, come back to me!" called Barbara, starting to worry now. Her daughter was in some kind of trance. It was spooky. Her color was good, but a large cumulus cloud had eclipsed the sun and thunder rumbled down the valley. The child sat erect and rock-still in her chair under the skylight. "MOSSY! COME TO ME!" yelled Barbara, leaving her dinner preparation and starting to panic.

To Barbara, it was a true miracle and manifestation of God's holy mercy. As she walked in fear, to minister to her daughter, the child stood up, unassisted with crutches. This stopped Barbara in mid-stride. "Mother! I can walk!" announced her daughter, closing the distance between them to hug Barbara as if she had just returned from a trip. Pulling away from the embrace the child looked up at her mother's awe-struck face and said, "And that's not all...Mother, I can run like the wind. I'm going out to play with Daisy before dinner!" The child ran out the door.

The sun was back, shining down through the skylight. Barbara hurriedly pulled the dinner off of the stove and put it on the table. She went to the phone and dialed the number of her mother in Oregon. "Muth...Mother?" she said in a shaky voice.

"Barbara, honey, is something wrong?" Barbara could hear the fear in her mother's voice.

"Mom...it's Mossy..."

"Oh, my God, NO," Mrs. Beyers voice was filled with dread for news that came like this, over the phone.

"No, Mom. It's good news! It's a...miracle. Mossy can walk..." Barbara's breath caught like she was about to cry. She looked out the window and first Daisy ran by and then Mossy, in full pursuit with her arms out, reaching towards the pet. "And she can ru...ru...run..." and suddenly both women were sobbing uncontrollably. Sobbing together: tears falling in two different states; electrons moving across more than 350 miles of phone lines to unite the two with the sound of their own sobbing. Sunlight coming through the window on the roof; the child chasing the dog; dinner on the table; the sound of her mother's joy on the phone; rainbows of color splashing on her brain from the sunlight which poured into the room...And as Barbara clutched the receiver to her ear, sobbing into the transmitter and hearing the sobbing of her phone, she conjured up words from a long ago high school essay which lay in a cedar chest under her bed...

৩৯

Langley High School
Creative Writing
(Walter Chester/Third Period)
September 21, 1967
Assignment: Create an emotionally impactive picture using every day, ubiquitous articles as literary props. Hold your composition to under 200 words.

Reaching a terminal velocity in 1.17 seconds, the celestial body moves through space and time at 25.2 feet per second. Like the living planet called 'Earth' its surface is mostly NaCl suspended in liquid H2O. Light pierces the sphere, breaking into a spectrum as wide as the circumstances incident to the conception of such a globe. Photons, in collision with electrons, create molecular activity: heat. The celestial body is steered by gravity on its course through the space-time continuum. It is the conflict between surface tension and gravity that gives rise to the mythical shape of a teardrop, for in its surrender to gravity, the body is a perfect sphere. Like the other celestial bodies scattered through the cosmos, steered by gravity, pierced by light,

133

and born of passions too deep to inwardly harbor, this falling sphere is a tear of joy.

Grade C- Phil, did you read the instructions to this assignment? "...using every day, ubiquitous articles..." What is this stuff you're talking about here? Save the science for another class and use plain English. It's easier for me to understand. See me if you're having problems with the language we use in Creative Writing.

ᔕᵒᵛᔋ

Hemp Hill Creek
Sunday, June 11, 1989, 12:20 hours

"Mom, put down the phone and come out and watch the fawn. It's already trying to run!" Mossy interrupted the sob fest on the phone, as if the wonder of the young deer's genetic memory was somehow more profound than the miracle of her own restored mobility.

"I'll call you back later, Mom. Mossy wants to show me something." Barbara put down the phone and followed her dancing, bouncing daughter out to the front pasture. A newly-born fawn was nursing from its mother. The broad white splotches on the fawn's hindquarters confirmed what Barbara had feared about the gene pool of the local deer population. Without the pressure of wolves or Native Americans to push them, the deer were inbreeding.

"What should we name the baby?" asked Mossy.

"Wild deer don't have names. Biologists would refer to an individual of a species as *A1* or maybe *D611* for a deer born on June eleventh. Calling a deer *Bambi* or *John Doe* is personifying a forest creature and detracting from its wildness..."

"But MOM! This is a SPECIAL deer. Look! We're both walking in the same hour," pleaded the child. "This deer HAS TO HAVE A NAME!"

"OK. How about if we refer to her as *June Eleven* which commemorates this special deer AND special day?"

The advancing humans intimidated the doe, who moved along with the fawn dancing and bouncing beside her. "Isn't she precious?" asked Mossy, somehow intuiting that the fawn was female.

"And so are you, Mossy...precious..." murmured the human mother. Barbara's joy and hope sparkled in the sun like the dew of birth, clinging to the fur of the newborn fawn.

ᔕᵒᵛᔋ

Merchant Road, Forks
Saturday, July 1, 1989

"ON YOUR MARK!" called out Wes Depew, the mayor of Forks, as fifty or so kids jostled and assembled to run the Children's Firecracker Fun Run. Mossy Stone took her place at the starting line between Janice Star, Amy Burt and the other hot-to-trot entries, ages 12 and under. Barbara stood nervously by the

Elks Club Building, with other parents. This was not Barbara's idea of an intelligent way to celebrate Mossy's new found mobility.

"This isn't the Special Olympics," Janice Star chided Mossy. "This is a real race with prizes for the winners."

"If you get as far as the school track, where the finish line is, don't stop running," coached Amy Burt. "You have to go twice around the track to finish. But it's a whole mile and a half before you get there..."

"GET SET!" Mossy leaned into the air over the line upon which the contestants were forbidden to step for yet another second. Science, nor medicine, could explain how a child who had experienced hemaplegia resulting from profound skeletal, neurological, and muscular injury, could present with spontaneous recovery. Her affected leg was still visibly atrophied from the dysfunctional period. It was pathetic to the parents and laughable to the other kids: a convalescent kid placing herself on the starting line with children who had been running every day since school let out. But in Mossy's heart, at this moment, lay the answer to the question insoluble to science and medicine. There was neither laughter nor tears, but there burned a fire to run. There was only running. There was only...

"GO!" and before the starting pistol cracked, Mossy's heart was across the starting line and falling like an ever-accelerating body to the finish line. Her heart was a pacing pony released from the stall of convalescence and stampeding into the wilderness of health and mobility.

And Mossy's flesh was pulled along by the gravity of the heart. Her legs pumping out a cadence even faster than the pace that had brought Mossy home from her spiritual peregrinations. The clean water of Hemp Hill Creek cascaded through Mossy's cardiovascular system, like a carousel carrying red blood cells through to the alveoli of Mossy's young pink lungs where the RBC's snatched brass rings of oxygen. The clean air of Mossy's environment passed in and out of the bellows of her lungs in great, heaving gasps. Glucose from Mossy's organic and natural diet poured fuel to each straight muscle cell like nitroethanol fuel from the carburetor of a fine-tuned racing car. While Mossy's flesh struggled to catch up to the lightning strike of her heart and spirit, air exploded out of her mouth with flecks of spit. Her face flushed with the exertion of self-propulsion. "Slow down!" came Barbara's voice from somewhere behind her, but the message never found its target in the aural processor, the inferior coulliculus of Mossy's brain.

By the time Mossy reached the track, ten minutes later, she was running by herself. As she came around the track for the second time, she realized that she was lapping the rearguard of the race. The last two persons she passed on her charge to the finish line were Amy Burt and Janice Star. Mossy gave a moment's thought to a smug remark, but, instead, controlled her breathing, and passed them like they were going backwards.

There was limited cheering when Mossy broke the ribbon 00:12:15 after the starting pistol had sent her on her way. As the crowd waited in embarrassment a full one minute and thirty seconds for the arrival of their favored winners, Barbara found a parking place and made her way through the crowd. As Mossy was led to the winner's circle, she began to focus on her hearing and she could pick out snatches of conversation from the crowd. "...kid can really run like the wind...wasn't she the gimp...the fastest time yet for this race...crazy mom must have put her on steroids..."

Mossy looked around for her mother and saw Mr. Burt standing next to Reverend Star, waiting for their daughters to finish second and third. "She's made a pact with Satan," said Rev. Star. "I know the work of the devil when I see it, and that child is running with the power of a demon."

Barbara got to her daughter and, partially blinded by the flash of Richard Stokes's camera, she missed seeing the blue ribbon draped over her daughter's neck. "Did you finish?" asked Barbara.

"Yes," said the child, in total humility.

"She won," said Stokes. "Your daughter set a record. I'd like an interview, if it's OK with you two."

"Mom, can we just go home? Please?"

Barbara told Stokes to call Mossy on the phone later in the day. The mother and daughter drove home with the award Mossy had gotten for first place in the race. Thomas Burt, owner of Thrifty Save, had donated a set of My Little Ponies with fluorescent manes. They were never even taken out of the box by their new owner.

From Crutches to First Place

Ten-year-old Mossy Stone is a medical miracle and athletic wonder. The child was critically injured twenty-five months ago in the school bus accident, which claimed the life of the driver, George Smith. Mossy was trapped under a tire with the entire weight of the school bus on her crushed pelvis. Her young life hung in the balance for two weeks. For more than a year she could not move her leg or walk without crutches. Two weeks ago, she began to use her leg. Today, she won the Kid's Firecracker Fun Run and set a new record for the event: twelve minutes and fifteen seconds.

"I prayed and it made the leg as good as new!" explained Mossy in a phone interview today.

"She may have experienced a spontaneous recovery from a form of hysterical paralysis," explained her physician, Doctor Richard Dickson.

"This is some kind of sign," explained Reverend Benjamin Star, of the Assembly of God Church. The reverend witnessed Mossy finish the last two laps of the race. "There are graver things involved here than can be explained by medical science."

Store owner, Thomas Burt, who contributed the gifts for the awards, also witnessed Mossy's finish. "I hope that Mossy Stone enjoys the gift of the My Little Ponies," remarked Mr. Burt. They're on sale in the toy section at Thrifty Save this week, so drop your crutches and hurry on down!"

৩৵৶

Hemp Hill Creek
Wednesday, July 5, 1989

"Mossy, are you done with this paper or do you want to send it to your grandmother?" Barbara called out from the shade of the barn to Mossy who was trying to work a posthole digger in the easy soil around the new garden. Barbara was using the copy of <u>Knives, Spoons, and Forks</u> she got in the mail to prepare the soil for her strawberry transplants. The newspaper would hold in the moisture and suppress the growth of weeds. When the new fence was done and it was time to move the strawberries, Barbara would cut holes in the newspaper and leave it to biodegrade in the sun, in the rain, on the organic soil.

"Naw, mom," called Mossy. "It was pretty bogus."

'Bogus.' That's a funny word for a kid to use, thought Barbara as she glanced over the article.

Barbara cut out the front page on the strawberry-patch-to-be without looking at the back page. "Mom, look!" called Mossy from the hole she was digging. "I'm finding all kinds of clam shells!" Barbara went over to inspect her daughter's discovery and, sure enough, at a depth of about eight inches there was a midden layer of fire char and shell. "Is this from one of the oceans that used to be here?" asked Mossy wondrously.

"No, honey. There were three different seas and three different mountain ranges which precede this point in geological time. You can find fossilized evidence on some of the high country in the Park, but this is very recent. I would say that Otto Seigfreid had a cook out..."

"Mom, look! Bones!" Mossy bent over to pick up some small bones from the pile of glacial till, char and broken shells. "Bones, Mom." The child instinctively put one of the small bones to her nose and reported, "Gross, Mom! It smells spooky!"

There was something about the bones that caught Barbara's special interest. Squinting in the bright sunlight, something told Barbara this was not a piece of cow cooked on a grill beside clams by an old German bachelor. "What does it smell like to you, honey?" Barbara asked her daughter.

"It smells like...(sniff)...it smells...(sniff)...it smells LIKE SLOPPY JOE!" the child shrieked, dropping the bone and pinching her nose in a display of disgust.

"Let's go look these bones up!" suggested Barbara. "Daisy, leave that alone!" Barbara scolded the dog who was chewing the orthopedic discovery which Mossy had abandoned. The family of two, plus dog, repaired to the cabin where Barbara pulled out a large volume depicting bones of common mammals. Barbara spent several hours pouring over the plates of small local mammals: otter, raccoon, fisher, skunk, mountain beaver, mink, weasel, Douglas squirrel...Though the bones were small, they were thick and Barbara began to search larger mammals: coyote, fox, deer, elk, bear. Barbara checked through sea mammals, cows, pigs, dogs. She came at last to a plate of the orthopedic structure of Homo sapiens. She went to the plate on the hand and THERE IT IS...

"Mossy it's a human phalange..." said Barbara with an undertone of fear that a piece of her deceased husband had been transported across the creek and into a pile of singed clam shells. Mossy's hand again went to her nose...

ॐ

Hemp Hill Creek
Bogachiel, Valley of the Muddy Water
End of Winter on the Day of Equal Light and Dark (March 21, 1891)

Twenty-one year-old Kwalet Toweleno, sat by the cooking-fire looking out across the smoldering fields. A group of Quileute youth had come out to this camp to burn out the prairie, hunt the abundant deer that gravitated to the open spaces, and celebrate their quickly arriving adulthood. Kwalet was the 'old maid' of the group, sent along as a chaperon. The elders of the Tribe had told the youths that they must prepare themselves for the challenges of their future. Already the strange smelling, white-complectioned, hairy, men-things that rode on large sailing vessels were insinuating themselves into the Quileute culture. *'Hoquat'* (or Feces Floating on Water) the Tribe called the men-things, for want of a better name. Already the Hoquat were introducing whiskey and glass bead baubles. The aliens were beginning to unravel the culture of the Tribe the way a cedar basket unravels once it has been asked to carry a rock which was too hot for the fabric of the wood lacings.

So the youth came to these meadows for the stated purpose of firing the brush that moved in upon every clearing, but with the concomitant agenda of renewing their cultural heritage through song and story. Howeshatta had brought some whale heart and rancid blubber from a beast his father had harpooned the previous week. The youth feasted on clams, whale and deer. Then Howeshatta disappeared into the forest to search out a cedar tree worthy of being made into a canoe to carry his bride-to-be, Kalaloch ("Good Place to Land"), back to their village at the mouth of the Three Rivers. Kalaloch was so beautiful and large. Her heft evidenced her slow metabolism, but was a sign of status for the young buck lucky enough to have her hand in marriage. The husbands of large wives and children were, superficially anyway, seen as the successful hunters, fishermen and providers for their tribe.

The tongue of these people knew no written form. So strange sounding were the words upon the white man's ear that a hundred years later, the name of Kwalet's people would be spelled four different ways within a half-day's walk of her village. It was in this tongue that Howeshatta called out to her as he came out of the forest. "Poor Kwalet still sits by the cooking-fire, starving, while we pass gas from our mouths and anus to keep from exploding. Her stomach is as empty and forgotten of food as this forest is empty and forgotten of cedar. But Howeshatta has another treat for the stomachs of the Tribe's youth. Boil the water, Kwalet, and we will partake of yet another feast!"

While Kwalet used sticks for tongs to drop hot rocks from the fire into the water-filled-cedar-cooking-basket, Howeshatta went to his satchel and returned with the remains of The Hand. This would be the last ceremony for this tired piece of flesh. It was what remained of a Makah warrior who died beneath the bastion of Akolot.[3] A decade ago, while the men of the tribe were preoccupied with the main frontal attack of so many Makahs who stormed the east end of the island, it was the children huddled over the horseshoe bay on the northwest aspect of the island who had detected a band of Makahs skulking up the cliffs above the bay. A few well-placed rock boulders had repelled the invading party and killed several. One body lay on a rock ledge and was inaccessible to the retreating Makah. This body was harvested by the Quileutes and had been used for ceremonial purposes over the last decade. A few pieces of flesh were boiled away from the tendons and ligaments that still consolidated the jigsaw puzzle of bones. "We will not honor the previous owner of this hand by using his remains for our bone game," and the naked skeleton was discarded into the dying cook fire with clam shells. The serving bowl was dipped and passed among the assembled youth, many of whom had participated in the child crusade against this fallen warrior.

As the serving bowl was passed, Kwalet watched to see if her two cousins from Ozette would partake. Geographically, the Ozettes were the neighbors of the Makahs, but their blood was separated by the water that had already come to divide the two Hoquat nations of Canada and the United States. The Ozettes drank and nodded that it was good.

The bowl came to Kwalet and before partaking, she gazed into the bowl upon the flecks of flesh floating amid the water of life. *It is the fate of us all*, brooded Kwalet. "Skinny Kwalet will consume it all!" someone joked. As she held her face over the bowl, inhaling the pungent vapor of the warrior-gone-to-soup, another smell came to Kwalet's olfactory. Looking up from the bowl at the smoke of the dying fire, she saw that, with evening, the wind was changing to move down the valley. A strange smell on this new breeze and Kwalet passed the bowl to give her attention to the scent.

She motioned the others to silence and pointed to her nose in such a way as to indicate the strange scent on the wind. It smelled like...**HOQUAT!** A Hoquat was up-valley from them! It was too much to believe! Was nothing sacred from the meddling, disease infested, stinking white, floating feces?

One after the other, the youth made the sign of holding their noses against the strange wind which blew down-valley...As if they could hold out the stench on the wind of the future: The strange wind which would give svelte Kwalet in marriage to the source of the stink, Chris Morganroth. The strange wind, which would call the Tribe "savages" and "barbarians" and prohibit the skirmishes which had provided their slaves and ceremonial soup. The strange wind which would blow a draft across the youth of the Tribe, sucking them into an army and sending them to far corners of the globe to die in battle without touching their ancestral enemies. As the Hoquat seemed to use his nose only to wrinkle in disgust, the strange perfumed and fumigated wind of the white man would cover all the smell of Nature and deprive the Tribe of the wonderful sense of olfactory

---

[3] 'Alkolot' means 'The Way Up' in the dialect of the Quileute. The island fortress next to the village was easily defended against the marauding Makah, who were more closely related to the natives from Vancouver Island. The island was renamed by James Swan to be more pronounceable to the Anglo tongue. See page 76, Gods and Goblins, Smitty Parratt.

which had existed for millennia as their primary window into the world. In the twentieth century, their noses would no longer lead them to elk, salmon and fresh water. The tribe would follow their noses into the wind of the future only because it was the forward-most facing protuberance upon their faces. The strange wind of the future would breathe across the tongue of the Tribe and would blow away the taste for the life-giving river and leave it thirsty for the poisonous beverages of Pepsi and Schlitz. The People would be blown from the river's corridor of transportation; and the asphalt highway leading to the Tribe would be scattered with empty bottles like the hollow vessels of the Tribe's youth. The strange wind will blow across your name, Kwalet, and you will be called "Susie Morganroth," just as the bogus wind will blow across the tongue of the Tribe and cause them to talk the gibberish of the Hoquat. The connection with the elk, whale, and cedar will be uprooted by the fierce blowing wind and the children of the youth who sit around you will blow along the Hoquat's asphalt highways like empty beer cans in the wind. In the wake of that wind...the great culture, the lifestyle...the glory of the Tribe, will blow down from the Tree of Life and lie like discarded skeletal remains on a pile of fire-charred midden.

Let go of your nose, Kwalet. Let go of your past. Behold the smell of your husband: the smell that has dominated the eastern territory for the last two centuries. It is the smell of your future upon a wind that will blow across the last corner of your continent. Let go...

ら﹏﹏

Hemp Hill Creek
Wednesday, July 5, 1989

"... of your nose, Mossy. You're being overly theatrical. It didn't stink to you that much before we discovered it was human."

"Yes, it DID STINK, too. I SAID it stunk, didn't I?"

"You said it smelled 'spooky.'"

"I said it smelled like sloppy joe!"

"OK. That's what you said. Sloppy joe wasn't invented when this hand went into the ground. You don't make sloppy joe with clams. How does this bone smell like sloppy joe?"

"It smells like meat that's been left in the pot so long you can't guess what it is!"

"You're way off. For one thing, sloppy joe doesn't have human phalanges in it..."

"It doesn't have heart valves in it either if you believe the recipe. These bones are scary!" The child poured water from the tap which was plumbed into the creek and gulped it down. "Mom, can I run up to the road and back with Daisy?" she asked, changing the subject.

Immediately the mother's protections asserted themselves. "No, honey, you're too young to be running on our road by yourself. This is cougar country and there have been a few incidents on the Peninsula of sick people trying to abduct pretty young things like you..."

140

"But, mom, you still let me ride the school bus and that's not safe either. We don't have any working locks on our doors, so you must feel that it's pretty safe out here. The road is where we live, too. Are we supposed to be afraid of where we live?" Barbara was turning the bones over and over, studying them for clues. "Mom?"

"It's too hot. You'll get heat stroke."

"Mom, that's bogus! We've been working in the sun all day and that's OK."

Barbara calculated the distance and realized that her daughter would cover the six miles in less than an hour. She could let the child start out and follow in the car to make a safety check. Why deny her the freedom of mobility they had prayed so fervently to obtain? "OK. Up to the end of the county road and straight back. No stopping to explore..."

"Yippie! Daisy, COME!" The child and canine exploded out the door and were gone like a changing wind. Barbara drank water and ambled out into the hot sun to finish the fence line.

Under the hot sun of a decade that had brought three of the hottest years in recorded history, Barbara dug the final corner post of her new garden site, while Mossy ran. Barbara fought down her feelings of protection for the child.

With each mouthful of the posthole digger, Barbara's tool bit into another century of the past. Each bite of dirt tasted a country that was three meters further from the advancing Pacific and thirty centimeters lower than the land being uplifted by the colliding tectonic plates, which pushed the face of the Olympic Peninsula into the erosive belt-sander of rain.

Barbara accepted the mystery of the skeleton hand with equanimity. As a person with a strong background in biology, she accepted that the mysteries of life and circumstance could not always be solved with the tools of science.

The sweat ran down Barbara's brow, dripping from her nose into the hole she dug, landing on sterile soil that had long ago forgotten human secretion. Barbara used the shovel to widen the hole, so she could get down five feet for the corner post, which would be the keystone of the new garden fence. The digging was easy in the glacial outwash, but the work was exhausting. She began dressing up the hole to accept the four-meter cedar post she had purchased for the corner post and her digger hit something solid as a Spruce limb. She hit it again and brought it up with the digger and let the blades drop their contents upon the enormous pile of glacial till. There, on the sand, under the sun of the twentieth century, was a fluted spearhead and what she recognized from her recent study of human orthopedics to be a tibia/Homo sapiens. This was evidence of Early Man! Pre-"Native" America. The ancestors of these bones continued south leaving what became a food-rich, mild environment to the nearer Mongolian throngs which would become the Quileute and other coastal nations of "Natives."

Barbara was excited and began work with a shovel. She cut through the grass to form a one-by-two-meter rectangle and began throwing the dirt into a heap. Digging and digging, the sweat was stinging her eyes so that she could hardly see what she was doing. Digging...

ॐ

Hemp Hill Creek
Monday, December 24, 1979

...and digging. Barbara could hardly see what she was doing: Cutting through the frosty grass, through the frozen few inches of ground, the tears stinging her eyes. What a strange way to be spending the day before Christmas: digging the grave for her husband.

It at least felt good to be back on her little piece of land. The morning had been spent on the pay phone by the Bogachiel Store trying to contact a human in the Governor's office to allow the burial she was about to effect. A recent wrinkle in State bureaucracy (R.C.W. 68.40.100) required a $25,000 endowment before a family could inter their dead into the ground of their farms. While the law provided for boxless burial with the family's choice of landscaping, from orchard to asphalt, the $25,000 provided for the maintenance of the plot in perpetua. No one in the Governor's office had agreed that respecting the last request of the deceased was more imperative than mowing grass. At noon, the office had shut down with the employees going home to their living families with whom they discussed the crazy woman's request.

Barbara had called George Redding and Rick Larson. She asked if they could pick up Phil's body, pretending to represent Mount Olympus Funeral Home. With the Forks Hospital calling in temps to work Christmas Eve and the hospital staff cut back to skeleton size, the scheme would probably work. She called Pastor Al Traces of the Prince of Peace Lutheran Church and explained her situation. The reverend put aside the final preparations for the evening candlelight service and began preparing for a simple funeral service.

The nurse at the charge desk led Redding and Larson to the only body in the hospital's mini-morgue and surrendered it without question. They wheeled the body out to the rear parking lot through the Emergency Entrance to find a Forks Police Officer putting a violation notice on Redding's pickup for parking in an Ambulance Only zone. They wheeled the body over to Larson's compact and surreptitiously put the body in the back seat. The Officer saw the body being removed and got Larson's license plate. He checked inside with the nurse and a call was made to the 24-hour Mt. Olympus number where they learned that the Stones were not clients of the only funeral service in town. While the officer chattered on the radio, Redding told Larson he had to stop off at Rod Hill's house. Redding would need to kick his coworker in the butt to get Hill to attend this impromptu funeral. Richard Stokes picked up the chatter about the Stone body-snatching on his police scanner at home. He made an educated guess about where the body might be going. With no immediate family or close friends to occupy this afternoon preceding Christmas, Stokes was in the mood to solve a police mystery. The cold, clear afternoon offered release from being cooped up indoors, holding out against the rain. Stokes took his overcoat and camera and got into his Volvo to drive south on Highway 101 to the address of the deceased on the upper Bogachiel.

Barbara finished with the two-meter-by-one-meter-by-one-meter hole and went inside the half-finished cabin to wash her hands and wait for the few funeral participants to arrive. Barbara removed the clothing she had kept in a cedar box. Her father had given her the box as a hope chest at Christmas exactly fifteen years ago. She got together a few keepsakes of her late husband, including some essays he had written, and placed them in the box. She filled out an order for a Paw Paw tree, to plant on the grave, and a Weeping Cherry as a birthtree for the child expected in six months. She sat beside the wood stove, waiting with the cedar box. She looked up at the blue sky, through the open rafters and began to cry. Barbara leafed through the few keepsakes she had of her husband. She selected an essay he had done in high school to read by the graveside. She looked at her watch and figured it might be another half-hour wait, which seemed interminable. She went out to her garden with the cedar box to pass the time.

Barbara was digging in the soil of her garden, mixing kelp meal and rock phosphate when a Volvo came down the long drive through the meadow. The car stopped and the driver rolled down the passenger window to say, "Excuse me, miss. I'm looking for the Stone residence. Is it back this way?"

"You're on it," said Barbara wondering if this city slicker had been sent by the Governor to mitigate the home burial which was about to occur without sanction.

"Then...you're Barbara Stone?" asked the dude, getting out of the Volvo.

"Yes. What's left of her."

"I'm sorry for your loss. I'm Richard Stokes. I'm the editor for <u>Knives, Spoons and Forks</u>. You get it delivered out here to your mailbox, I presume?"

"I've seen the paper," Barbara said, noncommittally, lapsing into silence and continuing to work with the soil.

Stokes got tired of waiting. "I heard on the scanner that your husband's body was taken without authorization. I'm wondering what you might know about why such an odd occurrence might happen."

"Not much that I'm willing to discuss."

"Mrs. Stone," countered Stokes looking suspiciously at the cedar box which sat waiting by the garden fence. "You wouldn't be considering cremating the remains of your husband on this property?"

"...."

"If you are planning some home service here, may I participate as an observer? It would make an interesting human-interest story."

"I'm not interested in the tragic details of my life being held up for public entertainment! There's no story here for you and your readers, Mr. Stokes. Excuse me if I don't invite you to stay."

"Mrs. Stone, let me remind you that I caught wind of this body-snatching on the police scanner. The cops may show up any minute. It may be in your best interest to have me here. The police aren't going to push around a bereaved widow with the press standing right there. Let me stay and I will respect whatever privacy you require while ensuring compassionate treatment in the event of police intervention."

Barbara mulled this over for a minute. "You can stay, but no pictures of where we inter the body."

"So you're planning home burial, not cremation?"

"Burial, of course, what made you think cremation?"

"That cedar box. I thought maybe it was to be used for an urn."

"It's some papers and letters from my late husband."

"May I look at them?"

"They're all kind of personal," said Barbara, leaving a smudge of dirt as she brushed hair from her tear-streaked face. She looked at Stokes and, for a moment thought she saw a man of compassion who wanted to understand her grief. "Yeah, go ahead..." Barbara went back to her digging and stirring.

Stokes opened the box and removed a logger's tin hat which had a crushed back rim. He looked inside and there was blood and what looked like some gray matter. "Jesus!" exclaimed Stokes, dropping the hard hat onto the soft dirt at his feet. "Excuse me," he said laying the hard hat beside the box and looking over the papers inside. He glanced over about 20 letters addressed to Barbara from the deceased and then studied a couple of high school assignments in creative writing class. There was a sheaf of technical notes labeled, *The Cosmic Clock.* "May I read some of this in the car?" asked Stokes

"Suit yourself," said Barbara.

Stokes took the essays into his Volvo and started the engine to heat up the cab. The writing was mediocre, but it served to excite the tabloid editor who featured himself as a creative writer. He was working on his own little bit of creative writing when the renegade funeral procession arrived in three cars: the Lutheran Reverend Al Traces and George Redding, followed by two vehicles driven by Rick Larson and Rod Hill.

৩৵৶

"*To every thing there is a season, and a time to every purpose under heaven:* I read from the book of <u>Ecclesiastes</u>, the third chapter." Of all the funerals over which Reverend Harness had presided, this Christmas Eve, graveside service was the weirdest. "*A time to be born, and a time to die; a time to plant, and a time to pluck up that which is planted...*" The widow had insisted that the clothing be removed from the deceased, which seemed pagan enough. The body lay next to the open grave with frost collecting on the gaping head wound. "*A time to kill, and a time to heal...*" Now a cold, freezing wind blew across the grave, causing the reverend to shudder. The widow had placed the collected clothing in a cedar chest and had taken out something, which she evidently intended to read. "*A time to weep, and a time to laugh; a time to mourn, and a time to dance...*" He would have to hurry this thing along if he wanted to be of any help with preparations for the candlelight Christmas service in town tonight. "*A time to rend, and a time to sew; a time to keep silence, and a time to speak...*At this time, let's lower Phil into his resting place."

The two loggers stepped forward leaving the widow standing next to the cub editor for the goofy town newspaper. They had a piece of manila rope, which they looped under the body. Good. For a minute the reverend thought they would just throw the body into the hole. As the head dangled from its balance on the rope, a large piece of gray matter fell out of the wound and hit the bottom of the grave with a soft thud.

"Holy Mary!" said the logger called Rod Hill. "That sounded like a turd hitting the floor of a shithouse pit!"

"A time to keep silence, Rod!" commanded the burley logger named George.

The body met the bottom of the grave, the rope was removed and the reverend reached out to gather a handful of dirt to throw on the body, but the loose dirt had frozen to a crust. The reverend kicked the frozen dirt, but it did not yield to his attack. He decided to dispense with this symbolic portion of the service. "Barbara, I see you have something there you want to read," said Reverend. "Why don't you proceed with that."

The widow stood over the grave. In the late, long-angled rays of the afternoon sun, tears sparkled like fire opals in her eyes. Her face was smudged with dirt and it occurred to the reverend that perhaps she had dug the grave herself. She was having trouble seeing the words on the page, through the tears. She spoke, "This is an essay about death that Ph... Ph... Phil wrote when he was in eighth gr... grade. His teacher didn't like it, b... but I always have. It so reminds me of h... h... him." She began trying to read, "L...L... Life is a ti... tiny school....... with two doors....leading.........."

"Ms. Stone," interrupted the editor. "I looked over that essay about an hour ago and enjoyed it very much. Would you like me to read it?"

"Yes, please," said the widow, holding out the paper for Stokes to join her at the grave.

ॐ∽♥

This was the best human-interest story to come down the road for Stokes since the blow of 1979, which heralded his arrival on the Olympic Peninsula. He could feel the writing juices in his blood coming to a boil. Widow Stone had pretty much put the kibosh on picture taking, so Stokes was trying to drink in everything with his eyes. "The Classroom, by Phil Stone," he announced before he even looked at the page. He repeated the sentence he had heard from the widow, "Life is a tiny school with two doors leading from it..." Then Stokes focused his attention on the document and tried to freeze it in his mind the way his toes were frozen in his loafers. Stokes was trying to drink the document like a college kid shotgunning a beer:

Langley High School
Creative Writing
(Walter Chester/Third Period)
December 19, 1967

Assignment: Create a metaphor (not a simile) on a subject of your choice using props that you might find in this classroom. Keep your composition to under 200 words and show that you understand the difference between the two literary techniques.

Life is a tiny school with two doors leading outside.

Warding over classroom are the stern and humorless teachers: Mr. Pain and Miss Fortune. The children of the Human Spirit titter and fidget in their seats as their teachers attempt to impress them with the grim reality of life. Occasionally, the children's ebullience exceeds the teacher's ability to control the mood of the classroom and the Principal is summoned.

"Silence!" yells Death, and the children obediently place their heads on their desks and wait in quietness as the lights are turned off and the blinds turned down on the windows. Death beckons the stern teachers from the building out of one door and discusses the intricacies of authority. While inside the classroom, the spring wind of eternity blows papers from desks and rattles the blinds. As one by one, the children cautiously raise their heads, they see the blinds blown aside and the other door to their school room standing wide open.

Death stands on one side of the school with Pain, Fortune and the family members, who are called whenever Death's presence is required. "See," says Death, pointing to the school. "The children always obey me. You cannot allow them to question your authority." While on the other side of the empty building, the children of the Human Spirit laugh, skip, and jump across the playground of the cosmos.

Stokes stopped reading out loud and his eyes again scanned the teacher's panning remarks:

GRADE: C- Phil, this is more of the same esoteric, depressive, far flung cow flop you were coming up with last September. You haven't proven to me that you know the difference between a metaphor and a simile. Without counting, I would say you went over 200 words and I resent your innuendo that the school staff here are somehow archangels of death and suffering. You should be proud to attend an institution which allows free speech such as your own. To get a better idea of what we want for this assignment, you may want to look at Sally Single's metaphor comparing the American flag in this room to a suit of armor or Hugh Helm's comparison of the windows of this classroom to different career opportunities.

Stokes stood in silence next to the grave of this young author whose career opportunity had led to Death at the young age of 29. Stokes waited for the reverend to bail him out of the awkward silence which had taken the funeral party in the cold, cutting wind of late December. Reverend Harness rose to the occasion. "Now would be an appropriate time for anyone who feels the call to share their feelings about Phil."

Rick Larson stepped forward to the grave. "I'll always remember Phil as being a great sport and fair player. He was a hero. I remember that blow last February when George's leg got busted. I remember Phil climbing those snags, without spurs, and tying off the tops..." Stokes' memory traveled back to his own harrowing experiences during that wind event. "He'll always be a friend to me and I know I'm going to miss him. George..." ended Larson inviting the burley logger to the open grave.

"I've never seen a man climb a tree like Phil," began Redding, as if being monkey-like was the highest manifestation of the species. "I've never worked with a more productive bushler, nor one that understood better how to make gravity work for him. I've never known a more intellectual man, not that that's saying a lot with the company I keep. In addition to being the most skilled faller I ever worked with, he was my friend. I was so ha... happy for Phil when Barbara and he got hitched." It looked to Stokes like the big man was going to cry. "What was he thinking when he dropped that spruce onto the top of that ma... maple? I'll miss him so..." The big brute Redding was actually crying. He stepped back and gave the logger Rod Hill a nudge to say some appropriate words in parting with his former coworker.

Rod Hill stood next to the open grave beside Barbara Stone and looked into the gloom of the grave on the lifeless face of Phil Stone. He looked like he was trying hard not to laugh. "As for what Philip - I mean Phil - was thinking...I'm guessing it wasn't logging. I agree with George, that this man had a talent for cutting and climbing trees, but he couldn't keep his big brain on the matters at hand and now its scattered on both sides of the river..."

"Rod! For crying out loud!" chastised George Redding. The widow Stone was walking away from the service with her hand to her face and the reverend and Forest Service biologist were chasing her. Stokes wished he had the camera he had left in the Volvo as the loggers went nose to nose. "Look what you did, Rod. You made poor Barbara cry!"

"I didn't make her cry. Her husband's dead, is why she's crying. I'm not going to lie about what put him in the grave. Besides, it's time to get back to our own families..."

The big logger grabbed up a shovel, which Barbara had left behind a tree, and pushed it into Hill's hands. "Go ahead and bury Phil. The police could show up and we want him underground. I'll go pay our respects to Barbara." Redding stomped off.

As Stokes began retreating across the bridge to the relative warmth of his vehicle, Hill took a couple of half-hearted stabs at the frozen dirt with the shovel. He threw down the shovel and looked both ways. Undetected, Stokes stopped on the bridge to ascertain what the logger was about. Both of Hill's hands disappeared in front of him and the sound of a splashing stream told the editor that the logger was micturating into the grave of his fallen coworker. This funeral was getting more bizarre at every juncture. Stokes returned to his Volvo to get his camera. He started his car and sat for a few minutes with the heater and fan on full blast. Hill came across the bridge, got into his car, and drove off. A few minutes later the Reverend Harness crossed the bridge, got into his car, and left. Stokes checked his camera for film. He got out with the camera concealed under his jacket. The biologist, Larson, and logger, Redding, were coming across the bridge.

"She's burying him by herself," announced the logger. "That's how she wants it, so we're taking our leave. Thanks for staying in case the police came to give us a hard time. But they never showed up, so maybe it's best if we all left."

"I'll just pay my respects and go home to get warm," answered the newspaperman. Merry Christmas," he called out to Larson and Redding as he walked across the bridge to where the widow was breaking up the frost-locked soil with a pick. He stood on the bridge quietly as Larson drove off with Redding. He pulled out his camera and shot several pictures: photons bouncing off the grieving woman and passing through the camera lens where they were frozen in time as they struck crystals of silver iodine on the cellulose film. The pictures of the widow, digging first with the pick, then shoveling with the spade, throwing dirt upon her dead husband - somehow they would be less poignant without the sobbing and crying which came from her direction. The smell of freshly-turned dirt on the frosty air reached the reporter's nose. Having filled in the hole with dirt, the widow began a wheelbarrow shuttle of wood chips to cover and disguise the grave.

It was cold. He had the pictures he needed. He returned to his Volvo, started the engine, and drove off. Just before he pulled out onto Highway 101 in the twilight of Christmas Eve, a Forks P.D. cruiser and Jefferson County deputy's wagon passed Stokes' Volvo on their way down the road. Stokes wanted to sit by his propane heater and write. He kept driving.

❧

The Garden of Grief
by Richard Stokes
December 24, 1979

In her garden of grief grow many weeds, flowers and a strange, bittersweet harvest. In the spring of grief, the weather is tempestuous with convulsive sobs and torrential tears. The low-hanging clouds and mist are so thick that the grieving gardener cannot see from one end of the plot to another. In the summer of grief, the garden begins to sprout unwelcome foliage: financial insecurity, behavioral change, family distress, anger and irritability. The gardener toils under a hot, dry sun of loneliness and celibacy to keep the weeds from over-running the bittersweet fruit of tender remembrances. The fall harvest of grief finds the gardener clutching a family photograph to her breast, trying to fill the aching emptiness that lies therein; returning to a cedar chest to feel and smell the clothes of her lost love for the ten thousandth time; looking deep into the folds and recesses of the recliner chair, trying once again to hang flesh on the spirit abiding there. In the death of winter, the garden plot of grief looks much like the neighboring plot of joy...but for the seeds in the ground.

❧

Hemp Hill Creek
July 5, 1989

Barbara was breaking up the soil with her pick and shoveling with her spade. She had to be careful of where she was digging because, through her sweat and tears, she could hardly see the exposed bones next to where she was striking. *Tears?* She had to think: *Why am I crying?* The ghost of a memory had visited her and left its calling card on her tear-streaked face and in the knot that clenched her stomach. She was trying to recall the memory that had so abused her when a little voice spoke, "What-cha-doeen, Mom?" Mossy had returned from her run.

"I've got something really exciting here, Mossy. I found another bone, but this one is REALLY OLD. That spearhead is evidence of tribes that arrived here just as this country came out of ice. HEY, GET THAT BONE AWAY FROM DAISY!"

The archeological treasure was rescued from the dog. Mother and daughter worked together digging out the site in what turned out to be a week-long project. Occasionally, the dog was used for digging out corners and tight spots. As they dug, Barbara began to appreciate the importance of the discovery. She considered calling the University of Washington, or Washington State University (which had managed the Ozette dig until it was reburied in 1980). But, she came back in her mind to the Manis Mastodon Site in Sequim, where a farmer had found a partially butchered woolly mammoth and spearheads similar to Barbara's find. The farm had become a roadside attraction. Barbara and Mossy decided to keep their find a secret.

When the site was roughly excavated, Barbara brought over a charged garden hose, with a fine nozzle, and old toothbrush. She began clearing the glacial till from the heap of bones that lay at the floor of the two-meter cube they had dug out of the earth.

After five days of work, Barbara and Mossy studied the matrix of bones. There was a story here. There was a pit within a pit where vertical cut lines defined the original pit into which these bones had been interred. It was a grave. There were the bones of an adult, malnourished female. The missing teeth and dimples at the back of her skull attested to her prolonged hunger. There were the collected bones of an infant male lying face down over the pelvic girdle of the adult female. The skeleton of a child lay beside the adult, also a female. On the ribs and entwined with the ulnas and radius bones of the child was another small skeleton; this a canine of some sort. This was the only skeleton showing trauma. The canine's skull was crushed as if by a rock. It made no sense that a coyote had been killed visiting the grave. Surely, hunters would have eaten it. It seemed unlikely that coyotes had established themselves on the Olympic Peninsula when primitive man threw fluted spearheads into the raging flesh of the woolly mammoth.

Two A-6 fighters from Whidbey Island rocketed through the sky over the farm, practicing dogfight maneuvers. There were a couple of tools and some oddities in the grave, as well. There was half of a huge bone, presumably that of a mammoth. Beside the bone were three stones, one appeared to be a flat piece of limestone with primitive stick drawings. Of the other two, one was fist sized; the other dish shaped. There were small seeds in the stone dish, and Barbara took two back to the cabin to identify. They turned out to be Engelmann spruce and Barbara put them in fertile soil to see if they would germinate. One of them would germinate and be planted as a dwarf tree next to the garden fence. A seed that fell asleep in the sterile glacial till when packs of wolves chased woolly mammoths across savannah and dwarf forests, had awakened into a world in which strange mechanical beasts roared across the sky, eating huge quantities of fuel refined from plants and animals that lay down in the ground many millennia before the birth of the spruce seed.

Barbara was standing in the grave, photographing the piece of limestone. "What can we make of this, Mossy?" Barbara asked her daughter as she loaded another 36-exposure roll of black and white Plus Pan X into her thirty-five millimeter camera. Mossy jumped into the soggy pit beside her mother and put her nose to the stone. "Hey, careful there! Don't disturb anything. I'm not done taking pictures."

"The rock smells like it's from the ocean and the blue stuff is berry juice," announced Mossy from her spectrographic nose.

"Well, I don't believe you can smell stuff that ancient, but the limestone would be from an ancient sea. There is rock out by Shi Shi beach that's 50 million years old. The blue ink could be berry juice and that would explain why it's etched into the stone: the acidic juice burned the alkaline stone. What do you see in the picture? Are those people? And what's that line running across the top? Is that the horizon?"

"Mom, the line is over there!" exclaimed Mossy, pointing to Reade Hill. And, sure enough, studying the inked line against the skyline, there was a match. One could make out the large granite erratic poised on the hill above the Bogachiel. "Only the line is flatter than the hill," observed Mossy.

"Well, Reade Hill would have grown almost a hundred feet in that time. The stick figures there remind me of you and me," said Barbara noticing that the taller of the two was ornamented with breasts. "Look at those big creatures in the picture where the elk hang out in the morning! Those are woolly mammoth! And that's the sun up on top of the horizon melting the ice upriver. What's that stick figure next to the sun? Is that supposed to be God? What does this say to you, Mossy?" Barbara asked, appealing to the child's imagination.

Mossy smelled the piece of limestone like a bloodhound. "That's the sun, but the guy next to it is like the father who died..." she smelled it again. "It says, 'This is a farm.'
It says, 'A warmer day is coming.' It reminds me of something I've smelled before."

"Let me guess: sloppy joe?"

"No, Mom. It's something even sadder."

"Mossy, you can't smell sadness. Sadness doesn't have a smell."

"Remember when I was in the hospital on my birthday and you brought Daisy and some get-well cards to cheer me up?"

"Yes," said Barbara, remembering the shepherd's pie hanging from the ceiling.

"It smells like the card my grandmother sent: the one she cried on. It's sadness like that with a great loneliness mixed in with it."

"Mossy, you can't smell sadness and loneliness. These bones and artifacts are over ten thousand years old. I'm not sure I believe that you smelled tears on that card, but you can't smell sadness that happened some ten millennia ago...Wait a minute! The infant is so small. It's prenatal. The adult died in childbirth. The young girl...she's got no sign of trauma. But the dog...it IS a dog...it's been killed. They were all starving, but they didn't eat the dog! The father of the family was lost. The mother died in childbirth and the girl was left alone with her dog. She dug a grave for her mother and killed the dog so it wouldn't suffer. She lay down beside...," Barbara was crying again and Mossy came out of the pit to hold onto her. The smell of the great loneliness followed her out of the grave. There was too much sadness for Mossy to feel vindication.

Eight

"A tree's a tree. How many more do you need to look at?"
- **Ronald Reagan** (b. 1911), U.S. Republican politician, President. Speech, 12 Sept. 1965. Quoted in: *Sacramento Bee* (California, 12 March 1966). Reagan later denied having made this statement.

Mossy and Barbara existed in relative bliss for the several years preceding and after Mossy's puberty. Theirs was a nuclear family reduced to the finite limit of two. It was like a hydrogen atom in it's basic simplicity. But their relationship was more akin to the orbiting of two sister suns: falling into one another with the same velocity as passing one another by; each body imposing equal gravity upon the other and behaving within those constraints.

To Barbara there were the garden and homestead chores on weekdays, Saturday hikes with Mossy, and Sunday talks with her mother on the telephone. There was the joy of Mossy's mobility and of raising her in an environment which pulsed with the pristine life forces of a major unadulterated ecosystem. Her finances were a balance of income won from selling produce once a week at the Farmer's Market, and State Labor and Industry support which would continue until Mossy's eighteenth birthday. The never ending complications of deer violating the garden fence or water escaping its plumbing were largely unobtrusive into the larger contentment of Barbara's life.

To Mossy there was the barely tolerable arena of school punctuated with blissful afternoons with her dog and mother. There was endless exploring to be had with either a microscopic or macroscopic perspective. To Mossy belonged the mobility of a child who has not been ensnared by the inactivity of television. On occasion, she watched educational movies with her mother, but, more often than not, the explorations shared on a Saturday afternoon were more active: into the woods and along the creek on nice days or into a greenhouse with a Ruper lens when it stormed. She celebrated her mobility with regular running of her dog in the woods and across a wide network of logging roads. That Mossy had no friends her own age or compatriots at school was no great burden for her, given the pleasant and healthful backdrop of her lifestyle.

In time, the sapling that was Mossy Stone ceased the apical growth that took her to a height of six feet. In the maturity of human tree-hood, she developed bosom boughs. While a pubic tangle grew at one end of her reproductive stem, no seed or fruit would ever issue from the other end.

Mossy became mildly obsessive about her running. Barbara worried about Mossy over-stressing the bones that had depended upon surgical pins for their mooring. In spite of the catastrophic injury years previous, Mossy grew stronger and more confident in her running. As a freshman, Mossy resisted attempts to recruit her into the high school track team. Her strength in movement was a personal expression of joy in her surroundings and a track seemed a poor arena for this exuberance. Weather was not an issue in her running and, as the crisp fall air of October surrendered to the monsoons of November, Mossy splashed across submerged logging roads, pushing through rain-laden salmonberry. The gray evenings grew darker and still Mossy ran into the evening. Stormy November gave way to occasionally icy December.

Running through temperate rain forest, on a path pioneered by Chris Morganroth, below the 48th parallel, during waning daylight, as the third planet reached mid-orbit around its mother star, Mossy came to a decision: She wanted to run another competitive event. She wanted a focal point for her training. She remembered the wind in her hair and the adrenal rush of the Firecracker Fun Run she had entered several years previous. She wanted to push the envelope forward and the target of the spring Olympia marathon seemed an appropriate address. Running hard toward a new year, breaking a skin of ice which had formed over an unavoidable mud puddle, Mossy's footprints stretched back across the muddy trail. Each footprint defining an epoch of time: footprints that stretched back across the joys and sorrows of this year of 1996; back to a single footprint framed by two crutch prints; back to the dancing exuberant footprints of a happy child; back to the wobbly first steps of the toddler; back to the first steps away from the mother who waited, in the growing darkness, in the valley below, for the return of her daughter...

෴

Hemp Hill Creek
Saturday, December 21, 1996, 16:40 hours

As darkness took the valley, Barbara set out dinner and waited for the return of Mossy. Her mood hinged on depression. The darkest night of the year carried an indelible memory of the winter solstice of 1979 and all that was lost on that short day.

Sixteen years later, there was still keening and a visceral tension that could constipate prune juice. On this day, Barbara's memory became like a finger held out over flame then dragged across the open eye.

She saw George Redding and Rod Hill on her doorstep with Phil Stone's crushed tin hat covered with blood. She stood at the open grave with the cold wind blowing over the naked body of her deceased husband. She sat crying in her rocking chair as Al Traces and George Redding tried to comfort her. Barbara is tearing at the frozen pile of dirt with a pick and throwing it onto the dead face of her husband, which is somehow wet and steaming. She feels something tickling the back of her neck. It is a wide, cold bed that waits for her on that Christmas Eve and a cold, hopeless morning that breaks the next day...

෴

Hemp Hill Creek
Tuesday, December 25, 1979, 09:15 hours

Barbara was overwhelmed by the enormity of the task of building a livable farm from the half-finished projects, which represented the fruit of the last three months labor. She took a hammer up to the rafters to begin nailing up the cedar tongue and groove roofing, but everything was iced up and she couldn't risk a fall.

The Hydraulics Project Approval for the micro-hydroelectric had arrived and Barbara dearly wanted lights for the long nights. She began to unroll the second of ten 300-foot rolls of two-inch polybutylene pipe. The pipe would provide the head and flow to the small turbine.

Anyone who doubts that Satan and the Power of Darkness has a physical manifestation on earth has never tried to work a coil of two-inch poly pipe by himself. Barbara tied the first running end to the cinder block race-box which Phil had built for the turbine. It took Barbara three hours to unroll the first section of pipe, cutting through the dense tangle of brush and roots to get the pipe as low to the ground as possible. On the second run, Barbara tried to anchor the running end under some exposed roots. She began to unroll the pipe and the running end escaped its mooring and whistled by her head to join the coil over her shoulder. She laid out a fallen alder limb to hold the rebellious end to its root anchor and again stepped into the coils to push through the sword fern and devil's club. The running end again defeated its fastening. Like her husband, four days previous, Barbara heard the whistling of the impending blow. The escaped end of pipe hit her in the back of the head like a flyswatter and she went down seeing colors and stars. She lay sobbing on the ground with the hopelessness of her effort.

This is how George Redding and Rick Larson found her. When they arrived at the property a little after noon, they looked around for the young widow. They wandered over to the hydroelectric site and saw the run of pipe taking off into the woods. Larson put his ear to the opening of the pipe and heard Barbara crying from 300 feet away. They arrived to help Barbara to her feet and say the words that somehow pulled hope out of the pit of despair. While Barbara rubbed her head and mumbled thank you's, the two men set about subduing the demon which abided in the flexed coils. In half an hour, they moved on to the next coil; in fifteen minutes to the next. By four p.m. the three had installed a temporary intake, wired the batteries to the turbine, the cabin to the batteries and turned on the two-inch gate valve to watch thirteen amps pushing out from the turbine into the batteries. Barbara began cooking dinner for the men in the bright artificial light of the new system, but they excused themselves: George Redding to his family and Rick Larson to his frozen dinner by the television.

The next morning the two were back and the subroof went up with the three taking care on the ice-slick rafters not to surrender to gravity. By noon, the downstairs roof was roughed in with a skylight and Barbara was tacking on the shake while Larson and Redding slapped on the loft roof and skylight. The cedar steamed under the gaze of the afternoon sunlight. By evening when the men left, the only view of the sky was through the glass in the roof. Where the windows in the walls were absent, plastic was stapled for temporary insulation.

Redding and Larson continued, on Thursday, helping Barbara put the homestead into a livable condition: water and electrical lines buried, hinged windows installed, a septic tank dug with a backhoe belonging to Mayr Brothers, light fixtures installed in the dark spots of the cabin. In five days of work, a focused but dynamic sense of mission had guided the three; and the homestead, while not finished, was cozy and inviting. That Sunday afternoon, Barbara argued with Rick and George that enough had been accomplished and that they should spend Monday in their own pursuits. She invited George and his family and Rick to return on Tuesday for a New Year's feast that she would prepare in the new habitat. Remembering that Rod Hill had been at the funeral, Barbara asked George to invite him and his family.

"The Hills have a new baby boy," commented George. "So Rod's been pretty busy lately. At least that's what he told me when I asked him if he could lend a hand out here."

"Well, go ahead and ask him, anyway," said Barbara.

Barbara spent Monday, December 31, 1979, cooking salmon, baking two pies, preparing salads and cleaning the sawdust from the few sticks of furniture she had acquired. An hour before the appointed time on New Year's Day, the feast was laid out on the table, firewood laid out by the wood stove, and the cabin made out to be as welcoming as such an outpost in the wilderness could appear.

First to arrive, much to Barbara's surprise, was Rod Hill, his wife, Ethel, four-year-old son, Brian, and baby Russell. She had not figured on this family accepting her invitation. The family went through the snacks and antipasto like a plague of locusts on the harvest. When the Reddings arrived, Brian was pulling at Ethel's skirt and complaining of hunger, the baby was crying, and Ethel was asking about the bathroom. Barbara was simultaneously trying to greet the Reddings while she showed Ethel the bathroom, explaining that she had yet to acquire a toilet bowl, though the sink worked.

While his wife labored in the bathroom changing the baby, Rod Hill, led the charge through the serving line, cutting a wide swath through the provender. Barbara had wanted to say a little prayer of thanks for the friends she had and the gift of shelter that she enjoyed largely because of them. Rod and Brian occupied the two available chairs, while the Reddings occupied the couch. When Ethel and baby Russell emerged from the bathroom reeking of diaper powder, Rod was already making a second swipe across the table. He grabbed his chair again and asked Barbara where his wife should sit. Redding's wife got up, dragging her kid with her, to make room for Ethel Hill. Before Ethel had finished her salad, her husband had served himself his second piece of pie. A few minutes later a fight broke out between Brian and the Redding kid over the last piece of pie. With his mouth full, Rod asked Barbara if there was another pie, which there was, I'm sorry, not.

Rod asked if the TV in the corner got reception so that they could enjoy the Super Bowl. Barbara said that there was no reception in the valley and that the TV was just for a VCR "What the hell is a VCR?" Rod wanted to know.

The sound of a car and Rick Larson arrived. There was no salmon left and only a little salad. Rod said, that with the arrival of the 'Forest Service bean counters' it was time for his family to take its leave. "Jesus!," he complained to Ethel, "Has Russell shit himself again? I swear that kid takes bigger dumps than his old man!" Ethel disappeared into the bathroom while Barbara apologized to Rick about the lack of food for his New Year's feast. As Rick was serving himself the leftovers, which consisted of jello salad, coleslaw and crusts of homemade bread, Rod was remarking, "Barb, you ought to get Ethel's recipe for coleslaw. She does it righteous!

"ETHEL!," screamed Rodney from where he sat, through the closed door of the bathroom. "WHAT'S THAT YOU USE IN YOUR COLESLAW? MIRACLE WHIP?"

"YEAH, RODNEY" replied Mrs. Hill.

"WELL, CLEAN THE MIRACLE WHIP OUT OF RUSS'S DIAPER AND LET'S GET A MOVE ON!" bellowed Rod Hill. "We're missing the Super Bowl," he offered Barbara in way of explanation.

The Hills left, followed shortly thereafter by the Reddings. "Thanks for the feed, Barbara," said George upon leaving. "It was really great." Redding walked over to where Larson sat on the floor pushing coleslaw onto his fork with a crust of bread. "I'm sorry that we didn't leave a fair portion for you, Rick. I guess we all got into a feeding frenzy. Rod single-handedly packed in enough chow to feed a starving African nation. Anyway, I've enjoyed working with you and Barbara the last five days. Good luck with your owls." Rick reached up to shake the logger's hand.

Barbara saw George and his family out. On the way back to the living room she stopped at the bathroom to turn off the light left on by Ethel. She saw two disposable diapers rolled up on the floor next to the open four-inch drainpipe where the toilet would go. There was baby shit smeared on the floor. Barbara took out her bandanna and wiped up the feces. Suddenly, she was sobbing...

ဆာင်္

Hemp Hill Creek
Saturday, December 21, 1996, 17:05 hours

Twilight had surrendered to darkness when Mossy came in the cabin and found her mother standing in the darkened bathroom. It looked like Barbara had been crying but she brightened at the sight of her daughter. "Dinner's ready as soon as you wash up."

"Mom, I'd like to run a marathon."

Immediately Barbara recollected her daughter as a nine-year-old child, exploding out from the starting line at the Firecracker Fun Run: determination chiseled on the young face and the wild fury of her puffed cheeks and pumping legs. "Maybe when you get to college you'll join a track team and they will help you train for it..."

"Mom! I don't need help training. I am training and I don't need to wait until college. I'm ready now."

"Your pins, Mossy! You were crippled for a year! Do you want to go back to that?" The words struck the child like a sloppy joe in the face.

"That's really low, Mother - to threaten ME with being crippled when it's my mobility that seems to threaten YOU. I'm sixteen-years-old and I'm in touch with my body. I can make my own decisions about these things. I'm whole! I want a focus for my running and a marathon's the right distance. The Olympia Marathon is in May and I intend to be in it!" Barbara saw dark clouds gathering over the mother and daughter like a cumulonimbus of shepherd's pie. Barbara looked for a compromise that might constrain her daughter from this reckless course to self-defeat and destruction while allowing Mossy the feeling of self-determination. A doctor would never sanction such foolishness.

"Okay. We'll go to Dr. Dickson and if he says the job they did on your hip is strong enough for a marathon and your leg won't fly off at the starting line, you can enter the race."

Olympia Marathon Starting Line
Sunday, May 25, 1997, 07:59:50 hours

"On your mark!" called the mayor of the state capital with a warm wave of Ben Gay and analgesic creams wafting on the air. With the mayor, at the starting line, was his college-aged cousin, Ned Adams. Another smell was overpowering the liniments and it took a few moments for the mayor to realize the fountain of fragrance was emanating from his cousin's girlfriend, Julie Smith.

Contestant 513 had already found her place based on her predicted time, fifteen feet short of the starting line and behind about a hundred runners who anticipated running 26.2 miles in under three hours. Mossy was exhilarated and began to focus inwardly on the task at hand.

From the sidewalk overlooking the closed street choked with runners, Barbara watched the expression on her daughter's face turn from adolescent exuberance to rock-hard determination. She felt the knot tighten in her stomach. What had Dr. Dickson been thinking when he refused to render an opinion on this foolishness? The family physician had merely said that he was not a bone doctor qualified to make decisions about sports medicine and recommended an orthopedic surgeon in Port Angeles. Barbara again wondered if Dr. Dickson's own polio-rendered disability had somehow tweaked his treatment of her daughter. After Mossy's accident, she was attended mostly by specialists until after her spontaneous recovery. On the few times in the last years in which Mossy had required a doctor, Rick Dickson had seemed somewhat uncomfortable and detached from his young patient. Barbara suspected that Mossy's almost immediate metamorphosis from cripple to child athlete had somehow awakened a sense of jealousy on the part of the kind, warm-hearted family doctor...

Sol Duc Clinic, Forks, WA
Sunday, May 25, 1997, 07:59:54 hours

Richard Dickson looked at his watch as he limped through the front door of his office to look through patient billing records. Business was hurting in the wake of the spotted owl issue. Money was getting scarce.

He thought of Mossy Stone, standing at a starting line on the opposite side of the Olympic Peninsula. As he struggled with a rising feeling of guilt, his heart flew out a thousandth light-second across temperate rain forest, over glaciated peaks, to join his young patient at the starting line in Olympia. Simultaneously, he was carried to a point in space-time where he overlooked the wreckage of a school bus and so many injured children. So much blood, so much crying, so few resources: the hopelessness of young Mossy's condition given the catastrophic nature of her injuries. Dr. Dickson had followed standard triage protocol in "No Coding" Mossy Stone. But medical discipline comes out of a book and human spirit is born out of the Heart of the Creator. From the moment of Mossy's birth, Richard Dickson had felt a strong affinity for the ebullient spirit and stony determination of his young patient. Pulling the plug on Mossy there on the Sol Duc bridge had been one of the hardest things of his professional or biological life. Mossy's survival, recovery and pursuit of athletic achievement was a constant reminder of the large rent between his medical profession and the human side of his practice. He could not make dispassionate decisions regarding Mossy's care.

"Set to face the day?" The doctor was surprised by his receptionist/ bookkeeper at the front desk, who had also come in to look for missing payments in a flagging medical business. Dr. Dickson was thinking of cutting roses from his garden and delivering them to Mossy's homestead on the upper Bogachiel...

త౾ఞ

Olympia Marathon Starting Line
Sunday, May 25, 1997, 07:59:58 hours

"Get set!" cried the mayor, pointing a starter gun into the air. The overcast sky was set to rain with light drizzle casting a sheen over the goose flesh of the throng of runners. The runners leaned forward, hands on the starting buttons of their chronographs. The mayor hoped that none of the runners would slam into the wall of Julie's perfume. It could knock them on their butts.

In the last month before the race, Mossy had increased her weekly mileage to 85. She jogged 10 to 16 miles six days a week and rested one day. She was ready for the race in condition and spirit.

The knot in Barbara's stomach cinched tighter. Barbara couldn't believe that Dr. Sam Baker had given the thumbs-up for Mossy's participation in a major foot race. X-rays had shown perfect mending of the crushed bone ends at the stainless steel pins at the surgical neck of her femur.

The doctor acknowledged that excessive stress could create play in the pin moorings of the bone. Dr. Baker agreed that a marathon would produce this level of stress and Barbara had thought this was the end of the discussion and appointment. But the doctor spoke with Mossy privately for a few minutes and the two emerged with a compromise plan for Mossy to attend this one race and hang up her competitive shoes, thereafter.

৩০৫৬

Port Angeles
May 25, 1997, 07:59:59 hours

"Go home!" Dr. Sam Baker was yelling at his dog, as he bicycled out off his driveway, attempting to set off on his regular fifty-mile, Sunday morning foray. He thought fleetingly of the young patient who would be running a marathon this morning.

৩০৫৬

Olympia Marathon Starting Line
Sunday, May 25, 1997, 07:59:59 hours

"MOSSY DON'T OVERDO IT!" Barbara was shouting to her daughter, as the drizzle turned to large drops of rain.
"GO!" screamed the mayor, BANG! went the starter pistol, and a wave of motion moved from beginning to end of the starting line. The drove of runners began leaving the station like the huge train engine it was. As Mossy pulled away from her mother, the rain intensified, driving the spectators off the street and into waiting coffee shops. Barbara stood on her tiptoes watching as the sight of her retreating daughter was engulfed by the crowd of runners. COME BACK! she wanted to yell to Mossy. "Go with God," Barbara said in a small voice, the rain dripping off her nose, which detected an overpowering scent of perfume.

৩০৫৬

Milepost 21, Olympia Marathon
Sunday, May 25, 1997, 10:31 hours

Pain. Pain splashing up from the pavement as her feet slapped down on the wet pavement. Pain raining down from a black sky driven by a cold wind that recalled winter. Pain dripping off her nose and running in rivulets down her aching back to where it soaked her tortured hips...her left femur pulling against its stainless steel mooring in a torrent of pain, pain, pain...
The spectators huddled under umbrellas and ponchos calling out encouragement to the vanguard of the race, which had been passing for the last forty minutes. "All men, so far," remarked one volunteer, setting out the Gatorade

160

and water so that it was immediately reachable by the contestants who already wore water like a shaggy coat.

Barbara Stone stood out holding a cup of Hemp Hill Creek for her daughter who disdained all drink except that which came from the drainage of her home. Barbara looked worried. "Slow down! Mossy slow down, you're going too fast!" The cup was whisked from her hand and Barbara's empty hand followed the course of her speeding daughter. "MOSSY, SLOW DOWN!" she screamed at the retreating figure.

Mossy was not hearing her mother, but was engaged in the deep prayer that is born out of physical pain and spiritual torment. "Creator of all things, be with us runners," she called out in her heart. "Help us to center on You in our hearts as we deal with our pain and discomfort. Be with the runner at the front of this race and with the runner in last place...and thank You for the gift of mobility that You have given us. Thank You for the control that You have given us over our feet, lungs and hearts...and be in our hearts. Amen. Amen. Aaaaaaaaaaaaaaaaaamennnnnnnnn..."

ೋ∽ಲ

Milepost 24, Olympia Marathon
Sunday, May 25, 1997, 10:35 hours

[You have stumbled out of your own reality and into this fictional work like a kid spilling out of an all-day matinee into the daylight, or a mole tumbling out into the larger world outside its tunnel.

It's still raining and the crowd, here by the aid station at the top of the last hill, has been thinned out to the attendants, two volunteer officials, and a few determined family members. One of the officials watches the oncoming runners and calls out their race numbers to the other who communicates by walkie-talkie to the finish line.]

"One-hundred-and-six!" yells the official looking through binoculars, while the second official fumbles through soggy paperwork, clutching his radio.

["Psst, you! Psst! Yes, YOU! You, reader, I'm talking to you. Come over here and join me by this last aid station."

Do you feel a little awkward being addressed by the author of the book you're reading? It's strange having the covers of a book holding you rather than you holding the book. We stand together, next to a pretty middle-aged woman in a drenched green 60/40, who anxiously searches the faces of the oncoming runners for her daughter. The woman holds a cup of water from a creek on the West End of the Olympic Peninsula. Her teeth are chattering from the cold and wet.]

"One-hundred-and-six," says the second race official into his handy-talkie. "Thirty-five-year-old, male, Boeing engineer from Renton. Personal record is two hours, forty-eight minutes..."

["Due to a miracle of modern fiction, you can read the thoughts of the race contestants before the thoughts even enter their minds. They are

161

cresting this final hill and heading down the last two-mile stretch of the race." And here is what the racer is thinking," says the author of <u>Between Forks and Alpha Centauri</u>:]

"God, this hurts! I'm not going to make two hours and forty-seven minutes. Why should I try so hard? If I'm running at nine miles an hour, forty percent of my body weight is flying. Only sixty pounds coming down on each foot. God, I hurt! I'm only in touch with the ground when my feet hit the pavement which is less than one percent of the time. The rest is flying. Mostly, I'm flying. GOD THIS HURTS..."

"Forty-eight!" calls the official looking through the binoculars.

"Zero four eight," says the second official into his hand-held.

"Twenty-eight year-old, male, music teacher from Bellingham, personal record is three zero hours which he is going to easily beat. He is number fifty - five zero - overall...

"God this hurts! Right, left, right, left...But I'm going to make it...In...out...in...out...in, out, in, out, in, out, in, out...I'm going to beat three hours...Right, left, right, left...Soon the race will be over and I can stop this awful music...In...out... in...out...in, out, in, out, in, out, in, out..."

"Five hundred thirteen," calls the official with binoculars.

"SLOW DOWN!" screams the woman standing beside us, spilling her Hemp Hill water in the frenzy. "SLOW DOWN, MOSSY! YOU'LL CRIPPLE YOURSELF!"

["Excuse me, miss..." says the author of <u>Between Forks and Alpha Centauri</u>. "But we're trying to have a conversation here!"]

"I'm sorry," says Barbara Stone, her concentration still focused at the oncoming female runner. "My daughter could damage her surgical pins...MOSSY, NOT SO FAST!"

["Aw, what the hell," says the author. She can't help yelling and I'm liable to disrupt your suspension of disbelief talking to her like that. It's pretty weird, anyway, two protagonists, a reader and an author, all on the same page together. But, like Phil Stone, I don't like to be ignored.]

"Five hundred thirteen is the first female," calls out the official with binoculars. "GO, FIVE ONE THREE!"

"Five one three," says the second official into his hand-held. "Seventeen-year-old student from Forks, Washington. It's her first marathon and SHE'S THE FIRST FEMALE RUNNER! GO, FIVE ONE THREE!"

"MOSSY, SLOW DOWN!" yells Barbara holding out the half-filled/half-empty cup of water for her approaching daughter.

["GO, FIVE ONE THREE! GO MOSSY!" yells the author, ignoring the flesh and blood bond of the agonized mother beside him. "Oh! What I was saying about a book is this: Your life is a book. It's a string of tiny pulses in space-time, which your brain translates into moments, just like you make words out of the strings of black and white on the page. Just like this page does not cease to exist once it is turned, any moment of our lives is, was, and always will be. The typos, the spilled coffee stains, the poorly chosen words, and misdirected literary license: these things are written in indelible ink on the pages of our lives. I hope you can savor and digest each page because it's forever. GO, FIVE ONE THREE!"]

Mossy streaks by us and snatches the cup of water from her mother's hand without breaking stride. Her head thrown back, she launches the contents of the cup partly down her throat and partly across her sweat- and rain-drenched face and neck. There is no reading her mind from the blank expression on her face.

[Allow me to show you the workings of Mossy's mind," says the author:

Mossy's mind is holographically flowing in the water of Hemp Hill Falls.

 It is the same water that flows through her veins. Unlike the other runners who have given focus to their discomforts with words like "hurt" and "sore" and "PAIN" she is freed from the joys and torments of the flesh and oblivious to our encouragement or the beseeching calls of her mother.

"But run in joy, Mossy, because your wonderful mobility will only occupy a few chapters in the book of your life. And you, dear reader, should run in joy and celebrate each chapter of your own life. If finishing <u>Between Forks and Alpha Centauri</u> is consistent with that, then I will retreat from the story line and wish you well with your reading. For each of us there is a last page. Of the four of us that came together on this page: Mossy; Barbara; you, dear reader; and myself, I know of only one of us who will be there for the last page of <u>Between Forks and Alpha Centauri</u> and I know of at least two of us that WILL NOT BE THERE. Adieu.]

༄

Finish Line, Olympia Marathon
Sunday, May 25, 1997, 10:51:59 hours

At first Mossy thought she was hearing a great roaring of wind through waving spruce boughs, but the bright colors brought her focus to the finish line that loomed 200 meters in front of her. The crowd was cheering wildly, accounting for the roaring din, and Mossy almost stumbled in the finishing chute as she felt the great pain welling out of her hip and over-stressed muscles. A woman volunteer came along side Mossy and supported her.

"Congratulations! Great run!" said the volunteer.

"Thanks," said Mossy, unaware that she was the first woman to finish. "I'm OK," she said, pulling away from the volunteer and looking for her mother in the crowd.

Barbara emerged, having barely arrived in time to see Mossy's finish. "Well, you're still walking, so that's a relief," said Barbara. "I brought some more water and some food, if you're ready to eat..."

"Mom, let's just go home," said cold Mossy, the energy drained out of her and her body aching mightily.

"You were the first woman runner," advised Barbara, in case this was somehow missed by Mossy. "There will be an award for you. Probably more interesting than My Little Ponies...I think it's a purse of several hundred dollars..."

"Mom, let's just go home. Please..." Mossy's teeth began to chatter.

On the way home, in the truck, both mother and daughter were on an emotional roller coaster, plunging from the heights of hubris to the valley of their exhaustion. Each one's tears setting off the other's as they dwelled in the pride of blood and the agony of flesh.

The rain and wind had not abated by the time they arrived back at their home. Mossy paused before entering their cabin to listen to the water coursing down Hemp Hill Creek and rejoice in the clean smell of the air.

Mossy fell asleep in her mother's bed shortly after their dinner. Barbara had been massaging Mossy's cramping muscles, but it was fine to lay beside her daughter on a stormy night on what would become the final spring of Barbara's life on Hemp Hill Creek. Barbara worried into the night about how fast Mossy was growing up, how soon she would be leaving for college and how lonely life would be without her daughter.

The rain stopped and the wind freshened. A starry sky peeked through the clouds and the long tail of the Hale-Bopp comet skulked over Reade Hill like a cougar over a grouse wallow.

Near the orchard, a pawpaw tree danced in the wind. Around its slender trunk were wrapped roses and a congratulations card left by Dr. Dickson, which had blown there from the front steps before Mossy and Barbara returned that afternoon.

 споре

Office of Dr. Richard Dickson
Monday, December 15, 1997, 12:45 hours

It had been months since Barbara had felt right. It was a little like the morning sickness she had experienced carrying Mossy, except sometimes when she threw up there was blood...and there was blood in her stool.

She waited in the front room with the other patients for Dr. Dickson to see her ...

споре

Hemp Hill Creek
Sunday, December 15, 1985, 12:45 hours

Barbara stood on the bridge over Hemp Hill Creek counting bald eagles. On Sunday afternoons, Barbara routinely scanned the back pages of the local newspaper for Forest Service and DNR timber sales. Since the sale which cut directly to the north bank of the Bogachiel and culminated in the death of her husband, Barbara assumed a watchful stance on local sales that might impact fish or her lifestyle. The second growth just below the granite boulder on Reade Hill was being harvested and there was disruption to the view-shed from the farm below. Reviewing the legal description of the "32-E Reade Ridge" Forest Service sale in the paper, Barbara realized that the old growth on the summit was now going on the auction block. She called Rick Larson on his day off to complain about the management of Olympic National Forest.

"On any given day this time of year you can make a dozen sightings of bald eagles soaring over Reade Ridge," she complained to the biologist. "Not just the same eagle. Yesterday Mossy and I saw eleven in the air at one time. They're roosting in the snags on top of the ridge! What happened to the SOMA[4] up there?"

"We adjusted the CHA[5] towards the Park because we got more answers to our calls out by Rugged Ridge. Nothing is chiseled in stone yet. The spotted owl may get placed on the endangered species list next year and then things will start to happen conservation-wise."

"Aren't bald eagles still on the Threatened and Endangered List? Next year will be too late for Reade Hill. Rick, the Forest Service will be selling prime habitat here for a few sticks of wood. Do something, for God's sake..."

An hour later Larson stood with Barbara on the bridge looking over the north pasture while five-year-old Mossy entertained herself watching video recordings, checked out from the Forks Library, at the cabin. Barbara and Rick counted eagles. Eight were visible in the air at the moment.

"Thanks for coming out, Rick. I've always been able to count on you as a friend. I'll never forget how you and George Redding took care of me five years ago." Two more eagles flew into view and circled lazily overhead.

"That's what friends are for," said Larson, logging the new sightings and moving closer to stand directly beside Barbara. The eagles soared closer together and cried out like a rusty screen door. Apparently, these two birds were about to mate as they soared higher and higher vying for more airtime. To the biologist, it was a sign.

Barbara likewise focused on the courtship of the birds and, as the birds connected talon to talon and tumbled through space, Barbara was falling through space-time to six year's previous, as she and her husband struggled together in the construction of the roof he never saw finished. Tears welled in her eyes and the biologist saw what he mistook for a sign of an impending breakthrough in his relationship with this woman. Two more eagles flew into view. The two that

---

[4]Spotted Owl Management Area

[5]Critical Habitat Area

were mating broke apart and flew off, circling one another. "Fourteen," snuffled Barbara.

"I can stop the sale on an administrative action. I'll have a retraction in the paper this Wednesday. If there is anything I can ever do for you, just let me know..." And suddenly Barbara was hugging Rick Larson. The biologist was feeling the warmth of the woman beneath her sweater and the clean smell of her hair against his cheek. His head was soaring like an amorous eagle. Just as he was winding up to kiss the top of Barbara's head, she broke off the embrace and walked purposefully back towards the bridge.

"Thanks, Rick," she called out in way of dismissal.

ぷℛ

Office of Dr. Richard Dickson
Monday, December 15, 1997, 13:30

"Ms. Stone," called Dr. Dickson, formally from the door leading to the exam rooms. "Please come in." Dr. Dickson looked older than his 46 years. He looked tired and discouraged: like a politician who had seen too much corruption, a cop who had seen too much crime, a doctor who had seen too much...

ぷℛ

Disease stumbles across the surface of the planet like a drunken logger. Sinking the cutting teeth of pain and debilitation into the trunks of the human forest, the logger (disease) staggers from tree to human tree. Here, a tree is felled to the ground; here the tree is sawn almost through, but healed itself enough to stand until the next great wind. The cut-line is a staggered, random path. The cut faces and backcuts are ragged and don't always meet.

The saw that cut into Barbara's flesh and buried itself deep in her trunk, was cancer.

ぷℛ

Olympic Memorial Hospital
Friday, June 12, 1998

"They're trying to cut the old growth on Reade Ridge just above our place!" This was how Mossy greeted her infirmed mother, seeing her for the first time in five days.

Barbara's face brightened at the sight of her daughter. "They'll have a time of that," replied Barbara. "Reade Hill is the center of a Critical Habitat bullseye. It would take a repeal of the Endangered Species Act for them to pull off a logging show on Reade Hill..."

"They're arguing mandatory education pre-existed and preempts Endangered Species. It's Forest Service land and they say that enabling legislation and traditional application of timber revenue to education takes precedence. They're talking about taking it to court."

"Who's *they*, anyway. That doesn't sound like Forks talking."

"The Washington Commercial Forest Action Committee."

"George Redding's not behind those arguments, I'll bet. He was gone from town for three years logging the Tongass, but he hasn't changed that much. Who's driving this?" asked Barbara.

"It's a bunch of lawyers from out of town, hanging around the office and telling George what to do. Every morning they arrive in a helicopter at Forks Airfield. Who knows where they're from or who sent them."

Barbara lay on her back looking at the ceiling. It had been a month since she had been out of bed, so the topography of the ceiling was well-known territory. "I'd sure like to get out of this bed and talk to George face-to-face. Maybe I can call him. Friends and community might be worth trading for a few trees, but you can't count on lawyers to look after the interest of a town like Forks. It sounds like big money and big money will run over Forks like Gestapo over a kindergarten."

"They're really mobilizing, Mom. A bunch of loggers who left town a couple years ago have arrived back in town. Who knows who called them or how they heard something was brewing? There's going to be a televised debate on TV next month."

"Where's Rick Larson in this? He should be very much a part of the debate."

"He's wearing a muzzle, I guess. The Forest Service says that it's become an issue of law. Conservation is a lesser issue. I haven't seen Rick around, but my guess is he may feel it's a conflict of interest to take a stand."

A nurse walked into the room and interrupted the conversation. "Your mom should be resting," she scolded Mossy. "She's on for chemo in an hour." The nurse adjusted the Darvon drip of the piggy back IV and went to the door looking back at Mossy meaningfully.

Mossy said brightly, "I'm going out for a walk. You rest for a while." Barbara grimaced in pain as her daughter started out the door.

"Mossy?" Her daughter turned at the threshold. "Have you noticed any fry in the stream?"

"I haven't seen any, Mom."

"You have to throw twigs in at the water to see the Coho... like I showed you."

"It hasn't been a good year for fish, Mom. You get some rest."

Just outside the door, Mossy sat in a chair by the door and stared inwardly at her dilemma. It was everything she could do to keep up the farm and stay in school. Mossy fetched a water jar from her tote and pulled a long drink of Hemp Hill Creek. The smell of trauma and disease were everywhere in the hall and exacerbated Mossy's agitation. She feared that the Department of Social and Health Services would intervene and take her from the farm. Her mother was dying and she felt friendless in the world. Mossy placed her hands over her face and sobbed miserably.

৽৵

Olympic Memorial Hospital
Friday, June 12, 1998

Barbara clutched feebly at the phone and, through the haze of painkiller swimming through her veins, tried to clear her mind for the call she was making. The nurse had dialed the phone. She recognized the voice of her friend George Redding.

"Good Morning, this is Washington Commercial Forest Action Committee."

"Hi, George. This is Barbara, how are you doing?"

"Barbara! It's great to hear your voice. I guess you know that I was away for three years logging where I could find work, and it's great to have this job back in good old Forks! How are you? How's little Mossy...well, BIG Mossy, now?"

Barbara spoke in a small voice, "Mossy's fine. I'm dying of cancer and am calling to make a dying request."

"Seriously, Barbara, how are you doing? I'm sorry that I haven't had a chance to get out to your place with all the stuff brewing with my new job..."

"Seriously, George, I'm dying. The doctors here at OMH give me another couple of months or less. I need to talk to you about this plan to log Reade Ridge..."

"My God, Barbara, how bad is it," Barbara's friend asked lamely, looking for a speck of hope upon which to cling. "OMH has good oncology. What are they doing for you?"

"Painkillers mostly. George, my guts are gone. They wanted to do a colostomy and have me come in to P.A. once a week for dialysis..."

"Sweet Jesus!" interjected George.

"...Hell with it! That's not living! And I'm not going to do it, but I need to talk to you about Reade Ridge. What's going on with this? Who are the guys in your office? Where's the money behind this?"

"You mean the lawyers that are helping with this thing? Well, it's a consortium of interests. I don't know all their employers. One of the guys lives on the Peninsula and works for Pope and Talbot out of Shelton."

"George, P & T are swinging over into developing their logged-out properties for housing. You don't want to be in bed with them. The people of Forks don't need out-of-town, high-priced lawyers telling them what's good for them..."

"Barbara, this is a chance to put people back to work in this community. I had to leave my home and family for three years to find work. There's plenty more like me in this community. We just want to work and live in our own homes with our families..."

"It wasn't spotted owls that ended things in Forks! Harvest was so far out ahead of yield that the timber industry cut its way into timber famine..."

"Don't get me started on that, Barbara. What I've been doing for the last two weeks is going over land allocations, re-prod rates, historic harvest levels and habitat issues...with these lawyers. They KNOW these things. I've got to be a spokesman for this community. Besides, Barbara, we shouldn't be arguing. You should be resting. What can I do to help you? Does Mossy need a place to stay?"

"Mossy is fine, George!" Barbara's voice was a little terse. "George, I'm asking you to reconsider your position. Logging Reade Ridge is wrong for the environment. You've done so many things for me, I hate to ask favors, but this is the last thing I'll ask of you: Please reconsider your position on this!"

"Barbara, if I could do that for you, I would. But I'm in too deep with WACK FACK[6] and you're asking me to turn my back on the interests of the community. Timber is the guts of this town. For this town to get by without logging would be like living without a liver..." George realized he had just stepped in dog manure.

"I know something about what that's like, George. If you would reconsider, I'd appreciate it. But, whatever the case, it's time to tell you that I appreciate everything that you've done for Mossy and me. It's been a great joy and comfort having you for a friend and..." Barbara paused looking for the right parting word to a friend... "Goodbye, George." She hung up the phone and closed her eyes wishing the painkiller could take away the raging fire where her guts used to be.

ॐॐ

Forks High School Gym
Monday, June 15, 1998

In the long night of unemployment, the debate about unlocking Critical Habitat drew logging families like moths to the light. It was Forks's biggest cultural gathering since Olympic Theater's showing of "Teenage Mutant Ninja Turtles" a decade previous. From the library to the Sea First Bank, pickup trucks and crummies filled the parking lots, demonstrating that Forks loggers searching for woods work, scattered from Alaska to Montana, had converged on their hometown.

Mossy followed hundreds of her near neighbors into the Forks High School to witness an event which would provide news bites across the United States and affect the mood of a country which deliberated how much it was willing to pay for the preservation of such species as the Northern Spotted Owl.

Among the crowd of Forks citizens pouring into the front door of the high school was a sprinkling of outsiders clearly identified by their dandified choice of clothing, which consisted of anything other than a hickory shirt and tin pants. The audience found their way to the bleachers set up in the gym and the wooden structure sighed under the weight of twenty-five tons of human biomass.

---

[6] Washington Commercial Forest Action Commitee

169

Phil Arbatrator, the mayor of Forks, stepped up to the public address system and began reading from his prepared speech: "We in Forks have come to depend on the timber industry for employment and support of our lifestyles much the way people in Olympia or Washington D.C. depend on government for theirs. The Federal listing of the Northern Spotted Owl as an endangered species, in 1992, has had a big impact on our fair, little city. Many of our townspeople have had to leave in search of work in the woods elsewhere. Of the fifty lumber and cedar mills that operated before the listing, less than five are currently in operation. The ripple effect across our economy has underfunded schools, stressed the county tax base, and depleted every kind of service from structural fire protection from our fire hall, to forestry management from the D.N.R. Olympic Region here in Forks. Our town is changing...and most of us don't like the direction we've been going..." The townspeople broke into applause and brief cheering.

The mayor continued, "Most of us see the proposed challenge of the Endangered Species Act with the Federal mandate to education as a reconciliation of priorities. As much as we love nature, most of us, given the opportunity, would choose the welfare of our children over the health of a bird that few of us have ever seen..." Again, a wave of whooping and cheering broke over the gym bleachers.

"Some of us ask: What were we doing before 1992 that was so all-fire wrong? We had about the cleanest air and water in the world. Walk two miles away from town in any direction and you're standing in the woods. Deer, elk and sometimes cougar are seen within our city limits. What were we doing that was so wrong? And more importantly, where are we going in the twenty first century?

"Here to help us answer those questions are two individuals representing different extremes of opinion. Recently returned to work in Forks as the Executive Director of the Washington Commercial Forest Action Committee is our own George Redding..." the audience broke into enthusiastic cheering and applause. The mayor continued, "I'm sure that George's family enjoyed his return as much as we do."

"At the other end of the scale, and representing a viewpoint which will require much studying and figuring on our part, is Peter Cienfuegos representing Earth First! and several other environmental... activists groups which have come to the Peninsula to help us... figure out our priorities...I guess. Mr. Cienfuegos is a graduate-engineering student at the University of Washington, studying energy. He and his father, Martin, were active in demonstration efforts to restrain MacMillan Bloedel's logging in Canada's Clayoquot Sound. They were among the 850 arrested in the largest act of civil disobedience in Canadian history. Thirty years ago, Peter's father, Martin, was active in the Save the Redwoods campaign in northern California, where demonstrators tied themselves high in the trees to prevent them from being felled...So let's give a warm Forks' welcome to Mr. Peter Cienfuegos of Earth First!"

As the young twenty-two-year-old speaker came to the microphone, the polite applause from a few of the town merchants was overwhelmed by the booing, hooting, and catcalls of the loggers. The young speaker smiled unabashedly at the hostile audience, "Thank you for the Forks welcome, folks. And thanks for the opportunity to clear the air about some of the misconceptions that you may be holding dear to your heart and viewpoint. And, speaking of clearing the air, let me first respond to Mayor Arbatrator's misconception that the air here in Forks is something of which to be proud. Check out the incidence of lung cancer in your little town. How many of your neighbors have been stricken down? The national average of incidence for lung cancer is 2 per thousand individuals a year, while here in Forks, a town of 3,000, about 200 cases were diagnosed from 1977 to 1990. That's three times the national average among a population that seems to prefer chewing to smoking. You're taking the cleanest air in the world and lacing it with poisonous cedar smoke and dust.

"When the glaciers left the lowlands of this country, retreating to the high crags of Mount Olympus and a few other Peninsula peaks, a succession of environmental and biological events led to savannahs becoming forests of stunted Engelmann Spruce which later developed into the magnificent stands of temperate rain forest which this town's people have cut as if there were no limit to this resource. A hundred years ago, temperate rain forest accounted for only two-tenths of one percent of the Earth's land area. In that hundred years, ninety percent of that rare environment has been harvested.

"At the turn of the century, the United States government convened environmentalist John Muir and Gifford Pinchot, the first director of the Forest Service, to draw boundaries for the Olympic Forest Reserve. The west-facing valleys all presented specimens of red cedar, Sitka spruce and Doug fir, that typically reached twenty feet in diameter and over 300 feet in stature. The two men agreed on boundaries that laid this rich forest resource in the public domain, then John Muir left to defend wilderness elsewhere. Within the first year, most of this great lowland forest, including the Quillayute and Hoh, the Queets and Quinault, was stripped from the Forest Reserve and given over to the private sector. With one swipe of the pencil, Gifford Pinchot surrendered more than 60% of the wood resource of the new Forest Reserve. When a million acres was withdrawn from the Forest and some adjoining lands in 1938 to create Olympic National Park, there was only a remnant of this great forest ecosystem. Though the Park acreage is mostly high country, the destruction of North America's west coast coniferous forest - previously, the largest in the world - was so complete, that five of the world's largest tree species are found in Olympic National Park.

"Temperate rain forest represents an important and immensely interesting theater of biodiversity. The endangered spotted owl is only an indicator species showing the stress upon this forest ecosystem. It's not JUST about spotted owls...it's about the last pieces of temperate rain forest in North America and all the other species that depend on this undisturbed environment. That's why the Park was declared a Biosphere Reserve by the United Nations. It's much more important than a few sticks of wood."

The young speaker turned on an overhead projector and a colored picture of the Olympic Peninsula came up on the gym wall. "So, I hear talk about sustainable yield and how withdrawing the last five percent of ancient forest from harvest somehow has disrupted the formula. This is a picture - not a drawing - of the Olympic Peninsula from space taken in 1987. All we did in the lab at the University of Washington was to enhance the color contrast with infrared spectrography. Now, outside the Park are three million acres on the Peninsula, of which about two million are in private or public forest, open to logging. If your signs along Highway 101 regarding fifty year harvest cycles were correct - and they're not - you could harvest two percent of two million acres indefinitely or forty thousand acres a year. Let's see what happens when greed colors this picture. I am going to put a plastic overlay on this picture sheet which will filter out all the forest that was cut in the decade between 1980 and 1990." About 20% of the entire peninsula disappeared. "Now I'm going to blot out what was harvested between 1970 and 1980..." about another 25% disappeared. "...and between 1960 and 1970..." about 20% disappeared. "What you have here is a rough map of the boundaries of Olympic National Park. In these three decades, cut limits were set 50% higher than sustainable yield would allow BY YOUR OWN CALCULATIONS OF FOREST GROWTH!"

Above the odor of 400 citizens packed into the high school gym, Mossy smelled the fear and wondered from what source it could emanate. She looked around at so many faces that studied the speakers with expressions ranging from boredom to rage, but there was not fear in this auditorium. She left her seat in the bleachers and walked by the Forks P.D. officer stationed by the exit. The cop had been dispatched to keep the peace in what would predictably be a tense confrontation between the community and the so-called radical extremists.

"Hi, Mossy," said Officer Fairbanks, smiling. "How are you tonight?"

"OK, I think," mumbled Mossy. "Excuse me," she said, passing through the exit and letting the door fall shut behind her. She found the source of the smell. A middle-aged man was being held by a group of three teenagers dressed up as loggers, while Russell Hill spoke to the man in threatening tones. The man wore a crooked, half-torn-off name tag that read HI, I'M MARTIN CIENFUEGOS, EARTH FIRST!

"First off," Hill was saying. "Let me assure you that we're not thugs. We're a peaceful community, really. But we get kind of riled when you talk about educating us about forestry, when we've grown up in these woods, and part of this education is closing down our work, and the other part is bankrupting our schools. We're going to spend a few moments educating you about what our feelings are on the subject. If we accidentally split your lips or loosen a few of your teeth....oh well. It's not nearly as painful as losing your life's work.

"Second off...HEY!" Hill was surprised to have Mossy Stone insert herself between himself and the enviro-puke he was interviewing.

"Let's go back to first off," growled Mossy, like a she bear defending her cubs. "First off, let this citizen go and disperse. Now!"

"What the fuck?!" hissed Hill. "Mossy, this has nothing to do with you. Get out of here right this shitting second!"

"This has everything to do with me, Russell. I live here. I'm not going to let you pretend to represent this town and strike out in anger against some innocent citizen. Let him go before one of you gets hurt."

Hill advanced on Mossy menacingly. "You'll be the one hurt in just a sec..." With an upward jab, Mossy shoved her fist into Hill's abdomen just below the xiphoid process in what might have been a perfect Heimlich maneuver except that his obstructed airway wouldn't occur for another ten seconds. The wind rushed out of Hill and he doubled over, unable to draw breath with his stunned diaphragm.

Behind Mossy, the three teenagers pushed aside the man they were holding and the largest of the three came up behind Mossy to restrain her. Anticipating the rear attack, Mossy withdrew her right fist from where it had embedded in Hill's gut and brought her arm straight back, following her elbow into a high rear sweep that caught the new assailant in the nose. There was the sound of a home run being knocked out of the stadium and the second assailant went down holding his bleeding nose. Mossy followed through with a pirouette in a low crouch, facing the two standing teenagers. Her hands were up, open claws, ready for the next move.

"Freeze! Police!" yelled Officer Fairbanks, coming out the door from the gym. Hill, who had been struggling to move air for the ten seconds it took his diaphragm to recover from the shock, drew a sudden, oxygen-starved gulp of air. Riding on a bolus of air was a big pinch of snoose which had dropped out of his lip and into his mouth as he had made attempts to move air. The snoose was propelled down his trachea and lodged at the bifurcation of his bronchi. Hill looked all bug-eyed as he regained a standing posture and faced his friends hoping for assistance. He coughed violently sending spit, phlegm and chew into their wondering faces and went down again. These two spray victims, in turn, backed away fast and began clawing at their faces, swearing.

Fairbanks walked into the melee. "You all right, Mossy?" he asked, laughing. "How about you, sir?" he asked the middle-aged visitor from out of town. Fairbanks sized up the situation in about five seconds and offered, "Lucky I got here when I did, or Mossy might have seriously hurt you boys. OK, if nobody wants to press charges, let's break it up and get back to our business." He helped Hill pick himself off the ground and went face to red-eyed, runny-nosed face with the logger-want-to-be. "And your business had better be your own and none of mine for the rest of this evening. And that goes for your buddies. Go home! Scram: out of here." The cop turned and went back into the auditorium as the young men gathered their snoose cans and wayward romeo slippers and slipped into the night.

Left alone with his young savior, the middle-aged man offered, "That was a remarkable form of self defense you exhibited there, young lady. What do you call that form of martial art? Aikido?"

"It's called fighting back and a couple of lucky shots," said Mossy, opening up the door to the gym. "They weren't expecting resistance, so I had a wide open window of defense. You had the same window. You could have kicked Hill and taken out the guy behind you by slamming your head back. Hey, look, I'm sorry this happened, but let me give you some advice. If you're going to behave like a sheep, which is OK, be sure to bleat like a sheep. There was a cop twenty yards from where they were hassling you. If you had yelled, Officer

Fairbanks would have been right there. I could have yelled, but it was fun getting in a couple of good punches first..."

"But those young thugs could have really hurt us!"

"No, sir. I'm totally against them shaking you down, which is why I came out, but they weren't lying when they said that they would do no serious harm. People in this town are very threatened by environmental sanctions. They are reaching out for someone to blame besides their employers; and environmental advocates from out-of-town fit the bill. But these people are not thugs...Let's sit together here..." Mossy pointed to where she had previously been sitting. The young Cienfuegos had surrendered the lectern to George Redding and had occupied Mossy's seat in the front row. The row compressed to make room for the two additional spectators.

"...looking at Washington State as a whole, the sixteen million, eight hundred and forty-two thousand acres of forest land represents about a third of the state's total acreage. Before 1992, the average annual harvest on these lands was about six billion board feet. The Washington Contract Loggers Association has estimated the annual growth of our commercial forests at ten billion board feet, so we were continuing to increase our timber resource at a rate of almost half a billion board feet a year. In 1991 almost three billion seedlings were planted in the United States which is more than ten for every citizen.

"Five percent of Washington's timber revenue was paid as stumpage tax to the Feds. That was sixty-three and a half million dollars in 1992. Before the spotted owl issue, a hundred and seventy million dollars a year was generated by DNR sales, much of which came back to our schools. In Washington State, the U.S. Forest Service secured thirty-five million to forty-million dollars a year for our schools and road districts. Think about it: the spotted owl has withdrawn four-million dollars a year from Clallam and Jefferson Counties schools and roads.

Peter Cienfuegos leaned over to remark to his father, "It's always about money with these guys. Everything that's not money is irrelevant..."

While Redding spoke, "Six million acres is preserved in Washington State forever as wilderness or otherwise protected land. Take our state's protected land and stretch it from Seattle to New York and you have a forest a mile and a half wide. Add to it the other wilderness designations and you have a swath forty miles wide from the West Coast all the way to East Coast. Why can't the spotted owl survive on a tract of land that big?

"Let's look at the spotted owl for a minute. The little guys live fifteen years or more and can reproduce annually from the age of three. What's killing spotted owls is that great horned owls are scarfing them up and barred owls are taking over their habitat. More than ten thousand spotted owls are known to inhabit the West Coast. They like old growth, sure, but they are well-adapted to managed forests with wildlife trees left to provide a multi-storied canopy..."

A man in a business suit came into the gym carrying a briefcase and a folded piece of paper, the latter of which he carried directly to George Redding. "Read it," the suit hissed before taking a seat with the six lawyers helping to prepare the case being put forward by the Washington Commercial Forest Action Committee.

"Excuse me a moment," said Redding, unfolding the paper and reading it to himself. Redding then refolded the paper and walked toward the front row of spectators. At first Mossy thought that George Redding would give her the folded piece of paper, but he passed it to Peter Cienfuegos and said in a whisper, "Better take care of it, Mr. Cienfuegos. Those lawyer jackals behind me will have you strung up if you don't."

As Redding walked back to the podium, Mossy glanced at the missive which Cienfuegos had unfolded to read:

The Jobs from Timber Legal Council has just received word that the opposition's speaker, Peter D. Cienfuegos (date of birth 08-30-74) has an outstanding bench warrant for a Failure To Appear out of the 9th District Federal Court. Cienfuegos is, therefore, a fugitive, subject to immediate arrest if the National Park Service (the citing agency) will extradite from Forks or pay the jail bill therein. Read this statement at the conclusion of your talk:
IT APPEARS THAT PETER CIENFUEGOS IS CONFUSED ON THE MANY ISSUES SURROUNDING TIMBER MANAGEMENT. SUCH CONFUSION IS TYPICAL OF YOUTH ON DRUGS, WHICH IS WHAT PETER CIENFUEGOS IS. IT'S COME TO OUR ATTENTION THAT THIS UNFORTUNATE INDIVIDUAL IS WANTED BY THE FEDERAL GOVERNMENT ON DRUG CHARGES. PART OF MR. CIENFUEGOS' AGENDA FOR THE NATIONAL PARKS INCLUDES USING THEM FOR ILLEGAL DRUG ACTIVITY...

"Jesus!" muttered Peter Cienfuegos, glancing across Mossy to Officer Brian Fairbanks who winked mysteriously at the young environmental activist.

George Redding resumed his part of the presentation. "Before our forests on the Olympic Peninsula came under human management, they burned every time there was a dry lightning strike. Dig down sixteen inches on the forest floor and you find the ash, which represents a fire that burned uncontrolled from one side of the Peninsula to the other. How is it unlike logging except that we remove most of the timber resource for jobs, where non-management would burn it and send it up as air pollution..."

"Dad, do you have three hundred and fifty dollars I could borrow?" Peter asked his father quietly, speaking across Mossy.

"This satellite picture and mumbo jumbo from space..." George Redding was saying.

"Sure," said Martin. "Unless you want cash..."

"...doesn't impress me. Trees grow, gosh darn-it. Get down here on the ground and look for yourself. Walk over a clearcut and come back ten years later. There's a young forest growing where you left stumps..."

"It's got to be cash, Dad," Peter said to Martin.

"What's this about, anyway?" asked Martin Cienfuegos of his son.

"...But if the environmental extremists want to flash around pictures from space, let's take a look," said George Redding turning the overhead projector back on.

"I got a ticket when a group of us were smoking a joint at our own campsite at the Sol Duc campground. They told me I had a month to take care of it and now there's maybe a warrant for my arrest..."

"HOW MANY TIMES HAVE I TOLD YOU NOT TO BRING DOWN THE CAUSE OF CONSERVATION WITH THE SORDID DETAILS OF YOUR PRIVATE LIFE..." Martin was winding up for a shout-out with his son in the front row.

"...Take a look at what the space satellite shows of the environment across the water in the land of eco-warriors! From space it's as brown as the floor of a pigsty! In their enthusiasm to remind us to leave our trees alone, did they forget to plant trees themselves? We replant; they repave...that's the difference here, if you want to get down to it..."

The audience began to applaud and cheer wildly. The voice of Peter Cienfuegos was drowned out, "Dad, can you loan me the money or..."

"...I don't have the cash and my credit card doesn't work in the ATM's in this backwater town," Martin was saying over the cheering.

"...They're going to ARREST MY ASS!" Peter Cienfuegos was saying.

Mossy felt stressed by the intrusion of big city problems into her small town life and reacted the only way she knew: blunt compassion. She stood up and said, "If you two need to continue this conversation, maybe you should sit together. If you need a safe place to stay tonight - the two of you - you can stay with me. But maybe right now you should focus on the here and now, which is that George Redding is winning the support of this audience. You need to be planning what to say that might reach the people of Forks. The first cut will be right at my doorstep and I wish you two could argue about that instead of your private predicaments."

Nine

"Most travelers content themselves with what they may chance to see from car windows, hotel verandas, of the deck of a steamer...clinging to the battered highways like drowning sailors to a life raft."
- John Muir, Founder of the Sierra Club

"The peculiar thing about a man's love of a woman is that it is tied in a tight knot with the man's concept of the woman's role. If the woman steps out of his perceived character of her for just a moment, the thread of his love remains tied to the role rather than the real woman."
*- **Barbara Beyers**, fictional character in a great American novel*
In a letter to her mother dated December, 1980

"Bogachiel Basin. Definitely, Bogachiel Basin..."
- Senator Dan Evans, when asked his favorite place in Olympic National Park

Olympic Memorial Hospital
Friday, December 18, 1998, 16:25 hours

*B*arbara Stone lay in her hospital bed awaiting death. In the dull, timeless dribble of indistinguishable events that entered her life like the morphine IV drip on the back of her hand, her daughter was the one bright drop. She managed to smile as Mossy came into the room.

"Hi, Mom," said Mossy, suppressing the disappointment at seeing her prayers unanswered and her mother another step closer to death.

"Hi, Mossy. How's my angel?" Barbara smiled and winced with pain in the same expression.

"Fine. I'm out of school until after the holiday."

"That's good. How are things on the farm? Are the coho spawning in the creek?"

"I've been watching from the bridge and I haven't seen any this year. I walked the creek last week and didn't see any spawned out carcasses..."

"Excuse me, Ms. Stone," came a voice from the door and Mossy turned her attention to the doctor standing at the threshold of the door. "I go off shift in about fifteen minutes and wonder if I could have a word with you before I leave?"

"Sure," said Mossy, pointing to the chair which had been set up next to her mother's hospital bed. Standing out of Barbara's view, the doctor shook his head no and wiggled his index finger, inviting Mossy out into the hall. "I'll be right back, Mom," said Mossy following the doctor out of the room.

"I'm Dr. Rubah from Oncology and I've been assigned your mother's case. I get many of the terminal cases here at OMH," said the physician in way of introduction. "We see a lot of suffering and dying, but we never get used to it and I can only imagine what you and your mother are going through...particularly, this time of year..."

The doctor paused for Mossy to respond, "Yeah, well...thanks."

177

"Most of our cases that get this far are referred to Hospice. Your mom seems ambivalent, but you seem to have some resistance..."

"They can't bring back my mother's health and neither can you. Hospice helps with feelings and I don't need help grieving. I'm doing fine in that department by myself..."

"Hospice can help with other things. Like...the funeral arrangements. I don't know if you've had time to think of that and it's awkward for me to deal with that end of things when I would like nothing more than to give your mom back her vitality."

"I can handle the disposition of the body. We've discussed it."

"In that case, I hope your mom's other affairs are in order. Her liver and kidneys are barely functioning. She's got maybe two weeks...at most...before total renal/hepatic failure. It could happen any time. Her pallor will get worse, her pulse will increase, her breathing will come in pants and the smell of her breath will change. These signs will indicate your mom has only a few hours to live...In the meantime, if her affairs are in order, I recommend that we increase the Morphine dosage on her IV. If you don't require your mother's lucidity, there is no reason to allow her suffering."

Tears welled in Mossy's eyes and, captured by gravity, rode down her cheeks where they escaped her chin becoming airborne: perfect round globules, sparkling in the bright artificial light in the hallway. "Go ahead, increase the dose..."

The physician pushed past Mossy to fidget with the settings on the electronic pump. "Good night, Mrs. Stone," he said to Barbara as if he expected the lights to be going out for Barbara imminently.

"I'll sit for a bit with you if that's all right, Mom."

"Please," murmured Barbara, with her respirations slowing under the influence of the strong narcotic.

As her mother slept, Mossy had only troubled thoughts for company. She had been somewhat guarded with the physician. The funeral arrangements were unclear. Barbara had said she wanted to be put in the ground beside her husband, which required the posting of a $25,000 trust with the State's cemetery board. The hospital bills had begun to arrive, dating back to Barbara's first month in the hospital, and the medical bills for the last six months had already exceeded the value of the farm on the open market. Mossy had gotten a card from one of Barbara's old neighbors in Rose Lodge telling her that her grandmother had died of breast cancer. Mossy was without support. She didn't have friend in the world apart from the one that lay dying in the bed beside her. All night, Mossy struggled with this reality.

In the small hours of the morning, Mossy's olfactory caught the acidotic, toxic scent of her mother's breath and Mossy knew that Barbara had entered the last chapter of her own book. Strangely, Barbara's right hand lifted from the bed and pointed at the ceiling. She was falling awake through space-time. "Look," she murmured. "They're mating." And her right hand closed in the clasp of a ghost.

৯৵৶

As had been her habit most of her life, Barbara opened her eyes with the first light of the sun, which, on this day, made it a little after seven. She saw her daughter stir in the chair next to her bed. "Did you stay the night there?" she asked Mossy, but could not quite hear Mossy's reply. "Are there salmon running in the creek?" she asked dumbly.

"It hasn't been a good year for salmon," she heard Mossy say and tried to see through the implications of that statement, looking at a world that was as tired and beat up as Barbara felt.

Her breakfast was hanging on the dorsal surface of her hand next to the saline/morphine drip. There was no morning coffee, no fruit from the orchard, no warmth from the cook stove, no morning walk with the dogs, no standing on the bridge watching the Coho fry strike at twigs...there was only the pain and the release from pain which was measured by a drip, drip, drip into her hand.

Barbara struggled to focus, and found that she could not. The brief moment of consciousness had exhausted her and she was falling back into the cloud of unconsciousness. She desired company with her daughter, but could think of nothing to say. "Please...," she said trying to focus. "Please...," she said trying to remember what it was that she was asking for...contact with her daughter; the sound of Mossy's voice; the feel of her daughter's warmth sitting next to Barbara; "God, I want to go home...tell me a story," said Barbara, not knowing what else to say.

Mossy sat silently for a moment and then began, "Well, once upon a time, there was a herd of wild little ponies that lived in a beautiful little valley in the deep forest..."

"A valley like our valley?" asked Barbara.

"Yes, just like the Bogachiel. A valley with grassy meadows and huge spruce trees. A wild, clean valley with sweet grass and crystal clear water...with fish." Mossy shut her eyes, and Barbara also shut her eyes, dabbing at the palette of her imagination and recall. "A fresh breeze always blew up the valley in the afternoon, blowing the tall sweet grass like waves on the ocean..."

"Just like hommmme," came Barbara's weak voice drawing out the word which was her center of the universe.

"Yes...and the frogs croaked, the owls called one another and, in fall, the ponies liked to stand in the meadow and listen to the elk bugle. It rained, just like where we live, and there were biting flies and sometimes the ponies tripped in holes made by the mountain beavers...But the ponies were very happy and glad to be alive. They had each other and they had the whole world to play in..."

"What games?" asked Barbara trying to focus beyond the pain that stabbed at her guts...seeing the valley through the clouds of her sedation.

"They ran as fast as they could across the wide, flat meadow and they played hide-and-go-seek in the surrounding ancient forest..." and Mossy went on to tell the story the way she remembered it from her mother's telling of the story when Mossy lay in a bed of hopelessness and endless pain. As Barbara's voice had then conveyed a promise of joy and freedom from affliction...

"The ponies prepared to fight for their home. They practiced their kicks and they sharpened their hooves and they prepared for battle. But they were peace-loving ponies and they could not make warriors out of themselves, so they sent the alpha pony out one more time to try to talk...I mean to communicate with the settlers that were flooding into the valley."

"Can you get the grasshopper out of my mane?" asked Barbara mysteriously. "My hands are like hooves." Barbara's breathing was coming in little panting puffs that sent messages through Mossy's nose that her mother was surely dying.

"There was no way for the ponies to defend their home or preserve their way of life..." Mossy stopped her story as Barbara's breathing stopped for fifteen seconds and then resumed. Mossy continued, "They smelled each other very carefully and made sure that they could find each other wherever they went by smell. They shared one last nibble from the grass that had lost its nourishment and a sip from the water that no longer tasted of freshness...they lay down in the meadow and they waited and waited..."

One by one the ponies woke up on the other side. And the White Pacing Pony of Barbara's soul stood naked without name, ego or pretense amid the other ponies. In joy, she recognized the spirit of the Father Pony she had lost as a girl and the Husband Pony she had lost as a young woman...The Mother Pony was there and even the Dog Ponies she had not seen since childhood...And together the wild creatures ran at the speed of light across the wide, curvaceous plane of space, hiding and seeking in the ancient forest of time...

"...by one the ponies woke up on the other side," Mossy was saying, when she realized that her mother had not been breathing for some time. Mossy felt for a pulse at her mother's neck and it was absent. A strange, peaceful expression faded from her mother's face and was replaced by the vacant mask of death. Mossy lay her head on her mother's still chest and wept for some time.

§◦◦§

Mossy pushed Barbara in the wheelchair toward the elevator and recognized Dr. Rubah getting into the wide elevator with a nurse and almost lost her nerve for her plan. The doctor held the elevator for Mossy and Barbara, so there was no turning back.

"Mrs. Stone, you're looking peaceful this morning," observed the physician as the doors closed. As the elevator made its two floor descent, the doctor flicked at the drip chamber attached to the IV tree sprouting from the back of Barbara's wheelchair and said in a quiet voice to Mossy, "Better have Jenny here check your mom's IV It's not running for some reason and the increased morphine dosage seems to be helping her to relax a bit."

"I promised my mom we would go out to feel the morning sun on our faces," said Mossy as the elevator doors opened. "You can do whatever you want with the IV in just two minutes," she protested, making for the outside door with her mother.

The rest of the school year had been the hardest time of Mossy's life since her accident twelve years previously. Being eighteen had allowed her to continue living on the farm and Medicaid had saved the farm from being sold to pay for her mother's medical expenses. Mossy had dug into the Farmer's Market business that her mother had maintained and taken a part-time custodial job at the Forks Library to maintain financial stability. Mossy acquired, Rufus, a large,

Newfoundland dog to help her with her loneliness and to protect the farm in her absence.

The physician waited with the nurse to give the mother and daughter a moment of privacy. "You know, I'm really glad we adjusted up the morphine for Mrs. Stone. She looks a lot more peaceful today..."

"She looked pretty stoned, really," observed R.N. Jenny Fox.

The medical personalities waited a few minutes before heading out though the outside doors where they found an empty wheelchair and, as promised, an IV, dripping onto the parking lot, waiting for their ministrations.

৩৵৻

Bogachiel Trail, Olympic National Park
Wednesday, June 9, 1999

The body of her mother lay next to that of Phil Stone's and eventually the state had lost interest in its whereabouts. While Mossy's classmates strutted across the football field in mortarboards and black robes to receive their diplomas, Mossy celebrated her graduation by exploring the river, which had been her friend through childhood and adolescence.

The first day was an easy trail hike up the main stem of the river to Fifteen Mile Shelter where a group of Boy Scouts were carving their troop's number in the old CCC shelter and breaking off pieces of the outhouse for fire starter. This was the first human contact Mossy had experienced on the trail, but she didn't linger. Crossing the glue-laminate bridge over the North Fork, Mossy saw the two adult scout leaders trout fishing in the cold babbling water above. Mossy took out her map and compass and laid one edge of the compass on a line connecting the Fifteen Mile bridge on the map with a waterfall shown on the trailless South Fork, about a mile distant.

"Lost?" called out one of the scout leaders, noticing the pretty young woman with her unfolded map on the bridge.

"Not yet!" replied Mossy, folding her map. "By the way, your clean, reverent, and brave boys are tearing apart the shelter back there," she added, stepping off crumbling, rotten cedar puncheon and plunging into the lush, green chaos of the untrammeled rain forest.

"The crazy bitch missed the trail!" remarked one scout leader to the other. "We'll probably have to rescue her."

"Not until we're done here," said the second, casting out into a promising pool.

Mossy plunged into the environment which was her namesake, and thrashed around on a general compass course until she found an elk trail through the living wall of jungle. As the sound of the babbling North Fork faded along with the shouts and curse words from the scouts, Mossy was enveloped by the all-quiet, all-living rain forest.

And it was, in a word: GREEN.

It was green, green, green.

It was green, over green, under green, ever green.

It was green, in between green, beside green, always green.

It was green on everything that sat still for more than a moment.

Green on every preposition in a sentence without a verb. It was green, hard-going green, through the devil's club, green,

And the vine maple, green, but beautiful, green, stumbling, tripping green.

Across the immense, green, tangle of the, green, forest floor of the green Ancient Forest: green, green, green.

Walking, staggering, sometimes crawling amid the huge stems of spruce, hemlock, and, cedar was like ambulating across the floor of a cage of dinosaurs. Mossy looked straight up in awe, frequently trying to catch a view of the tops of the tree giants. But their trunks and graceful necks disappeared in many vaulting ceilings of green, green, green.

As Mossy's nose took in the scent of the elk trail, the musk of a rotting fungus, the blunt fart of a bear stool, her ears likewise adjusted to the ambience of the rain forest. In the blanket of silence, she heard the distant drumming of a ruffed grouse; the staccato of a pileated woodpecker hammering on a hollow snag; and the excited chattering of a Douglas squirrel protesting the woodpecker's intrusion upon its space. And as Mossy's ears adjusted, she again heard the sound of tumbling water, now in front of her. She forgot the compass and walked, staggered, crawled to the hydraulic symphony. Crashing through the green barriers, the forest floor suddenly ended in open space, and Mossy looked down into the chasm of the South Fork Bogachiel. Above her was a mighty forty-foot waterfall, which would be the upward limits of anadromous fish. She held onto a vine maple and took in the spectacle. There was a dazzle of sword fern and devil's club climbing both flanks of the waterfall. The vine maple, slide alder, salmonberry and trailing vegetation grew over the lip of the gorge competing for open space. With the rays of evening light breaking through the canopy, it was like staring at the private parts of an Emerald Maiden, who protected her reticence with outstretched fingers bearing thorny nails. The deep green vulva of her gorge sheltering the silver salmon and steelhead that would add their nutrients to the fecundity of this forest jungle.

Mossy stepped back and found a flat spot where her nose told her that a deer had made its camp the night before. She pulled out her sleeping bag and sank into the soft moss. She ate muffins from the corn and raisins she had put up down-valley and closed her eyes, off and on, waiting for the night. The forest stirred restlessly in the waning light, likewise waiting for night to overtake twilight.

The distant pecking of the pileated woodpecker: the slap on the water of the late arriving steelhead to his ancestral pool below the falls, waiting for a mate that would never arrive; the distant bleating of a newborn elk separated from its mother; the green life erupting from the rot: there was, to Mossy, a sense of endless humor and interest; of ceaseless boredom; of conflict and resolution; of endless cycling...

To the author of <u>Between Forks and Alpha Centauri</u> who likewise sat on this spot of soft, dank, growing ground, (separated from Mossy by space-time and the thin membrane of a book's cover which sequesters reality from fiction) the forest experience was like watching endless summer re-runs of "I Love Lucy." In the frantic, red-headed antics of the pileated; in the "*Hoooohnieeee, A'Hm hooooohm*," of the steelhead; in the *"Bah-bah-Luuuuuuuuu!"* of the moss-draped alder; in the frantic, red-headed antics; in the *"Hoooohnieeee, A'Hm hooooohm*,"; in the *"Bah-bah-Luuuuuuuuu!"*; in the frantic, red-headed antics; in the *"Hoooohnieeee, A'Hm hooooohm*,"; in the *"Bah-bah-Luuuuuuuuu!"* of the moss draped alder...

ও৶৶

The next morning, Mossy was up in the dim light of the first bird calls and gathered her stuff sack of possessions and food from where she had hung it on a spruce limb. After her breakfast, she followed the gorge of the lower South Fork across the tangled jungle mat and gouged side canyons to where the river began to climb out of its ravine to lie on a lazy, winding bed through alder bottoms. The day grew warm and Mossy stopped frequently to feed on thimbleberries and salmonberries. In the afternoon she swam in the river in her clothes and then stripped, putting her wet garments on a sunny, hot rock to dry while she lay in the lush sedge to doze. Eventually the little bit of paradise was invaded by black flies and it was time to don damp clothes and push on.

By late afternoon the landscape was again turning to canyon country. The long shadows played invitingly across the glade of a small sedge meadow and Mossy decided to camp early, rather than enter steep country in waning daylight. Mossy's nose said, "Bear!" and, searching about for the most inviting spot to flake out her sleeping bag, she found the enormous scat piles which transmitted this message. She noticed a candy bar wrapper and aluminum foil in one of the piles and took extra care in hanging her food by counterbalancing the bag. Mossy rubbed elderberry leaves on her skin to cover her human smell and avoid attracting ursine company.

She lay comfortably in her sleeping bag and watched the waxing half moon in an evening sky of deepening hue. Eventually, the fresh, newborn light which had left the sun eight minutes and twenty seconds previous surrendered the theater to the ancient and mysterious light of the stars. From her sleeping bag, Mossy stared into the cosmos with the interest and intensity of a captain on the bridge of a starship. The *"who, who...WHO"* of a spotted owl punctuated the quiet. A cool, down-valley breeze from the subalpine basin above followed the river downstream to Mossy's home inviting the scrutiny of Mossy's nose which flared in wonderment at the smells of this new environment. The breeze carried the howling chorus of coyotes to Mossy's wakeful ears. Later on, Mossy's nose again alerted: *"Bear! Bear!"* and eventually she heard the grunting and farting which attended the procession of a sow bear and her cub into the meadow. Mossy caught the bear in her headlamp and the bear advanced on the light. Mossy got out of her bag and called, "Hey, bear. HEY!" but the two advanced to a spot directly under her hung food. She found a rock and pitched it at the sow, and the bear made a short charge, which affirmed what Mossy already suspicioned: that these were not wild bear, but bear from the heavily visited Sol Duc, accustomed to plundering human food. Noise did not intimidate the bear and Mossy stood by helplessly as the cub climbed the alder and bent down the branch supporting her food until it broke, lowering Mossy's food bag to the sow. In five minutes the bear had eaten Mossy's food supply for the next three days and proceeded downriver grunting and farting.

శారా

Upper South Fork, Bogachiel
Friday, June 11, 1999

Mossy had difficulty getting back to sleep. With the first hint of daylight, she retrieved her torn, slobbery, and empty bear bag. She picked several handfuls of oxalis and munched the tart, cloverlike leaves while drinking the cool water from the river. She packed her sleeping bag and began a slow cautious ascent into the canyon. She walked for a couple of hours through forest of enormous hemlock and dense huckleberry. In the early morning light, Mossy followed the hundred-year-old footsteps of pioneer Chris Morgenroth crossing to the south side of the river beneath a waterfall of indeterminate size. Warmed by her exertion, and thrilled by the roar of water, she dropped her pack and jumped into the pool, standing under the stinging cold rain of the falls. When she climbed out of the frigid water, her skin was tingling.

She donned her pack and climbed up a steep game trail beside the falls. In 500 vertical feet the forest community changed from the upper threshold of montane to a subalpine environment. She had left the oxalis at the bottom of the falls and walked amid a ground cover of wild vanilla leaf. Sitka spruce surrendered to mountain hemlock and subalpine fir. The falls benched and there was another falls...and then another. Daybreak brought a shifting of the diurnal breeze and the mist from the falls was pulled upwards in a mysterious veil. And after a last climb of several hundred feet, Mossy pushed through a gentle fence of salal and huckleberry and stood at the bottom of a natural amphitheater.

The orb of the sun broke over Bogachiel Peak and Mossy dropped her pack. She stood in awe watching the day advance on this magnificent basin. The rays of the sun struck her sweat drenched T-shirt and she spread her arms in welcoming. The cool mist from the falls tickled her back while the warm rays of the sun embraced her front. With her arms spread, a cross was projected in the cool mist at her back. The furnace of Creation warmed her front, while the water of Life cooled her back. The small hairs on her arms and legs horripilated and waved in the morning breeze like tendrils of an anemone in a tide pool.

And something extraordinary was happening inside her head. The oxalic acid she had taken on board with her earlier browsing, combined with the exertion from the climb, was triggering a chemical/electrical imbalance in her central nervous system. Opening her eyes and looking into the sun, Mossy saw an orange aura about the trees and herbaceous ground cover that carpeted the basin. She looked down at her legs and they appeared to glow with life and vitality. She could not see the birthmark on her left leg through the enveloping aura. It was like she was riding on a wild and free White Pacing Mustang. Her consciousness spread out over space-time and she was all places at once. If her eyes were mounted on pods and removed from her head like those of a banana slug so that she could look back at her face, she would see the same aura that burned around her legs shining in a halo around her face.

184

She was a beam of light; a crippled child taking her first step away from her crutches; a child in a drift boat hearing the story of a White Pacing Mustang that would never surrender its wildness. It was an event in space/time born in reality, stored in the mind of the father, conveyed to the soul of the daughter and somehow communicated to the spirit of the unborn child. Mossy's body quivered and quaked in a near convulsive state while her consciousness rode a wave of ecstasy.

She inspired a breath of the spring air and ten billion atoms moved across her sense of smell in a firm handshake with reality. The breath carried the scent of a pollen from the avalanche lily, elephant's head, shooting star, gentian, valerian, and other bold spring flowers that erupted from snow to find the sun that irradiated Mossy's young bosom. Her keen olfactory field-stripped the fragrance from the pollen like pretty wrapping from a Christmas package and studied the present of the underlying DNA.

She exhaled and inhaled ten billion more atoms. Her nose scanned the many musky messages scattered in scat and urine across the basin from bear, elk, and deer. The smell of the basin told her the marmot had been spring-cleaning and had pushed the accumulated dung of winter out into the blaze of the morning sunshine.

Mossy exhaled and hungrily pulled in ten billion more bytes of reality. The smell of the stream as the sun extorts its hydraulic tax to support the water cycle, even at the headwaters of the Bogachiel River; the pungent bleeding pitch of the subalpine fir in the wake of spring avalanche; the excited wind under the wings of the hummingbirds arriving in their summer home from a three thousand mile trip...

But in the next breath was a hint of something out of place: not of this valley; not of this reality. The something tried to smell like lilac, but, to Mossy's nose, smelled more like toxic waste. It broke the spell for Mossy. She lowered her arms, drank of the South Fork, shouldered her pack and continued into the basin heading for Bogachiel Peak.

ꝭ◌ꝭ

Bogachiel Peak
Friday, June 11, 1999, 10:00

It had been the worst night of Julie Smith's life. She hadn't slept all night on the hard ground beneath the tent floor and that had resulted in her having to "go to the bathroom" several times during the night. When her boyfriend, Ned Adams, had suggested the trip, Julie believed that he might be seeking the appropriate setting to ask for her hand in marriage. In the last month, he had been so busy with his Political Science finals at the University of Washington, that he had paid her no attention. She had envisioned a pleasant day of hiking followed by a night of making love under the stars. The pleasant day of hiking had been a torturous death march up winding, ankle twisting, precipitous mountain trail into a snow-clad environment. Before pitching camp on Bogachiel Peak, they ascended a steep, ice-filled chute on six snow-covered switchbacks. Ned had to take out an ice axe to cut steps to prevent Julie from sailing down the icy slopes to her death or disfigurement. She vomited Ritz crackers and salami halfway up. There had been a strange, wild, barnyard smell and Julie feared that *Eve's Secret* was, out of the bag, so to speak, but Ned made some remark about smelling elk - some kind of large, reindeerlike creatures(?!)... Then there were two more slopes that set Julie to dry heaving before they dropped their packs on Bogachiel Peak. Julie had immediately pulled out her sleeping bag and foam pad and lay down on the snow, shivering, while Ned pitched the tent. Then, when the tent was up, Ned helped her drag herself and gear into the fabric torture chamber, which had been the stage for the worst night of her life.

Forget lovemaking under the stars! For one thing, it was like winter up here with snow and ice dominating the landscape. For another thing: the ground, itself, which pushed up through the floor of the tent made the thought of any naked horseplay untenable. Then there was the damp, clammy sweat that followed Julie into the sleeping bag and persisted through much of the night. She had used up half a stick of *Secret Dry* in a prophylactic attempt that morning to curb the effect of exertion on her armpits, but sweat had welled from pores spread across Julie's entire body and, on the steep snow and ice, the *Secret Dry* had surrendered all authority over Julie's armpits.

The worse thing had happened the morning before the hike: Julie had started her period! She had douched with lilac *Eve's Secret* that morning before applying the *Secret Dry*, but she struggled through the night with a crushing paranoia that Ned would detect her biological condition through his loud snoring.

The snoring was a reminder that Julie was alone. She would wake Ned up to announce that she had to go to the bathroom and ask him for the toilet paper, and he would be back asleep two minutes later when Julie came back into the tent. Somewhere after midnight, her bowels began rumbling and predicting movement like the sulfurous venting of the Calawah Fault in the valley below. "Ned, I have to go to the BATHROOM!" she emphasized the final word hoping he would understand that this was a new predicament. Ned handed her the t.p. and settled back for another two-minute snooze. "I mean, I really have to go to the BATHROOM! It's serious this time!"

"Well, where have you been going? Just defecate there and bury it."

"I've been going just outside the tent..."

"Jesus!" exclaimed Ned. "Don't shit there!" he actually said the word "shit" to her.

"WELL, WHAT AM I SUPPOSED TO DO?" Julie exclaimed. "I mean, I can't go in here..." Julie started mewling which usually galvanized her boyfriends to action.

"Here, I'll go with you," said Ned, pulling out of the tent with flashlight, camp slippers, ice axe, and toilet paper.

Ned had led her down the steep, snow-covered way trail which led up to the peak. When he found a little piece of dirt sheltered by some huckleberry, he dug a slit with the ice axe and handed Julie the toilet paper. He turned his back to indicate that he was ready for her to commence her business.

"I can't make it work with you standing right beside me, Ned. You know that..." He began walking up the trail, with the flashlight, leaving her in utter darkness. "Wait! I need the flashlight!" called Julie.

"Well, how am I supposed to find my way up the trail without a flashlight?"

"You should have brought TWO flashlights. You're *Mr. Be Prepared.* Why didn't you think of that?"

"Just do your shit and get it done," grumbled Ned, saying that nasty word again. Surrendering the light, he retreated cautiously up the trail toward the miserable camp while Julie held the light on him.

When he disappeared from the cone of artificial light, she called his name to ascertain his whereabouts, "Ned?"

"Yes, Julie?" from 30 meters into the dark.

"You're too close. Move back towards the tent!" Julie ordered.

"Good Lord," came Ned's muttering as he retreated in the dark. "I'll walk off the other side of Bogachiel Peak, blind, and kill myself."

Julie had just pulled down her pants and was taking care of the business at hand when wolves just below her started howling. It scared her so badly she dropped the flashlight and started screaming. It seemed like it took Ned hours to get to her, and the wolves were howling right below her the whole time. What a mess! Intense embarrassment following on the heels of deep fear. Some minutes later, as they made their way back to the tent, Julie began scolding, "Why didn't you tell me there were wolves out here?! They almost got me!"

"Julie, those were coyotes and they were a mile from here. The last wolf was shot dead out of this country back in the twenties..." But the night hadn't gotten any better with that news and this morning wasn't turning out great, either. Before even preparing Julie's coffee, Ned was out with a plastic bag, picking up toilet paper from around the tent and muttering. It had seemed to Julie that the darkness would absorb the toilet paper and yellow snow, but there it was in the cruel morning light. Ned had even picked up and bagged the ultimate trophy in Julie's mortification: a used tampon. There it was, nestled in the clear trash bag, with the coffee grounds and instant oatmeal wrappers.

Julie had brought a cup of coffee and her *Secret Dry* down to the scene of the near wolf attack to freshen up. The coffee acted as a diuretic, just as the uneven ground had the previous evening, and she squatted to pee. As she threw down the toilet paper, which snagged on huckleberry shrub beside the way trail, she caught a reassuring whiff of lilac and smiled inwardly, knowing that *Eve's Secret* was still on the job.

Julie relaxed slightly, threw out the last gulp of coffee with grounds in the bottom of the Sierra cup and began to drink in the view. The red glow of the morning highlighted the West Peak on the Olympus/Mt. Tom massif like a pimple on a well-powdered nose. The great Blue Glacier poked its toe into the Hoh Rain Forest, like a well-shaven leg stepping into a deep green bath. Scattered subalpine fir escaped timberline like mismanaged hair along a bikini. Julie made a mental note to check her own bikini line. It was beautiful in a strange, feral way, but the same beauty was captured in a postcard or Ross Hamilton poster, without one having to pee on the ground or fall down in their own excrement in the face of wolf attack to enjoy.

With these ponderings, Julie shifted her gaze west, away from the Hoh, and into the basin of the South Fork Bogachiel. To her amazement, there was a hiker climbing up from the basin floor where no trail or apparent route existed. The hiker appeared to be climbing in their direction. "Ned! There's somebody down there," Julie called in a tremulous voice.

Ned called back from where he was washing out the breakfast bowls, "No surprises there. This is about the most used trail in Olympic National Park and everyone wants to see the view from Bogachiel Peak."

Julie looked down at the long hair and protuberant chest of the solitary figure and recognized womanhood. Why would a woman be hiking alone, particularly out from an area where no trail existed? "I don't think she is supposed to be down there," called Julie. "I think she's in some kind of trouble," she surmised to Ned, who came down to look for a moment.

"Yup, she's headed this way," was Ned's analysis. "I'll put on some more hot water in case she wants coffee or something..."

"Don't..." whined Julie, somehow jealous of the interloper who was advancing to steal this private moment from her and her lover.

ভ্ৰৎ

Mossy was climbing in earnest as she left the point where the Bogachiel River ceased being a trickle of cold water and became a large snowfield. She climbed for the highest point on the horizon, which she presumed to be the location of the now-gone fire lookout on Bogachiel Peak. The rich smells of the elk, pollen and bruised trees continued to assail her olfactory, but the other odor of chemical lilac grew in proportion and intensity. She became aware of two people watching her progress from a hundred vertical meters above her, and experienced a peculiar inner tickle. Most young women Mossy's age interpret the various aromas in disgust and feel a strong sense of self-consciousness in facing human society after a three-day stint in the wilderness. Mossy's T-shirt stuck to her chest and back with sweat. She ran her fingers through her hair and pulled out a few pieces of elephant's ear lichen and witch's hair from her long strands. She looked down at her legs and saw streaks of sweat running into mud where soil clung to the fine hair around her ankles and calves. She was a sight, she acknowledged to herself, but the part of her brain that might normally occupy itself with agonizing over personal appearance was engaged in processing the myriad of smells wafting on the warm morning air.

She pulled out her water bottle and realized she had forgotten to fill it from the stream before it ran into snow. She drained it and acknowledged she would soon face a decision to turn back or imbibe of water from a different drainage than the Bogachiel, which had exclusively hydrated her and carried her red blood cells for the last decade. She proceeded upslope to make this choice from Bogachiel Peak where a melting snowflake could choose between the Hoh, Sol Duc or Bogachiel for its ride to the ocean.

"HI!" called the man as Mossy approached voice range. "WERE YOU LOST?" the man yelled, as if this interrogation were too important to wait the two minutes it would take to close the distance between them. Mossy thought the question was strange and used part of her brain to formulate an answer. A greater part of her consciousness concentrated on the strange lilac stink and the unnatural smell of hostility that lay in the air like a turd in a scented tissue. Speaking of which, there was exactly such, directly beside the way trail, flagged by a used tampon hanging off the huckleberry bush.

"Hi," said Mossy approaching the couple who stood next to a boiling kettle of water a few meters from their tent. The lilac contagion was coming from the woman who stood slightly behind the man. "If this is Bogachiel Peak, I'm not lost. I've always wanted to explore this valley to its headwaters and here I am... Well, here WE are." Mossy's nose flared as she tried to determine the source of the hostility. It was the woman. The man's smell conveyed friendly interest, but the woman was angry for some unexplained reason. Mossy looked into the painted eyes and tried to find the human being there. "Hi," said Mossy to the woman specifically and smiled, trying to disarm whatever defensive mechanism was causal to the resentment. Mossy felt something tickle her lips from inside and realized that oxalis and some avalanche lilies clung to her smile. She retreated a few feet from the couple to offer personal space to the woman and dropped her pack and pulled out her wool flannel shirt.

"We have plenty of water. Would you like coffee or hot water for tea?" inquired the man.

Mossy considered this offer, "Where did you get the water?"

I hiked it all in from down below, so it's been chlorinated and safe to drink. Besides, it's been boiling for the last few minutes."

"No thanks," said Mossy, delaying her decision about where she would receive her next drink. She pulled her wet T-shirt away from her skin and pulled on her wool-flannel shirt to avoid the chill that would accompany the evaporation of sweat. She sat on her pack and began picking at her teeth to remove the latent vegetation which clung there. "A bear got my food and I've been foraging on some of the native cuisine. I think maybe I ate a little too much oxalis and lowered my pH."

"Hey, we have plenty of food! Want some instant oatmeal?"

"Thanks," she said. "Food's not a problem for me right now. I'm kind of picky about what I eat and I'm not big on *instant* anything." Mossy's nose continued to offer information about the ongoing encounter. The man was glad to see her; the woman was hostile and having her period. That's it: the toxic lilac was some sort of feminine douche! *My God, how could a woman put that poison inside her?* marveled Mossy. Under the lilac, Mossy smelled human urine and realized she had set her pack on yellow snow. She stood up and moved her pack.

"OK, suit yourself." said the man, slightly crestfallen. "We're locals from Seattle," he announced to Mossy. "Where are you from?"

Mossy's eyes scanned to the west and she picked out Reade Hill in the distance. "There!" she said pointing just south of the ridge. "That's where I'm from."

"What, Forks?" asked the man.

"No, seven miles south of Forks. There!" Mossy pointed again. "I own a farm a couple miles outside of the Park."

The woman finally talked, speaking with incredulity, "You hiked all the way across the Park? You're alone? You were way off the trail. Do your parents know where you are?" the stink of animosity was on her questions as well as in the air.

Mossy again smiled to quiet the woman's displeasure. "My parents are both deceased. I live alone. I don't have any friends that wanted to make the trip so I made it alone. Again, I wanted to see the drainage, not the trail, so I followed the South Fork all the way to here. It's beautiful!," said Mossy of her trip and looking around in awe. Her heart filled with a great love of this world and she almost felt like yodeling. "Did you hear the coyotes last night?" she asked.

"Are you sure those were coyotes?" asked the woman, still angry about something.

"What else would they be?" asked Mossy, smiling and showing open hands in an effort to convey a friendly question. The woman glared at her and Mossy retreated to ten meters from the high point of the domed peak to further consider the view and make a plan.

A thunderhead was rising in the eastern sky and eclipsed the sun for a few moments. Mossy's gaze traveled south down into the Hoh rain forest and up the tree-shrouded valley to Mount Olympus. She looked east across High Divide, which led out to the Bailey Range. She turned and looked out across the snow- and ice-choked Seven Lakes Basin and up at the brilliant white clouds in a bright azure sky. The woman was talking to her man friend in a hushed voice, "...got to tell the Park Rangers. She's probably a runaway or mental deficient hiking alone like that without any more equipment. She doesn't even have an ice axe..."

Mossy stood at this small summit as the thunderhead parted and allowed the rays of the sun to again bombard her with radiation. From this vantage, there were three hundred and sixty degrees of choice in direction, each offering three thousand, six hundred seconds of choice and each second providing unlimited opportunity for random exploration. She had arrived upon the field of limitless possibility and considered her options from an infinite menu. As the woman's hushed voice reached her ears and the smell of her enmity continued to grasp her nose, Mossy sought a state of mind consistent with the high field of possibilities she had reached...

I can control my appetite and hike many days without food, said Mossy of herself to herself. Amen. And I can go in any direction I please and drink from any water source I choose, amen, intoned Mossy, bravely divorcing herself from her relationship to the water of the Bogachiel below.

"...I mean look at that girl!" the woman was saying in anger to her partner. "When do you suppose she's last bathed? There's stuff growing out of her hair! What kind of equipment does she have for this environment? You said yourself a person would be nuts to be out here without an ice axe..."

And I can control my breathing, ahhhhhhhhhhhhhmen, said Mossy of herself, to herself, slowing her panting into deep, slow breaths...and heart ahhhhhhhhh...Mossy's heart slowed in measure to her breathing...And I have authority over what I let in through the windows of my nose and ears ahhhhhhhhhhhhhmmmmmmmen... The smell of lilac and hostility faded and the updrafting breeze again carried news from the marmots and wild flowers...of ozone from dry lightning in the distance...

The woman's voice was growing in decibels and hysteria, "Can't you smell her, for Christ sake? She smells like an animal: like a bear or a pig or something! Her legs are filthy, dirt..."

"Come to me," came a verbalization inside Mossy's head with the voice of Barbara Stone. *"It's time, Mossy..."* Mossy looked up into the mighty thunderhead that loomed like hands tented in prayer in the eastern sky. In her heart she felt the radiation of the sun striking the screen of this great cloud and the

stirring of electricity in its bosom. There were nameless spirits riding the strong updrafts of the cloud. Mossy was with her mother and with the father whom she had never met. Mossy was with Creation and with the Creator.

"Ah...Amen," she said. "Ahhhhhhhhhh..." as she looked out from the cloud at the world that unfolded from this threshold. She saw a line of 2,164,208 inches, which led back to her farm thirty-some miles downstream. "...mmmmmmm..." Following the spirit of her mother and father, Mossy looked down on this straight line, seeing the waterfalls, giant trees, and circuitous river that followed the general course back home. From the field of infinite possibilities, the-------line------led------home. "....mmmmmmmmmmmmmmmen. Hooooommmmmmmmmmmme," said Mossy out loud. Going back to the pack and taking off her flannel shirt in obedience to the voice in her head.

"Come to Me. Come home to Me," commanded the Voice.

"Hey," said the human male, standing next to the boiling pot, "Where are you going?"

"...she's definitely not right, Ned. Better leave her be. She may be dangerous...Just her smell is lethal...If I ever smell that funky, please, please, put a gun to my head and SHOOT ME..."

Mossy snapped out of her trance for a moment and said to the man, "I'm all right, but it's time for me to go home. It was nice to meet you." Mossy looked at the woman and said, "I just want to tell you that I smelled you first. I smelled you when I was way down there," said Mossy pointing to the distant roar of the falls. "It smells like you douched with the Love Canal!" Mossy donned her pack and was highballing down the way trail to the main footpath below.

The woman was crying hysterically, sobbing, "The bitch! The stinky little bitch! I hope she falls on the ice and slides ALL THE WAY TO HELL! The little stinky bitch..." But Mossy's concentration was upon the vectors of her feet as they skidded across the hard snow. One leg in front of the other: the birthmark on Mossy's left leg flashing like the broken centerline of a highway from a fast moving vehicle.

Running for home now, each pace consuming six feet of the 2.16 million inches that separated Mossy from her farm, one leg in front of the other. One leg in front of the other, hooommmmmmmmmmmmmme, one leg in front of the other, amen, leg, hooooooooooommmmmmmmmmmmmmme...Along the palisades above the basin she had traversed, aaaaaammmmmmmmmen; down the steep unmarked snow slopes to Deer Lake, hommmme; back up the ridge known as Little Divide, jumping on and off snow as the trail flirted with southern exposure, aaaaammmmmen, down the switchbacks into the rain forest of the North Fork Bogachiel, and along the trail passing Twenty One Mile and Hyak shelters to Fifteen Mile. Mossy's metabolism had been on the cannibalistic Krebs cycle since that morning and the fuel that powered her run down the trail was Mossy herself. She began mixing the jog with walking.

Below Fifteen Mile Shelter, she came on the scout troop she had met two days before. One of the scouts was being carried in a makeshift stretcher while one walked behind the stretcher with his right arm in a sling. Protruding from the sling was a hand wrapped in bloody gauze. Mossy walked for a while behind the troop before finding a flat enough piece of forest floor to skirt the group. "Hey, it's the lost girl hiker!" called the one leader to the other.

"So you finally found the trail!" said the second to Mossy.

"Yeah...whatever. Excuse me," said Mossy, pushing around the knot of hikers. *Hoooooooooommmmmme* said the voice in her head.

"Hey, Miss, if you can stay on the trail this time and expect to get out tomorrow, we need someone to make a call for us..."

Hooommmmmmmmmmmmmmmme, said the voice in Mossy's head.

"We have a couple of hurt boys here and only one stretcher between the two...Hey miss! Would you call the Park Service when you get out tomorrow? Miss!..."

Hooommmmmmmmmmmmmmmmme, commanded the voice, with Mossy transferring the command to her tired legs and feet. Slogging along the muddy trail to Flapjack and across the washed out meadow that used to be the site of the Bogachiel Guard Station. Hooommmmmmmmmmmmmmmme: out the last six miles to the trailhead, down the Forest Service Road which Barbara Beyers had first driven up twenty years ago on a fishery study at Bear Creek. Hooommmmmmmmmmmmmmmmme: Mossy caught a brief glimpse of her farm from the distance in what was becoming twilight and saw that the motion detecting garden lights were on. The old deer, *June Eleven*, must have jumped the six-foot fence again and be helping herself to the goodies therein. *June Eleven*: it occurred to Mossy that the date was on or near June 11, 1999, the tenth anniversary of her mobility.

Hooommmmmmmmmmmmmmmmme, until Mossy was running down the driveway towards the bridge, passing the garden... She stopped to watch the old doe jump the garden fence from the inside. Mossy went inside the garden and picked some plump strawberries for quick energy. She drank from the hose bib, gulping the water which had given her life and vitality. She called the Hoh Ranger Station from the phone at the barn and told them there was a scout troop in distress between Fifteen Mile and Flapjack.

The voice in Mossy's mind whispered, *come back to me*...and she hung up the phone. She walked to the dog kennel, eating strawberries, and released her old dog, Daisy, and big Newfoundland pup, Rufus who charged out to bounce around at her feet, wagging tails and rejoicing in the liberation and reunification. Come back to me...and Mossy was standing in the orchard under the weeping cherry which still clung to some of its spring blossoms...*come*. And Mossy dropped the remaining strawberries and sat on the mounded dirt that was her mother's grave and wept...the dogs licking the tears from her face and a daring mouse sneaking away with one of the berries. Mossy wept in grief for the loss of her mother and in joy for her place in the universe.

She was hooommmmmmmmmmmmmmmmme.

Ten

Space by itself, and time by itself, are doomed to fade away into mere shadows, and only a kind union of the two will preserve an independent reality
-**Albert Einstein** (1879-1955)

Space-time grips mass, telling it how to move, and mass grips space-time, telling it how to curve
-**John Archibald Wheeler** (1911 -)

Clallam County Courthouse
Monday, June 14, 1999, 13:00

"*N*inth District Federal Court of Western Washington in session, the Honorable Walter Greenway presiding," announced the Court Clerk, standing briefly while the judge took his seat.

Peter Cienfuegos shifted uncomfortably in his padded chair, recognizing George Redding, the man he had debated in Forks, along with the harem of lawyers which seemed to attend his every sneeze and fart. Suddenly the lawyers, followed by George Redding, stood up. "Please sit down," said the elderly magistrate, who sat himself at the desk above the court. In embarassment, Peter stood up out of respect, and Magistrate Greenway glared at the lone figure who seemed to countermand his reasonable request. "Do sit down, unless you're unhappy with your seat," intoned Magistrate Greenway. "Is Mr. George Redding in the courtroom?"

"Yes, Your Honor," said George, standing briefly.

"Now on the docket today, we have Mr. Redding, representing the Washington Commercial Forest Action Committee, forwarding an appeal of the 1990 finding in Judge William Dwyer's Court, which disallows a Federal Agency to conduct management action which further threatens an endangered species. The brief that you have filed presents the argument that the pre-existing legislation which created the Forest Service and provided for revenues to schools, coupled with Federal legislation mandating the State of Washington to provide compulsory education, conflict with Judge Dwyer's finding and are, therefore, illegal. Interesting... Is that the gist of it, Mr. Redding?"

"Yes, sir," said George, and then sat down.

The magistrate continued, "Is there a Mr. Peter Cienfuegos in the court?"

"Yes, sir," said Peter.

"And you're here today, owing to a charge by Olympic National Park Rangers regarding your possession of a controlled substance in the Sol Duc Campground and the further aggravation of said charges by your failure to appear in this court last month...Well, we're happy to see you in court today, Mr. Cienfuegos, because we take a dim view of drugs in this court and a dimmer view of people who don't deign to settle such charges against them." The magistrate seemed to be waiting for a reply.

"Uh, yes, sir," said Cienfuegos.

"Well, if there is no objection in the court, let's settle the matter with Mr. Cienfuegos first, since this seems to be a more straight forward consideration and requires less deliberation on the part of the court..." There were a few moments of silence in the courtroom. "All right then, Mr. Cienfuegos, how do you plead to the matter of possession of a controlled substance, an alleged violation occurring April 1, 1998 in the Sol Duc Campground?"

"Well, guilty, sir," Cienfuegos looked at the ceiling searching his memory about the civil rights issues which attached to his case. "But the charges came under circumstances I would like to discuss with you..."

"Mr. Cienfuegos, if you're prepared to enter a plea, please stand and face the court. How say you on the charge of possession of controlled substance?"

Peter Cienfuegos stood and faced the magistrate. "Guilty, but I would like to explain what happened."

"Now is the time," said Magistrate Greenway.

"Some friends of mine were smoking marijuana inside our wall tent. I may have also taken a couple of hits. A Park Ranger came by and must have smelled the pot. He ordered us out and searched the tent without a warrant. I feel that he should have had a search warrant to go in the tent..."

"I feel that you should have responded to the Court's first summons. If that is the best you can do in the way of explaining away the charges against you, I am prepared to pronounce sentence."

"Yeah, go ahead..."

"I sentence you to six months in jail and a $500 fine with all but two days of the jail term suspended, pending no further involvement with drugs. In the matter of failing to appear in court, I hold you to a $10,000 bail, to be cleared by this Court on October 10."

"Uh, Judge, that seems rather harsh. The Ranger came into my tent without a warrant and I feel that my rights were violated..."

"Young man. You're remanded to jail. Turn yourself in downstairs at the jail or I'll put forward a warrant for your arrest. Next case...Mr. Redding..."

George Redding stood. "Your Honor, you have read the brief. The position of the Washington Commercial Forest Action Committee is this..." Redding read from his own brief. "There is no legal defense for the Endangered Species Act on Forest Service lands in any of the 50 states which apply mandatory education and promise contributions to the school districts therein. When the United States Forest Service was created in 1897, only timber, grazing, and watershed protection are recognized aspects of the multiple use concept...

"Interesting," mumbled the magistrate into his microphone. "I wondered how long it would be before the timber industry tripped on the conflict of mission..."

"Your Honor..." George Redding waited for the magistrate to stop talking to himself.

"Yes, go ahead, Mr. Redding. I expected this argument to be raised by the community."

"The Forest Service has an integral timber production responsibility, central to its congressional mandate. The overlay of the Endangered Species Act cannot be allowed to interfere with the agency's core mission, staffing, budgeting, and management priorities. In short, the Forests belong to the American people first as timber, grazing and watershed resources. The long string of attending multiple purposes exists to enhance these paramount elements. The use of the Endangered Species Act by the environmental community to stonewall this core mission is inconsiderate of both Congressional mandate and such basic human community needs as the feeding, clothing, transporting and educating of our children.

"Your Honor, you can turn this injustice around. Sign a court order breaking the injunction on logging the parcel on Reade Hill known as unit 37-E..."

Peter Cienfuegos was out of his chair, "This is outrageous! You can't get around the Endangered Species by crying economic hardship! Otherwise there is no point to the law..."

"Young man," exploded the Magistrate Greenway, "I've had it with you! I order you out of the courtroom this moment. Clerk, call the baliff to remove the nuisance..."

☙❧

Hemp Hill Creek
Monday, June 14, 1999, 13:00

Mossy had felt disconnected ever since returning from her hike a few days previous. She had halfheartedly gotten several flats of strawberries ready for the Farmer's Market along with some greenhouse tomatoes. It felt good to be working in the garden and associated with her mother's previous industry. Mossy spent time at the cedar she had planted over her mother's grave next to the pawpaw, which her mother had planted over Phil. In the cabin, she missed her mother's company and found herself in imaginary conversations with the deceased. She had taken a few possessions of Barbara's and placed them in the cedar box under the bed she now used as her own. She opened the box and stood under the skylight examining the material items that sufficed for family heirlooms. She picked up what had been her mother's favorite shirt and smelled it. It was as if Barbara was in the room beside her. There were the wedding rings of both her parents, a crushed hard hat that still had the dried blood of her father, and an old hickory shirt that painted a picture for her nose of the father she had never met. In an old manila envelope, she found a document in her mother's handwriting which she had never seen before. She sat in the sunlight and read:

The Cosmic Clock by Phil and Barbara Stone

The following explain how the human intellect has misinterpreted sensorial information and created a totally erroneous picture of the relationship between space-time and matter, which we mistakenly call "reality."

* A second is forever. Time flies when you're bored or scared. That is because brain waves normally occur at 10 Hz, but are accelerated by boredom or fear. It is only the peak waves which yield conscious thought. Therefore, even if time were linear (which it is not) our perception of it is particular. Between the brief points of consciousness, represented by peak brain waves, is the vast space of other-consciousness.

* Time cannot occur without space, nor space without time. This is because movement defines them both. Picture a canvas with a line (representing time) on one face and a cube (representing three-dimensional space) on the other. The human brain perceives only one aspect of that canvas at a time. But the real picture can only be seen from within the canvas itself looking out upon time and space simultaneously.

* Picture a sphere alone in the dark in space-time. Envision that sphere traveling at a velocity of 1.86 mile per second (6,696 mph). Now envision the same sphere traveling at ten times the speed or 186 miles per second. With nothing external to the sphere to measure its travel, there is no difference between its condition in either state. If a ray of light is projected upon the leading hemisphere, then travel can be defined as either 0.00001 or 0.001 the yardstick of lightspeed. If two spheres exist alone in the dark of space-time, then their velocity and condition is measured in relation to each other. With no internal calibration (such as the whirring of electrons around a nucleus), space-time and velocity would be defined by the relationship between those two sole members of the universe. Neither time nor space exists beyond the realm of the material or energetic universe.

* Time is not a point on a line, but a spot in the curvaceous cup of time-space. A moment in time is like an address along a street or a sentence in a book. It does not cease to be when the observer is no longer in its proximity, nor does it come to be only as the observer approaches it. Witness a starry night which showers our planet with the ancient light of the universe.

* Take a stone and throw it into still water. A concentric wave travels out from the stone's impact with the water. The splash is an expanding, concentric ring defining an event horizon. Everything outside of the event horizon is nothingness as related to the splash. Consider the splash of the Big Bang, some ten billion years ago. As the universe is hurled outward, it forms the celestial splash of the known universe some twenty billion light-years across. Though our most powerful telescopes reveal the light of stars which are five-billion light-years away, we cannot stand on earth today and perceive light, which emanated before our five billion year-old planet. Advancing outward at the speed of light, some five billion light-years ahead of the hurtling stars and galaxies, is the expanding concentric event horizon of the Big Bang. At the edge of this concentric circle is the beginning of time. Outside of the growing ring is the nothingness of nonexistence.

* Take a burning ember on the end of a stick and wave it back and forth faster and faster until you reach the speed of light. The moving point appears to define a solid line, but we know that the ember is not at all points along the line. The line is an event shadow. Spin the line and the line defines a one-inch circle. Spin the circle and the circle becomes a sphere. In subatomic structures, the spherical impression of the atom is defined by the random occurrence of the electron(s) in unpredicted orbits within the tiny space of an angstrom, as the electrons move at the speed of light.

* What we see as hard reality is only the blur of movement in space-time. Hold a camera with a 1/60th second shutter speed as still as you can and take a picture of a fast moving truck. The background may appear well defined, but the truck will be blurred. Now take the picture again while you track the truck and the truck may appear defined while the background blurs. Increase the shutter speed to 1/1,000 of a second and both the truck and the background are perfectly clear. Increase the shutter speed to a strobe of 1/186,000th second and reality is defined by the one-mile tail in space-time of the orbiting electrons. Some sharpness is lost. Multiply the shutter speed again by 5,280 and the reality captured in the picture is a one-foot tail of the event horizon. The picture appears more ghostlike. Multiply the shutter speed by twelve and you look right through the one-inch tail of the event horizon into the vast, vacant space between. As the moment becomes increasingly constricted, the tail becomes shorter and shorter until it is the breadth of the electron at the threshold of inner space-time. At this point, reality totally disappears and our picture in time and space is of the same nothingness that exists beyond the 20-billion light-year-bubble of our universe. Deep inner space-time is the same place as deep outer space-time.

* The character of reality depends entirely on movement. The only difference between a cube of ice and steaming water, which would boil a lobster, is molecular movement. The difference between water and hydrogen and oxygen is based on the movement of a shared electron between two atoms of hydrogen and one atom of oxygen. If one looks into the fine moment of time between the sharing of the electron, there is no difference between a glass of water and two hydrogen balloons tied to an oxygen bottle...

ঙ৵৵

Hemp Hill Creek
Monday, June 14, 1999, 14:10 hours

The phone rang, pulling Mossy out of the mental contortion occasioned by the manuscript of her deceased parents. The usual call was a salesman for light bulbs for the handicapped or tickets to a firemen's ball, but Mossy received few enough phone calls in general to motivate her downstairs and to have the receiver to her ear in less than three rings. "Stone residence, Mossy speaking."
"Uh, hi, Mossy," said the male voice on the line. "This is Peter Cienfuegos. Remember me?"
"Sure. I've been thinking about you and wondering how the thing was going on Reade Hill. I heard rumors that WACFAC might try to get review in a local court and thought you should know about it."
"Well, by coincidence I was in Magistrate's Court today on another matter and it did come up. Magistrate Greenway broke the injunction that your mom got placed on the 37-E parcel and it looks like it's going up for bid in a couple of days."

"That's terrible!" cried Mossy. "It's lousy forestry! The land's too steep. It's going to throw a sediment wash into the river! That old growth is good only for habitat!"

"Mossy, you don't have to convince me. But I kind of need a hand here so I can get busy on trying to tie up the sale with further litigation. They need someone over eighteen with a permanent address to whom they can release me...Also, I need to borrow $600 for bail, but I can pay it back today. Is there any way you can help me on this?"

"Did the Magistrate slap a contempt charge on you for protesting his order?"

"Well, actually, as I said...it's another thing. But I need to take care of it before I can move forward on protecting the forest. I'm in the Clallam County jail. Can you help me?"

"The jail behind the Courthouse on Lincoln Street? I'll be there in two hours with $1000 cash."

"Thanks a lot, Mossy. I knew I could count on you."

"Peter, $1000 is about $150 less than all the money I have in the world. I need it to eat..."

"I'll get it back for you today. I swear it."

๛

Hemp Hill Creek
Tuesday, June 15, to Tuesday, June 22, 1999

Peter Cienfuegos had been good for his word and remunerated Mossy directly after being bailed out of jail. Peter had returned to Mossy's home on Hemp Hill Creek and made telephone contacts with environmental activists to set up a protest demonstration against the impending logging on Reade Hill. He spent the rest of the afternoon nosing around the Flying S Farm making observations about the utilities and energy systems. According to Cienfuegos, the two-inch flexible poly pipe, which Barbara had struggled to lay out nineteen years ago, was under-rated for the flow of water through the penstock. Peter said Mossy was only getting a tenth of the energy potential of the hydroelectric site. Mossy asked how much it would cost to replace the 3,000 feet of pipe. Peter called around and got a price of $2,800. Mossy said she couldn't afford even one-tenth of that. Peter checked a Government Sales Administration bulletin and disappeared with Mossy's old pickup. It took three trips, but Peter ended up stockpiling 3,000 feet of four-inch PVC, salvaged from Quileute Fisheries, for the price of $280, which he made as a gift to Mossy. The following day, Cienfuegos acquired the fittings, solvent, and glue to rework the line and set about the four-day task of the retrofit. Working together, they refitted the pipe, trestled it to the ground with rebar and large hose clamps and, finally, gated the pipe to the old system to flood it with water. When they turned the hydroelectric back on, it pinned the ammeter at 60 amps - six times what the system had been delivering. Peter asked if he could use the pickup to make another equipment run to Seattle. Mossy said to go ahead, but that the engine had over 200,000 miles and would need an overhaul soon, which would cost in excess of the $1150 of Mossy's lifesavings.

Cienfuegos returned the following day with a load controller for the improved performance of the hydro's output. He had two big battery banks that he had gotten cheap from the phone company, and a big box of new parts he had scammed from the University of Washington. The parts were two large direct current motors, heavy duty switching, wiring, instrumentation, and other wherewithal to convert an internal-combustion truck to an electrical vehicle. When Mossy asked about the price of the batteries, load controller, and E.V. conversion kit, Peter said that the batteries had been obtained for free, that the load controller was a project that he had built in school, and that the E.V. conversion kit belonged to the U. of W. It had been purchased by the University's Science and Tech Department with demonstration monies and had sat in its box for three years waiting for a target vehicle to occupy. Peter explained that the conversion would continue to be the property of the U of W. They would require an installation report, which he would provide; and three annual reports on miles driven, loads hauled, and so forth. For all intents and purposes it was a free improvement. It would cost Mossy nothing.

That afternoon they drove the pickup into the garage bay of the shop Barbara had built to keep the old truck out of the rain and hooked up a chain hoist to the engine. Mossy removed the bolts that mounted the engine to the frame of the old GMC, while Peter mounted the two large D.C. motors to the front wheels of the truck and explained the regenerative braking switch that would attach to the brake peddle. When he came out, Mossy was working on the last rusty bolt with a three-foot cheater bar over the open-end wrench. Her face glistened with the sweat of her exertion as she applied an ever-increasing counterclockwise pressure to the frozen bolt. Peter was stricken with the oddity of a young woman in this role: sweating, doing hard physical work, self-sufficient, totally disconnected from the skin care products and underarm deodorants. It occurred to him that Mossy was incredibly attractive to him. There was a sudden snap: the wrench fell out of the cheater onto the floor of the garage. They stood side by side looking into the engine compartment. "You sheared off a 3/4 inch bolt!" said Peter.

"Oh well," replied Mossy, reefing on the chain hoist and pulling the old engine out of its compartment.

By Monday evening, they had finished installing one of the battery banks where the old engine had rested and Cienfuegos followed Mossy into the passenger cab for a test drive. The truck glided silently forward and out the driveway and across the bridge. "Cool!" Mossy enthused. It occurred to her that this day was her 19th birthday and a trip to town in an E.V. would be a great celebration. When they got to the garden, Mossy stopped the truck.

"Why stop here?" asked Peter. "Let's take her all the way to Forks and celebrate."

"That damned deer has been into the garden again!" lamented Mossy. "I'll have to stop, fix the garden fence, and salvage what I can from what she knocked down and crushed. She's hell on the strawberries and that's my big cash crop this time of year."

"You say *'she'*. Do you know which deer is doing it?"

"Yeah, she's an old friend, but she's destroying me. I even got a wildlife nuisance permit from the State."

"What's that? A permit to keep pesky deer on your property?"

199

"No...a permit to get them off. I hope I don't have to use it..." Mossy's voice trailed off.

"Let's put up an electric fence from the hydroelectric," suggested Peter.

"I've tried electric fencing before and the deer don't seem to respect it."

"With the voltage and current you've got now, you could shock them into packing hunters into the forest."

"I suppose it's worth a try...but let's get the fencing tomorrow. I have to repair this damage. You can head back to the cabin, if you like, and I'll round up what I can here and meet you back there. You can have first bath with the water heated up by the diversion load. I'll make a fire when I come in for dinner."

Cienfuegos was setting up to take a bath when Mossy came in with the produce she intended for dinner. He had wanted to go to town, partially for beer, partially for his hankering for junk food, and partially to purchase some toiletries to see him through until he went back to Seattle. He picked up a bar of what appeared to be homemade soap from the sink and climbed into the warm, deep tub. Plants that Mossy was starting indoors, safe from slugs, forested the large open window next to the tub. "I hope you don't mind me using your toilet stuff!" called Peter through the shut door, hoping that Mossy would tell him where the hair conditioner was.

"Whatever you can find!" called Mossy, cutting up berries and stoking the stove with kindling.

"This is shampoo by the tub, right?" called Peter picking up the bottle to pour onto his grimy hair.

"Well, yeah, I don't know if you'll like it!"

Peter poured a couple of ounces onto his head and was aware of an earthy smell as he lathered it in. "What is this stuff? Did you make it yourself?" It wasn't lathering quite right.

"Yeah, it's aloe and pineapple sage, yarrow and sea kelp. I put in a little elk placenta for extra protein!" Cienfuegos plunged under water to try to get the mess off his head.

When he came out of the bathroom a few minutes later, the table was set and there were delicious smells coming out of the kitchen and from the food which was already laid out. He helped Mossy shuttle a large platter of salad, a crock of soup, and corn muffins to the table. "Do you mind if we have a minute of silence before eating?" asked Mossy, as they sat down.

As they sat under the skylight with the June sun washing over the table, Peter studied the chiseled good looks of his hostess: the sunlight sparkling off her long, golden hair; the smudge of garden soil upon the radiant and otherwise clean face that cast a grateful and reflective gaze downward to the table. Over the intense and pleasing dinner aromas came the blast of herbal-scented air from the small sun room built off the dining nook where Mossy raised spices and aromatic plants. Beyond the table and out the window was the brief strip of landscaped clearing before the green curtain of the immense stage of wilderness which extended east, unabated for 50 miles. Mossy looked up from her reflection and smiled and Peter realized that he had already developed very strong feelings for this young woman and the environment with which she was inextricably intwined. "This is great!" he said warmly.

"Amen," said Mossy and they began to eat.

Peter considered the various dishes before him and surmised, "So, you're a strict vegan vegetarian?"

"No, I guess I would be described as a Bogaterian."

"What's a Bogaterian?"

"I'll eat anything that I can grow, catch, pick or dig in this valley. I don't eat anything else. My diet changes with the seasons and with what's available."

"What do you do when you're traveling?"

"Pretty much..." and for a moment Mossy's soul raced out along the narrow valley walls in two directions. Her spirit overlooked the headwaters from the vantage she had visited two weeks earlier, while her soul crashed against the rock fortress of James Island where the freshwater met the salt of the ocean. "Pretty much, I don't travel...at least by most people's definition of the word. The world of this valley seems big enough to me."

They ate for a while in silence, Peter savoring the steaming aroma of cornmeal, wild honey, fresh butter, fava beans, vegetable broth, and tangy herbs. "Travel is not so important when you're complete in yourself and your immediate environment," observed Peter.

"There's a few small holes, here and there," murmured Mossy taking her dishes out to the kitchen where, to Peter's horror, the dogs provided the pre-wash and scrap disposal.

৽৽৵

Hemp Hill Creek
Thursday, June 24, 1999, 22:40 hours

The last trace of twilight had dissolved to unleash night upon the screen of the skylight over their heads. Peter and Mossy sat together on the couch which had served as Peter's bed for the last two weeks with the blue-green light from the grow lights in the sun room casting an eerie illumination into the darkened room in which they sat. The skylight window, which served to capture the precious sunlight that visited this tiny forest clearing, was now affording a view of the waxing moon. The east-facing crescent advanced into view through the skylight in obedience to the spinning planet upon which the couch depended.

Peter brooded about how he had fallen behind in planning resistance to the impending logging on Reade Hill. He thought about Mossy's garden. The fencing project had not worked. In spite of $200 worth of New Zealand ribbon fencing and a hot, 110-volt zapper, the pesky deer had made it through the perimeter and devastated the garden. Mossy had cried for an hour. Under the hot sun, Mossy had endeavored to water the injured plants and reconnect broken root tissue in the mussed-up soil. Peter tried to help, but mostly got in the way. As he was putting up the wire ribbon, which was pulled askew by the trailing foot of the high jumping deer, Mossy sweated under the work of digging and moving soil. She dropped the bib of her overalls, rolled up her pant legs and hiked up her T-shirt. "Do you ever do the Adam and Eve thing, naked out here in the garden?" called out Peter, playfully.

"Sure," replied, Mossy, still distracted with her salvage. And, to Peter's great amazement and awe, Mossy stripped off all her clothes and tended her garden naked.

Peter thought about shucking off his own clothing, but realized his sexual excitement, and was too self-conscious. Mossy was like a centerfold with her willowy, perfect figure and beautiful facial features. Unlike the generic centerfolds, Mossy's was the body of a farm-hardened athlete and her legs and underarms wore the downy fuzz prohibited by purveyors of American cosmetics. Also, there was something almost masculine in her countenance and muscularity. "Don't you worry that someone will drive up or be walking up the road and surprise you?" Peter called out to Mossy.

"No way!" replied Mossy, standing to retrieve some more cow manure. "Rufus can hear a motor vehicle a half mile away. If it's hot enough to be without clothes, there's an up-valley wind and I'll smell whatever is lurking down-valley..." Mossy realized that Peter was staring at her and felt a wave of self-consciousness. She turned and crouched down to her plants, hiding her nakedness.

In the near dark, now, with Peter sitting closely beside her, as moonlight overwhelmed the soft green glow from the grow lights, she wondered if she had committed some great social trespass in taking off her clothes. Who kept the rule book on such things? Who wrote the *Dear Abbey* column on the frontier? She sensed that she had blundered socially and regretted whatever distance she may have put between herself and this person she was seeing as a partner. But the distance on the couch was growing less and less. Mossy looked beyond the moonbeams to the ancient light of the stars, which flooded through the skylight, and tried to find poise and balance in this awkward, new, social situation.

"So...I would say you pretty well solved the energy situation here for at least a few decades. What's your agenda for the rest of the world? I mean...after the demonstration." Having asked the question, Mossy felt stupid.

"Solving the so-called *energy crisis* for the world is a lot like solving it here. With oil, we settled on the most exhaustible and most polluting of any energy scheme. All the great energy resources are untapped and renewable beyond depletion. The earth itself is a huge rotor spinning in the stator of space. Magnetism has unlimited energy potential. Harnessing the sun with solar space farms, capturing the energy of the tides or lightning, tabletop fusion...we will develop something that will offer unlimited energy. It's very close."But that won't solve the world's real problems and might make things even worse. Along with solving energy could come unparalleled growth and development and we can easily forget that energy is not the greatest resource..."

"Without soil, air, and water, energy would mean nothing," interjected Mossy and then fell silent not wanting to interrupt Peter's soliloquy.

"Yeah, that's what I mean. Without energy as a check, there may be no limit to the harm we can cause the biological systems of this planet. Just like the discovery of nuclear energy, the discovery of a benign and unlimited energy source could kill us.

"What I'm working for is to first live within our limits. A good exercise would be to tweak our existing systems to provide for our basic needs, while not creating major environmental upheaval. We should start with transportation.

Instead of huge internal combustion engines, Detroit needs to build E.V.'s like yours with small onboard charging-motors, or, better yet, hydrogen cells to go long distances between charging stations. I think that every Federal dollar that's invested in Interstates should carry the stipulation that a non-traffic lane for alternative, non-combustive transportation be developed. Sailplanes, combination kinetic and photovoltaic cars...frictionless bearing systems that allow for magnetism as a method for propulsion...All this is presently available and doesn't preclude throwing away what we already have."

Mossy realized that her shoulder was touching Peter's. He put his arm around her and for the first time in her life, the fatherless girl felt the touch and warmth of a man. Peter was saying, "But jet planes are absolutely destroying the stratosphere. We need to come back to earth with fast transportation. Bullet trains can get large numbers of people coast to coast in twelve hours, which is fast enough. The upper stratosphere should belong to the zeppelin of the 1930's, which can ride the jet streams one way and return under small engine propellers the other way. Imagine a world where, instead of jogging before you hurried off to work in rush hour traffic, you climbed aboard public transportation where everyone peddled to power the bus...

Peter was rubbing Mossy's shoulder, which felt strange and somehow wonderful. Mossy didn't know how to behave or what she was suppose to do about what she was feeling. "We need to learn to think smaller," Peter was saying. "We need to look at the technology of the past and present before charging ahead with the technology of the future..." Mossy unclenched her left hand and dropped it on Peter's knee, where it perched like a frightened rabbit. "I would like to explore that future with you," Peter said in a hot whisper in Mossy's ear, and kissed her cheek.

Mossy turned her face to Peter's and kissed him back...or, at least, thought she did. She had been sheltered all her life from displays of human sexuality. The nibbling, sucking motions she was making with her mouth were nothing like the kisses that she had shared with her mother...

And Mossy's sudden, unbridled passion was the dog, off leash, chasing the rabbit of her hand from Peter's knee along his thigh...Her want was the wet tangle of rain forest, damp and gasping air, as Paul's hand moved from her shoulder to breast...

,,,the creaking of the 2" by 4" floor as gravity guided the couple from the couch onto the floor under the full gaze of the moon and stars...Mossy lets out a noise which sounds a little like the snarl of a cougar, crouched on the back of the bull elk... And as the wildlife continues in its business of procreation, the barren, virginal human mistress engages in the only sexual encounter of her life...

[Pssssst! Reader! Reader, I'm over here by the door. I'm getting out of here and where I goest thou must follow. We step into the cool night air and walk down the driveway in the new light of the moon and ancient light of the stars. We stand under the moon and stars, sniffing the cool, down-valley breeze which would tell an olfactory such as Mossy's, a story much bigger and more complete than the tale contained in the pages of this book.]

There is a rustle in the dark and the garden lights come on to reveal the silhouette of a deer making a mighty vault of the high fence and toppling into the garden. As the deer browses on the little plants that Mossy has worked so hard to preserve, severing roots and breaking irrigation line, visible to anyone standing on the driveway would be the white rear end of the deer known to Mossy as June Eleven.

[We stand together watching, as the deer lays to waste the garden that underpins the foundation for Mossy's lifestyle. We can do nothing to intervene, since, within the context of these pages, we do not even exist. "Mossy isn't going to like this," I observe moronically.]

வ~ே

Hemp Hill Creek
Friday, June 25, 1999, 04:45 hours

BANG! The loud shot caused Peter Cienfuegos to sit bolt upright in the upstairs bed to which he and Mossy had repaired just four hours ago. He looked over to where Mossy had lain when sleep had overtaken the couple, but the covers were turned down and she was absent.

Worried, Peter leapt out of bed and looked around for his underwear. After a minute of futile searching he remembered his clothing was in a rumpled pile downstairs by the couch. He climbed down the steep stairs naked and clothed himself. The report had come from outside, over by the front barn. As he walked down the driveway, he saw Mossy at the rear of the garden and a red flash of blood, which caused him to start running. When he got to her, he couldn't believe what he was seeing. Propped against the barn was a .243 carbine and Mossy was dragging a bleeding deer from a puddle of blood in the garden to a block and tackle she had fastened to the low, side rafters of the barn. "What the hell is this!" demanded Cienfuegos, as if it weren't obvious.

"This deer got into my garden for the last time," said Mossy in a small voice, lashing one leg of the deer to the rope and pulling on the running end of the block and tackle.

"Jesus!" exclaimed Peter, as Mossy tied off the running end and plunged a knife into the deer's belly. "I thought you were a vegetarian. Don't you have any feelings for this poor deer?"

"Yes," said Mossy, as the guts spilled out on the ground.

"JESUS, GOD," exclaimed Cienfuegos, squeamishly. "That deer could be a mother," he protested. "Somewhere out there is that deer's mother...I've seen this deer around here with the spots on its rear. Don't you recognize her?"

"Yes," said Mossy. "I've known her all her life. She was born on June 11, ten years ago," she said in a broken voice, scooping up intestines and stomach with a grain shovel and carrying them to a hole she had already dug near the corn.

"If you had killed her two weeks ago you could have made her birthday her deathday...Wouldn't that be a great gift!" Cienfuegos said accusingly. Mossy came back to the deer and put her bare hands inside the gaping visceral cavity and scooped out the remaining contents. "Dear God!" exclaimed Cienfuegos. "Don't you have any feelings for what you're doing?"

"Yes," said Mossy, and she was crying into the open eyes of death that watched her from the face of June Eleven.

Peter turned and walked away in disgust back to the cabin. Quickly he gathered his few possessions into his daypack and headed back out the driveway. He paused where Mossy was pulling the skin off the deer carcass.

"This is too much for me," he announced. "I'm leaving. I'll catch the bus from Forks to P.A. and, from there, I'll get back to Seattle."

"Do you want..." Mossy's voice broke. She stood with her back facing Peter, blood dripping off her fingers. "Can I give you a ride to town?" Cienfuegos could barely hear her words.

"Naw!" he said in disgust. "I wouldn't want you to get blood all over the steering wheel. I'll walk or hitchhike," he said, turning on his heel and heading out.

"I've got to eat," said Mossy in a voice too small for Cienfuegos' parting ears. Mossy stood with a butchered deer and a butchered heart, sobbing in the early light of morning.

[God, I love this place," I disturb you again with my ruminations. . Do you hear that mewling sound out there in the deep grass toward the river? That's the sound of the newborn elk, looking for its mother in the tall grass. Hear the soft, bouncing note of a screech owl upriver calling to her mate? If I could hold on to this moment like a stopwatch in space-time and clutch the wild, loneliness of these meadows where the elk come to calve and the Indians faced their forthcoming adulthood...If I could hold onto that moment like a breath of that delicious breeze...If I could throttle down the Great American Engine which rumbles on the horizon with its thrashers of the 21st century...If I could gather together with the wild ponies and plan a strategy to hold off the human encroachments which loom on the horizon...But, alas, I wander ephemerally in space-time when NOW, this moment, is all that really matters]

Eleven

"It took over three thousand years to make some of the trees in these western woods...God has cared for these trees, saved them from drought, disease, avalanche and a thousand straining, leveling tempests and floods; but He cannot save them from the hands of fools."

"Pick up any thing in nature and pull on it. You will find that it is attached to everything else in the universe."

- John Muir
Founder of the Sierra Club

Reade Hill
Wednesday, August 25, 1999, 22:30 hours

*W*HUP, WHUP, WHUP, WHUP...The rotor noise penetrated the wilderness as the KOMO news helicopter flew downstream, the pilot shining the powerful light on the tree tops 150 feet below. Instead of following Highway 101 from Forks, the copilot had suggested a compass course to get to Reade Hill by 10:30pm, in time to get footage of the eco-freaks who had tied themselves up in trees to protest impending logging of the old growth stand in Olympic National Forest. Apparently, the course had taken them too far east, into the Park, and the helicopter was coming downstream to correct for the navigational error.

"I hope a God damned spotted owl doesn't fly into the rear rotor," grimaced the pilot over the intercom of his hot microphone. "I'll keep watching for tall snags along the river bar. You keep watching the skyline for the lights of those lunatic demonstrators."

The lights to which the pilot referred were kerosene and white gas lanterns. Thirty-six demonstrators had carried them into the high tree perches they occupied in anticipation of the media's interest in the protest of the planned timber management. Confabulating with the press, the protest leader, Peter Cienfuegos, had arranged to have all the lights burning for the visual effect it might impart to the Eleven O'clock News.

"There they are!" exclaimed the copilot as they came around a bend in the river and lights twinkled merrily from the top of a ridge. "I'll start rolling as we approach to get the effect off those lanterns. Christ! They'll be lucky if they don't torch themselves! When we get within 300 yards or so, put the light on them and I'll zoom in with the 1,000 millimeter lens. I want a close-up of one of the crazy bastards."

"Roger that," said the pilot, rising from view of the river and coming in for a slow approach.

໒∾໑

Reade Hill
Thursday, August 26, 1999, 07:15 hours

Sunlight danced merrily on the water of the Bogachiel River. Mossy adjusted the seat straps of her rappel harness to get the circulation back in her legs. From her perch sixty feet up in a large Douglas fir, she could see the state boat launch. Two fishermen were launching their dory, their hopes set on harvesting the last of the few summer chinook salmon which infrequently occasioned this section of river. A warm, up-valley wind had started shortly after sunrise carrying the distant voices of the fishermen. "Don't forget the salmon roe!" called the fisherman holding the drift boat to the one returning from the truck with a cooler. "I put the bait in with the beer so we couldn't forget it!" he answered merrily, as they launched the boat, rowing gently against the downstream current.

From her vantage below the top of the ridge, Mossy could look down and see her farm, the golden-brown meadows framed by the deep green of the rain forest. Waves rippled across the tall, dry grass as the up-valley wind puffed and gusted with the rising temperature. She saw a straight row of spruce a few hundred feet south of her property line and at first thought she was looking at a man-planted tree line, perhaps evidencing the hand of Otto Seigfreid, the old German immigrant who had first worked this land. She realized she was looking at a colonnade from a nurse log, one of the signatures of her rain forest home. A mature tree had pitched over in the forest, probably in the windstorm of 1979, and broken a small clearing in the canopy to allow the visitation of sunlight. Spruce seeds had germinated in the scaly bark of the decaying mother and a straight row of healthy young trees had grown merrily from the nurse log. It was peculiar how different the environment was just 700 feet higher on top of Reade Hill. The Douglas fir supplanted the Sitka spruce of the rain forest as the dominant species of tree. Doug fir depended on fire for its propagation and, without the influence of man, the Bogachiel Valley was usually too dank to torch, whereas the adjoining ridges caught the lightning strikes and burned. In the meeting to discuss the demonstration strategy, Mossy had briefly argued the wisdom of carrying kerosene and white gas lanterns into such a flammable environment, but Cienfuegos had promised a wide press response to such a visual theme and had remained obdurate. It was the first time Mossy had seen Peter since he stormed off her property in the aftermath of the deer incident. On the previous day, Cienfuegos had shot an arrow tied to parachute cord to pull a climbing rope over stout limbs about 50 to 75 feet up the trunks of the stately Firs. One by one the demonstrators climbed up the rope to the limbs where they set up their hammocks and tethered themselves, their lanterns and their overnight bags. Then the climbing rope was removed to set up the next demonstrator. There was no coming down to take find a toilet, which made for some interesting maneuvers in a rappel harness. There was no escape and the only fire drill was: burn with the trees.

ᖇᖇ

Reade Hill
Thursday, August 26, 1999, 07:45 hours

Bouncing up the 2932 Road in his new Ford pickup, it felt wonderful to George Redding to be back on his old stomping grounds. Until he had secured his current position as director for the Washington Commercial Forester Action Committee, he had been forced to seek temporary work in southeast Alaska, and Montana, and at times had resorted to drawing unemployment to keep afloat financially. Now, to be drawing the additional wage of a logging foreman for a new logging company called Bogachiel River Timber, he had been able to secure loans to buy a new pickup and a decent house for his wife. Breaking the prohibitory lock on heavy-handed environmental sanctions was a milestone in logging history to which Redding was pleased to be party.

Redding had a certain sense of respect for the environmental community. He believed, like they professed, that the woods were a special place and that incursions by man were creating upsets that could have planetary consequence. But few of these eco-freaks actually got out in the woods and really romped around. They would all grab their polypropylene underwear, Gortex hiking boots, and granola bars and head up to High Divide where they all bunched up and began tripping over one another. Instead of spreading out over the one million acre Park to find wild places, they clustered up and began bitching and moaning about how they needed more wilderness. Hell, they didn't need more land taken out of production...they needed to appreciate and understand what they already had.

As the head guy for WACFAC, George understood that political and public relation duties fell on his shoulders and that, in any confrontation with environmentalists, the media would stereotype the loggers as greedy, oafish, Huns of the forest. George remembered his old friend, Phil Stone, who worked with Redding, logging this country, and had settled just across the river. Stone would be a great enigma for the press: a nuclear physicist turned lumberjack. Let the press stereotype that! Redding had put together a few placards and signs for a counter demonstration, if it came to that. His sign read, LOGGERS SUPPORT WILDERNESS - WORKING FORESTS SUPPORT EVERYBODY.

Leading the convoy of loggers, Redding pulled into the trailhead parking lot for the Bogachiel, where he met U.S. Forest Service Ranger Chris Fairbanks, who unlocked the gate to let the logger caravan pass. Several news vans were set up in the parking lot and a couple of cameras caught the scene of the loggers arriving for work. "Good morning, George," said Ranger Fairbanks. "Did you see the Eleven O'clock News last night on KOMO? The Earth First!ers have themselves tied up in trees. They're about fifty feet off the ground! We're holding the press here until we figure out what we're going to do about it, but they have two or three news helicopters at the Forks airfield that will be arriving anytime. We'll let your bunch through because you've got a legal right to be here and we'll probably need some climbers in your logging crew to fetch down the demonstrators. It's a zoo up there. My husband, Brian, got detailed from Forks Police Department to work here as a peace officer. He's up there now talking to the leader of the group, Peter Cienfuegos..."

"He was the guy I debated at the Town Meeting last spring," interjected Redding. "Cienfuegos showed up in Walt Greenway's court when we appealed this injunction and raised a little fuss."

"We checked him out, and there was a Federal warrant on the guy for drugs which has been dismissed and some contempt of court stuff which was satisfied by a few hours in the jug, but we can hook them all for trespass and interfering with agency function. But first we have to get them down and Cienfuegos tells Brian they're not coming down for anything. The weather forecast predicts a chance of thundershowers. A few lightning strikes on the ridge around them might give the demonstrators a little shove to get down out of there...George, these woods are bone dry. The DNR must be feeling some political pressure on this, or they would have shut down the woods before this operation. When we get this sorted out and you start the felling, be super careful, and keep your extinguishers at the ready."

ভ৵৶

Morganroth Cabin, upper Bogachiel
August 26, 1919, 13:15 hours

Kwalet stood by the door of the cabin as thunder shook the floor. Her husband, Forest Ranger Chris Morganroth, promised that he would be home on what he called "annual leave," to spend time with their two children and take care of overdue farm chores. But he had broken that promise before. She felt that she had lost her husband and the father of her children to the Olympic Forest Reserve. Whatever promises Morganroth made to Kwalet, he satisfied them after extinguishing every smoking stump on the burned-over ridges. When he did make it on the long walk home from the Soleduck to the Bogachiel, all he talked about was building fire trails, setting up caches in the Forest and saving trees from the fire that seemed to inevitably catch them anyway. Morganroth had gotten funny in the head about fire and prohibited his fifteen-year-old son from keeping the evergreen berries and encroaching alder in check by burning out their little meadows. The forest was closing in and Kwalet longed for the open horizon of the ocean, which had been her front door throughout her childhood. The law had disbanded the coastal village of Ozette by requiring the children to attend public school in Neah Bay with their historic enemies the Makahs. Her children overwintered with her mother in LaPush for mandatory schooling provided there. Soon they would not be coming back and she would be alone in this rain forest that threatened to swallow her. She had promised herself: if her husband came back today as promised, walking through the little gate with his big backpack high with fresh meat and candy for the children...she would stick it out; she would explain her loneliness and plead for more attention, but she would stand by her obligation to her husband. But if today was another failed promise...she would leave for LaPush with her children. She would leave her errant husband and her name "Susie." She would leave this cabin of aching loneliness and return to the people. The thunder rocked the cabin again and Kwalet walked out on the riverbar in front of the cabin to gain a view of the high, west-running ridge just downstream of the cabin to check for lightning strikes. The fog along the banks earlier in the morning had gathered itself into low clouds held down on the ridge by the hand of high pressure which had dried the theater of the Olympic Peninsula in preparation for the spectacle of wildfire; the showtime of which was being heralded by the booming of thunder. It reminded Kwalet of what existed in LaPush before the white truant officer: the village crier dressed as Thunder Bird circulating through LaPush to announce the telling of the stories the children heard and reheard throughout their childhood, in this case the story of fire.

A strong downdraft forced a cool gust of wind down valley carrying with it the scent of smoke and the message to Kwalet that her husband would not be coming home. As the down-valley gust collided with the warm up-valley diurnal wind, small vortexes developed and Kwalet's fresh laundry was pulled from its line on the river bar and carried several feet into the air. The low clouds were whisked off the ridge and carried up into the high stratosphere, where the moisture stolen from the rain forest of the Bogachiel Valley would be carried away and fall as rain on a small town in northern Virginia. But the ridge was without smoke. The geological feature that would become known as "Reade Hill" would hold its fuel load for ignition at another point in space-time. Kwalet left the river bar to gather her laundry and pack the rest of her things.

༄༅

Highway 101, MP 183
August 24, 1962

From his vantage, just below Dead Dog Flats, next to the red DNR pickup overlooking the headwater of Dowans Creek, Jim Reade could see the wide plateau where two glaciers had come from the Hoh and Bogachiel to form an ice cap. In the direction from whence had come ice, ten millennia previous, was now coming black, roiling clouds connecting to the ridges with jagged, white lines of lightning. With his binoculars, Reade could count three smokes already burning on the south side of Willoughby Ridge and two smokes burning up the Bogachiel, inside the Park. One of the farthest smokes on Willoughby was proximal to the Park and not far from the Lewis Ranch. Reade smiled and hoped that this fire got pushed down the ridge to burn out that tired, old shithead, Charlie Lewis. A dark night a few years back, he and Charlie had agreed to meet in the woods below Willoughby Ridge to settle their differences once and for all. Both combatants had fueled their courage with alcohol, which had impaired their night navigation. They carried their weapons around in the woods all night without finding one another. The old blabbing, fart, Charlie had told the story to his neighbors.

The closer ridge on the Bogachiel, which would bear his name was currently clear of smoke. Reade was paying close attention to this ridge, because at the foot of it was the old Morganroth cabin which had been his home for the last ten years. His binoculars swept again from northwest to southeast until he was looking down the highway at the jagged peaks of the Vahallas visible through the corridor of the highway. He could see smoke with glowing embers going straight up from the spalts-burning igloo at Graham Brothers Mill almost a mile away. He would be driving his pickup that way to serve one of the brothers with a violation notice of the No Burn order, which his office enforced. He used the wireless in his pickup to call in the smokes on Willoughby and asked the Forks dispatcher to notify the District Ranger, Ted Sullivan, at Kalaloch, of the fires in the Park. When he glanced over his shoulder back toward his home, he saw a jagged line connecting with the ridge a mile outside the Park. He grabbed his binoculars and ran back down the highway to a vantage of the Bogachiel drainage several hundred feet from his pickup. For half an hour he studied the ridge for signs of smoke. Dust devils blew up around him as a cool down-draft from the invading cumulonimbus clouds collided with the warm up-valley wind of the hot afternoon. He studied the ridge. If there was smoke, he would risk getting in trouble driving the DNR pickup to his residence to pick up the cash and whiskey he had squirreled away in the cabin. After considerable time he satisfied himself that there was no risk to his estate and re-directed his attention to the columns of smoke coming off of the side of Willoughby. But, as the smell of smoke reached his nostrils, he realized that there was a fire much more proximal to him than the distant ridge. Looking fully to the south, he saw a column of smoke gathered straight up over the highway between himself and the mill on the other side of the flat named for the canine casualties claimed by the highway. A spark from the mill had fallen into the draw formed by the Dowans Creek headwater, ignited slash and "21-blow" windfall, and developed into a 30-foot flaming front driven by gusting winds blowing up the draw toward the highway. Reade ran for his pickup.

By the time he got to the truck, the paint was beginning to peel off the driver's door and the tires were puffed up like four weather balloons. He ran around on the passenger's side to access the cab and climbed into the broiling driver's seat. No keys! He fumbled in his pocket, but then realized he had left them in the glove compartment. Trees all along the highway started torching and he saw the top of the flaming front like the head of a giant coming up the draw as fast as a man could run. Keys in the ignition, the solenoid made a grinding sound indicating low battery. He had left the wireless on! A driver's side tire burst. The truck jumped and slouched down. He heard a hissing sound from the driver's side and realized the gas tank was venting hot, extremely volatile fumes. He got out of the passenger's side and was running north on the road, sucking hot air into his lungs, when the fuel tank exploded. Behind him, a giant fire-twirl rose, sucking burning violation notices through the broken windows of the pickup.

Two hours later, Jim Reade stood next to the blackened carcass of his pickup waiting for rescue from Forks. A flyover had spotted him a half an hour ago and it would not be long before his coworkers would arrive to cudgel him all the way back to disciplinary action at the DNR Olympic Headquarters in Forks. It was the most embarrassing thing that had happened in his life...excluding the time that Charlie Lewis and he had dueled in the rain forest.

᪐

Reade Hill
Thursday, August 26, 1999, 08:45 hours

Merrily, Peter Cienfuegos pendulummed from his hammock to the swinging bench he used for his office in the sky. Life was so good: the silver spike he wore as a necklace caught the reddish morning sun and flashed a joyous code in the waxing light. This is as good as it gets, thought Cienfuegos, looking across to where Mossy Stone hung solemnly from a Doug fir. She needed to feel the joy of the morning. She needed to lighten up.

Cienfuegos felt slight remorse for the way he had walked away from the relationship he was establishing with Mossy in the wake of her butchering the poor deer. In the few relationships he had sustained in his 24 years, the two weeks with Mossy were the most profound and wonderful he had experienced. If he could change the world, as he would this morning, he could convert Mossy from her bloodthirsty carnivorism to healthy vegetarianism practiced by such civilized environmentalists as himself. Mossy was a catch, and he would be a fool to walk away without making an effort to rekindle their romance. Cienfuegos pushed aside an oil lantern he had used to amuse the press and wrote on a piece of old "onion skin" typing paper:

> *Dear Mossy,*
> *I love you. I have always loved you. From the minute*
> *I laid eyes on you in the auditorium of the Forks High School*
> *I knew that you and I were destined...*

...Cienfuegos heard the armada of pickup trucks of the approaching loggers and a distant rumble up-valley, which may have been thunder or military jets.

> *...to be one.*
> *Love,*
> *Peter*

He put his note to Mossy aside. The first pickup truck pulled to a stop and Cienfuegos recognized his political adversary George Redding getting out of the pickup and walking toward the base of his tree. "For Gosh sakes, please come down and let us just do our job," yelled the son-of-a-bitch and then disappeared into the woods.

Before Cienfuegos could formulate a proper response to the insulting behavior of the illiterate, old logger who had vanished, another menace appeared. Getting out of the pickup was a logger that Cienfuegos recognized as the father of the dirty shitpaper that had beaten up his father. Rod Hill came to the bottom of the nearest tree, from which swung Peter Cienfuegos, and immediately began piling tree limbs and loose brush. He yelled, "All right, you fuckers, you have five minutes before I light this pile and burn you sons of bitches to crispy enviro-critters!" Hill looked aside and saw Mossy looking down in horror at what he was doing and yelled, "Uh, excuse me, Mossy! But you'd better get the fuck down! I'm about to burn out this pestilence!"

"No, Mr. Hill, No!" began Mossy.

"YOU FUCKER!!!!" screamed Cienfuegos. "YOU JUST TRY IT! YOU JUST TRY TO BURN US OUT, YOU STUPID FUCK!" Cienfuegos hushed briefly as Hill struck a match and lit the pile.

"...NO, Rod, NO! NO! NO!..." screamed Mossy, the ponies kicking in their smokey stalls, from her perch in the tree. Hill was astounded to see the pile catch and start to climb the tree. He ran to his pickup and grabbed a fire extinguisher, which he applied to the flame with immediate success.

"...YOU FUCKER!," Cienfuegos was screaming, noticing Hill's own respect of the fire he had created. Cienfuegos ripped the bottom off the letter he was composing to Mossy and dipped it in oil. He lit it and threw it down, flaming, at the logger with the fire extinguisher. "HAVE A LITTLE FIRE YOURSELF, FUCKFACE," screamed Cienfuegos. Immediately, Hill extinguished the flame with dry chemical left in his extinguisher.

"NO! PETER, NO! NO! NO!" Mossy was screaming..."

"WHUP, WHUP, WHUP," said the approaching KOMO news helicopter.

"rrrrrrrRUMBLLIIlllllllle," said a dry lightning strike from up-valley.

"YOU FUCKER!" screamed Cienfuegos. "YOU THINK WE'RE SCARED OF FIRE?!" Cienfuegos dumped the reservoir of his oil lamp onto the smoldering pyre below him.

Hill moved to cover the volatile fuel with his extinguisher and then checked himself. He smiled wickedly and looked up at Cienfuegos. "I DARE YOU TO THROW A MATCH, YOU ENVIRO-PUSSY, YOU!"

"NO! NO! STOP IT! NO! NO!" Mossy was screaming...

A strong downdraft of air from the approaching storm...the cumulonimbus clouds, flickering lightning. "YOU FUCKER, TASTE THIS!" screamed Cienfuegos and threw a bandanna soaked in oil, aflame, down to the pyre beneath him...

"STOP IT! NO, NO, NO!" screamed Mossy.

"KA-BOOOOOOOOOOM!" exclaimed the thunder.

"WHUP, WHUP, WHUP," another helicopter arrived and began filming the column of smoke as a wall of huge cumulonimbus clouds advanced down-valley, pushing wind and thunder.

"ENJOY THE FIRE, YOU FAGGOT!" screamed Hill over the growing cacophony of thunder and human noise.

"NO! NO! NO!" screamed Mossy.

"HEY, YOU BETTER PUT THAT OUT!" yelled Cienfuegos as the pile beneath him set aflame.

"FLASH/KA-BOOOM!" yelled Mother Nature. The fire climbed up the tree like a logger going up a spar pole.

"YOU FUCKER!" were the last words to leave the mouth of Peter Cienfuegos before the fir bough, which he was in, exploded into fire. "AHHHHHHHHHHH!" he screamed, dancing in the fire at the end of a nylon tether. His voice was cut off as he sucked in the superheated air. He dangled quietly for a moment longer before the nylon melted through and his body fell straight down into the bonfire that burned at the base of the tree.

As the burned end of the webbing continued to drip molten nylon into the blaze below, the fire in the tree jumped from limb to limb like a Doug squirrel chased by a hungry bobcat. On the ground, George Redding and the other loggers had run back to gather tools and were trying to put a line around the ground fire which was being pushed by the strong downdrafts in the advancing clouds.

The noise was deafening. The crashing thunder; the helicopters trying to get in for close-ups of the catastrophe; the loggers screaming back and forth; the human wail of the ponies caught in the burning barn. Above all: the roar of the fire itself as it gained momentum and strength in the dry fuel and quickening wind. But for a moment in space-time, the uproar subsided in Mossy's head and, as the boughs below her ignited in an explosion of flame, she heard the voice of her mother, singing, "...merrily, merrily, merrily, merrily..." Mossy felt the warmth of her mother against her skin, and smelled her mother's sweat and soap lingering in her flaring nostrils. Flames raced up the tree toward the body of the young woman, but Mossy's spirit was in the body of the child at another address in space-time. "Cut it loose," said her mother's voice. "Cut yourself loose from your tangle..."

The fire was all around her and burning in a wall of flame across the ground beneath her. She reached into her pocket, as if in a trance, and pulled out her pocketknife. She drew it swiftly across the tubular nylon tether and with a twang it released her weight and sent her, free-falling through burning boughs to the wall of flame below. Accelerating at 32 feet per second, Mossy was traveling at slightly more than 30 miles per hour when her left leg impacted a tree limb. Both limbs, human and arboreal, bent with the impact, but the cracking sound was not from the tree but from Mossy's femur cracking, creating new jigsaw pieces to her historic injuries. Mossy's acceleration was slowed, and the tree limb deflected her toward the tree upon which Peter Cienfuegos had depended.

Mossy hit the ground, headfirst into an exposed tree root, her body slamming into the ground with so much force that her diaphragm was shocked into paralysis. She couldn't breathe. Woozily, she pulled her hand out of the burning embers seeing some of the flesh pull away with burning debris. Her face flushed and burned with the heat as she rolled over on her back. Her hip screamed in pain. Mossy couldn't breathe. Hot embers from the burning canopy above her fell onto her upturned face and part of her long blond hair flashed in flame and sputtered out next to her ear. She heard the ponies screaming in their burning stalls. She turned her head to the side and laid her head upon the enormous hematoma that pushed up from the side of her head where she had impacted the root. On the other side of the flaming front, she could see a ruffed grouse - the village idiot of the forest - running back and forth trying to gather her chicks. She covered as many of her brood with her wings and body as she could before her feathers singed and burst into flames. Mossy couldn't breathe.

Mossy turned her aching head away from the flames and looked into the black. The superheated air shimmered and moved back and forth like an ephemeral curtain. She saw a desiccated mummy with two broken legs lying in smoking ash, looking back at her and smiling. The body was naked except for an amulet around its neck. She believed she was looking at the face of death, but was not ready to meet it. She couldn't breathe, but realized, when this hot air reached her lungs, it would kill her. She rolled back onto her stomach and, with her bleeding hands, dug a pit for her face. Beneath the hot ash, the soil was relatively cool. She couldn't breathe. Hypoxia and intracranial pressure were causing sparks to fly around inside her head. The ponies were screaming. She couldn't breathe. A fingernail was torn off as she dug.

And then her mother's voice said again, "Cut yourself loose, Mossy. Cut yourself free from the tangle of this story," and Mossy fell against the cool bosom of her mother and sucked the sweet smell of her into her pharynx, bronchi and lungs. "...merrily, merrily, merrily, merrily..."

$\wp\!\sim\!\wp$

The helicopters were being forced to retreat westward from the smoke and advancing cumulonimbus. This was as good as it gets, thought the cameraman in the KOMO news helicopter, as he captured a tree torching with a close-up of a demonstrator waving wildly with her cotton clothing on fire.

Death was throwing human dice on the bright orange and green crap table of the burning forest. Thirty-three Earth First! demonstrators would crap out.

As the diurnal up-valley breeze met the strong downdrafts from the cumulonimbi a gigantic fire-twirl greeted the happy newsmen who merrily recorded the greatest wildland fire disaster in history.

Unobserved by the newsmen, was a torn piece of onion skin paper that was carried high aloft by the hot air of the firestorm. The paper was slightly browned on the edges, but the handwriting would have been legible to any literate eye that scanned it. But the paper was carried over the cumulus clouds, catching the prevailing winds and blown out over wilderness where it landed with the voice of a tree falling beyond the range of hearing.

$\wp\!\sim\!\wp$

The U.S. Forest Ranger had come screaming up the hill as soon as she heard the first rumble of thunder. The storm came on so fast that by the time she got within sight of the demonstrators, lightning was striking the top of Reade Ridge and loggers were dragging out tools to attack a ground fire. The tree that Peter Cienfuegos had been in was fully involved in flame and the canopy fire was spreading to the tree, where hung the local girl, Mossy Stone. Fairbanks saw her husband running toward the woods to where George Redding was coming out. Ranger Fairbanks grabbed a fire shelter out from under the seat of her Bronco and ran to her husband. Redding and Officer Fairbanks stood together for a moment watching the horror. A human wail could be heard coming out of the woods from the demonstrators caught in the trees.

When Ranger Fairbanks got to her husband and the logger, Redding said, "Sweet Jesus, did you see that! Mossy cut her line and fell into the fire!"

"SHE HAD TO, GEORGE!" screamed Officer Fairbanks. "HER TREE'S GOING UP IN FLAMES! THE WHOLE WOODS IS LIGHTING UP! ALL THOSE DEMONSTRATORS..."

"WE GOTTA GET TO MOSSY AND GET HER OUTTA THERE!" hollered Redding into Brian Fairbanks' ears, which already burned from the radiant heat of the blaze.

"NO, BRIAN, NO, NO!" Ranger Fairbanks began protesting. From where they stood she could already see sweat turning to steam from the bulletproof vest worn by her husband. The hickory shirt worn by George Redding was already singed above his work gloves. Officer Fairbanks grabbed the fire shelter out his wife's hands and whipped out the aluminum tent. "NO, BRIAN, NO! THE HOT AIR WILL KILL YOU. IT'S 500 DEGREES ANYWHERE IN

THERE!" But Chris Fairbanks was yelling to an aluminum four-legged turtle that advanced into the holocaust against all odds and admonition. She wept for a few moments in fear and frustration before running over to organize the efforts of the battalion of loggers that fought in vain to control the blaze.

༄‿༄

"We can't help her...cough, cough. If she's alive, she'll be dead soon enough, cough," the words reached Mossy's ears, but the smell of smoke is what pulled her away from the security she felt on her mother's bosom. "Besides, look at her left leg, cough, cough. It's broken badly and we'd just get sued if we got her out, cough, cough...SHIT! LOOK AT THE DEAD GUY! That's Peter Cienfuegos! We've got to save ourselves. If we stay in the burned-over area we should be OK, cough!" The two would-be rescuers stumbled out of Mossy's ear range, but she could smell the fear as they retreated. She struggled to make sense of the words she had heard and place where she was and why her head and hip were throbbing with pain. Had there been another school bus accident? Was she in the hospital? Then, above the smoke and hot air, which flooded her nostrils - above the stench of charred flesh and burning feathers - was the smell of human fear mixed with something else...Something she had smelled as a girl on her mother...Something she smelled on the postcards from her grandmother... Something she smelled on the old, bloody hickory shirt of her father in the cedar chest under her bed: Mossy smelled human courage.

༄‿༄

George Redding and Brian Fairbanks were running, stooped over, in the blackened forest trying to keep their heads as low as possible. Fairbanks carried the fire shelter over his shoulder since things had cooled off a bit. They encountered two demonstrators heading into the blaze from which they had just retreated, "HOLD ON THERE!" called Redding.

"I climbed down the limbs and jumped," the one was babbling. "He jumped and landed in a dried-up frog pond."

"Are there others? demanded Fairbanks. "Did you see that guy Cienfuegos or the girl that was in the tree next to him?"

"Peter is a goner for sure! Mossy, or whatever her name was, is a goner, maybe..."

"We've got to get to them," said Fairbanks. "You two better stay with us. You were headed into big trouble. Stay as low as you can. The cooler air is closer to the ground..."

༄‿༄

Merrily, Mossy's left leg bounced along loosely attached to her shattered hip, as she was dragged and carried by Redding and the two other demonstrators. Fairbanks led the way, carrying the mummified carcass of Peter Cienfuegos wrapped in the fire shelter over his shoulder. At one point they stumbled going over a steep burned-over embankment to the landing where the ambulance and fire trucks waited. Peter Cienfuegos rolled down the hill towards the landing where Rod Hill and his son stood watching. The dried flesh broke away separating the lower legs exposing the shattered ends of the tibias and fibulas of the carcass. Merrily, Fairbanks picked up the mummy, wrapping it again in the shelter, and climbing down to retrieve the severed lower legs. "Leave it, Brian. Let's get Mossy to the ambulance. I'll have Hill come up and fetch those...pieces."

A few minutes later, the antiseptic smell of the ambulance filled Mossy's nostrils: the same hospital reek that had filled the nostrils of the young girl who lamented the death of the ponies in their burning stalls. Merrily, she heard the logger, Rod Hill, call out, "What HAVE we here?" and pull the desiccated remains of Peter Cienfuegos out from the fire shelter. Merrily, Hill stood the carcass up on its broken stumps in view of the open ambulance doors and took off his tin hat, putting it on the head of the carcass. Merrily, he got down on his own knees to have his son photograph him arm in arm with the mummy. Mossy recognized the tree spike and chain around the neck of the crisped human who, for one night, had been her lover. The ambulance door swung shut on this scene.

"Look, Dad. His dick got burned off!" said Hill of the only penis that Mossy had known, or would ever know in her life.

The ambulance pulled out and white fire exploded in Mossy's hip at every bump and chuckhole...of which there were ten million. Merrily:...*pain* screaming from throbbing head across her blistered face to her bleeding hands to the white hot, searing *pain* in her hip. "Or he never had one in the first place!" called Rod Hill, merrily. Merrily, merrily, Mossy escaping back into unconsciousness. Merrily, merrily...

Life is but a dream.

୨୦୧

Olympic Memorial Hospital
Thursday, August 26, 1999, 18:25 hours

Mossy opened her eyes and saw the bloodshot eye of the sun staring back at her through the west-facing window of the hospital. She knew immediately from the smell that she was in the hospital. Her mind groped: where was her mother; what had happened to Mossy; was it another school bus accident; had all the ponies been burned in the fire?

She was trying to make sense out of the cacophony of pain and other stabbing messages given to her by her senses. She smelled drugs on her own breath and wondered why she was back in the hospital. She smelled scorched hair and put her hand to her face and felt the bandages. *The fire...that had been real. The ponies: they were something out of her head...something symbolic of other casualties...* A picture flashed into her head of Peter Cienfuegos burning in the tree next to her and the screaming of other demonstrators as the fire swept over them. Mossy shuddered.

"Oh, hello," said a cheerful voice a few feet away. A young woman was looking up from her <u>Seventeen</u> magazine. "You've been out all afternoon. They finished operating on your hip a few hours ago. They wanted you out for that, but they were scared about the bonk on your head, so they did a CAT scan and pain reflex stuff to make sure they could keep you under sedation...

218

"Where am I? What all is wrong with me?"

"OH! I thought you knew that. Let's see, you're at Olympic Memorial Hospital and you fell out of a tree and got burned up in a big fire. You broke your hip on the fall and whacked your head and your face got kind of burned, but they say there won't be much scarring, thank God, and they can do some skin grafts to make you good as new and, let's see, I'm Amy, your Candy Striper, OH!, and I don't know who does your nails, but one of them is gone, I mean - OH MY GOD! gone - and the others look like you dug your way out of a grave, no offense, which reminds me, the doctors say your airway is OK, which has them WAY confused, because, like, you landed in a hot frying pan and, let's see, I told you my name is Amy and dinner will be along in a little bit and I saw them wheeling it in to the other rooms when they brought you back from surgery and it was something with potatoes and hamburger - I THINK -, I mean, it could be road kill for all I know - just kidding - which reminds me, thirty-three people died in that fire and...uh, I don't think they want you doing that!"

Mossy had sat up and was groggily undoing the restraints which lashed both her legs to a foam pad between them. "Amy, do you drive?" asked Mossy of the young verbal fountain.

"No, but my boy friend does. HEY, you better leave that alone! I better get the nurse..."

"Do you and your boyfriend want to make a little cash driving to Forks?"

"Well, sure," said Amy withdrawing her finger from the call button to hear the proposal without administrative interference. "I mean, like, I'm a volunteer here and they don't pay me so...HEY, you better not fool with that IV. They're giving you Morphine with that D5W and it's doctor's orders..."

"Push that wheelchair over to the bed and call your boyfriend," said Mossy, fully sitting up and pulling off the tape chevron which held the needle into her hand. "New doctor. New orders. Let's get out of here!"

"They're going to fire my ass for this," remarked Amy, without much regret.

ॐ

Hemp Hill Creek
Thursday, August 26, 1999, 20:40 hours

Mossy painfully dragged herself out of Amy's boyfriend's car into the wheelchair and sat looking at the sunlight play on the burned-over ridge above her farm. A distant rumble to the west made Mossy think that the storm had moved out to the ocean and she sniffed the air. There was no storm within thirty miles and she remembered that a new supersonic flyway was bringing commercial jet traffic up from South America to Seattle.

"Are you sure that there is nothing more we can do for you? I mean, I can cook at least as good as the food at the hospital and I could help you with your fingernails or Jerry could drive to the store and buy you stuff and do you really live here by yourself and OH MY GOD! up there is where those people all died, Jerry, honey, let's stay and help her..."

"Just let the two dogs out of their kennels and leave the door open so they can get water or food for the next couple of days until I can get around myself.

219

I'll stay downstairs with water and the door open. I've got crutches and know how to use them..." Mossy's voice trailed off as she looked up at Reade Hill. A red appendage of sunlight was licking the lifeless, smoking ridge like the lolling tongue of a cow upon the steaming carcass of its stillborn calf. "I'll be all right," said Mossy.

Twelve

"Thirty three eco-terrorists burned in wildfire.
A nation asks, 'Wisdom of God or wisdom of man?'"
- **Sign on marquis in front of fictional saw shop in Forks (no, not Jerry's)**

"You can log this country, or burn it, but give it time and the country comes back. The country can be washed away or covered under ten-feet of windfalls, but even that doesn't stop anything. Sooner or later the trees find their way."
- **Don Moser**, author/seasonal Park Ranger, Kalaloch about 1960

Highway 101, Milepost 183
Monday, August 30, 1999, 09:10 hours

Special Agent Fred Prue stood approximately where Jim Reade had stood forty years previously and looked at the blackened ridge named after a man who had lost a pickup on this spot. From a distance, it looked like any other fire scar on the landscape. The abundance of silver snags in the pockets of old growth on Willoughby Ridge attested to the participation of fire in the grooming and structuring of the natural forest. But this fire on Reade Ridge had taken an awesome toll in human life and the question remained, what started this fire? If it was caused by lightning, then the thirty-three demonstrators fell victim to Mother Nature, same as the silver snags. If, however, the fire was started by a logger, then it was the greatest violation of civil rights imaginable: the deprivation of right to life. That this deprivation of human life occurred in a National Forest, with Federal concurrent jurisdiction, meant that Title 18 of the Code of Federal Regulations applied. The town of Forks would feel the prodding and poking of a full Federal probe.

Yesterday, two of the surviving Earth First! demonstrators on their way back to California had agreed to meet with Prue at a Taco Bell in Aberdeen. The two Earth First!ers told a long and detailed story about how they had saved a local girl, who was badly broken up from coming out of a tree, and how they had heroically led a logger and Forks cop out of the holocaust. The first ambulance had pulled out with the busted-up girl and the Earth First!ers had waited around another hour for an ambulance which took them to the hospital in Aberdeen where they were held for 48 hour observation. They were weak on the details of the fire's cause, since they were on the other side of the ridge from the point of ignition.

Special Agent Prue had learned the address of this young female from Forks Police Officer Brian Fairbanks, who told a different story about the girl's rescue. Fairbanks said that she lived alone on a farm at the base of this ridge in Prue's view. He hoped that she would have more information of the type that supported an investigation of a civil rights violation.

He got back in his unmarked car, drove to Milepost 184 and made a right-hand turn onto the Dowans Creek Road. He drove to the end of the road and made several wrong turns looking for the Flying S Farm. As he drove across the bridge marked on his map as Hemp Hill Creek he heard dogs barking.

A big, black monster of a dog and a small, nondescript Chihuahua type, came boiling out of the front door of the cabin. Special Agent Prue waited while the two dogs circled his car barking and whooping like marauding Indians. Eventually, out limped his target, a 19-year-old girl on crutches with a burned-up face. Prue motioned to himself and pointed out the window, indicating that he wanted to get out. "Rufus, DOWN!" and the big, black thing dropped in its tracks like it had been shot with a buffalo rifle. As the G-man began slowly getting out of his rig, the little yapper came running forward and jumped up on the leading leg of Prue's $250 slacks with its grimy, little paws, wagging its tail wildly and smiling broadly with a gray muzzle.

"Daisy, DOWN!" and the small, white dog hit the ground still smiling and fanning the air with its tail. The girl hobbled over to stand next to the big, prostrate dog and began scratching its ear with an extended crutch. The big, black dog began to moan in ecstasy. The dog's eyeballs began to shift around in its head in apparent dissociation with one another like windows of a slot machine.

"Nice dogs," remarked the Special Agent, feeling the need for small talk before introducing the purpose of his visit.

"They're kind of an intrusion alarm, body guard, and pest exterminator rolled into one."

"I imagine you need them, living way out here alone," said the Special Agent, dusting off his pant leg.

"What makes you think that I'm alone out here?" asked Mossy, wondering who this dandified visitor was. The Jehovah's Witnesses had kind of stopped coming around since Mossy began espousing the philosophy outlined in her parents' dissertation and declaring herself a "Cosmic Creationist."

"Oh, I was told on the phone by an officer from Forks - let's see..." Fred Prue reached into his jacket pocket for his notebook and, mysteriously, the black dog's eyes stopped spinning and came to focus on the hand he placed in his jacket. Prue slowly pulled out the notebook and opened it. "...an Officer Brian Fairbanks? Do you know an Officer Fairbanks?"

"Maybe I do," said Mossy, not wishing to put any cards on the table before she knew the nature of the game being played here.

Ahhhh! So she's being cagey, thought the FBI man looking at the peeling blisters and burnt-off eyebrows on the pretty face of the young woman. Let's use shock and anger to get her talking. "Look, Ms. Stone, I know you live here alone. I know that you were injured in that fire on the ridge last Thursday and I'm here as a Federal Investigator, trying to get to the bottom of what happened. We think the fire was set. We think thirty-three people were killed and you were disfigured by person or persons, unknown. We need your cooperation. Now, do you agree that your name is Mossy Stone, that you live here alone, and that you were an eyewitness to the fire on the ridge up there that I'm here to investigate?"

"No." said Mossy.

"WHAT DO YOU MEAN, NO?" Fred Prue raised his voice in exasperation. The big, black son-of-a-bitch made a low-pitched noise like distant thunder and sniffed the air.

"Good, Ruffie," said the young woman, talking to the dog, instead of the Special Agent.

"Miss, I'm trying to get at the people who tortured your friends and burned up your face. I would like a little cooperation, please. What do you mean you don't agree?"

"I don't agree to anything until I know with whom I'm speaking and by whom you're employed. I need some identification..."

With his notebook in his left hand, the Special Agent jammed his other arm into his jacket and whipped out his badge and credentials into the face of the recalcitrant witness. "SPECIAL AGENT FRED PRUE, FBI," said the G-man with force, to gain the attention and respect of this unruly subject. Mossy stepped backwards on her crutches in intimidation and the black dog exploded in a fury of white teeth, flopping jowls and slobber. In his retreat to the open door of his car, Prue dropped his notebook on the ground and grabbed the wheel to pull himself into the seat. He closed the door and a tidal wave of black hair slammed into the side of his car. Quickly he rolled up his window. "CALL HIM OFF! CALL OFF THE DOG!" the FBI man yelled, but the young woman had lost her balance when she stepped back. The dog continued his frenzy on the vehicle like the roller on a car wash. She was getting off the ground in obvious pain and the little dog had gone nuts, as well. The little mutt that had muddied his pants leg was now on the hood of his vehicle, snarling at him through the windshield. No problem, there, but the black dog was bouncing off the driver's window leaving a froth of white slobber. The monster could break through at any second. Prue withdrew his 30-caliber handgun and both dogs went even more ballistic. "CALL OFF CUJO BEFORE I HAVE TO KILL HIM!" order the Agent.

"RUFUS, DOWN, DOWN! DAISY, OFF!" ordered the young woman and both canines hit the ground. "Here's your notebook," she said, holding onto her crutches and reaching down painfully to pick it up off the ground.

"Can you get in on the passenger's side a minute so we can talk?" asked Special Agent Prue, humbly, rolling down the window a crack to receive his notebook.

"It's not a good idea. The dogs wouldn't go for it..."

"The dogs wouldn't go for it! Miss Stone, this is a Federal Investigation! What wags what around here?"

"There's already been enough trouble here. You've upset my dogs. I think you should leave."

The black dog lay at the feet and crutches of the crazy woman. The dog lifted its lips and snarled. That's it! thought Special Agent Prue. He'd come back with Brian Fairbanks, if he had to, and feed the Forks Cop to the crazy bitch's mutts. He started the car and put it in reverse, "I'll be back!" he yelled out the crack in the window. "I'll kill these dogs if I have to..."

ഇ~ഏ

Forks Office of law firm, Mulligan and Mulligan
Tuesday, August 31, 1999, 20:05 hours

Rod Hill had little idea why he had been summoned by the national leadership of WACFAC to come to the law office at this time of evening. He presumed the worst: that it involved his participation in the counter demonstration and events leading up to the fire fatalities. Though the official investigation continued without resolution, he had been seen at the fire's point area by the Fairbankses, both city cop and ranger. Perhaps this was to be some kind of kangaroo court where he was punched raw by a room of hopping lawyers before being fed to the law.

"Thanks for coming at such short notice, Mr. Hill," began one of the lawyers. "There are matters that need to be addressed with deliberate expedition." Whatever that meant. "Perhaps, Mr. Hill, you have noticed that the winds of change are upon Forks..." The lawyer paused and Hill understood that some kind of answer was required of him.

"Naw, they seem pretty much out of the southwest like they've always been. Or am I missing something?"

"What we mean is that new economic opportunity is upon us. The vitality is draining out of the logging industry that has carried you and this town all these years. Men of character and sensitivity - men such as yourself - need to keep their noses to the wind to detect new opportunity. I wonder if you or the other good, hardworking people of this town have any idea what the reaction will be to this faux pas on Reade Hill with the dead demonstrators?" The lawyer again paused.

"Well, as near as I can make out, the folks here in Forks aren't losing any sleep over a bunch of goofy tree huggers climbing up trees and setting fire to the woods beneath themselves..."

"The Federal investigation has not revealed the cause of that blaze yet," interrupted the lawyer. "Perhaps you know something about how the fire started that you would like to share with us? ...but I was referring to the predictable national reaction to the incident which will be extremely detrimental to the timber industry. Are you aware that there will be a profound backlash which will further curtail logging?"

Hill still couldn't see where this conversation was going and wasn't going to offer up information about his involvement with the fire until he understood where the checker pieces were on the board. He stalled, "Well, as I see it, no one thinks it's a big deal. I mean, the signs in town are making it out as a joke and, if you think about it, a bunch of longhairs setting fire to themselves and the trees they were trying to save is kind of funny..."

"Mr. Hill, however amusing it may seem to you and the people of Forks, the rest of the world will NOT be laughing. There will be an outcry and logging on public lands will come to a halt. The impact of the spotted owl and marbled murrelet will be nothing compared to what lies immediately ahead. We, in this room, represent people who are ready to turn what may seem unfortuitous into the greatest pecuniary opportunity you or your town has ever dreamed of. Are you following this, Mr. Hill?"

"It would help if you'd talk English instead of Lawyerese."

"OK, I'll put it plain and simple," the lawyer paused for a moment to edit his thinking to be understood by a grade school dropout. "Everyone in this room - except maybe you - is going to get rich. Do you want to be rich?"

"Well, yeah, sure. Who wouldn't want that?"

"Maybe getting rich wasn't so important to the demonstrators who died in the fire. Already many Americans are angry about what happened on Reade

Hill and the Forest Service will feel that political pressure - that public anger - and not allow for the salvage logging that is currently approved. Bogachiel River Timber is under new ownership, which is here in this room. We have made arrangements to harvest and remove the fire-kill in three days..."

"That's impossible!" Hill interrupted. "We'll need ten days just to build roads before we can knock down the timber. Setting up the tower and yarding the logs will take another week."

"Mr. Hill, we represent interests that have the resources to do as I said: remove the fire-kill in three days. I mean, we CAN and WILL do it. But the lumber is not our big concern. We are becoming more interested in the land upon which the forest depends. I mean, in the future, there is more money in real estate than in logging..."

"You can't sell public land for real estate!" Hill interjected the one rule with which he was familiar which applied to State as well as Federal forests. "George Redding and WACFAC, who you work for, will never go along with..."

"You're not listening, Mr. Hill. We represent powerful interests who are accustomed to getting their way. Just today we contacted the Forest Supervisor's Office in Olympia and told him to hurry up on the Federal investigation so we could get our trees. Tomorrow, first thing, we will be taking the trees. We control the patent on a new process for a synthetic wood product which will revolutionize the building industry. We require a modicum - I mean, a little bit - of wood to run our first batch.

"We are going to OWN the Olympic Peninsula. Those that run with us will be running with power and those that get in the way will be trampled by our powerful hooves. Among our partners are the biggest real estate company in the United States, a major east coast newspaper and the Catholic Church, which gives us a cozy shelter for capital gains. Am I making sense to you, Mr. Hill?"

"Um...capital gains is a money thing, so you're going to hide money in a church?"

"Well, something like that. The Washington Commercial Forester Action Committee is under our immediate control. Mr. Redding will not be representing us. We need a personality that is more in touch with current trends and someone we can count on to do the right thing. We understand that your son made a heroic stand against the environmental extremists who tried to take over your town, and was physically beaten. We know you have a voice in this community and feel that you may have the personality and temperament to be among us.

"Mr. Hill, what's the most you ever made in a day of logging?"

"As a bushler, I've made almost $350 on a seven hour day before," Hill answered proudly.

"We are prepared to pay you $1,000 for every day we retain you for your services. If we only need you for a few hours a day, we will pay $150 an hour and, after you sign our contract, you will receive a retainer of $1,000 a week for conducting yourself in a manner consistent with our values. Am I getting through to you?"

"Where do I sign," asked Rod Hill. This meeting had taken an unbelievable turn. He was going to be rich. His mouth was dry and he wanted a drink.

ᔆᔆ

Hemp Hill Creek
Wednesday, September 1, 1999, 07:40 hours

Inside the cabin, the dogs started growling, indicating an intruder was approaching: maybe a deer; maybe a Jehovah's Witness; maybe the Federal Bureau of Investigation...Mossy leashed the two dogs and went to the door. In the distance, she heard an internal combustion engine approaching, but it sounded like a pickup. With the continued warm weather, there was already an upriver breeze and Mossy's nostrils flared as her olfactory sought a preview to the purpose of the interloper. "Friend," she caught the pleasant whiff of the visitor's intent. "Friend," her nose told her again and she hobbled out on her crutches to unleash the dogs and let them join in the welcome.

George Redding's pickup pulled up to the cabin and, as the dogs ran around and around it barking, Mossy studied the kindly, but haggard face of the old family friend. Trying to play logger and satisfy his duties with WACFAC was taking a toll on him. "Hi, Mossy," came George's voice as he dragged himself out of the pickup. His leg was stiff from its old injury and he viewed Mossy's crutches with suspicion. "How are you doing?"

"Alive, thanks to you and Brian Fairbanks."

"Oh, you remember our little jog through the fire?"

"I know you guys risked your life to get me out and I'll never forget it. I'm sorry I haven't called before now to thank you and Officer Fairbanks, but I've been kind of laying low."

"Sure, Mossy. We're not looking for thanks. Anyway, the word is that you pulled the plug on your stay at the hospital before they could treat your leg fracture. You may know that my leg got broken when I worked with your dad. It was his ingenuity in devising a splint that saved my ability to walk. You can't just ignore a broken leg, Mossy," the logger said kindly, but in a firm voice.

"Whatever..." was Mossy's reply.

"Anyway, the reason I came by, besides to check on you, is to tell you that Bogachiel River Timber is going ahead with the salvage operation on the ridge. We filed with DNR for an amendment to our Forestry Practice Act permit and got the go-ahead to take out the fire kill. I know you are concerned with what goes on up on that ridge, or you wouldn't have been in that tree, but the mills need the wood, the dead trees will just bring insects and other pests and, well, we need the jobs cutting down the trees."

"Whatever, George. The fight's gone out of me as far as that ridge. I wish you luck with the logging."

The dogs were called off their sentry of the old logger by a squirrel up in a Spruce. While the dogs ran around the tree and barked invectives, the squirrel chattered and threw down cones. "I guess your dogs know what it's like to want to lay down a tree," George Redding mused. Suddenly, the dogs gave up on the squirrel and began growling and barking at something they sensed across the river. "What's more interesting to those dogs than a squirrel, Mossy? Are they on to a bear or cougar?"

226

"Naw," said Mossy, picking distractedly at a burn scab above her ear. "They're picking up on the logging tower - or whatever the heavy equipment is you guys are hauling up to Reade Hill."

"We're not hauling anything for a few days. Last I heard there was still an arson investigation going on up there on Reade Hill and they were treating it like a crime scene. Some fools just can't understand that the fire was caused by lightning and you can't investigate God for arson..."

"The fire was man-caused," interrupted Mossy. "I saw the ignition. As far as whether you're hauling today, someone is moving heavy equipment on the other side of the river. I can smell the diesel exhaust. The dogs are barking because they hear the engines and we'll be hearing it ourselves in a moment."

"You SAW the ignition!? Who did it? Was it one of the demonstrators? Was it..." George Redding stopped in mid-sentence. He could feel the ground rumbling. Standing in silence for a moment, he could hear the growing growl of heavy machinery over the canine cacophony. In awe, George Redding stood frozen to the ground as Mossy and he caught glimpses of several heavy machines moving up the winding USFS 2932 Road to Reade Hill.

"Well, I'll be dipped in manure!" exclaimed Redding.

"What is that equipment?" asked Mossy. "They looked like wheeled harvesters."

"They WERE wheeled harvesters! I don't have the slightest idea what's going on, but whoever's taking them harvesters up there is wasting plenty of hours on their Hobbs meters. You can't use them things on old growth and on that steep terrain. Mossy, can I use your phone? This has to be some kind of big mistake or a trespass...or I just don't know what." The old logger bent over to begin taking off his cork boots to go in the house, but Mossy stopped him and brought him a cordless phone in a hand that grasped a crutch handle.

While Redding made his phone calls, Mossy hobbled over to gather the spruce cones the squirrel had thrown down, for fire starter. When she came back with a bag of cones tied around her shoulder, George Redding was looking like he had just been cut down and loaded aboard by a wheeled harvester. "They're planning on taking the whole salvage with those infernal machines!" Redding fumed.

"I thought you said that they couldn't operate in timber that size on those slopes."

"They modified Timberjack Harvesters some kind of way. They put some of them on legs like the machines in that old Star Wars movie to move on steep terrain. They plan to do face cuts on the big timber with the cutter heads. I still don't see how they can do it."

"You're the foreman for the job. Just say they can't do it."

"I did! They fired me!"

"They can't fire you. They'll lose their voice in WACFAC."

"They got me fired there, too! Mossy..." the old logger shook his head. "I got no pot to pee in..."

"Who's they? Who's doing all this?"

"Near as I can figure, it's those jackal lawyers that were standing by me for the last few months. They're calling the shots. Things have turned around. Bogachiel River Timber was taken over by something called Twenty First

Century. They plan a bunch more cut-and-run tactics and they need mechanized harvesters for the get and get away. Mossy, them sons of female dog lawyers'll ruin this landscape and every poor..." Redding caught his breath, trying not to sob. "...poor...fool of us left on it." Redding handed Mossy back her phone and stepped back to get in his pickup.

"Mossy, I'll lose everything...my home, my truck, my property... Unemployment can't carry my debt. I'll lose it all. What am I gonna say to my wife? The best thing I could do for her is DIE and leave her my life insurance..." Redding was back in his pickup and started the engine. "I'm sorry, Mossy. You've got some problems of your own. I shouldn't be blubbering so. Be with God, girl."

"And God with you, Mr. Redding," called out Mossy as the dogs barked and chased the retreating pickup to the bridge.

ৡৡ

Hang Ups Tavern, Forks
Wednesday, September 1, 1999, 21:00 hours

The stranger in a new hickory shirt and clean tin pants made his way to the bar and waited to be served. The bar was almost entirely full. Loggers reacted to the news of impending unemployment the same way they greeted news of impending employment by hitting the bars. Several stools down from the stranger, Rod Hill was buying drinks all around and filling the air with his beer breath. "Another round of beer for all these out-of-work-sons-a-bitches! HERE'S HOPING THE BASTARDS IN THE HARVESTERS ROLL DOWN THE HILL AND DROWN THEIR SCABBY ASSES IN THE RIVER."

The barkeep swept along the counter refilling mugs and putting hash marks on Hill's bill. When the barkeep got to the stranger, he smiled and asked, "What'll it be there, Paul Bunyan?"

"I'll have a draft on that guy's bill," the stranger pointed to Rod Hill. The bartender filled a mug and placed it on the bar in front of the stranger and then went back to Hill to report the arrival of the new pup at the beer teat.

In a moment, Rod Hill appeared next to the man and asked in a loud voice, "YOU WOULDN'T BY ANY CHANCE BE ONE OF THEM FAGGOT, CANDY-ASSED, TIMBERJACK OPERATORS WORKING UP ON READE RIDGE?"

"No, sir," the stranger replied in a low voice. "I got nothing in the world to do with them rascals."

Hill lowered his voice a little and continued the interview, "Then...lose your job today, sport. Because the beer in that glass was intended for those who lost work today and not freeloaders in spit-shined tin pants."

"As a matter of fact, the wind changed and my job was taken away from me today and that's why I never got a chance to get these clothes dirty. Anyway, take no offense. Let me buy the next round for all us out-of-work gents."

"Well, all right, then!" said Hill, glad to be sitting at the bar with a man of generosity such as himself. "NEXT ROUND IS ON THE LOGGER IN

STARCHED HICKORY!" he called out to the crowd. "THE POOR BASTARD LOST HIS JOB TODAY, SAME AS US!"

"Who'd you say it was who fired your ass?" Hill barely lowered his voice. He pulled a can of snoose from his shirt pocket, tapped it on the counter and stuffed a pinch into his lower lip. Hill offered the open can to the stranger.

"I didn't say they fired me. I said the wind changed and I kinda lost my job," the stranger replied conspiratorially, taking a little pinch and gingerly tucking it into his lip. "I'm not at liberty to discuss my employer, at the moment, but they're very big and you would recognize their name if I told you."

"Iz-zat-so?" challenged Hill, wondering if this dude could be emissary from the huge concern which now secretly employed him. He was beginning to talk like those high farting legal beagles. The stranger immediately looked sorry that he had applied the snoose to his mouth. He was looking under the counter for a spittoon, for Christ sake! The wind changed - was this some kind of secret password. Hill further tested the waters, "Would you call this outfit that... retains you...powerful?" Hill spit on the floor when the barkeep wasn't looking.

"Absolutely! Why do you ask?"

The stranger spit on the floor in full view of the bartender who came over red faced. "Mister, if you don't want me wiping the floor with your clean shirt and pants, I would appreciate you not spitting there!"

"Back off," growled Hill. This guy here represents powerful interests." The bartender scowled and moved down the bar filling up mugs and putting his hash marks on the spitter's tab. "So, it sounzz to me, like we may be anshering to the same powerful gizze," continued Hill, in a hushed slur.

"Maybe," whispered the stranger. "I already told you that my job has been changed, but I still have an employer. How about you? Are you still working for somebody?"

Bingo! thought Hill. This guy is legit! Whatever he wants, I'll give it! "Uh, yeah," he whispered. "Don't let it get out to these boozers I came in with, cause they think I'm in the toilet with them. Let's go over there and talk," Hill pointed to an abandoned table far from the drinking trough of the bar.

At the table, Hill asked in a run on slur of the stranger, "So why are you here? Are you guys checking up on me already, for Christ's sake?"

"We're looking for a little information about what you know about the fire on Reade Hill. We understand that you were there?"

"Shit, yes! You couldn't have been more there than I was and not be crispied! What the fuck do you guys want to know?"

"Well, for one, we're interested in how the fire got started. The investigation kind of got shoved aside to let those...those God damned harvesters in and screw up...I mean FUCK UP everything."

"Wait a minute!" A wave of suspicion crossed Hill's drunken countenance and he lowered his voice to a hissing whisper. "You are sent here by the same honchos that brought in the harvesters? Being pissed about the Timberjacks is just a show for these yodelheads." Hill waved at the unemployed loggers draining their glasses of the last of the free beer.

"Uh, right. Of course. But we want to know how the fire was started."

"Then ask your questions. I told you I was right there."

"Man-caused or lightning-caused?"

"Man-caused...or, really, sissy-caused."

"Logger or demonstrator?"

"I already told you it was started by a sissy! How many sissy loggers do you know that aren't riding around in wheeled harvesters...I mean you guys must think they're OK and that makes them OK with me, but the operators are still fairy faggots, no offense."

"So was the fire caused by one of the Timberjack operators and, if so, whom?"

"Naw! I already told your bosses about this. You must be further down the pecker pole than me, even. It was only real loggers going nose-to-nose with them eeeko-freako's." A sly expression passed over Hill's snoosy puss. "The way I reckon, you guys were figuring to have us loggers do the dirty work, breaking up the demonstration, and then bring in the Timberjacks to run our asses out of the woods. The fire wasn't part of the plan, but it's the icing on the cake for your bosses..."

"But, who set the blaze?"

"I already told your people: the fruity-headed demonstrator set the fire..."

"Peter Cienfuegos, Mossy Stone - which exact demonstrator?"

"The first one...Cienfegoose, or whatever. He lit the thing."

"But why would he do that, or how is that possible? He was in the tree. He was killed in the fire. Are you sure Mossy Stone didn't light it?"

"Hell no! She was one of us until the eeeko-freaks got their hooks in her. I used to work with her nutty-professor dad twenty years ago. Shit! She would never do something like that!"

"Well, why did Cienfuegos do it? He DIED in the fire."

"He needed a little help coming up with the right decision and I already told you that I was there. I may have coached him a little."

"OK, so what was your part in it."

"Well, I may have arranged a bunch of bone dry brush and slash under his tree and got him to playing around with fire a little."

"Why would he be playing with fire? Surely he must have seen the danger to himself and the other demonstrators?"

"These guys are crazy! I may have pissed him off a little. He may have thought that I would put the fire out if he threw a burning rag down into it."

"Why would he do something like that?" the stranger winked as he delivered the question.

"I may have put the idea in his head. I doused out a fire I set myself with a fire extinguisher."

"Oh!" the stranger winked again, approvingly. "So you provoked some kind of game with fire and then withdrew the safeguard of the extinguisher?"

"Yeah!" Hill laughed smugly. It started as a game of chicken and ended up as K.F.C. I couldn't figure out the other night why your bosses weren't more interested in my part in the thing. What am I going to tell the newspapers? Do you think they may want to give me some kind of bonus?"

The stranger laughed in kind and said, "I think they will want you to have a bonus, yes! I think they would use Title 18 of the Criminal Federal Code to describe it to the press. There you will find the definition of "manslaughter," to whit: any action OR LACK THEREOF on the part of the accused that leads directly or indirectly to the loss of human life. It carries up to life imprisonment, so, I would guess your bonus would be thirty-three times that..."

"WHAT THE FUCK ARE YOU TALKING..."

"I'm talking," said the stranger, pushing back his chair and standing up with a gun in his right hand and a badge in his left hand, "about Special Agent Fred Prue, Federal Bureau of Investigations! YOU'RE UNDER ARREST FOR MANSLAUGHTER! PUT YOUR HANDS ON YOUR HEAD AND TURN AROUND!"

The mute button turned off the bar noise and the silence was shattered by the barkeep yelling, "HEY! YOU CAN'T BRING A GUN IN HERE!"

"Another round of free drinks!" announced the stranger. Put it on Prisoner Hill's bill. Good night all!"

Thirteen

The only reason for time is so that everything doesn't happen at once.
-Albert Einstein. (1879-1955)

Time and space - time to be alone, space to move about - these may well become the great scarcities of tomorrow.
-Edwin Way Teale (1899-1980)

Bogachiel Way, Forks
Wednesday, September 8, 1999, 14:20 hours

The weekly edition of <u>Knives, Spoons and Forks</u> lay open on her dining room table as Angeline Redding called the number of the newspaper. She was devastated. Never in her life had she endured such suffering. Two days ago, she had called her son, who was attending his last year at Duke University back east and given him the news. He was using money he would need for meals to fly back for the funeral. When Richard Stokes, the reporter/editor, had phoned her a few hours after the body had been found, she was trying to reach her son and unprepared to deal with the man's probing questions. Now, waiting on hold, she had more than a comment to offer the town newspaper.

Stokes had to understand that he was sorting through and destroying the few fragments left in Angeline's life. The slant posed in this article would probably result in benefits being withheld from the life insurance plan, which would be her only source of income besides Social Security. It would color her relationship with the church. From where she stood next to the phone she could see the front page and the picture of her husband's body being brought out of the woods to the road in a wire basket. Next to the picture were other disturbing news stories, which chronicled the anxiety felt by her husband before he left to go "fishing" last Saturday. She could read the headlines; the story was emblazoned on her mind's eye...

Hill Appointed New Executive Director of WACFAC	Executive Director of WACFAC Found Dead
Rod Hill promises that he will be responsive to the need for adjustment and change in the management of public and private forests on the peninsula and that the doors to WACFAC will be open to all in the name of educating the public. "It galls me to think that those hippies in the trees on Reade Ridge had no idea about what logging is all about and how it keeps them in telephone books and toilet paper. Maybe they wouldn't have gotten burned up in the fire if they understood all that," concluded Mr. Hill. (See other article on Hill assisting the F.B.I. on arson investigation on page 2 and late breaking story on George Redding on same page.)	Fell, pushed or jumped? That's the subject of a Federal investigation surrounding the circumstances of the death of a local Forks man whose smashed body was found in the Calawah River last Sunday. "We're studying all angles regarding the death of George Redding," announced Forest Ranger Chris Fairbanks. A long-time, personal friend of the deceased, Fairbanks discovered the body with her search/police dog, Sig Sauer. The discovery of the body terminated an all-night search which followed the report by Angeline Redding that her husband had not returned from a fishing trip. (story continued, p 2)

Wednesday, September 8, 1999

Director Dead, cont'd from p 1 "We know that Mr. Redding went over the guardrail of the bridge from wool fibers we have found matching the pants he was wearing," said an F.B.I. investigator on the case. Special Agent Fred Prue, in the area pursuing another investigation (see article "Environmentalists Set Fire" on page 1), was brought in to assist with forensics of this death investigation. "From the study of the fiber compression we will be able to determine whether they came from the seat of his pants and whether they were dragged across the rail."

An anonymous F.B.I. investigator on the case and speaking off-the-record speculated that George Redding jumped from the bridge. "Study of the wool fibers through an ordinary magnifying glass corroborate that they were pressed not pulled into the steel. It appears that Mr. Redding sat for a few minutes contemplating the jump."

"George may have been a little upset about losing his position as Executive Director of Washington Commercial Foresters Action Committee," said Rod Hill, the man who was selected to replace Redding. Reading a press release from WACFAC, Hill added, "As the former director of WACFAC and a logger himself, Mr. Redding leaves behind a legacy of good will, honesty, hard work, and a concern for this land and its people."

Speaking as a long time friend and not representing WACFAC, Hill concluded, "I think the poor, dumb slob jumped."

Angeline Redding had no comment on allegations that her husband took his own life. A significant life insurance policy through Farmers Insurance was carried by the deceased payable to his wife. Local adjusters for the company are following the investigation with great interest.

Twenty First Century Merger (continued)

John Smith, spokesman for the Timberland Division of the emerging corporate giant, held a press conference explaining that the "countenance of logging would look much different on the face of the Twenty First Century." Smith explained that much less wood product would be required in the company's new process, which will produce "a durable, inexpensive, indestructible and *beautiful* resource, which will allow timberlands to exist undisturbed as habitat for wildlife."

The company's Timberlands rep also said that some of its newly acquired land will be used for

Knives, Spoons and Forks   page 2

housing starts for first time home owners and for time-share condominiums in areas which provide exceptional recreational and scenic opportunity. "Such occurs on the Olympic Peninsula in the state of Washington, where we are purchasing lands that afford the opportunity to *live* amid the splendor of ancient forests."

Another giant in real estate - the Catholic Church - has teamed up with Twenty First Century. Trading most of its non-church-related real estate holdings for a position in the company, Archbishop Ryan McGreggor spoke from the church's National Council saying that it was a financial miracle and that "in third world countries (the Catholic Church) can pass around collection plates allowing the poor parishioners to help themselves.

This newspaper and The Washington Host, were also purchased by Twenty First Century.

Forks Man Brings Information on Fire

Rodney Hill, the newly appointed Executive Director of the Washington Commercial Foresters Action Committee has stepped forward with information which may help the F.B.I. and other Federal investigators find the cause of last week's fire on Reade Ridge. Approximately three million board feet of timber were destroyed in the blaze. Thirty-three demonstrators also lost their lives in the fire.

Now it appears that the cause of the fire may have been the demonstrators themselves. Two weeks ago, to thwart the logging operations of Bogachiel River Timber, thirty-six demonstrators had climbed high into the trees and were resisting lawful orders Thursday morning to come down out of the trees. Rodney Hill, now claims to have witnessed the ignition. He says burning material was thrown out of trees by the confrontational demonstrators.

To government allegations that timber workers "allowed the fire to happen," Hill argues that loggers on the ground, including himself, put out spot fires with extinguishers until the dry chemical was used up and the loggers had to flee for their own lives. Hill points out that loggers and a Forks police officer re-entered the holocaust at extreme peril to themselves to rescue the three surviving demonstrators.

So valuable is witness Hill , he has been taken into custody by the FBI. Para-legals for TFC, which owns Bogachiel River Timber, claim that Rod Hill is too valuable to Forks to remain so sequestered, vow to have him home in a week..

❦

Forks Office of law firm, Mulligan and Mulligan
Friday, September 10, 1999, 20:05 hours

    In a small, smoke-filled room with big money, sat Richard Stokes, a small town newspaperman, talking about big plans for the future. Stokes was trying to make some small sense out of what John Smith, the bigwig from Twenty First Century, was saying: "We were blown away by your sensitivity and the depth of your investigatory reporting, both in the cases of the Reade Ridge tragedy and the unfortunate passing of Mr. Redding from your community."

    Now the incident on Reade Ridge was tragic or poetic, depending upon with whom you were talking at the moment. The circumstances surrounding George's death pointed pretty clearly to his self-destruction, though Redding's wife was pissing and moaning about the news and threatening libel. What these guys really thought about his writing, the news in Forks, or the smell of owl shit on a freshly cut tree stump was beyond his fathom. "Uh... I'm glad you enjoyed the stories."

    "I'm not sure enjoy is the word I would use," countered John Smith, who appeared to be the leader in this mob of high-priced lawyers. Stokes looked uncomfortably around the room from face to face trying to read where this meeting was going. Some of the men had sat with George Redding as WACFAC applied the legal lever to push the timber resources of Reade Ridge out of environmental protection and onto the auction block. In the end, these guys weren't there for George. "We, of course, share the...pain of what happened on Reade Ridge and the unfortunate end of our friend, George Redding. Not much gets by you unnoticed, Mr. Stokes, so you must be aware that many of us in the room, like yourself, knew Mr. Redding personally, as we worked, shoulder to shoulder, on the issue of breaking the timber deadlock..."

    Smith waved his hand flamboyantly at the pack of snarling legal wolves behind him and, one by one, their lips curled up as they muttered a word or two that offered Richard no clue as to why they were all here. "Truly tragic," said one. "Such a pity," said another. "A good man." "A loss for everyone." "If we had only known..." What were these guys thinking? Stokes was trying hard to read between the lines. He tried to formulate a phrase to show he was on the same channel. "Brrrrrp!" he said, as a nervous burp escaped his mouth.

    John Smith smiled, understandingly. "It's tough for all of us, but we continue to do what we have to do. In your case, you don't make the tragic news, you just report it. Tell me, Mr. Stokes - may I please call you Richard? Is your primary job as a newspaper man to unveil the whole truth of a given issue, or to tell the public what's in their best interests to know?"

    "Well...," Stokes tried to stall. "Brrrrrp...excuse me! I guess that would depend on the situation, wouldn't it?"

    "Ah, so wise, so wise," intoned Smith. "Tell me, in your training as a journalist, were you made familiar with the term pseudo-event - where the impact of an occurrence is controlled by the media? How public reaction to a perhaps trivial happening becomes the real story?"

"Um...I think so, brrrrrp, excuse me!"

"Now, what happened on Reade Ridge was no trivial thing, but how the media goes with the event and how the public reacts to it...that is the real story. We, in this room, have certain...expectations on how it will pan out. Can you see the big picture, Richard?"

"Er...I think so. How do you mean, exactly?"

"Ah hah!" chuckled Smith. "You're being very careful, answering a question with another question. What I mean is that there are always two sides to a story, if you look hard enough. I mean, either George Redding jumped or he didn't jump. Your investigative reporting puts him as jumping. But, assuming he jumped, did he just get tired of his wife, his job, his church...whatever, and jump...or did larger events conspire against him and he was a victim?"

"Er...I haven't gotten that far..."

"Good, good!" interrupted Smith. Some things are best left alone...both for the welfare of the bereaved and for the good of the community. What we're here to say is that what's good for the community is what brings jobs, and tax revenue, and property value...Do you agree that these are good things to bring to your community?"

"Well, sure, but brrrp..."

"And unemployment, an erosion of the tax base, collapsing property values are bad for the community, don't you agree?

"Yes, I think so..."

"What you tell people about any given event fills the windsock of public opinion and pushes it to one side or the other. It's like the stock market. Have you followed the progress of Twenty First Century?"

"Not really, I don't..."

"It's what people believe that makes it true. What they feel about Twenty First Century is unbridled optimism and extreme confidence. If the smallest thing came along to threaten that - just some misperception - the stock price could tumble and millions of investors would be hurt. Would you want that to happen?"

"Well, I don't even know these investors and I don't play around with the stock market myself..."

"Right! What I'm getting at is more personal. If you are a reporter sitting in a crowded theater and the person next to you decides to break the law a little by lighting up a cigarette, do you scream FIRE! at the top of your voice or just talk with the person about putting out the cigarette. If you scream FIRE! hundreds of people will be injured by panic, whereas, if you approach the... violator, and ask him to please extinguish his smoke, the law will be upheld and the peace protected. Don't you agree that, under these circumstances, it is best to...control the information you give the public?"

"Yeah, sure, but..."

"Ah hah! So we do agree after all! What you tell the public to some degree is guided by what is best for their welfare."

"Well, honestly, brrrrp, <u>Knives, Spoons and Forks</u> has always been influenced by what the community wants to read. That's what sells advertising."

"Excellent! So you are in the habit of coping with financial realities. Excellent! Let's change gears for just a minute. Have you heard about RIO 2000? As a journalist, aren't you intrigued by the stories that will play out down there?"

"Honestly, it's a bit beyond the scope of Forks. I mean overpopulation, polluted water, global re-warming, holes in the ozone...these aren't big problems in our town."

"Surely Forks will one day experience the influence of these effects. Our intention - in this room - would be to blunt the impact for your community and...well...turn a penny. But that's not the point I'm trying to make. How would you, personally, feel about an assignment to cover RIO 2000 for a prestigious, large-circulation newspaper?"

"I would love to go to Rio, but I could never afford it..."

"I'm not talking about being a stringer. I'm talking about an all-expense-paid trip with first-class accommodations over looking Copacabana. A salaried position paying $2,500 a week, whether we use your material or not, and, say, a $3,000 bonus for every story or piece of a story we use. The trip would last three months because we would want you to get down there and get settled before the ruckus started."

"I would LOVE to go to Rio! And that sounds like more money than I make in Forks in a year. But I can't get three months off my job here. Journalists aren't just sitting around the unemployment office or roaming the streets of this town..."

"We've already been in touch with your parents and, like yourself, they were sensitive to certain financial realities. We're closing the deal on buying Knives, Spoons and Forks as we speak. Tomorrow you'll be working for us, anyway, and we will be changing the name of your little newspaper and finding a suitable journalist to manage things while you're gone. But we are trying to look at a big picture and we feel that a person of your ability and temperament might be more valuable to the world with a wider readership. We can use this trip to Rio to look at one another. Perhaps you would be happier writing for THE WASHINGTON HOST?"

ھوﻻ

Over the Pacific Ocean
December 31, 1999

At 21:45 p.m., the Trans-Brasil supersonic Concorde left Rio International Airport with Richard Stokes and his pregnant wife, Jenny. "Chiggers," was the name Jenny used to refer to the six-month-old, squirming fetus inside her. Joining the Stokeses on this airbus ride were a handful of North American businessmen and a planeload of party-hearty Brazilian tourists.

The SST had left Rio in a lazy, diagonal northwest line toward Bolivia, coursing across the remains of the Amazon ecosystem, inhabited by some three million dirt farmers. From six miles up, Richard Stokes could see the jungle burning from farmers clearing more rain forest. The fire revealed more of the thin, soil horizon to the sun: a process that would offer marginal cropland for two or three years before becoming a dead zone. The enormous population below didn't stop the pilot from goosing the enormous kerosene engines above half throttle which pushed the craft over Mach One, laying out a sonic boom that would knock the natives right out of their thatched grass huts. Just as the celebrants began a Portuguese countdown of the last ten seconds of the twentieth century on their watches, the pilot interrupted to announce, in two languages, that the progress of the west-facing Concorde had pushed back the time in the cabin two hours. The plane would continue its northwest direction across the equator, which they would be passing in fifteen minutes. To spare the inhabitants of the west coast of the United States any disturbance, the craft would proceed north along the hundred thirty-fifth parallel, which would set back the advancing twenty first century six hours from the time on their watches. To assuage their disappointment, the pilot announced the implementation of free beverage service for the remainder of the flight.

The Concorde hurtled toward Seattle in the night at a speed seven times faster than a man jumping off the airplane would descend to the dark ocean below. Stokes brooded about the fate of the Olympic Peninsula, dozed on and off and tinkered with creative writing..

Oh you poor, defiled Emerald maiden. If I could only cradle myself in your mountainous, glacially-lactating bosom a moment longer and feel the beating of your wild heart. As you gather together the shreds of your torn skirt of forest, trying to cover the road scars we see from space upon your once innocent face, spitting out the taste of man at every river mouth into the ocean...As you are dragged by men like me who knew you, kicking and crying, into the Twenty First century, I want to ask you...

Stokes looked at himself in the reflection of the dark window. Ahead, in the dark, the flash of the lighthouse on Destruction Island was just visible, but Stokes looked at his silk suit, his natty hairdo, the golden chain around his neck, a future with The Washington Host, a condo in Sequim. His twenty years on the Olympic Peninsula had finally led to something. He had made it big time! RIO 2000 had been a journalist's paradise replete with Right-To-Lifer's slinging human fetuses they had acquired from an abortion clinic at the convention center walls. A young Amazonian had immolated himself by pouring gasoline upon himself and lighting a match on Copacabana Beach. He died in an effort to call attention to the plight of the stressed human population who consumed the jungle trying to etch out an existence from the poor acidic soil of the rain forest. Stokes knew the same fate waited for the Olympic Peninsula. This body of land was coming under the shadow of technology and big money, but for him, it had been a sweet ride.

I want to ask you, while you still have the clean breath to answer...while you still have the voice of the frogs in the swamp, the cougar cry in the night, the lugubrious lullaby of the screech owl...while pure water still runs in your veins of glacier, creek, lake, river, to ocean...was it good for you, too? Did you enjoy our little intercourse?

The Concorde continued its deceleration, increasing its rate of fall. Airspeed dropped and the dull boom rolled across the beaches and rocky cliffs like a sonic tsunami. What sounded like thunder to the human ear rang strange terror in the inner ear of the wild creatures. Harbor seals dove off rocks into the waning surf of the setting moon. A seal pup crushed its face diving onto an exposed rock in pursuit of its mother. The pneumatic wave rumbled up the river valleys and into the temperate rain forests, and across the still sparsely settled country of the western Peninsula. spotted owls fluttered from their perches. As the sound crashed upon their tiny feathered tufts, into their ear canals and upon their ear drums, it was translated to a pneumatic wave that pummeled the blood-rich beds of the owl's inner ear. By the same mechanism that causes hearing shifts in humans, the birds were losing their hearing. A raptor, which used its fine, dimensional hearing to determine the parallax of prey was being driven to extinction by forces that had little to do with the logging curtailed by this species' demise.

The plane had collided with the imaginary line of the 135th longitude, crashing into and through the twenty first century and falling down through space-time.

ᆑᆄ

The Washington Host

Volume 2002 Issue 12345   November 10, 2010

Ned Adams' Surprise Victory

Washington, D.C.- In a surprise victory over Republican hopeful, John Buck, Ned Adams, won the Sixth District seat to the United States Congress. In a District occupied by increasing number of Republican constituents, the 29-year-old candidate won the election on a platform that weighed heavily on environmental issues. In particular. Adams is calling for boundary adjustment and visitational constraints upon Olympic National Park, which occupies some 15% of the Sixth District. John Buck claims that such a platform violates the will and interests of the constituents and is making allegations of ballot box tampering. Senate octogenarian, Slate Gorton, is joining his voice to that of Buck's and is calling for a ballot recount.

Congressman Adams brings to Washington, D.C. his beautiful and flamboyant wife who dazzled campaign rallies with her tight skirts and pungent perfume. Particularly amusing to members of the media was Julie Adams remark, upon her husband's election. "As long as I'm in Washington, D.C.," said the previous fashion model, "the theater of female environmentalists will no longer be dominated by hairy, unwashed lesbians...or at least they won't occupy center stage."

Hanford Nuclear Reservation Spewing Radiation

Richland, WA. -Vat 44, a stainless steel tank, storing some 40,000 pounds of highly radioactive plutonium waste at the Hanford Nuclear Reservation, is again venting steam and threatening to turn the downwind Tri-Cities into Tri-Ghost Towns. Steam venting occurs when the cooling systems within one of these two hundred, underground super canisters is overworked or faulty and prevents the ultimate disaster of rupture or explosion.

An uncontrolled steam release forty years ago had wind conditions that carried a radioactive cloud over the local population. Hundreds, if not thousands, of cancer cases have been linked to that event. Another uncontrolled vapor release in 1981 contained deadly Tridmium, a biproduct of weapon-grade Plutonium.

Officials at the Hanford facility explain that this is why the Reservation is so geographically large - to buffer human populations. But the mayor of Richland, speaking from Forks, claims that the situation is like having a can of highly radioactive beans thrown into a campfire at a Boy Scout jamboree. "Sooner or later, the can will blow; the Federal government has an obligation to prevent what they let happen back in the '60's and '80's."

Congressional action is forthcoming. An evacuation plan is being implemented with temporary relocation camps on Olympic Peninsula National Forest lands, where evacuees can have absolute assurance of air quality. Twenty First Century Corporation, which controls extensive real estate on the Peninsula and provides moderate cost housing, is poised to accept a five billion dollar contract to provide permanent housing for the dislocated citizens.

Olympic to Receive Visitor Center

Port Angeles, Washington - In what may be the biggest corporate donation to a Government agency in the history of the world, Twenty First Century Corporation presented the National Park Service with a gift of 2.5 billion dollars to build a "Disney-class visitor center" for Olympic National Park. The check was presented to the Park Superintendent Dagmar Huffman by Julie Adams, wife of freshman Congressman Ned Adams, who is rapidly becoming the symbol for modern environmentalism.

The visitor center will be built to the specifications laid out in a Developmental Concept Plan, the engineers for which were provided by Twenty First Century. The visitor center will attempt to correct one of the major environmental problems facing the Park's "wilderness" which, put simply, is: too many visitors. Many of the ancient trees along road corridors within the Park are being threatened. Superintendent "Dog" Huffman pointed out that "many of the trees, which have stood in some cases before the advent of the desktop computer or even the television, are dying from root compaction and girdling of their bark. As people swarm around the trees and pick off pieces of bark for souvenirs, they are literally loving the trees to death."

Other problems associated with over-visitation include: vegetative denuding of alpine meadows, overwhelming of backcountry sewer systems, corruption of animal behavior from exposure to human food sources, and trash and litter being strewn to the far corners of the Park. "Our visitation has been something in the neighborhood of five thousand per cent above that which we can sustain without significant impairment to our wilderness resources," remarked Superintendent Huffman.

The new "gala-center" will offer holographic viewing of Park resources without impinging on wilderness. Forty-eight half hour performances will be offered every day in the proposed 5,000 seat auditorium, in hopes of providing a "wilderness experience" to the estimated 50 million annual visitors who swarm the beleaguered Park.

Mass Rioting South of the Border

Mexico City, Mexico - Mass riots in the streets of this city have killed several hundred people and injured thousands. The cause of the riots mystified police and other emergency personnel who have worked to quell the rioting. Interviews with arrested parties revealed one common grievance: television programming.

When the city's most widely viewed television station announced plans to replace its airing of fifty-year-old installments of the American sitcom *I Love Lucy* with a show for children with an educational theme, protests poured in. The station's program director even received threats and hate mail. The first street disturbance erupted Monday evening, immediately as the first children's show was aired. But the riots continued after the station discontinued the educational programming and the station worked with police by airing back to back episodes of the comedy series starring Lucille Ball and Desi Arnaz.

Scientists have now linked the destructive behavior to the air of this smog-choked city. According to Dr. Burt Comstock, a rage psychologist detailed to the incident by the United States Embassy, high levels of CO_2 in the blood stream of the arrested is the underlying cause of the destructive behavior.

Dr. Comstock theorizes that high CO_2 in the blood causes heavy breathing with a hyperventilation reflex yielding heightened anxiety. He believes that the panic that usually attends a hyperventilative episode is transferred to rage in a mob setting.

Though the death toll is still untallied, it is speculated that this is the greatest taking of human life in Mexico since the destruction of General Santa Anna and his troops by the Yellow Rose and the Texas Army.

༄༅

Hemp Hill Creek
January 1, 2000, 00:00

Mossy was awakened from a fitful dream by the boom. Smoke lingered in the atmosphere of the cabin. The downdrafting of a cumulonimbus cloud in the stratosphere had pushed smoke back down the chimney and into the cabin. It was suffocating to Mossy's acute olfactory. "Thunder?" wondered Mossy, at the boom which had shaken the cabin. "Damn Concordes!" said Mossy out loud, hearing the jet engines trailing the subsiding boom. Not far away, a pregnant cow elk lay with two broken front legs. The herd had spooked at the sonic boom and the cow had charged head-on into the tensioned wire of the farm's fence.

Mossy tried to settle back to sleep while the plane continued over the cabin, rattling the glass...falling to earth as it decelerated: the earth falling into the sun, the sun falling into Virgo and gravity ticking into space-time. The twenty first century had just overtaken the Olympic Peninsula.

ৡৢ

Hemp Hill Creek
June 11, 2011, 06:45

The woman leaves her crutch leaning against the fence at the edge of the garden and hobbles over to her work area using a shovel for support. Arriving at the spot from which she had quit the previous evening, she continues the job of digging up tired earth from the ground that sustained the high production of her 100 square-meter corn patch and creating mounds to be removed by wheelbarrow. She will replace the earth with fertile soil from the barn and let this part of the garden lie fallow. The corn that will sustain her through the year will be frozen and dried like the frozen, dried memories of her earlier life that visit her here in the garden.

She begins her work facing the rising sun and with her back to the silver forest of Reade Hill...the silver forest that represents for Mossy the death of Venus love, the end of adolescent idealism, the ball and chain of mobile impairment and the loss of sleep that either attends resting on bones which have never properly mended...or the vision of your lover mummified by fire.

This morning, to the list of these profound regrets is added another: As Mossy attacks the ground with her shovel, there is the rumble of heavy equipment and the cajoling of men arriving to work, as ground is broken for a high-rise condominium in the field between the Flying S Farm and the Bogachiel River. The cocoon of privacy and chrysalis of Mossy's soul are being torn open and laid bare to the eyes of the twenty first century. "Hey, lady!" cries a workman leaning on his shovel. "You work too hard over there! You should come over here and work for us...or at LEAST put on a bra!"

Mossy squares off over her work. Shovel full by shovel full, mound by mound, she attends the work and ignores the wolf whistles and sounds of paradise lost behind her. She leans into the work, forgetting pain, forgetting anger...for getting to the other side of this job must happen if she is to continue to eat...or, at least, to eat corn. Her shovel hits something hard and with some difficulty she lets herself down into the shallow hole and retrieves a bone...a deer femur. And from this bone, to the hologram of Mossy's mind are sent messages via olfactory imaging: a new born fawn gamboling across these pastures; a deer jumping over the citadel of this garden fence; a doe shot point blank in the head and the venison that commingled with human flesh but, somehow, never made up for that which was lost in the garden. Mossy holds the cold, dry femur to her face and lets the memory wash over her while workmen behind her stop shoveling once again to speculate at her activity. "Look at the dyke!" exclaims one. "She dug up her dildo!"

THE WASHINGTON HOST

Volume 101 Issue 3650 | January 1, 2019

The BIG Year of 2018 in Review:

Ground breaking for the Green Wall

Twenty First Century to defend the threatened resources of Olympic National Park by building a bastion of condominium time-shares around the Peninsula. Story: A-2.

Lawyers: number ONE industry in US

Department of Com-merce issued its December Report which confirms that lawyers and the paralegal industry are the biggest moneymakers in the country. This industry is followed by the prison/corrections industry which was privatized five years ago. Story: A-3

Energy solved Scientists at Massachusetts Institute of Technology confirm that energy will

not be a problem in the remainder of the Twenty First century. Harnessing tidal action and lightning will combine with tabletop fusion and new geothermal projects to provide a glut of energy. Story: A-3

Cienfuegos Project

in greater Yellow-stone

The first step in solving the Nation's energy shortage is a geo-thermal project sponsored by the Twenty First Century Corp. Using research done 30 years ago by a University of Washington grad student, TFCC was able to establish the "Old Faithful" 20 gigot system by controlling geysers that were identified by the National Park

See Urban Life Section –

Advice for getting your time-share on Washington State's pristine Olympic Peninsula.

Service as threats to visitor safety. Story: B-2.

Right to Lawyer assisted suicide

The Constitutional right of an individual to end their own life by abstaining from food and water was reaffirmed by the Supreme Court. Given the large legal consequences of such an act, the Court ordered that each death must be attended by a probate lawyer qualified to make decisions regarding the involved estate.

Barnacles: rare and endangered? New study

Pesky marine pests, put under control by a Twenty First Century Corp. patent, which led to the development and production of synthetic wood, have come under a new Federal study. Story: D-6.

Hemp Hill Creek
June 15, 2019

The woman walks the electric fence line picking up trash which was thrown over by her transient neighbors, 4,000 some people who own shares in Bogachiel Rain Forest Gardens, the huge time-share condominium between her and the river. Of the 4,000, less than 400 would be in residence at any given time exercising their thirty day, thirty thousand dollar lease, but, with them, would be a gaggle of friends and family and friends of friends and friends of family and friends of friends of friends...to which this valley had surrendered innocence and virtue.

For nine years she had not seen the silver forest of Reade Hill with the northern view eclipsed by the twenty-story condo. Had she been able to see through the tall edifice to Reade Hill, she would not have seen a forest in rejuvenation, as she expected. Instead, atop Reade Hill, she would see another bastion condominium, just like the one in her back yard. The entire Olympic Peninsula was girdled by them. And to the few perennial residents, like Mossy, is inflicted inflated property values and the crushing burden of taxation it carries.

She secures the trash in an animal resistant container and hobbles back to the garden where she trades crutch for shovel and begins digging a trench to carry irrigation to the strawberries whose thirst is no longer sated by that which falls from the sky. The woman works facing south with her back to her disappointments...looking forward to the success that can be coaxed from this little piece of land.

From where the fence line disappears into an alder hedge on the east end of the farm, some salmonberry is knocked down and a large black dog ambles along the fence on patrol. Arriving at the garden gate, he sits, hoping for admittance.

"Oh, all right Fif, it IS your birthday. The woman hobbles to the gate and lets the dog enter. The animal prostrates itself at her feet and she picks up her crutch, the end of which she uses to great effect on the side of the dog's head. As she massages the area around the ear the dog grunts and moans in ecstasy. The two-year-old dog was the son of the bitch, Samantha, who, in turn was daughter to Rufus. His eyelids flutter open and his eyes seem to be spinning independently. "Good, Fif!" coos the woman. "Good June Fifteenth." She finally puts down the crutch to pick up the shovel and return to her project. Fifteenth repairs to a corner of the garden where he is allowed to dig and commences prospecting for a deer bone.

꙳

Hemp Hill Creek
September 29, 2019, 16:00 hours

In a kerosene-soaked sky, a single sand hill crane makes its lonely flight south over the cement jungle. The genetic memory born with wetlands emerging from receding glacier promised meadow where now there is only asphalt and concrete. The bird puts down for a moment in this island of meadow just south of Reade Hill. The bird looks around confused. A woman working at the other end of the meadow stops her work to consider the bird. The bird nibbles some grass and hops around in search of water. Before the woman can get to the bird with a charged hose, the sand hill crane lifts off and again heads south following a promise given by the memory of its ancestors...A memory that had no place in reality and a promise that had now become a lie.

The woman stops her digging again to allow passage of a banana slug, which glides across the soft dirt in front of her on a fine layer of secreted slime. Unlike their exotic, brown, English cousins, the banana slug disdains garden produce for detritus in the forest and is welcomed by the woman as a neighbor. The slug cuts the glistening slime track of a previous representative of its species and changes course 90 degrees to follow its predecessor. Mossy's eyes jump ahead of the charging gastropod and find the second slug waiting out the afternoon rays of the sun under a squash leaf. In a minute, the second slug is joined by the first, and under the presumed privacy of the squash leaf, unfolds another strange story of a species sexuality. Mossy watches the second slug feeding on the slime plug of the first.

Shhhh! While her lithe body leans on the shovel her mind follows the slime track of her memory across two decades to the moon-drenched carpet under her living room skylight. Under the squash leaf the slugs engage sexually in a posture that resembles the Taoist symbol of the yin and the yang or the numerical symbol of 69. For the slugs are hermaphrodite and, to them, is the pleasure of the male and the female, the yin and the yang.

Likewise, is the woman's hermaphroditic memory set in the give and the take, the caressing and caressed, the kissing and kissed, of a moment twenty solar orbits distant in space-time. Though she has quit her work and leans on the shovel, a sheen of sweat glistens on her face. She is deep in the thrill of this memory...And, in the sultry shade of the squash leaf, as the banana slugs exude slime in the final throes of copulation, the hologram in Mossy's brain is locked on her only encounter with human sexuality.

Done mating, the slugs face a predicament known to town mutts and porn stars. They are entrapped in their sexual posture. For the envy of Homo sapiens manifests itself in the species and giganticism presents in their male organs. The slugs are locked in sexual congress and, as the angle of the sun changes to tickle their backs with its desiccating rays, they become earnest about disengaging.

What was it that called Mossy from her bed of bliss twenty years ago? Why didn't she abide in the commingling like these two lovers under the squash plant? And then she remembers: it was the garden. She had to rise from that wonderful bed to defend this garden from deer attack. This precious interface between soil, water, air, and edible biota was the only thing, which would have stirred her that morning. From that recollection comes the gnawing image of the gun, the blood, the disapproval of her lover...

The one slug is tethered to a penis leash and engages in what Nature has taught her/him is the only course to free her/himself: apophallation. The one slug is chewing off the penis of the other...

...as the fangs of remembrance sever Mossy's sweet embrace with the memory of sexuality and she is dragged up a tree with panic now beating in her heart. And, to the trees, is applied fire, and in the fire, is her love consumed. Apophallation has been applied to the sweet memory of her lover and she sees him now, through an ambulance door: naked, mummified and without a penis. Mossy drops her shovel to pick up her crutch and hobbles for the cabin. Her eyes sting from sweat and tears.

The two slugs slither in opposite directions.

ের

Hemp Hill Creek
June 11, 2020, 10:20 hours

Mossy stands next to an exotic mulberry bush planted next to her bridge tossing little bits of twig into the placid water of Hemp Hill Creek. She wishes beyond measure for an environmental miracle. With the casting of each twig, she waits for each bit to disappear into the murky water before tossing another. She prays for the erratic underwater bounce of the twig, which will indicate a salmon fry striking at it. On Thanksgiving Day, three years ago, after a rain event which reminded her of the weather of her childhood, she saw an adult Coho salmon hen waiting by her nest for the arrival of a buck. The sight had given Mossy hope to face the degradation which besmirched her home. Her eyes now sting as she strains to see into the dusky water and she curses the incinerator from the condominium bastion across the way. From its imperfect scrubbers emanate an all-pervasive smoke, which tinges the air and besmirches the taste of the water. The water of the creek below her farm has been fouled with algae and the carcasses of old refrigerators and stoves. It's too much to hope that a wild fish could navigate or survive such depredation.

Please let there be fish, she prays to the Force who created and maintained this valley before the human onslaught. Something tickles at the back of her neck and, in a rare act of self-consciousness, she glances north to the front gate to see if she has company. Only a stunted and bent Engelmann spruce stands by the gate where her mother planted it thirty years ago. The messages on the air of the valley had become too confusing for her nose to serve as an intrusion alarm, but she seems to be alone.

She refocuses on the creek. *Please don't let this creek die,* her eyes tearing in the hazy air as the once pristine valley chokes on the smoke of a hundred thousand garbage fires...the wild ponies sharing one last sip from the water that no longer tasted of freshness. She again senses a presence by the front gate and looks north to see her Newfoundland, June Fifteenth, finishing a patrol of the fence line and turning down the driveway in her direction. She smiles at the sight of her canine friend and calls, "Here, Fif! Here, boy!" She holds her arms open in welcome.

ের

Bogachiel Garden Condominiums
June 11, 2020, 10:25 hours

Finished with the adjustment, chewing gum, Rod Hill removes his gaze from the eyepiece of the spotting scope, which focuses on the inholding of a farm to the south. Tiredly, he rubs his eyes. How long would the Stone family thwart his agenda? First had been the big asshole, Dr. Philip; then his pain-in-the-ass widowed wife; and now the biggest problem: their pioneer daughter Mossy Stone. Imagine! The crazy bitch, Mossy, holding out for a lifestyle that was mostly over a century ago. And, now, Mossy Stone and her hillbilly farm lay in the path of the Twenty First Century Corporation like a big, moss-covered rock sticking out of the ground. The farm was twenty acres, for Christ sake! Each acre contained 40,000 square feet which, when applied to the traditional Twenty First Century formula of twenty stories and the bullshit requirements of equal 'open space' to living space required by high density zoning...each acre of this accursed farm stood in the way of 400 units which, on an average, brought in $1,000 a day.

For the hundredth time he punches the buttons on his hand calculator: 400 units times 365 days times 20 acres times 1,000 dollars = TWO FUCKING BILLION, NINE HUNDRED AND TWENTY GOD DAMN MILLION DOLLARS A YEAR (minus overhead) = WHAT THIS BITCH IS COSTING US! = JOHN SMITH WILL HAVE MY ASS IF I CAN'T MOVE HER! Hill snaps his gum and picks up the trigger for the digital camera, turning on the big screen TV which shows the woman standing on the bridge of the farm throwing something into the water.

What was she doing now? Feeding the condoms as they swam upstream? *Pop!* answers Hill's gum. At the thought that he might be observing some kind of environmental offense, his knuckles turn white on the trigger. The latest idea from headquarters in Washington, D.C., is to collect pictures and background data to make Mossy Stone a poster child for the lifestyle afforded by life on the Olympic Peninsula. There is nothing illegal about photographing a person in open view, assured the huge, overpaid Legal Unit of Twenty First Century. Still, there was the thrill of spying: She has the body and face to be on a poster or centerfold, agreed Hill as his big eyes explored her smooth, innocent face and scantily covered, nubile body. Twenty First's Behavioral Analysis Unit of the Public Relations Department postulated that privacy was a big feature for Mossy's refusal to sell off her property. If the glass in the fish bowl could be opened up a little to public scrutiny, she might cave. If nothing else, her health and physical attributes being what they were, she would make a great ad campaign. The trouble is, she is always working a shovel and wheelbarrow with her hands stuck in dirt, compost, or shit. That doesn't raise a hard-on in the modern world. Still, a little airbrushing of the smudges on her face and a change of attire by computer morphing...

The old man sighs. God knows, Rod Hill has tried to get along with the Stones over the years. Hill put up with all of Dr. Philip's bullshit and even went to the bastard's funeral (may he, please God, rot in hell). Hill helped out the Widow Stone in her hour of need, putting in (he-didn't-know-how-many) hours building her cabin and helping out with the utilities. He had even dragged his family along that Thanksgiving forty years ago...just trying to be neighborly.

How Mossy had mortified his family by ambushing his son Russell with a punch to the gut! Russell's snoose had gone down in his windpipe and chewed on his lungs. He had been there on Reade Ridge and seen how this little bitch could run with the enviro-creeps and turn on her own community. God knows, Rod Hill has tolerated more from this family than any man should be asked to suffer...How long will Mossy Stone be in our way? How selfish can one person be?

The woman's attention changes and looks directly at the camera and smiles as if in recognition of an old friend. Hill goes again to the window and sees the big, black hound from hell heading towards the bridge. The woman is holding her arms open in greeting walking around the mulberry bush.

Click! goes the camera. *Snap!* goes the gum. *Pop!* goes the weasel.

ও৵

Office of <u>The Washington Host,</u> Washington, D.C.
June 15, 2020, 13:20 hours E.S.T.

The old newspaper man had held onto his job, less out of interest for what he was doing and more out of a concern with what life would hold for him in retirement. He had more than enough money on which to retire. Twenty First Century had made him wealthy beyond his dreams. But to what avail was all that money if you existed in daily fear of your environment and the society in which you lived? The home he owned outright in the rich neighborhood of McLean, Virginia, was threatened by malaria, air riots, racial unrest and the terrorist target for every third world country stepping forward with biological weapons or a nuclear firecracker. But for sewers, there was no longer any such thing as wild, running water except in the beleaguered Parks. The sun's rays and the non-life-sustaining air did not allow for one to emerge into the outdoors for very long - which was OK with Richard Stokes. But he yearned for security in his home, and of his many holdings, only the time-share condo that was near his old home on the Olympic Peninsula provided such confidence. Unlike the Tri-City nuclear refugees which had lucked into permanent asylum in this paradise, Twenty First Century Corporation controlled its employees by dolling out days of ownership in this last secure nest. The fear kept employees in the traces until they dropped. Stokes would do anything to get more time on the Peninsula and at this moment he was preparing to meet his son and bring him in on his employer's latest scheme to rule the world.

There was a knock at the door and in entered the long-haired, wildly disobedient, C-, New York University student, poor-excuse-for-a-son, Chiggers Stokes. "Hi, Dad."

"Hello, Chigs. How are you coming on your summer internship?"

"I had something lined up with <u>The Washington Star</u>, proof reading subscription list data, but it fell through when they got some OCR stuff that could do it faster. I keep telling my faculty advisor at N.Y.U. that you're going to find something for me here with <u>The Host</u>."

"Well, for once, you're right," said the old editor of the Life Style Section. "As a matter of fact, we have the opportunity of a lifetime lined up for you..."

"Please, not cleaning the restrooms again, Dad! The last 'opportunity of a lifetime' made me want to upchuck and I could have made more money recycling pencil stubs."

"This is REALLY BIG, son," professed the father reassuringly. "I don't want you loafing around the house drinking my beer and letting in smog with all your comings and goings. I've arranged with The Host to really develop your journalistic talent, which is more than they're doing for you at that drug fraternity you call a university. We're going to send you to the last wilderness to do in-depth interviews with one of the last pioneers in the lower 48! We're sending you to the Olympic Peninsula to interview Mossy Stone!"

Chiggers' mind swam and spun, trying to take in the offer, like a flushing toilet. He had visited the Peninsula when he was ten years old - when they still allowed people to drive up to Hurricane Ridge and into the Hoh Rain Forest. He had longed to go back, but his father had never allowed him more visits to the family's time-share condominium since the person/days was heavily figured into the share. His mother needed the salubrious environment for health reasons. "Dad! That's great! What's the..."

...catch? As the thrill of such an environment flushed down Chiggers' brain stem and drained down to a tingling of his spine, his mind begin flushing another spin of excitement: the target of his interview - Mossy Stone. She was a beautiful and mysterious sensation of the media. It was the journalistic opportunity of a lifetime! Why me? It was like being with the Marlboro Man in the doctor's office as he is diagnosed with lung cancer, and photographing him riding off into the sunset with an O2 bottle tied to his saddle. It was like...

"Chiggers? HELLO! Earth to Chiggers! Is anyone home?"

"Dad, why me? Why give an assignment this rich in opportunity to a student intern instead of using it as a major perk for you or some other Host staff member?"

"Well, Ms. Stone has here-to-fore been unapproachable to the press. She has even put off telephone interviews and remains secretive. We need to know every little thing about her: what she watches on TV, whether her dogs are licensed and vaccinated, whether her shack is connected to an old septic tank like they used in the twentieth century. We need all the details of her life and you may be the only one to get close to her. Our research indicates that, by coincidence, you went to the same high school and screwy university as her father who may have learned more about writing than you ever have, by the way..."

"Mossy Stone's father was a writer?!"

"No. He dabbled in it. He studied nuclear physics, but worked as a lumberjack when he came to the Olympic Peninsula..."

"He worked as a WHAT?"

"Lumberjack, logger...the man cut down trees for the timber industry," explained the father impatiently.

"Oh! I thought they did that with a big machine."

"Well, they didn't when I lived on the Peninsula. When I first arrived, there were more men knocking down trees than bagging groceries, though that changed, even when I lived there. Her dad died working in the woods and I was even at the goofy funeral before Mossy Stone was born! That gives you some idea about how long I've been chained to this keyboard reporting the news."

"Dad, you guys don't report the news - you MAKE the news!"

"Whatever. Anyway, here's a picture of Stone, a research file on all the things we know so far, and a task list of all the stuff we want researched. Here are your tickets, company credit card, and reservations for three months at Bogachiel Rain Forest Condominiums. It's costing <u>The Host</u> about half a million dollars, so may I suggest you not blow it like usual. My neck is kind of on the chopping block along with your testicles. We expect you to call me every Monday morning without fail...and, oh yes, if you do screw up, don't bother coming home."

Fourteen

I mean, like, where goest thou America?
Where goest thou in thy shiny black car in the night?
- **Jack Kerouak**, American author/Merry Prankster

Welcome to FORKS - The Last Wilderness
- Road sign just west of Forks in 1940
Welcome to FORKS - Logging capital of the world
- Road sign just west of Forks in 1980
Welcome to Forks - A Nice Place to Live for a Week
- Fictional road sign just west of Forks in 2020

"It's more bearable being a woman living alone out here than any man might care to think."
- **Mossy Stone**, fictional character in the book in your hand

Bogachiel Garden Condominiums
June 17, 2020

*N*othing I have seen in my twenty-one years of life has prepared me for the sight of Mossy Stone. Her physical beauty is not made of the same stuff as the character in the poster or even flesh and blood. Through the 2,000-millimeter spy lens set up in Rod Hill's office, I can see that her complexion is absolutely clear and free of melanoma scars. But, unlike the poster, she wears no makeup of any sort. Her file says that she has a scar over her right ear from a burn, but it's concealed by her long, flowing, blond hair. She is almost forty years old, but she looks younger and more vibrant than the twenty-year-olds I dated back at NYU. I don't think I've ever seen a woman stand that straight or move with such purpose and natural grace...even with the crutch she carries.

My contact, Rod Hill, is a rectal orifice. I guess he's a pretty high muckity-muck here because he supervises the building superintendent and everyone calls him 'sir.' But he cannot shut up about Mossy Stone: how selfish she is for her land-consumptive lifestyle; how she wears dirt like "the farm pig she is," how her dad was a "certified psycho and her mom a lonely old lezbo..."

Watching her through the lens, as she moves along her fence line, picking up trash and stowing it in a bag tied to her belt...Even with that crutch, her body moves with the fluidity of a garter snake sliding over a rock or the rock rolling down an incline with slight irregularities along the plane.

Her appearance is like the physical manifestation of Joan of Arc, a rain forest Mona Lisa, Mary: the Mother of God...

"I had naked pictures of her," Rod Hill is saying as I study the quarry through the magnified lens. "When we were building this place, it took a while to sink into that stubborn head of hers that she wasn't the only one in this valley anymore. I had maybe fifty pictures, until I made the mistake of showing them to John Smith who kyped the lot..."

Watching her now work a shovel in the garden I try to drown out Hill's blasphemy with my attention to the lens. She does work like a farm animal! But with total economy of movement: the shovel blade stays low and moves in a concentrated arc over the work.

"I can still whip up computer generated morphs that show her naked and give you a pretty good sniff at what she looks like under those dirty farm clothes..." I continue to ignore Rod Hill. "...I mean, if you need those kind of pictures for the article you're doing..."

Watching her through the lens...it is a quality that is apart from her physical beauty and attributes. Watching her work this piece of land like her life depended on it...It is like the land stood up to defend itself. It is like the land took shovel in hand and began to groom itself in a declaration of its fertility. It had never occurred to me that such a relationship could exist: a person to the land and the land to the person.

"...so if you need the morph pictures, let me know, and these files here have everything you need on her background. These files gave us the connection between her crazy dad's schools and yours. Anyway, possible IRS infractions, sanitation violations, county tax records, it's all included...Oh! Here's an A.T.F. file because she started selling wine at the Farmer's Market, and we may be able to bring down the hammer on that." Hill's prattle is interrupting and disturbing. He talks like I'm part of some conspiracy to dislocate this innocent creature.

"Look, Mr. Hill," I say. "I'm just here to do a human-interest article on her. Whatever your problems are with her, legal or otherwise, they're certainly not mine. And I sure don't need or want any naked pictures..."

"If you feature yourself as a cub reporter on some kind of journalistic quest, you're as confused about what you are as she is," reprimanded Hill.

"I don't think that SHE is confused about what she IS. And I don't think I'M confused, either."

"You were brought here to be a spy and make no mistake about that. Whatever your toad-of-a-reporter father told you...you're a spy."

Again, I try to lose myself in watching Mossy Stone work her garden. As I watch, she stops her shoveling and looks up from the work. It is as if she could feel me watching her. She looks dead at the camera, though there is no way she could be seeing it. Her nostrils flare like a nervous doe's. Then she moves behind a tall hedge and is lost to my view.

ৡৄয়

Phone conversation of Monday June 22, 2020
Recorded on Bogachiel Gardens security system
Tap ordered by Rod Hill, Regional Director Twenty First Century

source: Hi, Dad, it's me.
target: Well, well, the first story from the cub reporter. Tell me how everything is going in my part of the world. How are the accommodations?
source: Everything's fine, dad. But things are a lot more developed than when you brought me here as a kid. It's not the wild place it used to be...

target: Well, that's what they call progress. That's what makes real estate work. Have you been briefed by Mr. Hill? Has he helped you come up with a plan on how to meet Ms. Stone?

source: I met Hill, who is one big asshole! I'm not about to waste my breath asking him for ideas on how to insinuate myself into her company. He acts like I'm here doing an article for Playboy. He wants to send me back with a bunch of naked pictures...

target: I had heard that those pictures had been confiscated by John Smith himself!

source: Dad, forget the pictures. Hill says that I'm here as a spy. I take that to mean that there is a plan afoot to remove Mossy Stone from her land and I am in some way a co-conspirator...

target: He's just playing with you, son! Just do as you're told and get us a story we can use here at The Host. But we need everyday details like the stuff we talked about: her farm operation, what she sells at market, how much wine she sells and what price she gets for it...That sort of stuff.

source: Dad, are you being straight with me? Are you sure big money isn't catching us both up in some diabolical plot to kick a decent, hard-working soul off her land?

target: Son, I swear to you I would know it if that were the case. I promise you that you're being funded by The Host and that we are, in fact, very interested in your story on Mossy Stone. You have every reason to believe that it will be published...

source: Dad, can you hold the line for a second. I've got another call coming in...

target: That's OK, son. Your mom's got my dinner on the table and I'll talk to you later on when you have something tangible to report. Good night.

source: Goodnight, Dad. (*end connection/new connection*)

Hello, this is room, um, uh 1255. Chiggers Stokes speaking.

target: Hello, Chiggers. This is Rod Hill calling just to make sure you're getting settled in OK. How is every little thing?

source: Fine, everything is fine. I like the room.

target: I am SO GLAD that you like the room! Say, I'm also calling to tell you what, I'm sure, you already guessed, that I WAS JOKING ABOUT THE SPY BUSINESS. THAT'S RIGHT: JUST PLAYING WITH YOU. You're here as a reporter just like your dad told you. And, OH! Have you given any thought about how you're going to make Ms. Stones' acquaintance? That's an important thing to consider.

source: I had an idea or two...

target: Well, what about this idea: Take a plastic bag from Maintenance tomorrow, tie it to your belt and patrol our side of her fence when you see her out picking up trash. Her fucking dog, excuse me, will snarl at you through the gate, but NOT TO WORRY, the chain link will hold him and he only kills what she sics him on, if you do get into the tarpaper palace.

source: Yeah, that idea might work...

target: Good! Call me if you need anything and welcome to Bogachiel Gardens! And remember: I was kidding about the spy business!

❦

Northern fence of Flying S Farm
Tuesday June 23, 2020, 07:45 hours

I am executing a good plan, but my timing is poor. I dressed in clothes fitting for dealing with rubbish and picked up my "litter bag" from Central Maintenance. I am waiting in Hill's office, watching through the lens until I see two dogs and then Mossy Stone appear on her bridge. While I hurry through the building and two security checks which put me on a road separating the Flying S Farm from Bogachiel Gardens Condominiums, I have arrived too late and Ms. Stone is half way along the fence line. I hurry to catch up.

How she can move! I am half running to catch up with her and there is no time to pick up the beer cans, dirty diapers and (oh-my-God!) used condoms which festoon my side of the fence. Her big, black dog is the first to see me and doubles back to check me out. "Good boy! Good Fido!" I call, as the dog swoops in from the other side of the fence. The dog immediately shows teeth and follows me making ugly faces and low rumbling noises on the other side of the fence. "Good dog!" I lie again,

By the time I am within voice range of this big, black bastard's mistress I am winded. "Good morning!" I call out and Mossy Stone turns to look at me. "Sure a lot of trash out here this morning!" I call cheerfully and bend over to pick up a Budweiser can. The black dog is now full-on growling and her little dog, seeing me for the first time, doubles back and begins barking.

"Shush, Chick!" she calls, and the little dog stops the alert. "I smelled him coming and what's wrong with your nose?" I'm not sure if the insult is intended for me, or the dog. "Easy, Fif!" she yells and the canine gorilla stops its ugly faces and pulls away from the fence in a happy-go-lucky race with the small dog back to their mistress. "Good dogs!" she exclaims with sincerity.

"I can't believe what people throw out here!" I exclaim, trying to close the distance between us. I am sweating with exertion now and, as she moves, I find it nearly impossible to gain on her. "Don't you just hate all this trash?" I yell my inquiry hoping she will slow down.

Over her shoulder she calls, "I don't feel one way or the other about the trash. I reserve my feelings for the idiots who throw it out here!" She comes to the end of the fence line shared with Bogachiel Gardens and does an about face, walking towards me at last.

I begin immediately picking up the more innocent pieces of trash along the fence, but she passes me without comment. The black dog makes a low rumble in its throat as it passes. I scurry along trying to keep up with the procession and picking up trash as best I can. They are again putting distance between us. I give up pretending to pick up trash and jog to catch up. When I come along side, the black bastard and the little bitch again begin growling and showing teeth. "Nice doggies!" I say, but Mossy continues her march. "Aren't you Mossy Stone?" I inquire moronically.

"Maybe I am," she says guardedly and the dogs growl and begin barking. "If you want to make a go of cleaning up your side of the fence you ought to bring a flatbed instead of a little bag tied to your belt."

"I need to talk to you," I huff.

"So talk," she says, stopping briefly to pick up a cigarette butt with her gloved hand.

"I am the son of Richard Stokes who I think, maybe, is an old friend of yours..."

"I knew him as the editor of our town newspaper twenty years ago. He was a pompous ass then, but I guess his ethics have been on a big downhill slide since those days."

"Yeah," I agree. "He's a pompous ass, but he's not evil or anything." Mossy ignores my defense and continues to walk along the fence. Both dogs are making ugly faces and I am playing to a really tough audience. "Listen, I'm a journalist intern from NYU, the same university your dad went to. I've been sent out here to do a human-interest story on you and I would really appreciate your cooperation."

"Goodbye," she says pleasantly and begins cutting away from the fence line, leaving me with the dogs. She is headed in the direction of her northwest garden gate 400 feet distant and soon she will be out of conversational range.

"Wait, please!" I call as she continues to walk. "Wait! I can tell you things!" She ignores me, but her dogs are still snarling. "Don't you know they're spying on you?" I yell in desperation and she slows slightly. "Didn't you FEEL them spying on you yesterday morning as you were shoveling in the same garden to which you are presently heading?" and my yelled message finally stops her.

"Yeah, I felt myself being spied upon. So what?"

What can I tell this woman that will make her open her door to me. She is self-complete: herself, the dogs, the farm land. I have nothing to offer her. Wait! I can contrive a threat. That will get me in the gate. "They're spying on you. They want to take away your farm. I can tell you things about their plans!" The dogs are putting their teeth into the wire mesh and flecks of slobber are dropping at my feet. But the hook is set and Mossy walks back to meet me at the fence line.

"DOGS, DOWN!" she yells and the feet drop out from beneath both canines and they lie placidly against the fence looking at their mistress for a sign of their release from this command. "What do you know about them taking this farm?" Mossy hisses.

"I know..." my brain races for the next move that will get me closer...that will yield a story. "I know a lot." A threat, a plot...something to make her cast her lot with me. "They have files on you! For example...For example...They are looking at how much wine you sell at Farmer's Market and may bring in ATF Agents to bust you!"

"I was told that I could brew 50 gallons a year, no questions asked."

"Well..." what the hell do I say now? "That's only if you don't sell it. They're going to make a case on you selling alcohol."

"I do it because the property tax has become so steep. I get $100 a bottle from the yuppies who own this town on time-share. They think it will cure cancer while getting them drunk. But I'll just plant more strawberries if there is a conflict with ATF. What else do you know," she asks, greedy now for information.

"Well, haven't you seen the poster campaign they use to sell time-shares at Bogachiel Gardens and other time-shares across the peninsula?"

"Yeah, well, I saw this ad in a magazine at the library and it looked like they cut my face out and pasted it on somebody else and then pasted that back on that bridge over there..."

"They were trying to BLOW YOUR MIND! But you didn't go for it..."

"I didn't GIVE A BOWEL MOVEMENT! What do you know about them taking this farm?" she hisses and her dogs whine to be released from the command so they can throw themselves back upon the fence.

I put my face against the wire and whisper, "They're watching us right now. Can't you feel it?"

"Yes," Mossy replied, looking like a frightened doe with her nostrils flaring again. "I know they're watching."

I whisper, "They're listening too. You need to let me in so I can tell you everything I know about this. I just want to tell you what they're up to so you'll know.... But you've got to let me in."

"All right," says Mossy. "Just follow this fence line down to the gate. I'll let you in."

ϑ~ℛ

Rod Hill's Office/Bogachiel Garden Condominiums
Tuesday, June 23, 2020, 08:00

"Christ, I can't make out what they're saying," complained Rod Hill, looking through the 2,000 mm lens. "How much do they get for one of them big ears? Put in a requisition, will ya? And put a permanent bug on room 1255. I want a total record of every little thing out of that yuppie shit's mouth."

ϑ~ℛ

Monday, June 29, 2020
Phone conversation of Room 1255
Recorded on Bogachiel Gardens security system
Tap ordered by Rod Hill, Regional Director Twenty First Century

target: Hello, this is Richard Stokes
source: Hi, Dad. Well, I'm in like Flynn.
target: Oh, hi, Chiggers. What do you mean? Are you saying you've made contact with the subject?
source: Yup. I've been taken into her confidence. I've visited her on the other side of the fence and even saw her place of residence. It looks like it's made entirely of wood. Can you imagine how much that would cost to build today?
target: What scam did you use to get in? Did she remember me?
source: Well, actually she didn't remember you kindly. So I played on her paranoia. She's pretty freaked about all the development out here and worries about them taking her farm.
target: O.K. That's not the approach I would have used, but if it got you in the door...

source: I'm more than in the door. I'm on my way to a story. Once I got through the gate and she told her dogs not to eat me...she was glad to talk. I have to do farm work for the privilege of sharing her space, but she is fun to be with. I'm getting my story.

target: Oh, there's one small detail you need to take care of for me. Rod Hill will give you the kit, but we need you to drop a little dye in her toilet and give it a flush...

source: Why would I do something like that? How is that connected to the human-interest story I'm working on?

target: Well, the big thinkers here at <u>The Host</u> are always looking to play the ironical side of things. So, if she has some ancient and out-of-date sanitation thing and her shit is going in the creek...well, that's a story. She's trying to play herself off as some environmental goddess...

source: Dad, she's not playing herself off as anything. She's just surviving and trying to keep asphalt off her gardens...

target: Look, son, I'll make this one warning: Don't get emotionally involved with your subject. Just give your readers the news. And put the goddamn dye in the goddamn toilet before I have to come out there personally and rip up your goddamn press card and privilege pass...

source: Dad, I've got another call again.

target: That's all right, I'm done. Just do what you're told. Good night.

source: Good night, Dad.

Room 1255, Stokes.

target: Oh, hello Chiggers. Rod Hill here. I just wanted to say good work getting inside the gate to the tarpaper palace and I've been asked to send you out tomorrow with a little kit for checking out Stone's sanitation system.

source: What's that got to do with a human-interest story may I ask?

target: Well, I kindda wondered the same, but you're the big shot reporter so YOU TELL ME! ASK YOUR DAD, IF YOU FUCKING DON'T HAVE A CLUE! I mean, I'm as bewildered as you. The kit came from <u>The Washington Host</u>. Isn't that who you work for...<u>The Host</u>?

source: Yeah, I'll be by tomorrow to pick it up before going over there. I told Ms. Stone I would be coming back at nine, tomorrow morning. And, by the way, I need to look over those files before going over.

target: Whatever. We're all just tickled pink that you got through the gate.

Front gate of Flying S Farm
Tuesday, June 30, 2020, 08:15 hours

They serve real food at the Bogachiel Gardens Restaurant so I snuck out a couple of pieces of meat to placate Mossy Stone's dogs. After breakfast, I stopped by Hill's office to pick up the dye they want me to dump in her toilet and sneak away the file on Mossy's wine-selling operation, which is the bait I have used to insinuate myself into her hospitality.

I come to the front gate at the appointed time and have but a moment to wait before the electric solenoid clicks and the gate swings open. I look around for a camera, but instead hear feet thundering across the bridge and see the dogs Mossy calls "Fif" and "Chick" coming for me like canine emissaries from hell. Quickly, I fumble in my belly pack for the sausages and almost drop the glass vial of phosphorescent, day-glow dye. I hold the sausages out like a brace of pistols and, when the dogs catch whiff of what I have, they turn tail and highball it back to their mistress who is now coming across the bridge herself.

"Please close that gate behind you," Mossy calls out and proceeds out to meet me with a dog heeling at either side.

After closing the gate, I again take the sausages from my bellypack and hold them out as a peace offering to the dogs. Both dogs again run back to their mistress and begin whining.

"Please don't try to feed the dogs," Mossy said. "They're trained to only eat from my hand. Otherwise, they would have been poisoned long ago."

"How did you teach them THAT?" I ask in amazement.

"We don't like to remember that. It's one of those painful lessons that survival requires." She held her hand out to receive the meat offering and broke one in half. She threw one half to the small dog, Chick, and one and a half sausages to Fif. Fif caught both pieces in one snap of his mighty jaws. Chick and Fif took off running circles around us in wild exuberance over their treats.

"We don't get too much company on this side of the fence, so I don't have the opportunity to develop a bunch of ground rules for visitors. But one thing I will ask: don't try to give anything to the dogs except through me. If you want to give them a treat, give it to me first. Same thing if you feel the need to kick them."

Mossy and the dogs begin walking back to the bridge and I follow. I look back one more time in confusion. "Um, Ms. Stone...uh, Mossy, I don't see a camera back there. How did you know I was at the gate?"

"I was working in the orchard on the other side of the bridge," she said in way of explanation. "I rigged up that gate switch for the UPS man." But, as we approach the bridge, I can see that the orchard is still another 300 feet from the bridge and out of sight entirely from the gate.

"But how did you know I was at the gate?" I persist.

"There's a breeze blowing off the river and they're not burning that infernal incinerator this early in the morning. The dogs and I smelled you."

"Yeah, right!" I say, perceiving that I am the brunt of some joke. "Anyway, that incinerator has state-of-the-art scrubbers on its stack, so you shouldn't smell anything. It powers a one and a half megawatt steam generator. It powers all the lights you see at night in this valley..."

"It doesn't power the lights on this side of the fence, I can tell you. The license to operate that incinerator is tied to an arcane state law passed back in the days when watts were more precious than water. One and a half megawatts may drive the lighting, but the real loads, such as heat and air conditioning, are satisfied by the grid. The scrubbers haven't been changed in about two years and sulfur dioxide is escaping into the atmosphere where it mixes with moisture in the air to form sulfuric acid. See that brown on that weeping cherry tree and those dead leaves on the pawpaw next to it? That's acid rain caused by that infernal incinerator. They don't need the power. But they are too cheap to take the garbage to the land fill, so there goes the neighborhood."

Yesterday, on the bridge, I had pointed in the direction of the surveillance camera and whispered words of paranoia and how I could share files that would help Mossy to keep her farm. Now, as an invited guest, I was being taken to the sanctum sanctorum inside her cabin. As we stepped through the door, Fif was left outside on guard duty. I looked around in disbelief. Herbs were hung everywhere, living and dried; houseplants, edible and ornamental; aquariums; sprouts; grains; a beehive with a glass window built right into the wall! Light streamed through skylights in every room of the house and the walls, ceilings and floors were built entirely of wood. "Wow!" I stammer. "I've never been in a place like this before!"

"It's what I've grown up and lived my life in. I can't imagine how dreary it must be to live in that walled prison across the fence," Mossy said, almost in pity.

"Well, people pay upwards of a thousand dollars a night for the privilege of staying in that prison, but I'll admit this place has much more food for the soul."

Enough bull manure, Mossy cuts to the chase, "Did you bring that file?" she inquires.

"Sho' nuff, sweet stuff," I say trying to conjure up some sense of familiarity with this strange woman. I carefully dig into my belly pack, trying hard to keep the vial of bright Zenker/Formalin dye from being detected or falling out on the floor and breaking there upon. "Here be dat file, sugar." I passed it to her. "Ya'll let me know if dey be any mo' dem files yo be needing."

Mossy begins glancing through the file and says off-handedly, "Did that fancy breakfast they served you across the fence not sit well with you? Forgive my directness, but you sound like maybe you're about to throw up. The bathroom is right there," she points to a closed door just to the left of a ladder/stairway leading up to her upstairs.

"Well, I'm not sick," I protest. "I'm just affecting an accent from my home state of Ol' Virginny, but I do need to use the bathroom," I say, not wanting to lose the opportunity to get this goddamn dye off my person and into its intended target. I slip into the bathroom and waste a few moments looking for a lock on the door which is entirely absent. I go straight for the eight-ounce vial and remove the top, which is an eye dropper. I dump the bottle and immediately the water goes opaque blue-green, like paint. I am scared to piss in it for fear it will splash or explode or something. So I flush the toilet and get myself ready to piss so there will be some recognizable sound to explain my trip in here. It's no good! The water still has a bright blue-green tint, though this time a little more translucent. It looks like I've stained the porcelain! I frantically look for a toilet brush while the toilet is recharging. I flush again, and still the water is blue-green! I find the toilet brush and begin scrubbing madly. Some of the blue-green comes off the inside of the bowl, but when I pull out the brush to flush again, the brush is bright blue-green!

"Is that toilet stopped up in there?" inquires Mossy from just outside the door. "I've got a plumber's friend under the kitchen sink."

"No...Uh...," I am panicking. "No, everything's fine in here." I flush again. Still blue-green!

"The last time it wouldn't flush was about five years ago," she was talking from just outside the door. "The thousand gallon tank was totally filled with solids and I had to pump it out with a sump pump I rented..." she pauses while the toilet flushes again. "I bought a five hundred gallon stock tank to move the solids from the septic system to a 20 foot by 20 foot fenced off plot where I could desiccate the mess. It took a year before I trusted it as fertilizer, but I had zucchinis that took a wheelbarrow to move..." the toilet interrupts her again. "Are you sure you're all right in there?"

No. I'm not all right! The toilet brush is stained, the toilet bowl is stained, I've got blue-green spots on my shirt and spatters on my face! I call out cheerfully, "Oh, everything is fine in here. I'll be out in just a second. Um, so you used your own shit for fertilizer, is that what you said? I thought there were laws about that kind of thing..." I've wiped everything down with toilet paper as best I can and flushed about six times. It's the best I can do.

"Whatever the law is, this is what I did: I used the sun as a pasteurizer for a full year, turning it with a shovel once a week. After a year, it was the consistency of peat moss and I put some in a coffee filter and ran a pint of water through it. I took the water to the county for a test and there was zero E. coli. You could safely eat it if you wanted to, but it tastes better and is more nutritious to grow food with it first." I come out of the bathroom looking sheepish and Mossy steals a glance into the bathroom registering the disappearance of a toilet tissue roll and the new fluorescent hue to her toilet brush. "Are you sure there wasn't a problem in there?"

"No, everything is fine. Have you made anything out of that file?" I say, trying to change the subject.

"Yeah, I'm stuck with a hundred bottles of strawberry and Cascade berry wine. Oh, well...I'll just sell the berries straight up. It's a pity though. I was getting $100 a bottle for the wine and I'll have to tie up more land in berries to make up the difference. But it's not worth giving them a lever to jack me off this property. Say, would you like some dandelion tea and do you have more of these files you can share with me? And here's a bottle of my wine to take back with you."

This was working out better than I could have expected, given the circumstances of the blue-green toilet bowl. "Thanks!" I say. "Thanks a lot! Sure I can bring you more files. They're definitely trying to jack you off your property. God, those are ancient video recordings. VHS, right? That kind of technology was gone before I was born!"

"Yeah, they belonged to my dad who I never met. He got them back in the late 1970s when they first developed the system of recording from cable or antenna. When I was a kid my mom recorded educational movies from the library and, occasionally, I still do it. I don't get TV out here and it's fun to use the system my folks used to use to educate myself."

"How did you get permits to use the creek for electricity and to use a twentieth century sanitation system?"

"Well, there's a permit for the hydroelectric, but nothing on the sanitation system. It's the old thousand gallon septic tank with 200 linear feet of drain field that has worked forever. I already told you that I had to remove the solids from the tank about five years ago. It's great technology, just like those ancient video recordings. Whatever Bogachiel Gardens is doing, they've killed the creek."

"They send all their waste to Forks for processing," I say almost defensively.

"Well, enough of it leaches into the creek to create huge algae blooms and goodbye everything else."

"You're saying that Bogachiel Gardens is poisoning the water and air in this valley?"

"Bingo! They're also transporting all available living soil into the creek! Check me out on this...Of the 200 thousand acres currently owned by Twenty First Century Inc., less than 500 acres show a positive factor on the sustainable solid threshold. I've thought about drafting a lawsuit against them, but they have such political clout it would be like trying to sue God."

I spend that morning helping Mossy with the endless chores that comprise her life alone on the farm. It is the beginning of the most powerful and profound friendship I have experienced with any human being. And the longer I stand on her land, the more hold it has upon me. It is like jumping or falling off a high place upon soft soil wearing farm boots. The land is swallowing me...

"It must be hard and lonely being a woman and living alone with only this work for company," I remark preparing to depart for the day.

"I've got more than work for company and it's more bearable being a woman living alone out here than any man might care to think."

That gives me a good quote for the story I am writing for The Washington Host.

Front gate of Flying S Farm
Tuesday, July 7, 2020, 08:15 hours

The latch pops open and, as I close the gate behind me, I worry that Mossy will be angry. This morning Rod Hill has accused me of sharing privileged information and locked the files, most of which Mossy had already seen. He has a big ear/unidirectional boom mike set up in his office, but he also wants me to plant a bug in her cabin. At first I refused, but then it occurred to me that it might offer something Mossy could play to her advantage.

As I approach the bridge I get a strong whiff of shit and check my shoes to see if I have stepped into one of Fif's giant piles. Nope...shoes clean. The smell gets stronger as I approach the cabin. I see Mossy out front setting up a sump pump next to a 500 gallon stock tank loaded into the back of her antique GMC/EV pickup.

"Say, here's just the guy to solve a little mystery!" she calls out. I realize with a sinking heart that she has dug up and removed the concrete manhole cover to her septic tank. "See those Golden Willow planted along the drain field? Yesterday, I noticed that their leaves were curling and tinged with blue. Later in the day, the toilet wouldn't flush and when I pulled the lid on the tank, this is what I found!" She pointed into the bright blue-green cesspool. "You killed my septic tank! I would like to know WHY! Are you spying on me or what?"

I pull the electric gizmo out of my belly bag and mouth the words, "It's a bug." Then I say in a loud voice, "Gee, Mossy, I don't have any idea what happened to your septic tank! It looks like blue-green algae to me!"

Mossy takes the bug from me and gently sets it on the two-cycle engine of the sump pump. "Blue-green algae," she says in a small voice and I can envision Rod Hill turning up the volume of his headset, greedy for every word. Mossy continues in a small voice. "Maybe I can sell it at the Farmer's Market. People are always hankering for blue-green algae." Then she hits the start switch and I can hear Rod Hill scream from a quarter mile away.

While the pump runs she takes me aside and says in a quiet but stern voice, "What you've given me here is 500 gallons of toxic waste. I know you have allegiances and obligations across the fence, but I can't have you coming around here playing spy games on me. Do what you want and say what you will on their side of the fence, but on MY side, you're on MY SIDE, OK?"

"OK," I say humbly.

"I've got some Russian olive that I planted for bird habitat and a privacy screen against those prying eyes from the other side of the fence. It's starting to run away so I figure on digging a five hundred gallon moat around it and fencing it in with this blue-green shit. Judging from what it did to the willow, it should slow down the olive. Let's get started."

Digging a 500-gallon moat is a piece of work even when you have Mossy Stone for a digging partner. Both dogs join the project in hopes of exhuming a bone or, better yet, a mole. But it still takes two hours of backbreaking, callous-building, blister-popping work.

When we get back to the septic tank, the pump engine has long ago died and most of the blue-green sludge has been transferred to the stock tank. "The last 50 gallons has to be transferred by hand because the pump can't draft that high...At least that's how it worked out last time I did this chore." She fetches an old wooden ladder from the shop and two plastic five-gallon buckets. She lowers the ladder until its feet sit solidly on the bottom of the tank, sets the five-gallon buckets and a plastic bailer next to the manhole. She looks at me expectantly.

My mouth goes dry and I start to stutter, "Mos...Mossy, please no. No, no, no. Please don't make me go down there! There's got to be another way! Surely it's not worth it!"

"The only other way is ME going down there," she reasons. "If that seems fair to you, then step aside."

"But I don't have rubber boots," I plead. She kicks off her rubber farm boots and tosses them to me.

Glumly, I put on the boots, take the buckets, and climb down the hole. I stand on the bottom rung to keep Mossy's boots out of the sludge and fill both buckets with the bailer. I am coming up the wood ladder with about seventy-five pounds of shit when the fifth rung breaks from the new weight and down I go, riding the rail of the ladder, kerplunk!, up to my knees in the soft sludge. My feet are stuck fast. I feel dizzy and claustrophobic. I begin climbing out in my stocking feet like a scalded dog.

"Oh no you don't!" countermands Mossy. "You can't leave my boots in there!"

"But, Mossy," I plead. "They're stuck fast!"

"Stick your feet back in them," she orders. "I'll come down and help."

I climb back down the God-forsaken hole and insert my feet into the tops of the boots. Mossy puts on my shoes, climbs down and is standing on the bottom rung with her hands grasping the boot top. "One! Two! HEAVE!" she yells and the bottom rung gives way leaving us both standing knee deep in the shit pit. Mossy pulls up her right foot and my loafer is down in the muck. She climbs to the second rung and the left loafer is gone, as well. Then she starts laughing. "You were right," she is struggling to talk and I start laughing, as well. "It's not worth it! Let's get the hell out of Dodge before all the rungs break and we're left down here with nothing to eat but blue-green algae." And we struggle up the ladder, carrying the empty buckets, and laughing so hard we are nearly choking.

Once we are out, Mossy collects the bug microphone from off the sump pump engine. With some difficulty, she stops laughing and clearly enunciates into the mike, "And I want to thank you for helping me in the marijuana patch behind the Russian Olive. As you can see I'm going to be quite rich, soon selling pot to the kids in Forks. I won't miss my little wine sales one twit." She tossed the bug into the septic tank, kerplunk!

Then, laughing again, she hoses off her feet and goes into the house. She comes out with five bottles of wine. "And, you were right about there being another way!" she says, popping the cork on one of the bottles. She takes one sip and then pours the rest into the tank. Likewise with the other four bottles. $500 dollars worth of wine! "It's an aggressive and hearty yeast that gives my wine its bouquet. I'm sure it will do well in there. Anyway, that should be enough bugs to get life re-established down there."

We are both laughing as she hoses me off and sends me home with another bottle of wine while she deals with disposing of the waste in the stock tank herself. They give me a hard time at the gate for the smell that is coming off of me and spray me down with disinfectant before sending me straight to my room.

When I check my answering machine, there is a message from Rod Hill advising me to stay in my room and congratulating me for the material I got with the bug. I call 375-0001 to ascertain if he is joking or pitifully mistaken, but the line is busy.

I am soaking in the tub, drinking the gift that Mossy gave me, when I hear a helicopter come low overhead and land. I hurry to dry off and get dressed but the incident is over in a couple of minutes. I call upstairs to Hill and he growls, "You'd better get your ass up here right this second. You have some explaining to do to the Drug Enforcement Agency that is currently stinking up my office.

Upstairs, the whole floor reeks of shit. Three DEA agents stand in the threshold of Hill's office dyed blue-green from the waist down. Their flak jackets, which say "Federal Officer" in front and "DEA" in back are all spattered blue-green. One of the agents has the seat of his pants torn off and I expect to see the fabric on Fifteenth's trophy shelf the following day.

The agents are blaming Rod Hill for an ambush that resulted in one of them being attacked by a monster dog, one of them losing his assault rifle, and all three getting dunked up to their nuts in blue-green shit. There was not and never had been a grow operation on that twenty acres. If Twenty First Century wanted the property seized, they could send out a posse of their sleazy lawyers to do the job, but leave the DEA out of it, because they were a busy and dedicated bunch of guys and how the fuck were they supposed to get back to Seattle because the pilot wouldn't let any of the three on board and where was Hill's stretch limo because this was a police emergency and three officers required transport back to their duty station and WHAT THE FUCK WAS HILL THINKING WHEN HE CALLED THEIR 1-800-POT-BUST HOTLINE WITH AN UNCONFIRMED TIP THAT RESULTED IN THREE OFFICERS BEING DIPPED IN SHIT...

I slink back to my room and finish the bottle of wine, laughing, and toasting the window looking out on the Flying S Farm.

ഏൟ

Flying S Farm
September 4, 2020

I sit on the living room couch under the skylight watching the Congressional Hearings on adjusting Title 16, United States Code, which, I was making Mossy understand, will have profound repercussions upon her resistance to selling her property. I had borrowed one of Mossy's ancient Cassettes to record C-Span coverage of the hearings and am playing back a section to Mossy as we sit drinking dandelion tea and eating cornbread and honey. The last two months has been the finest of my life and I feel a kinship with Mossy that goes beyond friendship and deeper than family. Having submitted to my father the copy of the subject matter of "A Day in the Life of Mossy Stone," my room lease and restaurant privileges will soon be canceled. I need to be making my plans on returning to school to finish up missed requirements so I can graduate. But walking away from this lifestyle will not be easy...

And I don't like what I was seeing on TV and what it portends for the Flying S Farm. Fifteen years previously, in the wake of the collapsing timber industry, much of the land base of the National Forest System had been given over to the administration of the National Park Service. Some half a million acres had been added to the Park, mostly from the Forest Service, but a lot of land was acquired by private timber companies when legislation was passed imposing severe back taxes when forest lands were sold for development. The USFS lands acquired by the Park carried the land ethic of the previous land manager ("the greatest good, for the greatest number of people"). Twenty First Century was instrumental in the committee meetings and legal process and, when Congress conferred the land to the Park, stipulation was made that the Developmental Zone of the Park would be extended to provide for a concessionaire structure sufficient to provide recreational and spiritual renewal for a significant percentage of the Nation's urban-locked citizenry. A citadel managed by Twenty First Century had grown around the Park. Now Twenty First Century was hungry for the little inholdings of private property that got in their way and was anxious for the Park to flex its mighty muscle of acquisition by eminent domain.

On the VCR, Congressman Ned Adams, head of the Interior Committee on Parks and Recreation, is querying Mrs. "Dog" Huffman, superintendent of Olympic National Park, about previous boundary changes and the readjustment of the "Developmental Zone" in the Park's Land Management Plan. The Congressman looks tired and worn, but the Park representative seems lively and awake.

"I am not taking away from the many contributions that Twenty First Century has made to Olympic National Park and our visiting public. But from the perspective of responsible resources management, ours has not been a relationship built in heaven. While the billion dollar Virtual Park visitor center in Port Angeles continues to provide a daily Park experience to twenty-five thousand visitors, on any given day, forty times that are quartered within the Park in time-share condominiums managed by TFCC. With the gross revenue collected on this time-share scheme, TFCC could fund a Virtual Park visitor center in black ink every day of the year in perpetuum.

"Twenty First Century Corporation looks at the wonder of Olympic National Park and, instead of seeing a wild elk, they see a cash cow. Our euphoria over the Virtual Park concept and the TFCC lobby efforts which resulted in the 2010 Forest Addition has been tempered by our realization that the Park has been targeted as the home plate over which is hurled the hard sales pitch of the Olympic Peninsula. Without the marketing of TFCC we might still enjoy some of the remoteness and some of the wildness which was the hallmark of our Park in the late twentieth century.

"Twenty First Century wants to complete the concrete collar that it began putting around the neck of the Park shortly after the Forest Addition. The ecosystem of the interior Park cannot function as an island. The few farms that remain on the outskirts of the Park still provide critical habitat to the endangered elk and other wildlife resources. In addition to the benefits to wildlife, these farms are a page from the cultural history of the Park and its environs. The language of the Developmental Concept Plan forwarded by TFCC suggests tampering with Title 16 to effectively dislocate lifetime residents from their homes and farms when their lands come within Park jurisdiction. It is the policy of the National Park Service to preserve idyllic and historic lifestyles when they do not conflict with Park resources and values.

"The Land Protection Plan of Olympic National Park is an administrative document developed by professionals who are closest to the resource and in the best position to provide guidance in the mapping of such things as the Developmental Zone, drawn boldly as a collar in the Developmental Concept Plan presented by TFCC.

Olympic National Park refuses all offers of managerial assistance from TFCC We reject the D.C.P. forwarded by TFCC We ask that Congress abide by its own decision in 1916 to allow the National Park Service to go about the business of managing and protecting the resources within that system for the enjoyment of Americans, but, most importantly, for the preservation of those resources for the benefit of generations yet unborn...if there is to be any future at all for anything. Thank you."

On the screen, the superintendent gathers a few pages of notes and leaves the lectern for a nearby seat. On her way to her seat, she is passed by the C.E.O. of TFCC, John Smith, who many consider the most powerful political/economic figure in the world. They appear to make eye contact and the C.E.O. leans in to say a brief word to the Park Superintendent before taking the lectern himself.

"Can you catch what Smith says to the Park superintendent, there?" Mossy asks, moving closer to the screen and punching the rewind.

"No," I reply. "There are no microphones within range and the noise within the Congressional chambers is all you hear."

"I mean, can you read their lips?" she says, as if I was a big dummy. She pushes Play and you can see the sleazy smile and his mouth makes an utterance of perhaps one sentence. " 'It's too bad...' he is saying." Mossy hits the rewind button and watches the clip again. I think I am able to count ten or twelve syllables. " '...new tricks,' he says at the end." She rewinds again. "He says to the superintendent, 'It's too bad you can't teach an old dog new tricks.' But that's nonsense, because you can teach any dog new tricks."

Mossy reclaims her seat beside me on the couch and lets the action resume to John Smith laying out his speech on the lectern. "Ladies and gentlemen of Congress and people of the United States, for those that view these proceedings via television, the time has come for innovative management of our National heritage. The bureaucracy given to us to protect these treasures is steeped in tradition and blind to new approach. So it was with the witness that just left this stand. Ten years ago it was the private sector, the very company that I represent, which approached Olympic National Park to identify their problems of over-visitation and present them with an alternative to the human flood which threatened their every resource. The answer: a Virtual Park, which satisfies ten million visitors a year and imparts a human impact on the Park resources of exactly zero.

"But this proved to be only a temporary fix as an increasing population and visitor base placed inexorable pressures on undefended boundaries of Olympic National Park. Trees were being stripped of bark; moss and ferns being torn from the ground; bird nests pulled down from trees and the chicks scattered on the forest floor to feed the invading rat population. Owing to budget constraints that originated within the walls between which I am speaking today, the NPS has never been able to field the army of Park Rangers required to deal with such problems.

"In cooperation with Park staff, Twenty First Century used a modified Developmental Zone - only about three percent of the land added to ONP with the Forest Addition - to provide a satisfying Park experience to many millions of our condominium clients. An enduring benefit to Park resources is the ironclad protection our compounds have extended to vast sections of ONP's boundary.

"Now, we need to finish the job we started. Where the boundary encounters private lands, Park resources are undefended. Where TFCC's protections are absent, wide portholes exist that conduit poachers, trophy hunters, forest collectors, and other illegal visitors into the Park.

"Superintendent Huffman's eloquent remarks about NPS's policy of protecting the lifestyle and culture of the Park's inholders notwithstanding: you know a common tax-dodge trick used by inholders is to donate lands under Title 16 and receive, as part of the compensation package, lifetime leases for family residents. While these farms and other so-called improvements may require caretaking, it is the position of TFCC that they require the appointment of professional custodians and that it is unfair to the American people to accept lands to which great indemnity has been attached, which could otherwise be acquired, fee simple, by exercising eminent domain.

"For two decades, Twenty First Century Corporation has had an unblemished record of serving visitors to Olympic National Park and protecting the resources therein. While well-meaning bureaucrats snooze by the stove and - forgive me, Dog - chase their tails, TFCC has provided leadership and hard planning. We need Congress to reaffirm our partnership in the stewardship of this, and other, national treasures by implementing long-overdue correction to Title 16 and providing incidental legislation - a rider, I would think - to break the fruitless deadlock between Olympic National Park and Twenty First Century Corporation - that we might protect these splendid resources for future generations. Thank you, Mr. Chairman, Congressmen, and people of the United States."

Congressman Ned Adams seems unconvinced by the arguments offered by the CEO from TFCC and begins making insinuations that many of the visitation problems experienced by the Park were the result of the huge company's publicity and greenwashing of everything that touched Adams' constituency, the Sixth District of Washington.

Mossy begins putting out lunch for us on the table under the skylight, while half watching the proceedings. "We used to see that big-monied butthead, Smith, around Forks quite a bit," she remarks. "He is quite the master of double speak. Because of TFCC, our lifestyle here on the Peninsula and, particularly in this valley, has gone down the toilet. To hear him talk, it's the fault of the Park Service and the few farmers who are trying to hold onto their family spreads. He would have these farms, if it weren't for a couple of little things called the Constitution and Congress." On the screen Congressman Adams is launching into a full blown attack on TFCC while the big-monied butthead smiles paternally while inwardly collecting a pile of sticks and stones. "I feel like I've met Congressman Adams somewhere, but it may be just his mugshot on all the junk mail I receive in October, once every four years."

We eat in silence for a few minutes and then the footage cuts to outside the rotunda, where reporters have found an interview with Mrs. Adams, the Congressman's wife. Dubbed as "the Green Mink" by the media, Julie Adams emerged as a glamorous and photogenic spokesperson for modern environmentalism. Her lobbying efforts for such groups as the Sierra Club, were well-funded and mainstream. She sported an endless wardrobe of suave outdoor clothing, provided by Eddie Bauer, L.L. Bean, and Lands End, while revolutionizing the fashion industry by wearing hiking boots to clomp around the halls of Congress. The fragrances of perfume she wore lingered long around the Rotunda and Clayburn Office Building like a breath of pine trees blowing on a spring wind, or an expensive deodorant plug in a men's' urinal. Whatever...she was politically well-connected, the darling of the media, and a pillar of strength to her husband's career.

"My husband and I share different views on the legislative package being studied by his committee," the Green Mink was saying, as Mossy brings in a dessert from the kitchen. Mossy sees the image on the screen and her nostrils flare like a horse smelling a stalking cougar.

"I know this woman!" Mossy exclaims and stands before the screen trying to make a connection from a far-off memory.

"Of course Ned and I have had a love affair with the Olympic Peninsula from long before it was...well, discovered. It was our backpacking and mountaineering experience in the Olympic Mountains where we fell in love, not only with the wonderful pristine environment...but with each other as well..."

Mossy still stands spellbound, half listening to the Congressman's wife, as she scans her memory. "Somewhere before...long ago...I met her..."

"So we both remember the late twentieth century on the Olympic Peninsula, particularly in the Park," the Green Mink was saying. "Before the Green Wall, as we call the protection afforded by TFCC, the Park was over-run by homeless, tripwire vets from the Vietnam conflict, and other indigents. Poaching of wildlife and plant material from the Park was big business, but a few courageous employees of TFCC dared to stand up to big business and say, 'Enough! Keeping the precious resources of Olympic National Park intact for future generations is worth more than the big money you make poaching...'"

"Excuse me, Mrs. Adams," interrupts one reporter with a voice familiar to me. "But isn't TFCC presently the biggest business in the solar system?"

"Perhaps presently," replies the Green Mink, icily. "But NOT in the late 20th century, which is the period I was discussing, if you were listening..."

"But when TFCC built the Virtual Park Visitor Center and began its so-called Green Wall project..." the dissenting reporter continued his attack and suddenly I recognized a classmate from NYU performing another internship. "...didn't Twenty First Century have more assets and greater cash reserves that any corporate interest in the world..."

"I know him! I know that reporter!" I yell excitedly at Mossy.

"Shhhh," says Mossy.

"Shhhh," says a <u>Washington Host</u> reporter standing next to my NYU compatriot.

"If the press is done lecturing me on technicalities, I would like to go on with my personal observations," the Green Mink again claimed center stage. "Before Ned and I were married we hiked and climbed all over the Park. Once we had climbed an extremely remote and dangerous summit next to Mount Olympus called 'Bogachiel Peak'...

"What is she talking about!" Mossy exploded. "Bogachiel Peak is a domed, walk-up and it's on the other side of the Hoh River from the Olympus massif!"

Released from silence, I share my big, good news again, "I know that reporter! He was in my class..."

"Having bivouacked on the peak itself the night before, we were having our mountaineers' breakfast before packing up and down climbing from the summit..."

- Mossy again interrupts with her own ruminations, "When I hiked up there from the South Fork maybe twenty-five years ago, there was a young couple camped where the old fire lookout used to be..."

"I know that reporter!" I tell Mossy: a record broken by excitement.

"...and imagine our surprise, when along came this poor young, homeless waif: No rope, no ice axe, no food, no equipment! How she got there I haven't a clue..."

"OK, Chiggers, so you know that reporter. I have the same feeling about Mrs. Adams, though to hear her talk, I can't believe she has ever been to Bogachiel Peak or the Park, for that matter. Anyway, when I was coming out of Bogachiel Basin, I caught a whiff of something that reminded me of a 55 gallon drum of Pine Sol being flushed down a toilet."

"...I could smell the poor little thing long before I saw her. When she emerged on the summit's peak - well - of course we were terrified for her safety with no ice axe or equipment! She had no water and had not eaten for God-knows-how-long. We tried to feed her, but the sad little girl was too wild to eat nutritious food...Maybe if we had brought along some sugar cubes we could have given her something. We asked where she lived and she threw her arm out over the expanse of the great Olympic wilderness, letting us know that she had no home, as such..."

"That business about tripwire vets in the Olympics was a media hoax back when I was a kid," interjects Mossy. "Sounds like this woman swallowed the bait and is coughing up a bigger hoax of her own. I can't believe she's ever been to Bogachiel Peak, to hear her talk; and I'm sure I've met her before and could place it in a second if they had developed teleolfactory instead of television..."

"I'm trying to remember the name of that reporter," I offer in way of conversation. "I was in two different classes with the guy and he was always shooting his mouth off to the profs."

"...which led us to believe that the hungry little creature had been eating from the forest! Imagine today's great sea of homeless and indigent washing its hungry way across the Olympic wilderness and you can appreciate the need for the Green Wall.

"She staggered precariously off the mountain and gave us one more look, as if to say 'Please, help me. Help me to be normal and whole and not this wild jungle creature I've become...'"

"I'd go with the jungle creature if it were me," quips Mossy. "The faces on Mount Rushmore have more human content than the made-up mask on that political siren."

"ROBERT TOOL!" I exclaim. "That's the name of my friend! You know: the guy that gave her a hard time?"

"...and back in the late twentieth century - at least in this forgotten wilderness - there was no cell phone service and we had no way to call for Park Rangers. So we had to report it after we climbed and hiked the nine miles out; and the Rangers had seen so much of this kind of thing and were so understaffed that all they could do was to send up some kind of volunteer college student with binoculars.

"This underscores the point that all thinking environmentalists have been saying for more than twenty years:"

On the screen, the Green Mink pauses for effect and I punctuate the silence with a loud fart, and laugh. Mossy moves her chair slightly away from me without comment and continues to wait for the woman on the screen to start making sense.

"You can't have an open, unprotected boundary between wilderness and the modern world without a huge army to defend it. Taxpayers won't tolerate the burden to support such effort, so some form of privatization is the only answer..."

"That's horse pucky!" exclaims Mossy. "If you build a wall around a wild bear, it's no longer a wild bear...it's a stuffed bear that hasn't stopped breathing! If you put wild land in a cage, whether the bars are made of concrete or Park Rangers, it's no longer wild! You can't protect wilderness in a cage."

"Which brings me to the uncomfortable position I find myself in today," continues the Green Mink. "If the strand of political rope, which for two decades has belayed my husband and I across the precipitous political peaks and valleys of the other Washington, separates into two braids...one braid representing my reasoning on the matter and, the other, a well-frayed braid of environmental extremism..."

In the pause I interject another flatulent punctuation.

"...to which strand dare I tether?" asks Mrs. Julie Adams, in the last statement she will ever give to the press.

"Tie them both around your neck!" sighs Mossy in disgust, taking empty dishes toward the kitchen.

"Your boot laces are untied!" exclaims Bobby Tool, finishing his internship with the <u>Washington Host</u> in disgrace. "Tie them and then decide!"

ᓚᢀᕗ

Bogachiel Garden Condominiums
Monday, September 7, 2020, 07:45 hours

It will be the biggest day and most pivotal point in my life. How you wake up one morning with the phone ringing and stumble across the floor to pick up the handset, already knowing through the fog of your sleep that your life has changed...that when sleep finds you again, it will be in a different head.

"Room 1255, Stokes." I answer with phlegm in my voice.

"RISE AND SHINE, NATURE BOY. WAKE IT AND SHAKE IT!" It's the voice of Rod Hill screaming into the phone. I had expected my father calling from Washington, D.C. to announce the publication of my human-interest story on Mossy. "GET YOUR ASS UP TO MY OFFICE PRONTO. THE LEADER OF THE FREE WORLD IS HERE TO TALK TO YOU."

Confusion washes over me along with a whiff of a hangover from drinking another bottle of Flying S wine last night. "The President wants to see me?" I ask incredulously.

"NO, YOU DUMB SHIT! THE PRESIDENT'S BOSS: MR. JOHN SMITH! PUT ON A TIE, SCRUB BEHIND YOUR EARS, WIPE YOUR ASS, AND HUSTLE UP HERE, PRONTO! This could be your big break, same as it was for your dad twenty-one years ago."

"Did my article come out, is that why he wants to see me..."

"HEY! WE ASK THE QUESTIONS! JUST DRAG YOUR LAZY, LATE-RISING ASS UP HERE FIVE MINUTES AGO!"

I am disappointed to find that the only tie I own has been used to mop up some wine spilled from a bottle. I find that this helps it to match my crumpled dress shirt, which has been the drop cloth for wine spilled from my mouth. I compose myself, as much as my attire will allow, and proceed upstairs to meet a man who dumps political mountains into socio-economic avalanche with a yawn.

I knock on the door of room number 0001 which is opened by Hill, revealing the man I had seen on TV a few days previously, seated in an office chair with a newspaper spread open on his lap. No attempt is made at introductions, the assumption being that I will recognize the most influential individual of the human species and Mr. Smith makes no pretense of disturbing himself as I come into the room. He throws the newspaper over on another chair in way of invitation for me to sit. "Well, congratulations on being published in a national newspaper. I believe your career may be well on its way. But me being the CEO of the company holding controlling interest in the periodical currently employing you and your father, I thought we would have a little chat..."

I catch a glimpse of the front page as I pick up The Washington Host and scan the headlines: Congressman Arrested for Slaying Green Mink Wife glares the lead story. In the subheading, "She was sleeping with my enemy and I smelled it on her," the Congressman confesses. "So I put a gun to her head and shot her."

I notice an article authored by my dad on the front page, Olympic National Park Announces the Retirement of Superintendent Dagmar Huffman. The subhead goes on: Long time resident and lawyer, Lawrence Mulligan, recruited to lend legal expertise and familiarity with economic needs of area.

Another scary headline: Congress Meets in Emergency Session Today/Measure to Extend Park Boundaries, Mandate Developmental Zones, and Modify Land Donation Expected to Pass

"You can see that the news is rather explosive this morning, Chiggers," so you will forgive The Host for the necessity of burying your little human-interest story. You'll find that on the last page of the Life Style section." I turned to the Life Style section and leafed through articles thrown together by my dad, eulogizing Julie Adams and extolling the virtues of the Forks lawyer stuffed into a gray and green uniform to fill the cordovan shoes of the woman who dared stand up for Park resources and briefly oppose the interests of TFCC.

I find the article which is illustrated with another computer generation of Mossy attired with clothing I think the now deceased, Green Mink, may have sported for the media's loving attention. The title has been changed from: A Holdout From the Twentieth Century to: Hold Onto the Twentieth Century. The open-arm welcome Mossy once innocently offered to her dog is again given to the world and, hanging from the left hand of the computer confabulation, I recognize the bottle of wine, the picture of which I sent back along with the copy to my father. The computer image of Mossy is decked out to look like some boozy bimbo. I begin reading the first line under my name, more fascinated to see my name in print than to be sitting with the most central figure of the global power elite.

On the subject of TTFC acquiring all or part of Mossy's spread I had quoted her as saying, "I wouldn't take a million dollars an acre..." to which my father, the Life Style editor, had inserted that the offer currently on the table from

Olympic National Park was 1.5 million an acre. "I...I didn't wri.. write this!" I stammer in outrage.

"Well," intoned John Smith. "I understand the copy you sent your dad was pretty rough and needed some work. Still, it must be gratifying to see your name in print in a newspaper read by a hundred million pairs of eyes.

At this point, the article totally departs from anything I wrote and goes on to discuss what I know to be a lie: that negotiations with Mossy Stone would result in application of new Federal law which would allow TFCC to acquire the Flying S Farm as an inholding to Olympic National Park, to concrete over the land in a 2,400 unit condominium which they describe as "low-density housing", and to bring back the ghost of Mossy Stone to reside in this cement cemetery like the hostess in some quaint bed and breakfast. "Mossy will never go for this," I observe. "And this article is a crock..."

"She doesn't have a choice," said John Smith, icily. "Or more accurately, her choice is the same as your's: Get on board or get run over. It's come to my attention that you have been accessing files relative to Ms. Stone from this office. While you borrowed the material under the guise of research for your article, we know from our own sources that you were, in fact, sharing sensitive documents with Ms. Stone and, thus, undermining the position of your employer's parent company. It's the time for you to make your own choice. Do you stand with your father's name to represent the interests of your family, your employer, and the American public? Or are you going to continue to sneak around helping this poor, misguided woman to resist the inevitable?"

"What...what do you want from me?"

"Mossy Stone appears to trust you. Explain to her the hopelessness of her resisting our offer. We don't want to kick her off her property. Far from it. We want to purchase the property, yes, and to make many necessary and overdue improvements to protect the environment that Ms. Stone finds so dear. But we want to have Ms. Stone continue to reside on the premises and would be happy to employ her in a well-salaried position as a hostess and already popular personality. We want what's best for the American people AND what's best for Ms. Stone and her precious tract of land. Can we count on you to help us avoid having Ms. Stone removed from the premises by the police?"

A deep well of regret was flooding my heart. It was so unfair! I have never had a friend as close as Mossy Stone and I have never known another person in the modern world to imbue the charisma that is born of simplicity and hard toil. "Ffffffffff....." I am searching my soul for a verbal response to a proposition which would trade my future in this modern world for a fleeting friendship with an eccentric farm woman. "...fffuuuuuuu....." A response is rising from my guts up my throat like a turd that forgot to ask directions. "....uuck YOU!" I stammer.

"Excuse me?" inquires the CEO of the five trillion dollar TFCC. John Smith appears amused at the apopleptic expression which is clouding my normally befuddled look.

"FUCK YOU! I SAID. FUCK HIM, TOO!" I say pointing to Rod Hill, who likewise smirks at my outburst. "I'll tell Mossy Stone to sic Fifteenth on any one of you suits that comes within a whiff of her farm." I stand up with the newspaper cascading off my lap and onto the floor. "FUCK YOU!" I say again for good measure.

"We had our psychiatric team do a profile on you and Ms. Stone and we anticipated that there was a 50% chance of such an unnecessary scene as this," John Smith intoned. "You'll find Security representatives out in the hall, who will be happy to relieve you of your privilege card and help you move yourself and your personal belongings off TFCC property. Oh! And by the way, within 24 hours that will include the Flying S Farm, so don't get toooo comfortable..."

I am moving towards the door, which Rod Hill is holding open for me like a 70-year-old bar bouncer. "...Oh! And one more thing I almost forgot: a signed little note from your dad. I had hoped it would say some congratulatory little remark about your piece on Mossy Stone."

It was Hill who passed me the piece of paper which read, "Chiggers, don't ever come home. We are no longer family and will have no further association with one another. - Richard Stokes."

Rod Hill leaned close to my ear and said in a low, whoopy-cushion of a voice, "Fuck you, too, Chiggers. WAY...about to...fuck you. And it WILL BE A PLEASURE!"

Hill pushes me out the door and slams it, where a couple of tough-looking security guards grab me, throw me in the elevator, and virtually drag me to the "temporary" gate. Just before pitching me out they grab my wallet, pull out my security card, and throw the wallet at me as the electronic gate slams down like a guillotine. "Have a nice day!" one of them calls out.

I gather my stuff and trudge over to the gate of the Flying S, where I am rung through. Fif and Chick come running over the bridge, apparently glad to see my tear-streaked face. I follow the dogs out to the family cemetery where Mossy is working on a pawpaw tree. "Hi, Chiggers," she calls cheerfully. "It smells to me like you're having a bad day. See if this cheers you up: this pawpaw is going to have fruit this year! I can't figure it out...A bee from the east coast transported on a jet plane, or bits of pollen attached to a carbon particle escaped from an east coast incinerator scrubber...but, what do you know, even in the twenty first century, life wants to be and will defy all odds to persevere."

"I'm tired of defying odds," I say glumly. "Mossy, they're coming to take your farm. Big things are happening over there..." I point behind us to the southern concrete skyline. "They're coming for this farm in the next 24 hours."

"Nothing new," Mossy says, dismissively, shoveling her fertilizer into a shallow trench by the pawpaw. "They have been coming for this farm for twenty years. They can't have it."

"Mossy, the outside world has changed. I just got thrown out of Bogachiel Gardens," I say pointing at my little baggage. "My family just disowned me. That cement tsunami that you see poised behind us will be crashing down on this farm by tomorrow."

"A little thing called the Constitution of the United States has always been a significant deterrent. Plus, for the last few years, Fifteenth has helped a little bit. Hey, are you hungry? I skipped breakfast when I saw this tree trying to fruit out. Let's have a nosh together and see if it cheers you up. Anyway, you can stay here until something else comes along for you. You're getting to be an OK farmhand and we could use some new smells around here."

"Mossy!" I protest as we begin walking to the cabin. "This is serious!"

The phone is ringing as we come to the front door and Mossy answers it. "Oh, hi, Brian!" she says brightly to some old friend, but then gets somber in hearing his message. She fetches a piece of paper to take some notes. After about ten minutes of listening, she says, "Well, thanks for making me aware of it and you can come over if you want, but I guess it's time for me to prepare for a little venture away from the farm."

Mossy hangs up and comes back to the kitchen. "Oh, well," she says casually, beginning to fill up a five gallon water urn. "Looks like I will be going to jail for a few days. Say, you got thrown out of Bogachiel Gardens at an opportune time for me. I'll need you to take care of the dogs and water some plants before I get home..."

Fif and Chick explode out the open front door barking and Mossy sets the water aside to follow the commotion out to the front porch. She stands a moment sniffing the air and then hits the solenoid to open the front gate.

"They're coming already!" I say, in a growing panic.

"Naw, it's a friend of mine," says Mossy, coming back to the sink and sponging up a little water which she carries to a thirsty, little plant by the porch. "I'm not sure who it is, but whoever it is, they are my friend."

"How would you know something like that?" I ask as the old forest biologist, Rick Larson drives up in his electric vehicle under close and noisy canine escort. I recognize him from old photographs Mossy shared with me while I was preparing the biographical sketch so wildly distorted by my father. "Hey, Mossy! Long time!" he calls out. "Hey, there," he says to me in way of courtesy to a stranger. "I brought you today's newspaper and need to talk to you about what it means." He gets out of his car with the same edition that had fallen off my lap an hour ago as I was being evicted. "Can we talk?" he asks Mossy, looking at me suspiciously and peering around the property warily for spies.

"TFCC had a BIG EAR in their office when I got thrown out an hour ago. They have been trying to bug this place for a while. Best to go inside," I say with authority.

Once inside the door, Larson asks Mossy, "Just this morning there has been legislation which mandates the Park Service to make certain adverse takings by eminent domain...

"If they try that, I'll donate the land with the standard clause that blocks development while allowing the donor life-time residence. There's a beneficial tax angle to it that..."

"They've got a new spin on that," interrupts the old biologist. "Listen, I hate to pry, but, just in case...are there any conditions out here that could lead to your arrest?"

"Well, yeah. I just got a call from Brian Fairbanks. He retired from the Forks P.D. a few years back, but still hacks round on the Secure Internet and found search-and-arrest warrants against me. Here's the list of violations they suppose they are going to find," says Mossy handing Rick the handwritten list she took from ex-Officer Fairbanks. I see:

"Jesus!" I exclaim. "Those are all taken from the biographical sketch I submitted on you, Mossy!" I felt devastated. "They used me as a Judas Iscariot on you!"

"It's OK, Chigs. We'll figure something out..."

→ *Multiple copyright violations*
→ *Illegal toxic waste dump*
→ *Growing controlled substance*
→ *Canine leash law violations*
→ *Transportation and illegal interment of human remains*
→ *Nonpotable and untreated water creating public nuisance*
→ *Using human waste on food products sold publicly*
→ *Unsafe septic system*

"You're in a legal jam here, Mossy, and I see TFCC paving over this farm as an inevitability..."

"NO! THEY WON'T PUT THIS FARM UNDER CONCRETE! NOT WHILE THERE IS BREATH LEFT IN MY BODY. THEY WON'T..." and suddenly Mossy is sobbing. I have never seen a pathetic side of Mossy and it's a scary sight. Rick and I exchange nervous glances and he shrugs. I reach out and put my arms around the sobbing woman and we embrace for a few moments while she collects herself against the enormity of the external threats upon her unique lifestyle.

"Mossy, we need a legal battle plan. How much money do you have saved up that we can dip into as a war chest for lawyer fees?"

Mossy snuffles and breaks my embrace. "After taxes, that amount would be...uh...zero."

Rich Larson rubs his chin. "How about The Trust for Public Land? They helped save some of the trail country and wetlands east of here twenty years ago by acting as the mediator between private landowners and the government. They could give you the best free advice on how to donate the land without giving up the lifestyle...if there is still a way."

Mossy disappears into the living room to make several phone calls, while Rick Larson and I wait in the kitchen. We hear Mossy's solemn and earnest voice, but can only make out snatches of words. "I can't see a way out of this for Mossy," says Larson, to avoid eavesdropping. "TFCC cited every case of fugitives fleeing through or abiding in National Parks from the Nez Perce's Trail of Tears through Yellowstone to the arrest of Charles Manson in Death Valley. Free-roaming arrestees won't be tolerated on Federal lands..."

Mossy comes back into the kitchen and picks up the five gallon urn she had been previously filling. "Chiggers, can I talk to you for a second?" she asks, carrying the water out to the thirsty, little plants in her sun room. I follow. "Chiggers, you mentioned that you needed a place to stay for a while. Well, I need you to be here right now and wonder if you would make yourself available for a while."

"Sure, how long do you need me?"

"Well, for the rest of your life would be the best for me, but I need you to sign a contract that guarantees you'll stay for at least twelve months."

"Sure, I'll sign up for twelve months, but you might get tired of me being here after that, so let's just see how it goes..."

"Chiggers, I can guarantee you that, in twelve months, I won't be tired of you living here. Anyway, I called back my friend Brian Fairbanks and he's going to pick up some paperwork prepared by The Trust for Public Land and bring it out. In the meantime, we need to go over some maintenance things, since all indications are that I will be in jail tomorrow."

For several hours, Mossy showed me breaker switches along the transmission line of the hydroelectric, maintenance logs and tools for maintaining the small fleet of farm machinery, watering schedules for the garden and orchard, feeding and care of the chickens and few head of livestock, harvesting schedules..."Mossy this schedule takes us all the way through December. Why should I concern myself with this when you'll be back in a couple of...Well, how long will you be in jail?"

"I can't see any way that I'll be in jail for more than ten days. Chiggers, you have to apply yourself and learn how to take care of this farm like it was your own." Back at the cabin, Mossy goes to drawing up more specific instructions and extemporaneous manuals. The dogs tear out of the cabin, barking frantically, but Mossy sits quietly writing in the old-fashioned way, with a pen and paper. As din of barking proceeds away from the house, I can hear a car engine in the distance out by the front gate.

"They're coming!" I say, with my heart in my throat.

"Naw," says Mossy nonchalantly, reaching up to press a switch to release the gate. "It's Officer Fairbanks arriving with that paperwork The Trust for Public Lands said I needed."

The engine noise and dog barking begins advancing towards the cabin and, I suppose, as my ears told the story of an unknown person driving an internal-combustion vehicle under dog escort, Mossy's nose tells her of the concern, compassion, and sense of duty in the blood pumped from the heart of an old friend.

Fairbanks arrives, the dogs are subdued, we are introduced, the old cop passes to Mossy a closed sheaf of papers, and she serves Larson, Fairbanks and myself lunch, before going to her desk to begin the paperwork with a pen. I argue that documents are not legally valid if not prepared on computer, but Mossy has already checked on this and knows differently. She sits alone brooding over the work while we eat. Toward the end of the meal, she brings in three bottles of wine, upon which I lead the charge. The old cop asks for my I.D., claiming that Mossy can't afford any liquor law violations, what-so-ever, but once assured that it's a legal drinking party, joins the ebullition. His understanding is that the warrant will be served the following morning and he wants to be on hand, so he plans to sleep over. Larson has the same idea, so our little wine party begins counting down from the ninety-nine bottles of wine on the wall. By the time Mossy comes to me to sign the paperwork she has been filling out, I am smashed and am having a good old time with these good old boys. They are telling stories about windstorms, a wildfire, and Mossy beating the crap out of Rod Hill's bully kid. The afternoon wears on to evening and we are having a high old time. The old biologist breaks out a sleeping bag and heads for the couch. Fairbanks goes out to his car to fetch his bedroll and lay it out protectively by the cabin door. I hold on to the party a little longer, finishing an open bottle and then drinking what's left in the glasses of the fallen celebrants. The last thing I remember is Mossy helping my drunken ass up the steep steps to her bed. I am confused. Am I being seduced? But I am asleep as soon as my head hits the pillow and Mossy steps quietly over the slumbering body of Officer Fairbanks to walk on her crutch around the land and reflect upon her brief future.

It seems like just a few hours later that the dogs are sounding an alarm and first light has brought the first intrusion from the outside world. My heart is pounding almost as vigorously as my head as I come down from the steep steps to find Officer Fairbanks and Rick Larson already observing the meeting between Mossy and a lawyer sent over by The Trust for Public Lands. We repair inside for tea and some breakfast snacks that Mossy has set out. Mossy presents me with a sheaf of instructions and protocols for the farm and I try to surmount my hangover with conversation with the green snake of a lawyer. "So, what are the chances of beating these trumped-up charges and getting it cleared for Mossy to stay here on her farm."

"I would say..." the lawyer appears to be looking for an exact percentage. "...zero."

"What the hell kind of attitude is that?" I exclaim. "How are you going to prove her innocence and save her lifestyle if you don't have any faith it can be done?"

Once again, the dogs announce visitors and I put my hands over my ears to save my brain from the piercing chorus. I almost miss what the lawyer says as he gets up to follow the party outside. "I really wouldn't know anything about her innocence. Her lifestyle is irrelevant," he says falling in with the party going out the front door to meet the new company. I can barely make out what he's saying and take my hands from my ears subjecting myself to the explosive commotion. "I was brought here as a right-to-die lawyer."

Slowly my mind turns over as I collect myself to go out the door. "Right-to-die lawyer - ?????," my brooding is further disjointed as I realize that I am hearing a procession of vehicles coming across the bridge and that this is finally THE BIG ONE. "Right-to-die lawyer-!!!!?!!!!?!!!!!?" a growing sense of panic is enveloping me as I see the lead car pull so close to the cabin the dogs, which are heeled beside Mossy, go nuts. My mind is sputtering, "!!!!!! right to !!!!? lawyer!!!!!!! right-to-die lawyer...???????!!!!!!!!"

A suit jumps out of the passenger seat of the lead vehicle. He's grabbing a badge in one hand and what looks like a real handgun in the other. "Fred Prue, FBI!" he shrieks over the din of the dogs. "Those dogs move an inch and I shoot!" he screams menacingly, pointing at Fifteenth.

"Dogs, down!" says Mossy and both Fif and Chick release their bodies to gravity and begin falling to earth. The FBI spook fires his gun at Fifteenth and the big, black dog lands with a thud, shot in the head.

"RIGHT TO DIE LAWYER!" my brain has finally put it together, though I am out of sequence with what's going on around me.

"Why did you shoot my dog? He was totally under control!" asks Mossy of the assailant.

"I warned you not to let your dogs move. Nothing has changed since I was here twenty years ago and that big, black bastard tried to kill me!"

"RIGHT TO DIE LAWYER!" I exclaim out loud. "What are you doing here? Who called for you?" Nothing is making sense.

"My black dog wasn't even alive twenty years ago," Mossy protests.

"Then, like I said..." snorted Special Agent Prue, "Nothing has changed. And I'll kill the small one if it moves while I place you under arrest. Leave the dogs where they lie and step forward while we place you under arrest. You, in the mob," said Agent Prue, waving his gun at all of us, "put your hands up and identify yourselves."

"Rick Larson," says the old forester, raising his hands. "Personal friend."

"Brian Fairbanks," says the cop, with his hands already up. "Forks Police."

"Chiggers Stokes," I say, trying to puff myself up. "Reporter."

"Berry Mulligan," says the man beside me with his hands up so high I see the band of his underwear. "Right-to-die lawyer for the defense."

"RIGHT-TO-DIE LAWYER?" exclaims Fred Prue. "Who called you?" and suddenly I was getting back in sync with the unfolding events. "Anyway," says the agent, putting Mossy in handcuffs, "it doesn't matter whether Ms. Stone elects to live or die. Upon this arrest, the government is seizing her farm and, in the absence of custodial pre-arrangement, we will be placing it within the jurisdiction and discretion of the National Park Service. And with us is our own lawyer who we have brought to seize the property and make restitution to the arrestee."

"Au contraire!" says Berry Mulligan. "This farm is already the property of the National Park Service. Here is the signed and notarized donation papers and title. We have an appointed caretaker with lifetime tenancy, so the Federal government will not have discretionary power over this property and it will remain a working farm and not time-share condominiums." Mulligan puts down his hands and slowly reaches into the briefcase at his feet to pass over some papers.

"Who is this appointed caretaker?" asks another suit, evidently the Assistant U.S. Attorney who wades into the fray, sensing that all physical threats have been neutralized by the FBI and other storm troopers who flank Mossy and her small living dog.

"Him," says Berry Mulligan pointing at me.

"All right, whatever..." says the U.S.A., passing back the papers to Mulligan and folding his arms on his chest. "OK, hook up the woman and anyone else that's standing next to a violation."

The FBI agent moves forward and seizes Mossy by the arm. He drags her unnecessarily to the prisoner transport vehicle and grabs something out of her left hand, which I recognize as the Beyer's family Bible.

"Please put the Bible in the vehicle," implores Mossy of the goon who has just assassinated her dog and, without warning, she throws her crutch toward the weeping cherry tree.

The brave Special Agent covers his head with his hands, anticipating an attack while the crutch lands with a thud in the family cemetery. "Pull a stunt like that again and I'll knock you shitless," he hisses. The F.B.I. agent handcuffs her arms behind her back. "Excuse me just a moment," Mossy says to the assembled officers and stands quietly for several moments. Her eyes follow the skyline of the tall spruce growing along the southern perimeter of the property. A summer storm is on the air, promising much needed moisture. The wind freshens and the chimes hung from the cabin peal like church bells at a wake. The river of air from the south blows the long hair from around Mossy's face - a face unchiseled by stress or pollutants, a face that could belong to the Mother of God. Mossy's feet remain planted on the ground while her upper torso sways with the spruce boughs: the uppermost growth of the Stone/Beyers conjugal tree, blowing freely in the wind in the last few moments before being bulldozed by progress. Her eyes are dry and her voice is steady as she speaks to me her last instructions, "Bury my dog in the orchard, please. If you don't do it soon, the kids from across the way will desecrate the carcass."

The G-man gets tired of waiting and opens the door of the prisoner carrier. He pushes her into the compartment and swings the door closed. The police pull out in a caravan and I walk out across the bridge to see about twenty of Mossy's neighbors cutting through the fence and pressing into Mossy's yard. This is the last view that Mossy has of the garden which had sustained her life since she was weaned from her mother's breast: looters digging up her plants and carrying off every green, living thing. The whole neighborhood had been hovering like buzzards, waiting for the power structure to break Mossy's claim on this twenty acres and the resources it held.

Fairbanks and I drag Fif's body over to the orchard and start digging a hole. A mob of seven kids amble across the bridge past us and walk right up to the porch like they own the place. They find the puddle of blood, left behind by the murdered animal. "Neato!" said one of the miscreants. "The cops wasted somebody!" The punks stick their fingers in the blood and began drawing streaks on their faces like war paint. So much for AIDS awareness.

"Get the hell out of here!" yells Fairbanks, dragging the dog into the hole we've dug. The kids ignore him and go inside the cabin. While Fairbanks leaves with the shovel to mix it up with the punks, I am left alone to finish the job with the dog. I fetch over the crutch, which lies ten feet away, and throw it into the hole with the carcass. I climb into the grave with one foot on the crutch and the other on the body of the dog that had learned to like me. I pull soil in with my hands. As I cover Fif with the soil Mossy had always held in such reverence, I begin to cry. This dog had never bitten a human...and (sniff)...Mossy had shown compassion and respect for these neighbors all her life...(sob)...what justice or hope is left in this world?

The kids come running out of the cabin with their arms full of jars of produce, which Mossy had put up earlier this summer. Fairbanks comes out chasing them with a bloody nose. I try to get out of the grave to come to the old cop's assistance, but my feet won't move. One of the punks has blipped him for trying to stop their theft. Once outside, the punks stop and spread out like a pack of wolves trying to blindside Fairbanks. The old cop begins swinging the shovel in a wide figure eight defending a 180 degree aspect. One of the flanking teenagers moves in for a strike and Fairbanks shifts quickly, catching the young hoodlum squarely in the elbow. The kid shrieks, "Ow! You crazy ol' freak! I'm going to tell my lawyer on you!"

And I am standing in the grave with my feet on the dog and crutch, having pulled fresh dirt in on myself up to my knees, crying like a baby.

❧

Flying S Farm
Friday, September 18, 2020

It's the picture of Mossy being carried away in the prisoner transport van that haunts my sleep and makes it easier to stand out here near the orchard, waiting for dawn. The stars are so bright this time of morning and the cold, crisp air makes everything feel clean.

I got a call two days ago from the National Park Service confirming my appointment as Warden over this twenty acre Park Reserve. But it seems too late for the National Park Service (and the gauze and glitter that the power elite use) to fool the masses into believing there is still a future. I heard on the radio last night that there were more air riots in Los Angeles and New York. There was water rioting in Phoenix and El Paso and food riots right across Mexico.

Last semester at N.Y.U., I took a course called Great Mistakes of the Twentieth Century. The prof held that our planet was basically environmentally intact all the way into the 1990's. He argued that it was simple economics that killed this planet: that trees could be extracted without the ruination of a forest, but the homeowner would not bear the price of that lumber; that wheat could be grown without using up the soil, but the consumer would not pay the price of this bread. A political overlay was in place and the opportunity existed to banish war forever from the planet. Humanity chose instead to persist in battles with fellow man, rather than to make peace with his environment. The prof pointed to the 1990's and said, "That was the crossroads, after which there was no turning back. There is no escape for us from the mistakes made in the 1990's and it is easy to predict that humanity will not see any part of the twenty-second century."

The prof said that there was some kind of self-proclaimed environmental movement all the way through the latter twentieth century. He talked about affluent, yogurt-sucking, tofu-munching yuppies that destroyed oceans of air as they drove from meeting to demonstration in their oxygen-gulping, carbon-monoxide-coughing internal-combustion machines. Through it all, the so-called "environmentalists" were shitting in drinking water and wiping their asses with trees right along with the loggers they decried. The environmentalists procreated as fast as the industrialists: yuppies breeding like guppies. At N.Y.U., the administration wasn't ready for students to hear this message and they fired the professor.

If I could only go back in time to the 1990's and hold up a sign for humanity as they approached the crossroads. Would they ignore my DEAD END sign and speed by me in their vehicles driven by fossil fuels? How could they argue with me, if I told them that there were limits to everything? That even the vastness of time and space folds back upon itself. And that, of our planetary resources, there must be left enough to heal the wounds from our extractions.

It makes me angry with my father's generation. Everyone had to have as much or more as the generation before until finally there was nothing left of the clean water, air, and soil the planet needs to survive. Our dreams are drowned in sterile mud like a salmon redd in silt. Our future is dried out and dead like a nurse log desiccated in the relentless sun. In the end, without soil, air, and water, we are all as vulnerable as Mossy or her precious trees.

I'm standing here in the starlight, next to the orchard, trying to think what it must have been like to live back then in the 90's, when there were five families at this latitude sharing 60 square miles; when the Bogachiel ran like a liquid jewel, sparkling clean and full of wild fish; when the cry of the elk trumpeted through a tangle of fern and moss and vine maple...when the future was as vast and unfathomable as a starry sky. When there was a future...

I am the author of Between Forks and Alpha Centauri and, as the nearest star to our solar system twinkles on the other side of the globe, I can see many things. I see a deer, sneaking into the orchard from the spruce grove on the south side of the farm. I see starlight beaming through the window in the cell in Forks where Mossy lies unconscious, waiting for her end, attended only by a lawyer and a small dog that licks Mossy's face that is too dry to bear tears. I see her heart tire of pushing the thick sludge that has become her blood and the flat line on the screen of the control room, indicating to the jailer that Mossy's room is ready for occupation by a fresh violator.

"Oh, Mossy," sighs the susurrant wind that whispers up-valley to the Park.

"Mossy, Mossy," babbles the creek in the bubbling froth under the bridge.

"MOSSY! OH, MOSSY!" grieves the green rock by the river's edge.

And as the land laments, I hear the shrieking of John Smith as he storms around Rod Hill's office calling him every name on a restroom wall. Patiently, he has waited for Mossy's end to bring him title to the twenty acres which she tied up in a donation to Olympic National Park; and he has worked in vain through the night, calling in political favors, and trying to take the Farm Reserve into the Developmental Zone by court injunction.

I can see that I am as safe here with John Smith's hit men and the last trees as I would be back in the food, air, and water riots that will be exploding in this nation's capital and every other city across this tired land next summer.

I can see beyond the covers of this book, which define the beginning and the end of this story. I see three white ponies running into the horizon of eternity with their tails high in the air. I see the anadromy of Mossy's spirit returning to the Godhead and the headwaters of Creation. All these things I can see...What I can't see, dear reader, (and thank you for your patience with this book) is how we came to surrender the fish, the elk, the trees, the homesteads: everything in this country which was wild, pure and free...How did we find it in our hearts to trade it all for a late-model vehicle, a big screen TV, a gas-guzzling S.U.V., and the privilege of uncontrolled procreation?

ৡৣৢ

By the weeping cherry tree I stand, where once stood a child admiring sunbeams on flowering buds of hope and joy. In the heartwood and bosom of this tree is the growth ring drawn from the same placenta that nourished the child and, to its outermost ring, I commit the cremated cinders that is all that remain of that human twirling of energy. And to the consciousness of this tree, the hope and joy of the child are simultaneous with the ash of ages. I turn and walk back to the cabin in the fading light.

❦

The deer noses around the base of the leafless pawpaw tree looking for another sweet fruit like the one it found earlier this fall. A human voice calls through the dark: noises that mean nothing to the deer. "I see you, you sneaking, stinking piece of venison. Get out of there or I'll fetch Mossy's gun!"

The deer squats and micturates. It sniffs one last time at the base of the tree, where it sees a tiny little tree still bearing leaves. "Go on! Get," comes the obnoxious, human noise. The deer bounds off through the orchard and a dewdrop jangles on the end of a leafless branch of the old pawpaw.

The drop of dew hangs pregnant over the thirsty, little tree. Four days ago, the winds blew and the skies darkened, but the clouds did not deliver. In a struggle between gravity and surface tension, the bead of water pulls and churns in the starlight, sparking like a jewel.

If this photon arriving from Alpha Centauri could see, which it can't, it would look down on the brown and gray crust which had become the surface of the third planet from the sun. There are a trillion, trillion obstacles between Alpha Centauri and the earth's sun, that lie in wait to gobble up a photon. But there were a trillion, trillion, trillion photons that left Alpha Centauri for the sun in that light-inch four earth years ago and, without a sound, the photon enters the dewdrop. The photon is absorbed and converted to molecular energy or heat, which breaks the tension and sends the drop of water falling. The quark of the photon is spun and re-expressed as a graviton.

The graviton rides two hydrogen atoms attached to oxygen through a soil of composted Doug Fir chips. It is these same Doug fir chips that broke the fall of Phil Stone some forty-five years ago. Approaching the roots of the young tree, the water molecule encounters the rich soil that is the earthly remains of the aforementioned deceased. In joy, the graviton delivers the water to the thirsty root hairs. There is much joy for such a tiny essence. The graviton has come home. The graviton holds the key to time. In the endless eons of the past and future; in the vast gallery of the galaxy; there could be no doors closed to it.

Thank you for reading this book.

About the Author...

Chiggers Stokes was born in Rio de Janeiro on March 21, 1950, the first day of fall in the southern hemisphere. A contrarious thread connects the events of his life and imbues his writing. Raised in the woods of Langley, Virginia, the construction of the CIA and the National Park Service's George Washington Memorial Parkway, were the first obstacles in the author's childhood explorations of the natural world. During the course of the author's formative years, suburban sprawl would digest the undeveloped fields and forests which typified the Potomac Valley in the '50's and early '60's.

The author was influenced by the Society of Friends, marching with Dr. Martin Luther King in August of 1963, being eyewitness to the civil rights leader's speech, "I have a dream..." Later, in the 60's the author read the names of Viet Nam war dead in front of the U.S. Capitol building and participated in "pray ins" in front of the White House.

In the later '60's, the author studied journalism at the University of Miami, Florida and New York University, Washington Square campus. He reported on large and sometimes violent demonstrations through college radio stations and politically oriented newspaper. In April of 1970, the Ohio National Guard opened fire on students of Kent State, killing four. Universities across the United States closed down for the political climate to settle, and so ended the author's formal education.

Chiggers Stokes was hired by the National Park Service as a Resource Educator and worked at the Chesapeake and Ohio National Historic Park for several years before becoming a River Safety Technician on the Potomac River. He transferred to Olympic National Park in 1977 where he worked as a protection ranger until retiring on April 1, 2000.

Since 1978, the author has lived on a portion of the *Flying S* homestead, settled by German immigrant, Otto Siegfried, before the turn of the twentieth century. In 1982, he electrified the property by a micro-hydroelectric scheme on Hemp Hill Creek and writes by the lights and power from this alternative energy project.

Bogachiel Beth Rossow & Author

Between Forks and Alpha Centauri is his second novel, written in 1997.